Kimble's TOP

For Emma

With happy memories of our reading group days!

Best wishes

Vicky Joynman.

Kimble's TOP

VICKY JOYNSON

AuthorHouse™
1663 Liberty Drive
Bloomington, IN 47403
www.authorhouse.com
Phone: 1-800-839-8640

This is a work of fiction. All of the characters, names, incidents, organizations, and dialogue in this novel are either the products of the author's imagination or are used fictitiously.

Published by AuthorHouse 02/16/2013

ISBN: 978-1-4817-8481-8 (sc)
ISBN: 978-1-4817-8482-5 (e)

This book is printed on acid-free paper.

Prologue

BURYING GINA

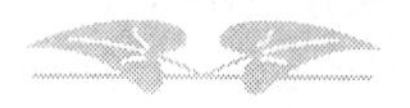

They buried Gina where she would have least expected it, in the town cemetery with the red-brick houses of Doddington Road behind her and the pale square outline of the prison ahead.

William watched as the light oak coffin was lowered out of sight and could imagine his daughter sitting up in it with a tight-lipped, 'Oh yes?' The familiar prelude to fifty years' worth of family battles.

Not that Gina would have found anyone to take her on that day.

As soon as the final 'amen' had been pronounced her three brothers were in retreat, turning away to lead the black tide of mourners in a general surge towards the parked cars.

William saw Maurice, far ahead on the tarmac path, thin and worried-looking, glancing back for a moment through the winter coats and dark uniforms of the Girls Brigade. Richard was up to his right, hands deep in his pockets, taking the steeper route through the shadowy columns of yew.

Both sons looked unfamiliar in their suits. Only Tommy ever wore a suit and he was nowhere to be seen.

Even with his stick William couldn't keep pace with the crowd. He stopped for breath along the path and stood looking around at the place, thick with trees and the uneven lines of grey, mildewed stones.

He searched for Tommy's face among the stragglers coming towards him with smiles of sympathy and words of condolence, nodded them silently on their way and looked beyond for his son's broad shoulders, the familiar turn of his head, but saw was no sign of him.

The December sky was a charcoal scrawl now, the temperature dropping by the minute, and an icy wind stirred the trees and gathered force in the branches, ripping with a sudden gust through the skeletal rowans along the whole length of the path.

William turned his back against it and saw the spindly branches bow ahead of him in a single flowing curve, all the way back to the red brick chapel at the far end of the path, all the way to where Tommy stood in the shelter of the Gothic buttresses and Robyn was at his side; the two of them, talking.

He saw them clearly now that the mourners had passed. Tommy was speaking in that measured, deliberate way of his and Robyn was actually listening, nodding assent even. Her blonde head was close to Tommy's dark shoulder, her eyes on his face, taking in every word, and whatever it was Tommy was saying, Robyn was consenting.

William stared, fascinated, at their sudden connivance, just stood there looking on while the cold rang in his ears so that he didn't hear the priest come up behind him, only felt his touch and turned to see him, this young Roman Catholic none of them knew, offering his arm in support against the wind.

Another freezing blast assailed the trees making the priest's hair stand up jagged and he smiled at it, a sudden smile with an air of mayhem to it, so that he looked to William like a comic book boy and the hand he offered was a gardener's hand with broken nails and the red snakes of bramble scars disappearing up into the black sleeve of his cassock.

1

SPINNING OUT OF CONTROL

It was just after two o'clock when William opened his front door and stood looking along the terraced street towards the main road at the far end.

They were still in the blustery days of early spring and the gutters were strewn with pink blossom, limp from the morning's rain. The sky was clear now though. Sunshine gleamed on the red brick facades of Hartley Rise and the white dog-tooth edging round the windows and doors. Air this mild would be easy on his chest and the afternoon seemed full of possibilities.

He thrust his fingers into the letter box, pulled the door to with a bang and set off along the street, leaning heavily on the stick in his right hand and stopping for a rest every few houses, longer outside number eight with its rail by the front door that he could lean on for a few minutes.

The sun was warm on his back as he stood there catching his breath. His own six foot shadow stretched ahead of him along the pavement and the street around him was quiet. Heavily parked at night, it was empty of cars at this time of the day with nothing to be seen but the regular succession of doors and windows and the grey wheelie bins crowding the narrow pavement.

Suddenly, with a terrific clatter, an empty can flew round the corner of the end house and into the gutter, followed by a group of schoolboys with ties off and shirts hanging out. They walked towards him, laughing, down the middle of the road, kicking the can between them. William watched it fly from foot to foot, red and white, turning over and over, echoing in the empty street.

As they drew level, the can bounced off the kerb and landed close to him. William leaned all his weight on the rail, aimed the walking stick and whacked the can hard. It cartwheeled noisily ahead to a beanpole of a lad with the wide strap of a canvas bag draped across his narrow chest.

The boy raised a languid hand in acknowledgement. 'Cheers, mate!'

'Yeah,' joked the others, looking back turned towards William: 'Cheers!', '*Mate!*'

He watched them saunter along to the far end of the street where a jitty crossed the railway, their voices resounding in the narrow brick alleyway as they walked over the cutting that made Hartley Rise a cul-de-sac, and with all his heart he felt like playing hookey himself, could have smoked a cigarette with them in Ise Meadow or kicked the can all the way up to South Hill Farm but an illicit trip to the corner shop was the extent of his misdemeanours these days.

That took him longer than he'd thought. His breathing was ragged as anything by the time he got there and he stopped inside the door, inhaling hard, reaching for the deep breaths that never came.

Better to keep going.

He moved down the aisle towards the biscuits and it was there among the labyrinth of shelves with the fluorescent lights buzzing overhead that it happened without warning. One minute he was clutching a packet of bourbons under one arm and reaching in his pocket for a handful of change and the next the pink and cream tiles were looming up to meet him.

The stick slipped sideways. He reached for the wire rack of cards but it spun away from him and crashed. Silver coins bounced ahead of him on the hard, dirty floor. His elbow smacked down first, then his chin and, turning, he felt pain shoot through his lower back.

A familiar, dark face was close to his. The lips moved but he couldn't take in the words. An arm moved under his shoulders and neck. He thought it was the shop's owner but when he twisted his head he saw sequins on a pink sari and realised it must be the wife.

They wanted to call an ambulance but he wasn't having that so they helped him into a wooden chair instead and he sat and stared at his long legs stretched awkwardly in front of him, dust marks all over his dark trousers, while his heartbeat thumped against his ribs and reverberated at the base of his throat.

The pain in his elbow had brought tears to his eyes and as he raised his hand to his chest he saw that it was shaking.

Mr Ramana was at his usual place behind the counter, mobile phone wedged under his ear. He was talking rapidly in his own language, smiling briefly at the customers and ringing up the change through a steady stream of conversation. Every now and then he looked across at William.

They'd rung for a taxi. The driver was middle aged, exchanged a battery of remarks with Ramana in their own language before helping William out to the bright yellow cab.

At Hartley Rise he pulled in close to the front door and insisted on taking William into the house, squeezing with him past the old bureau in the narrow hallway.

William sank down into the high-backed chair beside the fireplace in the front room and struggled for the wallet in his pocket but the driver just raised his hands and moved towards the door: 'No problems, forget it!'

William leaned his head back against the faded upholstery of the chair and closed his eyes, just needing to get his breath back. The curtains as always were half pulled across the bay window, lifting occasionally in the draught from the open vent at the top and making a soothing pattern of light and shade across the walls.

He must have nodded off then because a familiar sound woke him, three loud knocks on the front door followed by the key turning in the lock, and when he looked at the clock on the mantelpiece it was twenty past three. Too early for Tommy yet there was his black Audi parked right outside the window.

Hearing his son's heavy step in the hallway, William began to rise in protest but Tommy was already crossing the room and leaning down to kiss him, the only one of his sons who ever did. From his dark suit and silk tie he looked as if he'd come straight from the board room.

Before William could say anything he'd turned to the sideboard and opened the top drawer. 'Where's the doctor's number?'

'I'm not going down there wasting people's time.'

Tommy had the phone in one hand and the medical centre leaflet in the other. 'Ramana said you ought to have had an ambulance.'

'He'd no business ringing you.'

His son had got through to the clinic and was talking to the receptionist, all the while looking at William, his dark eyes scrutinising. After a few words he hung up with a frown. 'Surgery's over. I'll take you down there first thing in the morning.'

'I don't do first thing,' said William in alarm. 'Not by your standards.'

Tommy smiled cynically. 'Half past nine then.'

He disappeared off to the kitchen, returned with the tea tray and William sipped slowly whilst his son leaned his backside on the dining table, hands in his pockets, and quizzed him about what had happened.

Apparently satisfied, he finally turned to go with a single parting shot from the doorway.

'I don't know what Gina will say, you going to the shop on your own like that!'

'If you want to be useful you can pay that taxi driver!' snapped William.

Tommy's laughter echoed back from the hall followed by the bang of the front door.

William sat back gingerly, his elbow and back throbbing from the fall, and his wife's dark eyes regarded him mischievously from the photo frame on the lower shelf of the mantelpiece.

'*Funny turn indeed!*' her voice sounded irreverently in his head. '*They'll be carting you in a bath chair next.*'

'*You wouldn't have worn any better,*' he retorted. '*Old age has nothing to recommend it. If you'd stuck around a bit longer you'd know that.*'

She gazed back at him unperturbed from her twenty first birthday portrait, black and white with a studio background. She'd posed elegantly, her long hair swept up and backwards in a style that was old fashioned even in those days. Not that she'd ever been one for fashion; more interested in freewheeling on a bicycle down Ludlow's farm track or giggling over a glass of port too many at the village pub.

As he looked at her, his own face stared back at him, reflected in the glass. It was always the way now that the social services had raised the feet of his armchair on wooden blocks so he could get in and out more easily. It unsettled him to see his shadowy face lurking over hers, haunting her youthful features, frozen there for an instant in time and forever lost to him.

He glared into his own eyes, taking in the deep lines around them, the overhanging brows and the same old twist of grey, matted hair in the middle of his forehead. His cheeks looked thin but it might have been a trick of the glass. He turned his face from side to side and noticed the dark shadow on his lower, left cheek.

'*Missed yourself shaving. Again!*'

He slept badly that night and woke to the unnatural silence of the house. After seventeen years on his own he still hadn't got used to it: the cold emptiness of the place in the morning.

Familiar furniture stood all around: the bow-fronted wardrobe; the dressing table on Alice's side of the bed with her rose patterned hairbrush, mirror and comb laid out ready, as though she might take them up again and sit brushing her hair, looking back at him in the glass and talking through a mouthful of hairgrips.

His four children had all been born in this room and Alice had lain here for weeks at a time with one bout of illness after another.

'Weak constitution,' the doctor had shrugged. 'Too many wartime pregnancies. Influenza. The winter of forty seven.'

For years his family had filled this house. Gina, from her youngest days, ruling from the kitchen in her mother's absence with Maurice always at her beck and call, kneeling at the table in the back parlour with his comics. Tommy had shunned them both for the solitude of the front room and Richard had spent his waking hours next door in the boys' bedroom listening to his records.

Now there was no-one but William.

He struggled downstairs to shave at the kitchen sink, half sitting on a high stool listening to the breakfast show on the radio. His elbow still hurt from yesterday and his back was tender but there was nothing wrong with him really. When Tommy came he'd tell him to forget about the doctor's.

As soon as he heard his son at the front door, he tapped his razor clean on the edge of the chipped window sill, threw it into a nearby saucer and wiped his face with a rough, old towel.

'I'm not going,' he called towards the hall. 'There's nothing wrong with me.'

Tommy smiled at him from the doorway, the smile he reserved for old people being difficult.

The clinic was a modern breeze-block building with louvered windows set high up and it reminded William of a wartime pillbox. Red signs issued dire warnings against parking in the doctors' spaces so Tommy dropped him at the main door and went off to find somewhere in the surrounding streets.

'Er, you'll call me, will you?' William asked the lady behind the desk.

He never could remember how it worked. There were four waiting areas and lines of red and green lights along the walls.

The receptionist was already reaching to answer a ringing telephone. 'When the last person in front of you has gone in, you wait for the green light and it's your turn.'

She waved him to the left where a number of people were sitting on plastic chairs and William glanced around trying to fix in his mind who was in front of him.

'You ought to go private, Dad,' said Tommy after they'd been there for nearly an hour.

William nodded absently, his eyes on a woman in a pink spotted dress, wondering if she'd been there or not when he first arrived.

'It's not that expensive and you wouldn't have to sit through all this.'

The doctor's door opened and the previous patient came out. William looked for the green light, one eye on the pink spotted lady. Was she expecting to be next? She sat flicking through a magazine.

He watched for some minutes but the red light stayed on over the doctor's door. He half turned in his chair and looked back anxiously towards the desk, but the receptionist was on the phone and he couldn't seem to catch her eye. By the time he turned back, the light had changed to green and a young woman in tight jeans was disappearing into the doctor's room. The lady in pink turned another page of her magazine.

'I think that was my go,' he murmured to Tommy.

'Oh, what!'

Tommy threw his copy of Autosport down on the wooden table and headed for the reception desk. William heard fragments of a heated conversation. A few people turned round to look but he kept his eyes fixed on the red and green lights.

'Have you noticed if your breathing's got worse?' the doctor asked when he finally made it through the door.

'No,' he lied.

She pushed the stethoscope into her ears and listened to his chest and back. William sat breathing and coughing as directed.

'Not a smoker are you, Mr Allbright?'

'Not since the war.'

The doctor nodded. She seemed more interested in his breathing than in what had happened at the corner shop and that reassured him. It was obviously nothing to worry about.

She looked at her computer screen.

'Your emphysema's deteriorated since we last saw you. I'm afraid there's not much we can do about it.'

William nodded apologetically. 'Coal dust from the railways,' he said. 'I'm eighty three, you know.'

Outside, Tommy was waiting for him beside the notice boards at the main entrance. 'I wish you'd let me come in with you.'

'I'm not doolally yet.'

He wanted to fetch the car but William was buoyed up by the doctor's lack of concern about his funny turn and thought a short walk might do him good which was how they came to be making their way out of the car park just as a grey haired woman in a cream anorak turned from paying off a taxi at the side of the road.

William could see straightaway she'd recognised Tommy and was waiting for them and from her face he thought she'd been at Lister's in the early days when Tommy first took over. She must have survived the lay-offs too if she still had the time of day for Tommy Allbright when she met him in the street.

They said hello, she asked after Bryony and the children and Tommy made a few polite enquiries in return but he jingled the coins in his pocket all the while she was speaking and when the woman started to say that of course she'd seen Gina too only last week, he interrupted.

'I'm sorry, we'll have to go. My dad's had a long morning.'

She turned to William with a sympathetic nod. 'Yes, I'm sorry! You must be feeling it, yourself. Not that she's one to complain, your Gina. Even when things are bad.'

William didn't really follow but Tommy turned back sharply: 'Where did you say you'd seen Gina?'

'Up at The Briers. Tuesdays. My sister's in and out, I'm afraid.'

Tommy nodded and stood watching her go down the path to the clinic, then looked at William: 'Did you know?'

'Know what?' William still couldn't get the gist of what she'd said.

'The Briers, Dad! Oncology. That's where she's seen Gina. Chemotherapy? Radiotherapy?'

He spoke impatiently, his eyes on William's face.

William thought hard. 'Gina's not ill,' he said slowly.

Tommy led the way towards the car. 'Well we can soon find out. She'll be over to yours for lunch soon. We'll ask her.'

'I'm not sure she'll like that,' said William. 'Not if she hasn't already told us.'

'It sounds like half the town knows!' said Tommy angrily. 'What is she thinking? Letting us hear it from a stranger!'

'We don't know the facts,' said William and, as Tommy began to argue; 'I think you'd better leave it to me! I'll talk to her.'

But the morning had gone and when they turned into Hartley Rise Gina's blue Citroen was already parked outside number fourteen.

Tommy pulled in close behind it.

'You're not coming in,' said William warningly. 'I mean it, Tommy! Just leave it to me.'

2

GINA'S NEWS

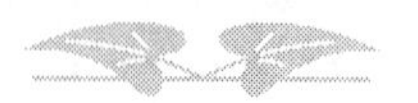

William pushed the car door open with the single aim of stopping Tommy marching into the house in search of Gina but before he'd even put a foot on the pavement, Tommy was at the passenger door helping him out.

Their faces were close as William struggled to gain his feet. His hands trembled against his son's but Tommy's movements were careful with a carefulness that meant he was seething.

Meanwhile the front door had opened and Gina stood on the threshold.

William pulled his arm free from Tommy and began making his way towards her, sensing her eyes on his every step as he picked his way with the stick while Tommy watched from behind so that he was caught, for one uncanny moment, like a toddler whose progress is monitored by anxious parents.

At the front step he turned back and saw Tommy still hesitating beside the car, one hand on its shiny, black roof.

'What's the matter with him?' asked Gina.

William stepped into the hall without replying and went into the front room where she came and arranged the cushions behind him in the armchair.

'Are you all right?' she asked.

'I haven't had a cup of tea all morning.'

She brought two cups through on a tray from the kitchen then set about watering the plants in the bay window, white plastic jug in hand, all the while asking him about his fall at the shop and what had brought that on and what the doctor had had to say.

She had a way of asking without making a song and dance about it and so he told her everything while she fussed round the plants, pulling the dead leaves off and gathering them into a pile on the windowsill.

'So what was the matter with Tommy?'

She was turning the pots this way and that to catch the sun when she spoke and he told her to come and sit down for a minute, gesturing to the low backed sofa next to his chair.

She sat with one arm propped on the back of it, her head resting on her hand and her long white fingers buried in her hair.

'There was this woman outside the clinic,' he said. 'Used to work for Tommy. She said she'd seen you up at The Briers.'

She was silent at first and afterwards her words seemed unreal. She talked about her oncologist and radiotherapy but all he could hear was the controlled tone of her voice. 'It's not as if I found any lumps. Just bleeding. And then when they had a look: it was everywhere. Aggressive.'

Listening to her, it was Alice again in front of him. His wife, drained and defiant against the white pillows, pulling William close and whispering while the young doctor wound his stethoscope round itself to stow away in his leather bag. 'I'm not going in there!'

Hardy Reynolds Ward it had been called then and changing the name hadn't changed what everyone his age knew: go in there, you come out in a box! Somehow he'd kept Alice out of it, argued with a man half his age and with twice his learning.

Alice had died upstairs in her own bed, William sitting at her side. Ten thirty five on a bright November morning.

He'd faced it calmly at the time but the loneliness afterwards was another matter. It had broken him slowly like water that freezes in the crevice of a rock and expands to crack it from the inside. It was the cold empty side of the bed every night, the solitary start to every new day, the curse of sole occupancy. The sense that no living being shared his roof.

But Gina had been here. A widow herself, she'd come every day to cook lunch and eat with him, the radio between them on the table tuned to their favourite programmes. And now here she was talking in familiar terms about The Briers.

His tears rose in a burning tide. He pressed his fingers against his eyes, too late to stem them, and Gina's hands closed around his arms: 'I didn't know how to tell you.'

He felt sick but she insisted on lunch: 'If I can so can you,' and as the smell of steak and kidney pie filled the house he got up and went to find a fresh tablecloth so he could lay the table properly the way she liked.

For once they left the radio off and, inevitably, they talked about Esther.

'I meant for her to hear it first,' said Gina. 'But nothing's ever straightforward with Esther.' She poured gravy over her potatoes and carrots. 'She was supposed to be coming home and I wanted to tell her face to face but then it kept getting put off. I tried calling but of course she's never in. Then I thought, maybe I should just wait until I know more anyway.'

William watched her eating, his strong resolute Gina, and thought she can't possibly be ill.

She stopped talking then and smiled as if she knew he hadn't been listening. 'We'll have to sort out your lunches, I might not be able to get over here every day.'

'Never mind about me,' he said. 'You just concentrate on getting better.'

He saw straightaway that he'd said the wrong thing. She put her knife and fork down very deliberately. 'I'm not going to get better, Dad.'

He could see he was supposed to have known that. It was what she'd already told him. 'Right!' He nodded as definitely as he could.

She got up to take the plates to the kitchen and he rested an elbow on the table and sank his forehead into his hand feeling pain like a lightning blow that had struck dead centre and left him wasted.

His breathing turned funny then so she stayed on into the afternoon, sorting through his kitchen cupboards and re-packing the freezer so she could make a list of things he could do with from the supermarket.

He'd gone up to use the bathroom when the phone rang. He heard her answer it and she was still speaking as he came down the stairs.

'Tommy,' she said, 'he's coming round.'

His heart sank but she was smiling, her eyes as hard as emeralds and an all too healthy colour rising in her cheeks: 'Well, if he's upset, we might as well have it out.'

Tommy's three loud knocks sounded as usual on the front door but for once the key didn't turn in the lock afterwards.

William stared at Gina. 'What does he think? I've got a butler?'

She laughed abruptly and moved towards the door but then they heard the key and she shrugged and went to the window instead, standing waiting with her arms folded.

It took him back forty years. Gina, arms folded, on a Saturday evening waiting for Tommy to come home, waiting to see him empty his pay packet out on the table for his mother, so she could berate him one more time about what he thought he was doing working at Orton's, when everyone knew he was worth more than that. And if he wanted to be a shop boy, for heaven's sake, then he could get himself down the Coop where they trained their lads up properly and gave them a uniform.

Not that Tommy had cared. At fourteen he'd enjoyed outfacing her, smiled maddeningly every time and heard her out without a word in his own defence.

There was nothing of the cocky teenager about Tommy now though. It wasn't just his fifty four years:

Tommy had an air of authority about him. He came through the door in his Savile Row suit and he looked mature, sober and thoroughly conservative.

Antagonistic too, he glanced at William with barely a nod then turned on his sister. 'Is it true?'

She nodded.

'For God's sake, Gina! I don't expect to hear that kind of thing from a stranger. What the hell do you think family's all about?'

'I was waiting to tell Esther.'

Tommy slipped his hands into his pockets and stood facing her with his back to the sideboard. 'How bad is it?'

'It's terminal.'

Tommy's breathing was audible even over William's own. 'So what are we talking about? Weeks? Months?'

'Either. Maybe. Who knows?'

'Well find someone who does know! It's not as if you haven't got the money. Don't trust your life to some second rate local . . .'

'The Briers has the best treatment going. And it's not down to money.'

They stared at one another across the room, Gina's eyes bright with satisfaction, thriving on the conflict, while Tommy's face was closed, his manner cold and dismissive.

'At least get someone in to look after you,' he said at last. 'Give yourself a fighting chance.'

'I already have,' smiled Gina.

'Properly trained, though?' said Tommy. 'Not just some foreign au pair?'

Gina had pulled a chair out from the dining table. She sat down with an air of calm resolve. 'Robyn's moving in.'

'You've got to be joking!'

'She's already been a brilliant support.'

'Oh, I'll bet she has!' his voice was bitter with fury. 'There's nothing Robyn likes better than a drama. Especially if she's at the centre of it.'

'You know that's not really fair, Tommy!'

'You want proper medical care!'

'What I want is someone close who cares about me! I happen to like Robyn. And I'm not having you bad mouthing her.'

Tommy laughed in utter disbelief. 'I've held back for years on Robyn!'

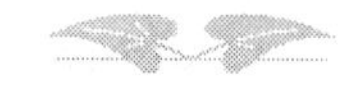

3

Robyn

Tommy had been the first to leave, abruptly conceding there was nothing more to say. Gina had been reluctant to follow but William had insisted he'd be all right and eventually she'd got her things together and gone.

Now he sat alone in the quiet of the room, utterly worn out, listening to his breathing.

It was early evening and the sunshine still fell in golden squares across the green swirls of the carpet. For once the silence was soothing. Everything around him old and familiar. His eyes passed from one piece of dark wood to another; the dining table with its twisting, turning legs, the long sideboard against the wall beside his chair and the tall, fringed lamps in the corners. Furniture that was too big for the room but Alice had brought it from her parent's farmhouse when they'd first married: it had stood for years in the stone floored passages and draughty parlours she'd once called home.

'Just as well you never lived to see this!'

Yet, selfishly, he longed for her to be there. It reminded him of another such day, the day his call-up papers had landed on the doormat. She had come and stood by him at the front door. He closed his eyes and felt her again; their breathing mingled as she put her arms around him, the press of her forehead against his own and the same sick turning in his stomach.

He opened his eyes to stop the flood of memories but wasn't quick enough. Two bodies were face down in water, spinning gently in a river's current. The grey uniforms had turned black with the wet and a cheery English voice was saying; 'Not ours, thank God,' as if it simply didn't matter.

War.

His children had brought him back from all that. Their happiness and energy had seized him, brought him tumbling back into life until he no longer thought about the solitary darkness of the regiment.

Their photos were all around him in the room. He went to stand at the sideboard, knuckles pressing down heavily on the smooth dark wood while he looked at them.

Tommy and Bryony, with their son and daughter, smiled out of the frames along the sideboard; early shots of their children with neat fringes and the burgundy and gold uniform of the local prep school.

A bigger collection of pictures hung on the wall above them. Richard's family, mostly of his daughter Robyn, and it was she who'd arranged them for William into multi-frames of squares and circles.

Four of them hung in a line along the picture rail and in the earliest a sturdy, five year old Robyn met his gaze. She was grinning up at the camera over the head of her baby brother, grasping him competently under the armpits while he kicked haphazardly at a football.

In the early days, when William's children had started their own families and begun gathering at each other's houses for tea on Sundays, the grandchildren had been very much in the background. They'd gone off to play quietly in some favourite corner of whichever home was playing host led by Tommy's two, who'd been brought up to behave that way, and Gina's daughter, Esther, had been the same. But as Robyn grew up, she'd been different. Robyn had liked to be where the adults were, ideally the centre of their attention, and never more so than when her two younger brothers had come on the scene.

William remembered the day Richard had first arrived with her brother, Paul, in the carry cot; Robyn had refused outright to go off with the other children into the garden and instead spent the afternoon rummaging through the baby's things and interrupting the adults' conversation. *'Mummy, where's his blanket?' 'Mummy, you haven't brought his rattle!' 'I think he's waking up.'*

By the time Paul grew strong enough to pinch and push there had been angry tussles and cries of *'Mummy, tell him!'* and Robyn's second brother, Lee, had been even less amenable to her constant attention, giving way to squalls of crying and protest whenever she came near.

By then Robyn had begun to tire of childhood anyway. In the next photograph she appeared at the age of nine in a black top hat and fishnet tights, tap dancing in a school concert. It was a routine they'd sat through repeatedly in the weeks running up to the show: *'You've all got to watch. And everyone's got to score, out of ten.'*

While her cousins had grown into serious adolescents preoccupied with homework, exams and school sports, Robyn's interests had been pop music, fashion and make-up. She'd badgered her aunts into a Sunday afternoon ritual of practice manicures and hair styling.

Tommy had disapproved. Where he'd initially simply endured her childish interruptions to the adults' conversation, now he brought the Sunday papers with him and sat on at the table after tea, barely looking up from their pages as long as Robyn was around.

Things were destined to get much worse.

In the later photos Robyn had begun to fill out, posing for the camera in fashionable jeans and crop tops. Her hair had remained childish though, pulled back untidily in an assortment of decorative clips and coloured bands.

For a while she'd begun to make regular money babysitting, they'd seen less of her on Sundays and among the family faces now in the pictures were unknown infants; bright-eyed, thumb-sucking children who snuggled up to Robyn in living rooms he'd never seen. One boy in particular had a familiar look to him; the same sharp blue eyes and narrow jaw of another, much older, lad William had seen Robyn with in town when she should have been at school. When he'd asked her about it she'd laughed and said she had free lessons. It had been just before everything came to a head.

William looked on at the photos, remembering Easter Monday the year Robyn turned fourteen.

He'd eaten lunch and was expecting Richard and the family to take him to Claydon for the afternoon, but an hour ticked by and there was no sign of them.

He didn't think to phone and see if something was wrong because he knew what Richard was like for time-keeping. So he just sat on in the front room looking at the weak sunshine struggling across the sky and listening to the wind filling the trees along the railway line with noise.

It was nearly four o'clock when Richard arrived alone. William left him sitting on the sofa, elbows on his knees, while he went to make tea, putting biscuits out on a china plate as if it were Gina or Tommy visiting and not his recalcitrant youngest who drank with his fingers wrapped round the cup and liked to put his feet up on the furniture.

'Robyn's pregnant,' Richard said flatly as William returned with the tray. 'Doreen's in a state. And the boys have disappeared off to some friend's house. God knows what the others will say!'

William concentrated on setting the tray down on the table.

Richard sat staring at the floor. 'Am I a lousy Dad?'

'No.'

'Tommy'll think so. Can't imagine this happening to one of his, can you?'

William sat down slowly. 'Is Robyn all right?'

'Well I don't think she's exactly surprised.'

'And the father?'

'Could be one of several apparently,' Richard shrugged. 'There is one she sees a lot of, babysitting for his brother. But I don't think even she really knows.' He took a biscuit and crumbled it between his fingers without eating. 'Doreen's on about taking her to Cromer for a while. To her sister's. Let the dust settle.'

'We had our honeymoon there,' William said without thinking.

Richard glanced up: 'I don't suppose Mum would have approved.'

William laughed to himself, remembering the icy New Year's Eve he'd offered to walk Alice home, more because her brothers were drunk than because he'd ever thought he was in with a chance. She'd stopped beside the rails of the frozen millpond and turned to face him, arms spread behind her along the wood, her cheeks mottled with the cold.

'Aren't you going to kiss me then?' she'd said. 'There's no-one around.'

Their icy mouths had touched and he'd felt her cheek soft against his own, her slight body drawing close. Then, with sudden warmth, the unmistakeable press of her hand where no nice girl's hand had any business to be. She'd been all farm girl had Alice Ludlow but he didn't think he'd tell Richard that.

The next day Tommy came to see him.

'I suppose you've heard?' he crossed the room and dropped his door key on the table. 'Pregnant! At her age.'

He seized the tea tray without waiting for a reply and headed for the kitchen to make a fresh pot, turning back momentarily from the door. 'I told Richard if she were mine I'd be prosecuting.'

William leaned his head back against the high cushions of the chair and listened to the rush of water in the kitchen sink as Tommy filled the kettle.

'Thirteen years old!' he'd returned to the doorway.

'She's fourteen,' said William.

'Three months gone. She was thirteen. Richard ought to be ashamed. What does he think fatherhood's all about? It's not just bedtime stories and cuddles.'

He went back to the kitchen and returned with the tea.

'If she'd been born on the wrong side of the tracks you could understand it. But she's had everything in life. And now she'll amount to nothing.'

'Motherhood's hardly nothing,' protested William.

'You know what I mean.'

Richard had arrived soon afterwards. William thought he must have known Tommy was there because he looked relieved rather than surprised to see him. He probably wanted Tommy to get it out of his system without Doreen and Robyn there.

His youngest son brought a cup from the kitchen and poured his own tea while Tommy watched him, one hand thrown behind his head against the back of the chair.

'So who's the father?' he demanded as soon as Richard had sat down.

'It's none of your business, Tommy.'

The clock on the mantelpiece ticked the seconds away until Richard broke the silence. 'Look, we're not going to fall out over this, are we?'

'We're here if you need anything,' shrugged Tommy.

'What we don't need is advice.'

'Oh come on, Richard, you can't exactly be pleased about it?'

'These things happen, that's all.'

'No they damn well don't,' said Tommy. 'Not if you bring them up properly.'

'So we are going to argue then.'

William could feel Tommy's exasperation even across the room.

'Just give it time to settle down,' said Richard at last. 'We don't want anything said that'll make things worse.'

After they'd gone William had looked through the old bureau in the hall and dug out Alice's necklace; a tiny black and white cameo on a long chain. He'd wrapped it in tissue paper and put it in a card with roses on that he'd thought Robyn might like. When they'd all finally made it down to Claydon a few weeks later he took it with him.

They walked away from the Georgian house, down through the wide meadow that sloped to the river. On the opposite bank a similar stretch of green rose as far as the eye could see. He'd known the others would draw ahead and leave him and Robyn trailing behind.

They stood together at the river's edge while he caught his breath, looking at the reflection of the trees in the grey water. The only sound was the patter and dribble of the foraging swans.

'Uncle Tommy thinks I'm a slut,' said Robyn staring tight-mouthed at the river. 'Just because I'm not prim and proper like his precious daughter.'

'That's not true.'

She pulled her bulky anorak closer round her chest and stared out across the water. 'I heard Mum arguing with Dad about it.'

He took the envelope out of his pocket and handed it to her and when she'd read the card he helped her fasten the necklace round her neck. There was no 'thank you' but she managed a half-smile as she stuffed the card and envelope into the back pocket of her jeans.

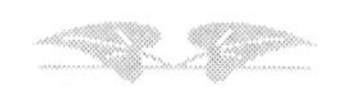

Things had never recovered after that. If Tommy expected penitence he was to be disappointed. Robyn had blossomed with motherhood and become more confident than ever, basking in the attention of her mother and aunts all through her pregnancy and even more so with the arrival of baby Laurel.

In time she'd adopted a scathing sarcasm towards Tommy and he'd responded with icy civility.

And so it had gone on.

William looked at the final frame of pictures over the sideboard. Robyn had put on weight but lost her teenage slouch as she smiled over Laurel's head: her little blue-eyed girl with the crooked smile and streak of blonde hair perpetually hanging over one eye.

The most recent was William's favourite. Robyn standing tall in a long, black skirt with pink flowers, five year old Laurel sitting on her hip, wearing a yellow dress and big white sandals. The shutter had closed seconds before the pose had been properly struck and had caught Robyn smiling warmly at her daughter. Laurel's chubby arm was raised half across her face, shielding her eyes from the sun and dangling in the sunlight was a black and white cameo on a silver chain that she'd been allowed to wear for the first time because it was her birthday.

4

SATURDAY

It was after midnight and still he couldn't face going to bed. He fetched a blanket down instead and sat in the front room, the photos of his family all around him.

There was raucous laughter in the street outside, the echo of high heels on the pavement as a couple came home from a night out and over by the window the streetlight shone through a gap in the curtains and fell directly onto the silver frame of Gina's wedding photo in the centre of the windowsill.

It had been a stormy Saturday in June 1971. Arthur, in his dark suit and glasses, looked positively windswept as he stood at the foot of the church tower with Gina stately and unmoved at his side. She wore ivory silk with an embroidered bodice. Arthur had paid for it and for the string of pearls round her neck, an engagement present, as if a diamond ring hadn't been enough.

His daughter looked so calm and permanent staring out at him on one of the best days of her life, a day they'd shared, walking down the aisle together.

William got up and went to put the kettle on for tea but changed his mind when it boiled and filled a hot water bottle instead, something he hadn't done for years.

He sat with it on his knee in the front room, smelling the hot rubber, and he must have dozed then because he thought he was a child again curled up by the kitchen stove, watching his mother fill hot water bottles while his older sisters plaited their hair for bed and his Dad rolled the final smoke of the day from the dock ends lined up along the mantelpiece.

He woke in the dead of night, the house creaking occasionally around him, and Tommy's angry voice came back into his head.

What the hell do you think family's all about?

He should have been used to it, the arguments that had gone on in this house over the years, but it had always been Gina asking the questions back then. Gina, desperate to know what Tommy was up to; how he'd met these contacts in London who got him the latest stuff for the markets, who it was buying him drinks at the Conservative Club and the Working Men's Clubs and the Band Club and what he found to talk about, sitting with James Wilcox into the early hours in that big, posh house of his down Midland Road.

He'd silenced her one Sunday afternoon, though, walking through the back door with beautiful Bryony Richardson on his arm when everyone still thought she was Alex Whitby's girl.

William remembered Gina, dumbstruck, pouring the tea while Alice reached out a dress-maker's hand to touch the silk of Bryony's rose patterned shirt.

Tommy and Bryony had married soon afterwards, for all that George Richardson was Director of Operations at Whitby's and set on marrying his girl to the company son and heir.

The arguments at Hartley Rise had finally ended then, at least until tonight.

The hot water bottle had gone cold. He dumped it on the floor and closed his eyes, fixing his mind on Robyn and Laurel. He visualised the photo: Robyn's long skirt with the pink flowers, the sunlight on the two blonde heads and, pulling the blanket around him, willed the warmth of that sun to wash over him and draw him into the close embrace of the living.

He woke before eight with an aching side, his jaw stiff from grinding his teeth all night and the whole desolate morning stretched ahead of him.

Normally he went up to Richard's on Saturday afternoons, his son picking him up around lunchtime, but he couldn't sit here alone dwelling on things.

He pushed the memory of his fall at the shop out of his mind and decided to walk up to Richard's house. He'd be all right as long as he took it steady.

Outside the sky was dazzling blue and the breeze blew behind him from the railway, carrying the seaweed smell of diesel on the air. It was nine o'clock on a Saturday morning and there was no-one about, no sound of traffic. The Victorian streets were as they had been years ago and in his mind's eye he was back in the Wellingborough of old: the town of his youth and of courtship.

William had known it first as an impossibly long word on the front of the charabanc that left his village twice a day and as the place where the trains were heading that whistled through the low meadows and piled up white smoke beside the picket fence of Castle Ashby station.

He'd learnt at infant school that it was built on the confluence of two rivers, where the Nene met the Ise and could be forded, named for a Saxon called Waendel whose people farmed barley on the lowlands and sheep on the uplands and for its many wells: *Redwell, Ladywell. Stanwell, Buckwell.*

It had become a town of shoemakers like every other town in Northamptonshire and also of brewers and even the expansion that had come with the railway had barely changed that.

Boot and shoe had been everywhere when he'd first come here to work at the age of fourteen. Factories and shoe works stood prominent on street corners and between the houses; three storey buildings with arched windows and small, square panes of glass. They'd resounded with the noise of heavy presses and machine sewing rooms and the upstairs din of clicking and closing, welting and finishing, while all around wooden hand barrows had rattled along the back alleyways, delivering leather uppers to the outworkers who still offered closing in their back yard workshops.

He'd come to the biggest works of all: J C Coleridge and Sons, a towering chequerboard building of red and yellow bricks behind a high wall and iron gates. It had been the most advanced of all the works; a quality outfit that smelt of full grain leather and machine oil, where engineers tested innovations in welting and clicking presses that might one day rival Goodyear and McKay and managers dreamt up radical processes to solve the age-old problem of the closing room bottle-neck.

Not that William at fourteen had cared much for industrial advance. He hadn't cared much for an apprenticeship in boot lasting either. What William Allbright had cared about was riding the charabanc out of a village that had little more to offer than a crossroads, a Saxon church and the grassy remains of a castle motte. His mother hadn't liked it, mind, and not just because of the expense.

'You needn't go getting above yourself, riding that bus every day.'

She didn't see why he couldn't follow his dad and sisters in the walk across the Piece every morning and learn boot lasting in the village works like everyone else. But that had all been down to James McNee.

Growing up among his neighbours' children with two older sisters beating every trail before him, William had gone off to his first day at the Council School confident that he already knew everyone in his class. But he'd walked through the old wooden doors to find a dark-haired boy no-one had ever seen before sitting at a desk by the window. A boy whose high forehead made his black eyes stand out, giving him a sensitive look, and whose thick wool jacket still had the marks of a sergeant's stripes on the sleeves, removed when the coat had been cut down for him.

McNee lived in the furthest flung cottage on Ludlow's farm, where his uncle was head cowman, and he'd walked well over an hour to join the others in the high-windowed classroom of the Council School.

Every aspect of William's little world had seemed to fascinate McNee: jostling round a football in the empty streets, the lines of village houses joined one to another and the bell that jangled when you pushed the shop door open at the Provident and Co-op. But what McNee had loved most of all was to sit at the Allbright family tea table and listen to William's dad, George.

William came from a family of talkers and his dad was the greatest talker of them all. He talked on his knees at the kitchen grate, twisting newspaper into kindling and coaxing a flame from among the coals, he talked with his sleeves rolled up at the kitchen table, the tin of polish and wooden brushes set out ready to black his boots, and he talked at the sink in the mornings, stripped to his waist and splashing in cold water while the porridge cooked on the stove.

And what George Allbright liked to talk about was trade unionism and the self-evident truths of socialism, together with the true significance of the historic trade guilds and the need for a revisionist approach to national history.

'It's your craftsman built this country, James. He might not know books but your working man, he's master of his own environment. He learns with his eyes and his hands and he's always changing things. Changing them for the better. It's your working man made this country what it is. Arkwright. Lyman Blake. Frank Chase. Ingenious,' a tap of the forehead; 'Always adapting and improving things.'

William had heard it all before. He sat quietly when George Allbright was in full flow, leant a forbidden elbow on the table, hand pressed to his ear and kept a watchful eye on the last slice of bread and jam that was meant to be his dad's but would be his for the taking if only James McNee asked enough artless questions.

McNee, it turned out, had many questions and a sympathy for the dignity of your working man, the potential of industrial revolution and the bright prospects of technology in proper skilled men's hands.

So when it came to them finishing at the Council School there was nowhere McNee would apply for an apprenticeship but Coleridge's, the innovative, forward-looking shoe works, and with George backing him all the way it made sense for William to go too.

Which was how they'd arrived at the village bus stop on an autumn morning in 1933 to find two girls huddled against the ancient stone wall of the pub; Alice Ludlow of Ludlow's farm buttoned to the neck in black garbardine and Margaret Fowler in a bright, fashionable coat that flapped open to show her thin blouse.

Margaret had been smoking a cigarette. She'd drawn on it with the sensuality of a film star and breathed out wreaths of blue smoke with the simple delight of a child.

'Don't mind, do you?' she'd said to William and McNee. 'Only some people think it's unladylike.'

'Not the way you do it,' McNee had laughed.

He'd turned away to joke with her and left William with Alice who was going to learn dress-making from a woman in Great Park Street because she wasn't up to farm work.

William could believe it. Alice looked thin and fragile, not like the girls he'd seen working behind the threshing engine, throwing sheaves into the drum and catching the wheat in bags, trousers tied at the ankle to stop the mice running up.

Stevens their old classmate had shown up then, wearing the black jacket and red stripes of the Grammar School. He'd approached them with a bright smile in the cold morning air, leaned against the wall next to Margaret and begged a smoke.

And so they'd become quite the gang: the five of them riding the damp, jolting bus every day and on Saturdays, when they'd all finished at lunchtime, they'd made the town their own.

In winter it had been the tepid water of the Council Baths, the Saturday double bill at the cinema or teasing one another across the table in the Cosy Café. In summer they'd walked through Swanspool Gardens or lay and smoked under the horse chestnuts in Castle Fields.

And somewhere in those six years of standing at a wooden bench, working leather for ten bob a week, Alice had become for him the standard by which all girls were judged. McNee and Stevens occasionally eyed up the other girls they knew but William was noncommittal, none of them compared with his growing ideal: an old fashioned look, a face lit easily by a wide smile and the glint of humour in small dark eyes.

Not that he'd ever thought he had a chance with her. She'd surprised him beside the mill pond that New Year's Eve and with war on the horizon no-one was waiting around. Not even her Dad.

'Not a time for the faint-hearted,' he'd said when William had stepped into the cold north-facing sitting room at Ludlow's to put his case. 'And it's you she wants.'

He'd paid the deposit for them on the house in Hartley Rise because by now Alice thought herself a regular town girl and so that was where William had left her and where he'd always thought of her waiting for him.

By the time he came home from the war, he'd been away as long as he'd known her and everything had changed.

McNee had gone first. Unbelievably. In the early days on the frenzied race for the coast. William had last seen him running for cover under the timbers and thatch of a woodshed minutes before a mortar hit it.

Stevens had drowned in the freezing black waters of the Atlantic when his convoy went down in the March of forty three.

Margaret had come through, though, working in munitions down south. They heard she'd married a pub landlord twice her age and planned to stay down there.

Coleridge's was a ghost of a place by then, half the wooden benches and managers' desks empty, and William couldn't face walking back in there without McNee. He'd gone down Midland Road and shovelled coal on the railway instead.

He'd anchored his life by those iron tracks; his days revolving around the brick sheds, the grit and shovel and the occasional glance upwards at the high wall of the cutting, where his house stood and his wife played with their children.

Wellingborough had grown after the war. Orchards and fields had given way to concrete estates and the place was expanding again now with great developments of dark brick houses crammed up against another. Down his end, though, by the railway, all was pretty much as it had been. The brick sheds where he'd once worked were dormant but undeveloped. The terraced streets stretched in the same neat lines around the old station building with its honeycomb windows and fancy iron pinnacles along pitched slate roofs.

Two of his children lived round here. Tommy on the other side of the cutting, where thirty years ago an ambitious developer had built an avenue of stunning houses within the wide, sparkling loop of the river. The plots had sold at laughable prices to retired bankers and directors even before the houses were built.

Richard lived this side of the line in one of the solid interwar semis along Eastfield Road. William walked slowly past their front gardens, picking his way across the slabs that rose like a tide over the roots of the cherry trees all along the grass verge.

Richard's wife, Doreen, was reversing her silver Corsa down the drive as William arrived at the house. She wound the window down straightaway. 'You've never walked up!'

'I thought it might do me good.'

She looked unconvinced. 'We heard about Gina. Terrible news. Mind you, Robyn's been over there no end. We wondered if something was wrong.'

At the far end of the drive the front door opened and Richard came out.

'Well, as long as you're all right,' said Doreen.

He watched her swing the car backwards into the road, smart and professional as always in her hotel manager's suit. She'd always insisted on keeping her Saturday shift at the Old Bakehouse Hotel even when the children were born.

'Weddings! They're our showcase events. Definitely not for the junior staff.'

Her own wedding had come months after Richard's previous sweetheart, Julia, had joined the Merchant Navy.

'I do hope he's not marrying her on the rebound,' Alice had fretted.

'He's not marrying her at all,' Tommy had remarked. 'She's marrying him.'

William had been surprised by that. Tommy held marriage sacrosanct. He'd always taken a dim view of Richard's casual approach to girls. But then there had been something about Julia: a joie de vivre.

'You'll lose her,' he'd heard Tommy warn Richard when Julia first talked about wanting to go abroad. 'If you don't buy her a ring, someone else will.'

But Richard had done nothing about it, Julia had disappeared off to Southampton and then Doreen had appeared on the scene: Doreen who owned a car and earned good money and had somehow made herself indispensable in Richard's easygoing life. Once they were married and there was a deposit to pay on the new starter home up Gleneagles, she'd even persuaded Richard to sit for professional exams, something he'd always resisted in his job at the council offices. After that there was the house here at Eastfield Road, a much bigger, older place and they'd ended up owing her dad money for that. Doreen set great store by a nice house and in time Richard had risen some way through the ranks of his accounts department.

He was smiling at William now, coming down the drive to meet him in washed out grey cargo shorts and a faded black t-shirt with his black hair wet and spiky from the shower.

Still too handsome for your own good, William thought.

His son flung his arm wide in a gesture William recognised as more an offer of hospitality than an invitation to embrace. 'You're early!'

They made their way up to the house where the living room curtains were still drawn and his grandsons, Paul and Lee, were slumped in armchairs, spooning cornflakes as they watched the roundup of that week's premier fixtures.

William was glad to join them. Saturdays had long been a boys' day at Richard's, nothing too taxing in the way of conversation.

On the television a group of smart young men was talking game plans and qualifying hopes, in between footage of goals. William sat back in the armchair listening to the wild roar of the crowd and watching the fast moving shapes against the background of green grass and goal posts.

First kick-off was at a quarter to one and they ate lunch while they watched: bangers and mash and not a green vegetable in sight, though when William helped carry the plates through he saw Doreen had left carrots and broccoli in a dish by the microwave.

Afterwards Richard went out to the garden for a cigarette and William followed. When Doreen was around Richard smoked at the far end of the garden, sitting on an upturned barrel behind the greenhouse, but on Saturdays he sat on the low wall of the patio at the edge of the grass.

William propped himself against the back of a wooden bench with a view down the long garden.

'Apple tree's a mess,' said Richard. 'Should have taken more height off it. Garlic's coming through all right though down the far end. Put some hard neck in this year and it's not bad. Apart from the watering.'

William smiled, remembering long days with Richard helping him on the allotment.

'You planted gladioli once in a bed I'd dug for onion sets,' he said suddenly. 'Esta bonita. Salmon pink.'

'And sweet dream,' nodded Richard. 'Pink and white. You went ballistic.'

'Those were hard times. We were digging for the table.'

'We did all right. Didn't Tommy sell them for us?'

'Oh yes. Tommy always got you out of trouble.'

Richard smiled up at him from the low wall, lifting the cigarette to his lips and drawing on it without haste.

'I'm worried about Tommy and Robyn,' William said.

But Richard shrugged it off. 'Tommy knows it's no time for an argument.'

His son took a final drag on the cigarette and bent down to stub it out against the wall. 'Do you remember when everyone smoked? And that's all life was? Just a smoke and a pint and a laugh with your mates.'

5

Kimble's Top

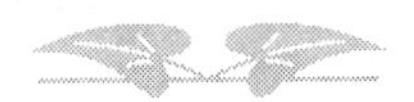

On Sunday he went to church. Jan Wright gave him a lift, white-haired, retired and a good twenty years his junior, she talked non-stop as she drove at speed along the terraced streets and William sat at her side nodding absently. He never had been able to follow what she was saying.

She stopped abruptly in the middle of the road to drop him off right outside the Victorian church and he joined the gaggle of people on the steps, squeezing in through the glass doors and ducking to the left to avoid the minister who was always on at him to join the men's fellowship group. William had no time for everyone knowing everyone else's business.

The front of the church was noisy with young children running around the old wooden pews. William sat down at the back, leaned his stick against the wall and threw a hassock onto the next seat to save it for the young woman who always came in halfway through the first hymn with her little boy.

She took her place as usual with a grateful smile and when the singing had finished the child crouched at William's feet playing with a red and yellow farmyard horse that he banged in a haphazard gallop along the wooden seat.

The minister got up to speak from the pulpit and William settled down to his own thoughts. He couldn't always follow what was said through those crackling lapel mikes. Sunday morning was thinking time.

The sunlight streamed through the high windows and there was a subdued quiet all around him. He stared at the lines of dark shoulders and backs of heads in front of him and thought about Gina.

Some people railed against God at times like this but he'd never felt anything one way or another towards God if he were honest. He came to church out of habit and because Alice had thought it mattered, especially at the end.

'It'll all come right,' she'd said to him in those final days when he'd mostly just sat, stretched out on the bed beside her. 'Hold on to that.'

So he'd kept on coming even after she'd gone. And if he had little faith in the young minister with his ready handshake and over familiar smile, he trusted Alice and what she'd believed in.

'*Gina's going to die. And there's nothing to hold onto.*'

She'd understand, he knew.

He stretched his legs out and watched the pattern of diamond panes shimmering across his dark trousers, while at his feet the child turned the pages of a cardboard book and glanced up at him between times, with his happy toddler's smile, sharing the farmyard pictures with him.

Gina had left him a casserole for lunch. He felt better for eating and afterwards sat leafing through the Sunday paper until it was time for Tommy and Bryony to come and pick him up for tea at Kimble's Top. When the car pulled up outside, though, he hung back, wanting Bryony to come inside for him.

She let herself in at the front door and came into the room with a smile, holding out his red scarf which she must have taken off the hook on her way down the hall. 'Wrap up warm, there's a real nip out there.'

She had on a white wool coat with a high collar and a black silk scarf imprinted with dots. When she turned her head to drape his own scarf round him, he saw the clip holding her blonde hair back was covered with the same material. Something she'd probably put together herself in one of her 'spare five minutes'.

'How's Tommy?' he asked.

'He took Gina out for lunch yesterday. I think they've made their peace. And the really good news is: Robyn won't be around this afternoon. She's taking Laurel to a party on the other side of town. Not worth her coming all the way back in between.'

She helped him on with his coat. 'Tread carefully though, our Tommy's still not best pleased.'

William could see that as soon as he reached the car. His son watched silently as he settled himself in the passenger seat and started the engine without a word.

'So how was church this morning?' Bryony asked from the back as they pulled away.

'Lots of children,' said William.

'Catching them young,' remarked Tommy in a cynical tone.

'It didn't do you any harm.'

'Sunday school's one thing. After that it's the weak and feeble minded who keep religion in business.'

'And which category are you putting me in?' asked William tartly.

'I'm talking generally, Dad.'

'Generally, religion brings a lot of comfort to a lot of people. It makes sense of things.' He could hear the annoyance in his voice even as he spoke.

'You won't win,' Alice warned in his head. *'He'll keep at it longer than you can!'*

William bit the rest of his words back and looked out of the window instead.

They drove in silence along the Embankment and onto the dual carriageway for Northampton. He watched the countryside flashing past while, at his side, Tommy drove with his fingers spread across the centre of the wheel and one elbow resting on the window ledge. He too seemed to have lost the desire to argue but then it had always been this way with Tommy, ever since he'd bought himself the Audi A8.

When his son had first brought the car round to show him, William could tell it was the dashboard he was meant to find impressive. They'd sat together in the front and when Tommy started the engine the whole thing had lit up with red and white lights, enormous dials and fine needles flickering over luminous digits.

'That's the one thing about this car,' Tommy had said. 'The way it lights up like a cockpit.' He'd sat looking round at it all then added with obvious satisfaction: 'That and the fact that it's the most technologically advanced car on the market.'

William could believe it. The engine started at the touch of a button and Tommy had only to come near with the key in his pocket for the doors to unlock automatically. He'd no idea what the point of that was, but it was clearly very progressive.

He'd sat there, casting around in his mind for something adequate to say. It wasn't easy. He'd never so much as driven a car in his life. But he'd stared long and hard at the wide dashboard with its walnut veneer and by sheer good luck had come up with the very thing.

'I suppose that's all this newfangled satellite stuff,' he'd said pointing to some little round dials.

Tommy's smile had been one of pure happiness as he'd reached across and gently pressed a button.

'No, Dad,' he'd said, as a screen slid up in front of them. 'That's the sat nav!'

They'd gone through every option on the screen and William had been impressed without following any of it. It was enough that the car enthralled Tommy and his son had waited a long time for it.

Thirty odd years ago it had amused Tommy's brothers no end that he was still a passenger in his wife's little run-around long after they'd all bought their first cars. Of course, that had been in the early seventies, the days of the cramped flat at Havelock Street when Tommy had gone out on a limb to buy Orton's. By the time he'd opened a second shop at Rushden, he'd been running a battered white van with 'Orton's' in big red writing on the side. Not that William had seen it but then he hadn't seen much of Tommy either in those days.

He'd heard a fair bit about him though, from his work mates and neighbours. How Orton's was the place everyone went now for anything new and fancy: hairdriers, food mixers, radio cassette players, televisions. Tommy got all sorts in. From all over. Apparently.

But what they'd talked about most was that anyone, pretty much anyone at all, could get credit at Orton's on a weekly chit. It had lost Tommy the old time customers but there were plenty of newcomers on the big estates to take their place.

Things were changing by then. The Labour government had gone. There seemed to be money around again and soon it'd be video recorders and personal stereos.

Meanwhile, a smart new chain store was taking over everywhere, buying up the independent electricals, and soon its shiny red signs had gone up over Tommy's two shops.

Now, when people talked about Tommy Allbright, they talked about how he'd made a pile of money and Richard, his brother, talked about a Porsche 944 that Tommy was supposedly buying: metallic black with a three litre engine, flared wheel arches and a chrome trim.

But Tommy's world had changed then, changed unexpectedly, unspeakably.

And after that came Lister's.

'But why?' Alice had said, appalled, when Tommy stopped by late one night to tell them he'd agreed to take on the old shoe works. 'It's been going downhill for years. You'll just end up taking the blame.'

Tommy had heard her out but clearly his mind was made up. In the hall on his way out he'd turned back to William. 'It's the end of the Porsche. Can't be seen driving a car like that through the gates every day. Not when half the workers have got to go. Even then we'll be lucky to keep going.'

William couldn't remember what Tommy had driven after that. He'd been a long time pulling Lister's through the aftermath of quotas and foreign imports until the day when he'd finally pulled up outside Hartley Rise to show William the sleek black Audi.

They'd reached the turn-off for Hunsbury and the big car began winding its way along the block paved roads, slowing for the speed humps.

When William had first known Hunsbury Hill it had stood isolated among the fields; a mound of mounds with nothing on top but windswept grasslands and the upturned earthworks of the iron ore company. Now the developers had covered the lower slopes with a labyrinth of modern housing. Yet for all the changes it was impossible not to feel elated by the sense of height and distance when you reached the top.

At the summit they passed between the twin white pillars printed with Kimble's Top in neat black letters. The drive was overshadowed by magnificent rhododendrons and it was only as they swept round the final curve that the clean aspect of the house presented itself.

William got out of the car and breathed in the fresh air. His son-in-law had obtained the topmost plot when the hill was first ear marked for development and up here, on the edge of the country park that preserved the site of the iron-age hill fort, he had somehow managed to retain something of those dignified, watchful ramparts.

William gazed at the straight white lines of the innovative house Arthur had designed, the flat roofs stretching away at different levels and the series of long, thin windows identically hung with Venetian blinds. Everything felt ordered and serene.

'It'll cost a fortune to heat,' Alice had said when Arthur had brought them to see it, a couple of weeks before he married Gina. The main living space was all open plan, its different areas defined only by the angles of the building or brief partitions of opaque glass bricks.

The journalists had passed more enlightened comment; '*possibly the last and most perfect expression of modernism*' he recalled, and something about '*harmonies of shape and functional space*'. In time they'd got used to seeing it in the papers when Arthur won the Bartlett Prize and the photographers came from miles around.

Inside the women had congregated in the kitchen under the guise of 'getting things ready' and his sons were in the long living room off to the right, where the blinds had been raised to the top of every floor length window and the green light of the garden filled the room.

Richard was flipping through a line of CDs on the built-in shelves and Maurice sat nearby on one of the white leather sofas, complaining about early starts and contractors who'd have them working more hours than there were in the day.

William raised a hand in greeting and wandered over to the window to look out at the view. The L-shape of the living room made a half-enclosed quadrangle of the space closest to the house and the newly cut grass there was spotted with daisies. In the distance the main garden extended across the hilltop and he could see early flowering shrubs tumbling over stones in the rockery. The sun was high and the whole place seemed alive with the moving shadows of the surrounding trees.

He looked straight out to the furthest point where a V-shaped gap had been left among the aspens and white poplars to reveal the rooftops of Northampton below and, dead centre, the jagged outline of the Express Lift Tower.

'*A step beyond Corner Green*,' Tommy spoke mockingly in his ear. '*From the semi-enclosure of the private household to the open embrace of the wider community*.'

Tommy always had been one for remembering things exactly. William recalled the article he was quoting, a folded broadsheet they'd kept in the top drawer of the sideboard. Alice had shown it to Tommy.

'What does it mean?' she'd asked.

Tommy had read it through. 'It means they like the view.'

'There must be more to it than that,' she'd argued. 'The house is on a hill. Stands to reason there's a view.'

'Not with these people, Mother. They're all high on their own rhetoric.'

William had tried again with Arthur. 'What exactly is Corner Green?' he'd asked.

'Social housing in Blackheath. 'Best of the Lyons developments.'

And they'd been none the wiser for that.

William turned away from the view of the spring garden with a smile. 'Well,' he said. 'Whatever the theory, it's quite a spot!'

At teatime he made his way along the line of black leather dining chairs to sit with Richard and the boys at their end of the table. Everything had been laid everything out ready: plain white crockery and three white teapots placed at intervals down the middle of the table with bowls of green salad, tomatoes and baskets of sliced baguette.

He'd cast an appraising look at Gina on his way through from the living room. It was the first time in ages that he'd seen her out of her winter sweatshirts and she didn't seem to have lost weight. He noticed the others doing the same, surreptitious glances all through the meal, watching what she ate and how much, but if Gina was aware she didn't show it, just sat unconcernedly peeling an apple, spooning home-made pickle onto slices of ham and nodding at the conversation around her.

On his right Paul and Lee began talking indignantly about the launch of some internet game and a website crash that had left them marooned on separate servers. Doreen, at the other end of the table, was updating Gina on the threat of parking charges in Wellingborough town centre to a chorus of heated comments.

Tommy had gone over to the sideboard to carve a few more slices of Gina's home-cooked ham. It was her special recipe, cooked on the bone, criss-crossed and glazed with marmalade. The citrus and cloves of the marinade combined perfectly with the flavour of the meat. It reminded William of Christmas when the children were young.

He was remembering those days and that's why he didn't really hear the front door bang, only registered it in retrospect with the closer sound of keys being dumped on the hall table and high heels approaching the dining room.

He looked up as Robyn entered.

'Hi, all!'

Her large hoop ear rings banged on William's cheek as she leaned down to kiss him and he had a fleeting glimpse of a silver bead necklace and a long, green skirt over leather boots.

Doreen had stopped short in the middle of spooning pickle onto her salad. 'I thought you were staying to bring Laurel back!'

'She's decided to sleep over.'

'On a school night!'

'Oh, Mum, that's what they do these days!'

At the sideboard Tommy had carried on carving the ham without the least change in expression. Robyn reached into the cupboard for a plate. 'You can cut me some of that. I'm starving.'

She stood silently at Tommy's elbow while he sliced the ham then sauntered down the table to sit by Gina.

Doreen was fussing around pouring second cups of tea and Gina got up to fetch more milk.

'One of you could go!' said Robyn sharply to Paul and Lee. 'We all know Gina's not well.'

'I am still capable of walking to the kitchen,' protested Gina, waving Paul down as he pushed his chair back.

'You're supposed to be taking it easy,' said Robyn. 'That's what the doctor said.'

At William's end of the table Tommy had returned to his seat with his own plate of ham and glanced across at Robyn with a cynical smile. She seized on it straightaway. 'If you've got something to say you'd better say it.'

'On the subject of . . . ?'

'Me looking after Gina.'

'Make the most of it,' he said. 'When Esther gets back she'll have you out of here like a shot.'

'I'll be here as long as Gina wants,' Robyn began but Tommy cut her off.

'So when is Esther coming home?' he asked Gina.

She'd finished gathering up the little milk jugs, two in each hand, and just gave him a wry smile on her way out of the room.

The conversation stalled after that and as soon as Paul and Lee had finished eating, Richard reached for their empty plates. 'Weren't you supposed to be going head to head with Tommy on some computer game?'

'Road Rage Three,' said Lee with a wicked smile at Tommy. 'Basically, you're going to die.' He thumped his brother on the shoulder and led the way out of the room.

'Why do you all let him get away with it?' complained Robyn when only she, Gina and William were left at the table.

'Tommy's not going to change,' laughed Gina with a hand on Robyn's arm. 'You're too much like me, girl. Confrontational!'

William left his last cup of tea half-drunk on the table and went to sit in the living room with Richard and Maurice but the room was full of sun and he dozed off while they talked.

He woke with a dry mouth and stiff shoulders to find he was alone. One of the French windows was ajar and he could hear voices out in the garden.

He struggled to his feet and went outside. As he crossed the immediate quadrangle the voices became louder, away to his left, beyond the side of the house where there were greenhouses and a croquet lawn.

Turning the other way, past the white walls of the house, he saw Tommy on the far side of the lawn, heading for the narrow path that ran along the garden's perimeter.

William gripped his stick and followed.

It was a sandy path running beside a wire fence and the deep red ditch filled with leaves and roots that separated the garden from the country park. Beyond it, as far as the eye could see, old trees waded in ivy and the woodland paths snaked between them. From somewhere in the park he heard distant voices and the smack of a football.

The path meandered behind the shrubs and herbaceous borders of Gina's garden, through the trees, and ended at a circular rose bed that swept outwards from an old brick wall, close to where the drive had once met the road.

Tommy and Bryony were there, standing with their backs to him, arm in arm. Bryony was tall, her blonde hair almost touched Tommy's dark head.

As he drew near, William smelt the roses on the breeze and saw petals drifting down around the white, marble statute of a boy that stood in the centre of the flower beds. From his tunic and pan pipes he was recognisable as Peter Pan though he was neither slightly built nor long-legged. He was stocky and real with thick boyish hair, a fringe over his brow and curls round his cheeks. His strong arms and legs made him look healthy and robust.

The boy was stepping carelessly over a tree stump which rose up alongside him. His right hand rested on the trunk and as he stepped, he looked up and away, the pipes in his left hand held thoughtlessly aloft as something in the distance caught his attention. He was poised in the very moment of childlike curiosity, his mouth slightly open and his expression alert, listening as well as looking.

It struck William then that the boy always would look away, beyond them, searching for that adventurous thing in his own childish world that had called his attention. It made him feel distant, as if the boy's world were unattainable and foreign.

Tommy turned, hearing him approach and William saw fleeting surprise on his face. His son reached an arm out and Bryony did the same until they'd drawn William into the middle of them and he stood there with them, looking down at the unconcerned figure of the little boy who never grew up.

6

Esther

Esther came home three weeks later, arriving on William's doorstep on a Tuesday morning in the middle of June, having told Gina she wouldn't be back until the end of the month at least.

Tuesday was washing day. William had emptied the machine and was arranging damp shirts on hangers along the picture rail in the back parlour. When the doorbell rang he thought it was the postman with a parcel for next door.

He struggled down the narrow hallway with his stick and opened the front door to find his grand-daughter there. She looked pale, he thought, for someone who lived in Spain, thin too in her brown stripy t-shirt and narrow jeans.

'I ended up getting an earlier flight,' she said and as no further explanation seemed forthcoming he led the way into the house.

He supposed that was how it was these days with their cheap flights and casual arrangements. She'd caught the train up from Luton and must have put her things in left luggage at the station because all she carried was a square canvas bag that banged on her hip as she walked.

'Okay if I ring Mum?'

She fished a mobile out of her bag and he went through to the kitchen to put the kettle on.

The parlour smelt of damp clothes and his black socks and pants were still in a jumble all over the table but they'd have to wait. He made her tea in a mug the way she'd always liked it and when he carried it through she held the phone out to him. 'Mum wants a word.'

William held the tiny silver thing to his ear wondering how it would pick up his voice when it reached no more than a third of a way down his cheek.

'Nothing's ever straightforward, is it?' Gina's voice sounded distant. 'Why can't she just make an arrangement and stick to it?'

His daughter thought she'd better come over and they could all have lunch together but she'd have to wait for Robyn first, because she'd taken some pain killers and couldn't drive.

'I thought Mum did your lunches anyway,' Esther said putting the phone back in her bag.

'It's mostly Robyn now.'

He wondered how much she knew but it seemed dangerous ground so he changed the subject and asked about her journey instead. She told him about the early morning bus to Malaga and the English girls on the plane still hung-over from a hen weekend.

Her auburn hair fell over her face like a curtain when she talked. He'd never seen it so long, Gina had always insisted on her wearing it short: *'She's slow enough in the mornings, without having to worry about that.'*

Soon they'd run out of things to say and in the silence William caught a tell-tale murmur on the wind. Within seconds the London to Sheffield train was thundering through the siding at the end of Hartley Rise; the blast of the engine followed by the long drawn-out rocking of the carriages.

The deep ticking of the clock sounded twice as loud afterwards.

'I love this house,' said Esther. 'I always wanted to live on the way to somewhere. Not stuck up on some dead-end hilltop looking down on everyone.'

William smiled and got up to find the postcard she'd sent him when she first went to Spain. It was somewhere in the sideboard.

'Is this on the way to somewhere?' he asked, pulling it out.

She laughed. 'I can't believe you've still got that old thing!'

'It helps me picture where you live.'

'Oh I'm not really anywhere near there now.'

She came and perched on the arm of his chair and showed him a series of tiny photos on her mobile phone. He expected to see picturesque villages or the beach but they were all of people, clinking glasses at a long wooden bar or posing round the tables of an outdoor café. One couple appeared often.

'Steve and Anna,' she said. 'You know, Josie Deacon's brother.'

William did know. Josie had been Esther's closest friend when she was about fifteen. They'd known each other through friends, if he remembered rightly, not through school because Josie was a Wellingborough girl from somewhere up Kingsway and Esher went to school in Northampton. Either way they'd hit it off and Esther had been over at Josie's house nearly every day in the summer holiday that year. Once or twice she'd popped in to see William on her way to catch the bus home.

'Don't tell Mum, right,' she'd said, curled up on his sofa in a t-shirt and shorts, her slender arms and legs pink with sunburn. 'But we're not really helping with the decorating. Josie's got this hammock at the bottom of the garden and we just read and chat. Josie's Mum's really laid back.'

Two years later she and Josie had gone out for the Easter holiday to stay with Josie's brother, Steve, who ran a bar on the Costa del Sol. And it seemed they'd offered Esther a job because when the two weeks were up she'd stayed on in Spain instead of flying back with Josie to sit her 'A'Levels.

William looked with interest at the couple in the photo. He'd imagined them to be brash or sleazy, but in fact they looked as wholesome as a pair of country ramblers with their matching red sweatshirts and candid smiles.

He could see how they'd helped put Gina's mind at rest. She'd gone straight out to Spain when Esther failed to return but had come back without her.

'It's not what I wanted but she might as well get it out of her system,' she'd said to William. 'Anyway, I can't see her sticking at washing glasses and wiping tables for long. She'll be back.'

But Esther hadn't come back. The family hadn't seen her more than a couple of times in the last four years.

'Steve's really into cooking,' Esther went on flicking through the photos. 'That's why the bar's doing so well. We've moved to a bigger place.'

William watched face after face in the pictures; trendy youngsters and, just once or twice, Esther in the middle of them, unsmiling, her chin propped on her hand and the camera picking out the dreamy sea green of her eyes, so different from Gina's sharp emeralds.

They ran out of things to say again after the photos and he put the radio on for a travel programme he thought she'd like.

She smiled now and again at the commentary and sipped her tea and that's how they were when he saw the blue of Gina's Citroen pulling up outside. The passenger door slammed and the car pulled away again but he saw Gina go past the window and then heard her key turning in the front door.

Esther got up when Gina came in and they exchanged the traces of a hug. After that she stood awkwardly by the settee with her hands jammed into the pockets of her jeans.

'Where's the rest of your stuff?' Gina asked with a glance at the canvas bag and it dawned on William then that there was no left luggage at Wellingborough Station.

'I can't stay,' said Esther. 'We're building up to high season.'

Gina unbuttoned her cream fleece jacket and hung it over a dining chair. 'So when are you going back?'

'Friday.'

'I'll have fun explaining that to everyone on Sunday,' said Gina sharply and, as Esther shrugged, 'It's called family. Whether you like it or not, it comes with expectations.'

'I'll be back after the summer,' said Esther. 'I can't just drop everything.'

Gina just nodded and turned towards the kitchen to start on lunch. 'You might as well sit and catch up. There's only room for one in the kitchen.'

When she'd gone William reached across with his stick and nudged the door shut. 'You know, Esther,' he said. 'She's really not well.'

'I know. She told me. I am going to come back, Grandad.'

'Don't leave it too long.'

She'd slumped down on the sofa again and was sitting with one knee drawn up close to her chest, glancing at him through the overhanging fringe as he spoke. 'She looks okay.'

'Yes, she does,' said William. 'I'm afraid that's often the way.'

In the background the radio was still playing and foreign travel gave way to the lunchtime news.

'Why don't you lay the table,' he suggested. 'That'll please your Mum.'

Robyn arrived shortly afterwards with fresh groceries and went to join Gina in the kitchen. Soon they brought the lunch through: pork chops with potato and swede mashed with butter and fresh peas.

While they ate Robyn asked Esther about Spain and Esther talked on about the midweek quiz they'd introduced at the bar, about happy hour on Mondays and the new karaoke machine that was bringing people in.

William sensed Gina's annoyance growing as she picked silently at her food beside him. There were shadows round her eyes as if she hadn't been sleeping well.

'You could easily get a bar job round here,' Robyn said to Esther. 'There's loads of clubs in Northampton.'

Esther shook her head. 'It wouldn't be the same.'

'Oh I don't know,' said Gina. 'Sleeping 'til midday. Earning a pittance. It can't be that different.'

Esther just shrugged. 'I like what I'm doing. What's wrong with that?'

'You might be happy going with the flow now,' said Gina. 'While you're young and carefree. But sooner or later you'll want something behind you. You've got no qualifications, no prospects and no security.'

Esther propped one elbow on the table and went on eating just with her fork, eyes on her plate.

'If you want to live abroad, fine!' Gina went on. 'But for goodness sake do something with your life. Get into a company that'll teach you something. Give you a career.'

'Like you did?'

William's own food was suddenly hard to swallow.

'You just worked in a shop, Mum. It was good enough for you.'

'Well work in a bloody shop then!' snapped Gina. 'Get trained up in buying or merchandising.'

'Like you did?'

'I had no choice. In my day you took what you were given. But you! You've had everything on a plate and you don't even know what to do with it.'

Esther had put her fork down and sat silent.

Gina raised a glass of water shakily to her lips. 'I'm sorry,' she said. 'I'm tired. It makes me tetchy.'

No-one was eating any more. Robyn got up to clear the plates. 'I was thinking of going home to Mum and Dad's for a few weeks,' she said to Gina. 'Give you two some time alone.'

'No need,' said Gina. 'Esther's going back on Friday.'

Robyn stared, halfway through collecting the plates into a neat pile.

Esther got up and took them off her. 'I'll wash up.'

'Let me come and dry then,' said Robyn and followed her out of the room.

William and Gina were left alone at the table.

'How is it I'm so good with everyone else's kids and so useless with my own?' asked Gina.

'Oh, I wouldn't say that.'

'She's such a dolly-daydream. Drifting through life. What's going to happen when I'm not here?'

'Don't think like that!' said William, appalled.

But she shrugged and gave him a weak smile. 'I have to, Dad.'

They had a cup of tea together and soon afterwards Gina thought they'd better make a move. Robyn had been a long time out in the back parlour and when William went through he found she'd ironed all his shirts, something Gina normally did for him.

'You know, if you washed on Fridays,' she said putting on her coat, 'I could do your ironing with ours at the weekend.'

He wanted to say, 'Tuesday's washing day,' but held back. She was only trying to help.

The others had already gone out to the car and as she got her things together she smiled at him.

'Oh well. It'll be one in the eye for Tommy, won't it? Wait til he hears Esther's been home and just gone straight back to Spain again!'

William followed her out to the pavement and watched them pull away: Robyn in the high driver's seat of the Picasso and Esther raising a hand and a half-smile from the back as they drove off. He felt exhausted and it was only halfway through the afternoon.

Tommy rang him on Friday night. Hearing his voice, William trailed the thin cable of the telephone over the sideboard and took the phone back with him to the armchair.

'Just what is she thinking?' Tommy was saying as he sank down into the cushions. 'I rang Gina to see if they wanted to borrow the old Mini for Esther. Apparently she arrived on Tuesday and went back today. Did you see her?'

'Yes.'

'Well does she know how serious things are?'

'Yes.' William leaned his head against the back of the chair, his chest still rising and falling with the effort of having got up to answer the phone.

'She can't know!'

'She went back to sort things out.'

'What's to sort out? She's pulling pints in a bar!'

'Oh Tommy,' said William wearily.

'Can you honestly say you're not appalled? The fact is, even if she had her own business out there she damn well ought to be back here given what's going on.'

'Are you talking about Gina or the fact that Robyn's running the show?'

'Both, since you ask.'

William sighed deeply.

'Well I'm not going to lie to you,' said Tommy at the other end of the line. 'You know how I feel.'

'Oh go and talk to Bryony!' said William. 'I'm too tired for this.'

On Sunday Gina had a headache and she and Robyn stayed at home all afternoon instead of joining the family for tea.

The rest of them gathered at Richard and Doreen's house though and it didn't take long for the conversation to get onto Esther.

'Has she really gone straight back?' asked Maurice's wife, Lorraine, reaching over to place a marble cake she'd made at the centre of the table.

'Well I can't say I'm surprised,' said Doreen with a glance back towards Tommy in the kitchen. 'Not everyone's cut out for the sick room. Robyn's unusual. She's very caring and practical.'

'It's got to be more than that,' said Lorraine. 'Still it's never been any secret how much Esther hates Kimble's Top.'

'That's complete nonsense!' said Tommy through the open doorway.

'No it isn't,' said Lorraine firmly.

William, sitting at the end of the table, looked up in surprise. Lorraine wasn't much for challenging anyone, least of all Tommy, but she stood facing him now, a willowy figure, mousey and unremarkable but for the striking blue and lilac of her summer dress.

'What would you know about it?' said Tommy.

'I got quite close to Esther once. We had some days out after her GCSEs. She hated living up there in splendid isolation, her friends afraid to visit. Gina's made Kimble's Top a showcase.'

'That house is unique.'

'No-one's going to argue with you about that, Tommy,' said Lorraine. 'I'm talking about Esther. And if she wasn't happy here when everything was fine, why would she want to come back now it isn't?'

'Well Gina obviously knew how she felt,' said Doreen said. 'She once talked about leaving Kimble's Top to Robyn. After Laurel was born and Esther disappeared off to Spain.'

Tommy laughed mirthlessly at that.

'I suppose you tried to put her off the idea,' said Doreen.

'I didn't have to,' said Tommy. 'Robyn could hardly keep a place like that going on benefits. And Gina's no fool.'

'There's rents,' said Doreen defensively. 'From the flats on Chelmsford Walk. Arthur had them put in trust so they're all tied in. He meant it to be self-sustaining.'

'You don't even know the meaning of the word,' said Tommy.

'All the same,' said Lorraine. 'It might be best, if Gina wants the house kept in the family. There's nothing to stop Esther selling it.'

William had had enough. He pulled the patio door open and went to find Richard in the garden. He was at the far end, watering tomatoes in the raised beds that surrounded the shed and greenhouse. Seeing William he put the watering can down, came to sit beside him on one of the upturned barrels and lit a cigarette. They'd only been there a few minutes when Tommy appeared at the end of the path.

'I can't believe you're still smoking those things,' he said to Richard. 'They're going to kill you.'

'Not if the beer gets me first!'

William watched Tommy prowl round the vegetable beds where lettuces sat in clumps on the light brown earth and ridged Perspex tunnels covered green leafy plants.

'What's the deal here then?' asked Tommy.

'Gardening,' said Richard with an amused glance at William. 'You should try it sometime. Helps you relax.'

Tommy gave him a black look and stood with his hands in his pockets gently kicking the wooden border of the vegetable patch.

'Esther couldn't have realised how serious things were,' he said to William after a while. 'Are you sure Gina told her straight?'

'Yes.'

'I don't suppose she left you a phone number?'

'I'd leave well alone, if I were you,' said Richard.

'You can't approve of her going back!'

'I neither approve nor disapprove since it's none of my business. Anyway, no point getting wound up over things on a nice summer's afternoon.'

'Oh well, that's you all over,' said Tommy roughly. 'God forbid you should actually take life seriously or show some responsibility.'

Richard got up from the barrel and flung an arm round Tommy's shoulders, ignoring his angry frown. 'Look, Tommy. I am not going to fight with you. And you are not going to fight with me. Eighteen years I shared a bedroom with you, remember? You don't frighten me!'

Tommy looked at William and rolled his eyes heavenwards, half-amused. But then another thought must have crossed his mind. He frowned again. 'Would Esther really sell Kimble's Top?'

William hadn't been home long when Robyn rang.

'How was tea?' she asked brightly and he guessed Doreen must have told her all about it. 'Anyway,' she said, 'I'll see you for lunch tomorrow. And don't forget you're washing on Fridays from now on. I was thinking about Sunday teas as well. Gina and I will pick you up next time. After all, we'll be passing the door.'

'No.' he said. 'It's all right.'

Tommy and Bryony had always picked him up for Sunday tea.

'But it makes more sense!'

'Robyn,' he said weakly. 'Do you think we could just leave some things as they are?'

When she'd gone he took Esther's postcard out again and sat looking at the picture of the bar where she'd once lived with its white archway, aluminium tables and red umbrellas filling one side of a cobbled square.

It was the nearest thing he had to a photo of Esther. She'd hated having her picture taken and contrived to spirit away even the regular school portraits they'd been given, much to Gina's fury. In the end Alice had stepped in and they'd agreed to keep the photos upstairs on her dressing table, but Esther had taken even these when Alice died.

He thought of the steady looking couple she'd shown him and the succession of young, smiling faces and wondered what she found over there among all those strangers that she couldn't seem to find here among her own.

7

Through the Summer

Afterwards it seemed to William as though he'd spent all of the summer at Kimble's Top. Robyn liked to fetch him mid-mornings and bring him over to the house for lunch so she could get on with things.

For two long, drawn-out weeks of July he didn't see Gina. She was on the Hardy Reynolds ward having chemotherapy and didn't want visitors. 'Plenty of time for you all to run around after me when I'm out.'

Robyn phoned the hospital every day for an update but otherwise they just ate lunch together and waited for Gina to come home.

Most afternoons he wandered in the garden. For years Gina had paid an old pensioner to keep it tidy, a retired groundsman commonly known as Stan for no other reason than that his surname was Matthews. He'd gone into a home a couple of summers back so now Gina had found some young fellow to take it on and Robyn had her doubts about him.

'Do me a favour and keep an eye on things will you?' she said to William on his first afternoon there. 'Only, I don't know what I'm looking at.'

He suspected it was a ruse to keep him occupied but went outside anyway, heading instinctively for the greenhouses; he had about as much idea as Robyn when it came to flower beds and summer borders. Vegetables were much more his thing.

He glanced into the first greenhouse. The white painted vents had been propped open and the humid smell of tomato plants greeted him. They were lined up in pots, climbing a good five feet up the canes and the shoots all cut back above the flowers. The compost looked dark and damp enough too.

Back outside he carried along the gravel path to look at the runner beans and the bed in front of them which was crowded with wigwams of colourful sweet peas. The soil all around had been freshly hoed.

The sun was high in the sky, its warmth like a blanket on his back and shoulders. He was beginning to sweat despite his short-sleeved shirt and light trousers. Up ahead was one of the shadiest spots in the garden: a ridge of red earth at the side of the hilltop with a circle of trees, four dark firs with spindly branches thrown upwards. William made his way slowly over and stood among them. Even on hot days this place still held the chilly damp of woodland. His grandchildren had loved to play here when they were little, calling it an enchanted circle because of the way the trees stood, but it was the panoramic view of Kimble's Top that drew William.

In front of him lay the whole garden; tall trees all around standing up straight from the different levels of the hillside and stretched between them, dwarfed by the great trunks and the wide reach of the branches, the velvet spread of the lawn, clusters of shrubs and the long flower beds where, here and there, the remarkable blue of borage and morning glory caught his eye.

He stood and stared across the quiet scene, envying its stillness.

By the time Gina came home in mid July the garden was in full summer flow and its beauty filled the house too; Robyn had put flowers everywhere and the fragrance of sweet peas wafted through the open spaces.

At the top end of the living room near the kitchen she'd covered one of the white leather settees with an embroidered throw and cushions. A couple of glass-topped tables had been pulled close with framed photos and a pile of magazines. William noticed Gina's reading glasses there too and a box of tissues.

He'd never seen such a personal corner at Kimble's Top, its interior had always been carefully minimalist: the curved white walls broken only by occasional alcoves with built-in shelves and the spotlights shining down on expensive glassware and rare ceramics. There had never been anything as normal as homely clutter to be seen.

Gina seemed to like what Robyn had done though. She came home in good spirits and settled back on the settee with a smile.

If anything she actually looked rather well, William thought, and as they sipped tea together he felt rather sorry for Robyn's well-meaning efforts. Gina had never been one to sit anywhere for long.

That was before the nausea started. The first few days they'd eaten lunch on the terrace and walked in the garden afterwards but he arrived one morning to find Gina lying full length on the sofa. For days afterwards she slept through the long afternoons, curled under a blanket and breathing deeply, her forehead covered with perspiration.

Robyn had bought a little white cabinet to stand behind the settee, an elegant affair with fancy fretwork and scrolled edges that held all the medicinal stuff out of sight but close at hand. She'd amassed a pile of dietary books too and spent most of her time sitting on a high stool at the kitchen counter, working through them and scribbling in a notebook. One afternoon William stood looking through the titles. *Fighting back with diet. A practical guide for managing nutrition. Understanding your cancer. An Oncology Handbook.* They were thick books with close type and business-like covers. All this learning, he thought, and no-one can just make it go away.

'Gina's worse now than when she came out of hospital,' he said to Robyn.

She looked up briefly from her notebook. 'It's like that sometimes. The side effects come afterwards.'

He went back to the living room. The windows had been thrown open but the blinds were down to keep the full sun off Gina. He sat in the leather armchair Robyn had brought through from Arthur's study. Gina stirred as he laid his stick on the floor but her eyes only flickered open for a moment and, as he sat watching her, his own head nodded and they dozed together.

It must have been her sudden movement that awakened him. He opened his eyes to see her sitting bolt upright, shuddering, calling for Robyn.

There were tears in her voice and Robyn must have been listening out because she was already there, bowl in hand, leaning over her. William's own mouth went dry as

Gina heaved. But it was the misery in her voice that hurt him most. It came back to him afterwards in the silence of Hartley Rise when he sat propped against his own pillows unable to sleep.

'I can't stand this, Dad,' she said to him one afternoon as he sat beside her.

'Try a drop of tea or something.'

'I just feel so sick all the time.'

She pressed a hand against her face and dissolved into tears and all he could do was sit by, listening to Robyn in the kitchen mixing things in the blender as she tried some new combination that might work for Gina.

By now it was August and there was still no sign of Esther coming home but Gina seemed to prefer it that way. 'The way I feel I'd end up saying something I shouldn't. And she'd have to live with that.'

You'd have stuck around if it had been her. William thought it but kept his mouth shut. No point in any of them saying something they shouldn't.

Just when he'd begun to think it would never end, the sickness passed and towards the end of August Gina began to look better. She put it down to Robyn's persistence with the milkshakes and for all William knew, she could have been right.

Now she sat up on the sofa with the blanket neatly folded beside her and one day he found her looking through a box of old photographs Robyn had produced. She smiled as he came to sit with her.

'You wouldn't look twice at him, would you?' she said holding up a snapshot of Arthur. 'That's exactly how he was the day I first laid eyes on him. Carnival Parade. 1969. Just a middle aged man in a suit with a big brown camera.'

William sat down beside her, taking the little photo carefully by the corner.

'He wanted a picture of his niece,' said Gina. 'Waited ages. The girls' band was a rabble. I was meant to be handing the drums out, getting them into line. The minute he opened his mouth I thought, you're not from round here. Far too nicely spoken. Can't imagine what he ever saw in me! Not exactly alluring, was I?'

William smiled. It was true Gina had never been one for getting dolled up and partying. She'd gone straight from school to Crosby's Bakery on Hammond Street; a real old-fashioned place where people still took their Sunday roasts on a Saturday night to have them cook in the heat from the ovens. If Gina was known for anything in the neighbourhood it was for the thin cotton frocks she wore in all weathers and her habit of letting the gate bang shut when she pulled her bicycle out of the back yard for a four o'clock start every morning.

Arthur had seen something he liked though. Gina had been twenty nine by then, well past marrying in most people's book, but then Arthur himself was over forty. Old enough to have money, friends and successful business contacts. It had been quite a wedding. They'd filled St Luke's to the very back pews and made a real racket in the lounge at The Hind afterwards. William remembered the smell of champagne, Chablis served at the top table and his sons under strict instructions to stay off the beer at least until the meal was over.

Not that Arthur would have worried. He'd always taken them for what they were. He was a man who knew his own mind and did things his own way. Middle aged before his time perhaps, but then he'd been an adolescent in the war and William had seen that before: lads too young to fight but old enough to feel the burden of it all.

If anything Arthur was more susceptible to the horrors of war than men William had known at the front. Totally averse to violence. Unlike William's sons, Arthur listened attentively when his elders talked about those days, always turned out on Armistice Day and bought a round of drinks in the Legion afterwards.

Arthur had set ways of handling things and he handled them well. He'd been quiet, unobtrusive and old fashioned.

William wondered what he'd have thought about Esther staying away at a time like this. But then if Arthur had still been around perhaps Esther would never have gone off to Spain in the first place.

Gina reminisced a lot now. They sat out on the terrace under the blue August skies, the buddleia in purple bloom at the edge of the lawn and white butterflies flitting everywhere, casting their rapid shadows on the ground.

That sheltered space with its view over the lawn seemed to awaken all her happiest memories. Anywhere else a terrace of those proportions would have seemed grand but at Kimble's Top it was a gentle place of white stone with a simple curved balustrade, semi-circular stone seats and white globes for lights all the way down.

She talked about the parties they'd held there for Arthur's colleagues, for his business friends and the shareholders of R S Gypsum. They'd always held the annual summer party and Robert Scholt himself had presided. William had seen the photos in the County Recorder: elegant women in jewellery and evening gowns with long gloves, men in dinner jackets drinking whisky and Scholt himself, of course: a short man with strong features, downright ugly but for his money. High class in his white tie and silk scarf and sometimes an opera cloak thrown eccentrically over his shoulders.

Scholt had been one of Arthur's oldest associates and a big name in the building trade with a fortune made from plasterboard, ceiling panels, paint and welding compounds. William suspected the company's dividends had funded a good deal more than the summer parties at Kimble's Top.

'What did happen with R S Gypsum in the end?' he asked Gina. 'Weren't the Americans going to buy it?'

'There was talk of it,' her tone was non committal and she seemed reluctant to elaborate. 'You know,' she said, 'for all the parties we had here, what Arthur liked best was when just the four of us went out to some country pub.'

William smiled, remembering their Saturday drives, he and Alice sitting in the back of Arthur's blue Morris Oxford, feeling like a young courting couple again. They'd always ended up at some village pub on the way home.

He'd held Arthur back at the bar once; 'Let me pay, at least for the beer if you won't take anything for the petrol.'

But Arthur had shook his head, pocketing his change, then lifted his foaming pint glass. 'No,' he'd said. 'I like to treat you. I never got the chance with my own Mum and Dad.'

At William's side Gina's thoughts were following their own tack.

'I wasn't at all sure about coming here,' she said looking out across the garden. 'I couldn't imagine being away from Hartley Rise and all of you. But once I got here, I didn't miss home at all. Even with Arthur out all day. He was so keen on me planning the garden. I used to look at the new houses going up around the hill and think, none of their gardens will be a patch on ours. It was something I could give back to him.'

The sun had dropped behind the trees as they talked and the air was sweet now with the fragrance of tobacco plants.

'I must have planted tons of those things over the years,' Gina said. 'Arthur insisted on having them right outside his study window. Never did any good. Full sun all day long, they just dried out every time.'

She began to gather her things up to go indoors then stood for a long moment looking out again across the garden.

'You know it's not a bad legacy. The house from Arthur and the garden from me. And Esther's even started phoning now, a couple of times a week. That's more than she's ever done.'

Esther phoned regularly but she still didn't come home and even William began to think that perhaps Gina was putting a brave face on things when they talked. He asked Robyn about it in the car one evening as she drove him back to Hartley Rise. 'The high season must be nearly over. Isn't that what she went back for?'

Robyn laughed. 'You're getting like Tommy.'

It was a rare allusion. They never mentioned Tommy between them and William knew he and Robyn hadn't met for weeks. The family gatherings on Sundays had been disrupted and when Robyn brought him home from Kimble's Top every day she hung around at Hartley Rise, dusting and hoovering and generally fussing about. William knew it was so she'd avoid seeing Tommy when he visited Gina after work.

He hadn't seen much of Tommy himself over the last few weeks but he'd seen the signs of his son's visits to Kimble's Top: a couple of red leather photo albums, dog-eared postcards from years gone by and once or twice a vase of Albertine roses that he knew had come from Ise Avenue. All the things he'd brought stood on a separate table in the living room and Robyn made a point of never moving it.

It was hardly surprising, though, if Tommy were fretting about Esther coming home. He was up there frequently at Gina's, seeing what William was seeing.

Gina's health was failing. She didn't always have the energy to make it onto the terrace, she was listless sometimes, disinterested even in the garden, and her face had a fragile softness to it now. She looked more than pale, the skin was drawn in delicate lines over her cheeks and round her mouth. She looked how Alice had looked near the end.

In the middle of September she was due to have a scan. The rest of the family talked of it constantly as though everything were hanging on it. They talked of Esther too with lowered voices and meaningful glances and wondered if one of them should ring her.

Tommy, as usual, was one step ahead, pursuing his own logic.

A few days before the scan he arrived at Kimble's Top around midday. Robyn took one look at the black Audi pulling up on the drive and went off to her room without a word.

'You might as well know I saw Esther yesterday,' Tommy said pulling an upright chair close to the sofa to sit by Gina. 'I was over in Portugal seeing a supplier. It was easy enough just to cross the border into Spain.'

'You never did know when to leave well alone, did you?' said Gina.

'She ought to be here.'

Gina dropped her head back against a cushion and closed her eyes. She'd taken a handful of tablets when William had first arrived and was looking drowsier by the minute.

'Well come on,' she said at last. 'Let's hear all about it. Did you see her flat and everything?'

'Briefly. She's living over the bar. Seems to have things the way she wants them. People dropping by, that kind of thing.'

Gina listened, nodding, but within minutes she'd fallen asleep. William followed Tommy out to his car.

'Esther's a strange one, living above that two bit bar,' his son said. 'She couldn't care less that Kimble's Top is going to be hers.'

'You never talked to her about that!'

Tommy turned to look at him. 'She brought it up. I told her she needed to come home. She said she was home. It went on from there.'

'So is she coming? Soon?'

'I wouldn't bet on it,' said Tommy. 'I'm beginning to think Gina's been right all these years. Dollydaydream's not far off the mark. She's totally self-centred.'

'Don't get like this over Esther,' said William. 'It's bad enough the way you are with Robyn.'

'Well fortunately she's had the sense to stay out of my way,' said Tommy and with that he got in his car and pulled away down the drive.

William went back inside. In the living room Gina was sound asleep and there was no sound from Robyn's room. He turned the radio on low and sat listening to a discussion about chemical additives and food allergies.

At five o'clock he got up to make some tea and took a cup along the corridor to Robyn's room where the door was ajar. She was lying on the bed but sat up as he pushed the door back: 'Thought you might like some tea.'

She looked weary as she moved to clear a space on the bedside table and when he put the cup down she slipped an arm across his back. 'We're doing okay, aren't we, Granddad?'

William felt a sudden affection for her. He put his arm around her shoulder and they stayed there together for a moment. Then she turned away to the sink in the corner to splash water on her face and he left her there and made his way back to the living room in case Gina awoke and found herself alone.

8

TWO WINTER NIGHTS

Gina had her scan on a Wednesday lunchtime. William spent the day alone at Hartley Rise and it was after five when Robyn phoned him.

'We're back but it's taken it out of her. The results are next week.'

When he went up to Kimble's Top the next day, though, Gina didn't seem too bad at all. They even walked out in the garden. The weather had turned with the middle of September; the sky was colourless and there was damp in the air although it had stayed mild. A few leaves blew around as they crossed the grass.

They made it all the way to the perimeter path where yellow lilies had come out, planted back in May for a bit of late colour. William had his eye on a wooden bench further along, beside a patch of purple michaelmas daisies but it was too far for Gina. They turned back to the house.

Gina had an afternoon appointment to hear the results of the scan so Robyn cooked William an early lunch and he stayed at Kimble's Top on his own waiting for the two of them to come back. They'd bought a sack of autumn crocuses for the pots on the terrace so he took himself off to the greenhouse and stood at the wooden bench, pushing the bulbs down in the dark compost and listening out for the sweet trill of a nearby robin in between the warbling of the wood pigeons.

When they returned Gina's progress from the car to the living room was slow. She took careful steps as if afraid of falling and her arm was tight through Robyn's all the way.

'Not good news, I'm afraid,' she told William when they reached the living room. 'But then we knew it wouldn't be.'

She hadn't sat with him for more than a few minutes before she decided to go and lie down.

'I'll make a hot drink,' said Robyn getting up too as Gina left the room.

She pulled a notebook out of her handbag and passed it to William.

'Have a look at this. I wrote it all down in case we forgot something.'

William sat looking at the rough jottings but they made little sense: *CT computerised using X-rays Abdominal shows spread enlarged nodes Staging primary tumour T-3 Inguinal lymph nodes and major organs T-3 N-1 M-2.*

He left the notebook on the table and went to find Robyn in the kitchen. She'd put the teapot ready with cups for the two of them next to it, a separate mug for Gina, and was grinding a pile of narrow seeds in a pestle and mortar.

'Did you read my notes?'

He nodded but said nothing.

'Basically it's spread despite the chemo.'

She put the little mash of seeds in a tea strainer and poured hot water from the kettle slowly through into

Gina's mug. William wrinkled his nose at the smell of aniseed and she laughed.

'It's good for the stomach. And makes the water taste of something.'

She put the mug on a tray and went to knock the seeds out of the silver strainer into the compost pot.

William sat on one of the high stools watching her. She wore a light coloured skirt and a soft pink top that folded casually down at the neck round three buttons. A selection of smart bangles jingled on her wrist as she went moved around, warming the teapot, bringing the kettle back to the boil and making their tea. As she arranged the tea cosy she spoke again.

'They said it's not about how long now. Just making every day the best we can.'

She picked up Gina's mug and turned towards the bedroom, the liquorice smell of the fennel reaching him again as she passed.

By October the district nurse was coming in every morning and Robyn came later to Hartley Rise, picking William up around midday. The relentless business of going out every day was telling on him now. His chest hurt and it took him longer than ever to get going in the morning. He said nothing to Robyn though. There was no question of staying away from Kimble's Top. Not now.

October had brought winter with it: only the very tops of the trees reflected the sun on the drive out to Hunsbury Hill and the grass verges were patchy, littered with circles of orange and yellow leaves, like a threadbare eastern carpet.

Robyn was showing the strain too. She looked tired and pale behind the eyeshadow and bright lipstick she always wore.

One day though she was brighter than usual when she came to collect him. 'Esther's finally booked a flight,' she said. 'She'll be back next week.'

William wondered if Tommy knew.

His son hadn't been the same since he'd gone out to visit Esther back in August. He'd dropped in late at Hartley Rise a couple of days ago, on one of Gina's worst days yet, gone through to make the tea for William then come back to stand in the front room, drying teaspoons on a linen cloth and talking angrily.

'Two centuries of medical science, all the latest technology and the best they can do is take a bloody photo and say, yes, it's spreading.'

When the kettle whistled he'd gone to fetch the tea, then stood silent at the mantelpiece, kicking a foot against the grate where as a boy he'd once sat too close, shrinking crisp packets in the flames, and Gina had berated him for singeing the sleeve of his pullover.

'She's on twice the medication and it's not even touching the pain.'

Sitting in the car beside Robyn, William stared out of the window. The wind was getting up as they turned down the Embankment, the swans on the river bobbing about in a swell of dark grey ripples.

'My God,' Tommy had said before he left. 'No wonder they all leave their money to cancer research.'

But it was more than the way things were with Gina that had upset him. Tommy had a perplexed look, William thought, as though he were trying to work something out that made no sense to him. William had never seen him so troubled.

By the time Esther came home, Gina never left her bed. On the good days she was restless with fatigue and a nagging backache. The worst times brought pain that set her face tight and closed her eyes in a breathless silence. Her lips shone with lip salve but she complained that they were permanently dry.

Robyn had moved all the personal things into the bedroom now: the glass-topped tables with the photos and magazines and Tommy's collection of albums and postcards. The little white cabinet was there too beside the wash basin. An armchair stood on each side of the bed and the bedside cabinets had vases of fresh flowers. When the wintry afternoons set in Robyn bought a collection of little lamps to put around the room.

She had all sorts of ploys for taking Gina's mind off things even for ten minutes at a time: CDs of Tony Hancock and Round the Horn, crossword books and even an H E Bates' novel, *Love for Lydia*, that she offered to read to her because it was set in Rushden and she thought Gina might like it.

Most successful of all though was her suggestion that Gina teach her to knit. She spent several afternoons wrestling with a tangled pile of blue and white wool and a long needle until, finally, she held it up and Gina thought it was time to admit defeat.

'That whole thing needs unravelling,' she said managing an amused smile at William. 'You haven't really got the patience for it!'

William had lost track of time. Bonfire night had come and gone and there were boxes of Christmas cards in the corner shop but it all seemed far away. It's never really like a Christmas card, he thought, looking out of the car window one day at dark figures hunched in black overcoats, their faces set against the wind. Always just another dismal winter.

His world had shrunk to Gina's bedroom, with an occasional change of faces among the district nurses to vary the same old routine of himself, Gina and Robyn. When Esther arrived she fitted into it all in her own peculiar way.

'She's not even sleeping at the house,' Robyn told him a few days after Esther had come home. 'Some old school mate picks her up every night. She's staying with friends.'

She'd declined the offer of Tommy and Bryony's old Mini and William got to know one face in particular among the youngsters who drove her around: a thin lad with a pony tail who sat on the drive in a battered red Peugeot with the radio turned up high.

'I need to get out sometimes,' Esther told him. 'Be with my own friends. Anyway, Mum doesn't need me there at night.'

During the day, when she joined them in Gina's bedroom, she mostly sat in the armchair on the other side of the bed, knees drawn up to her chest, saying little even when they made an effort to include her. Whenever Gina slept she disappeared into Arthur's study to chat online with friends.

'She just can't hack it, can she?' Robyn said angrily to William one afternoon.

'It must be hard,' was all he could find to say. 'I suppose she needs a break.'

'What about Gina?' said Robyn. 'When does she ever get a break?'

She went off to the kitchen by herself and William stepped across the hallway and stood at the entrance to the study watching Esther on the computer.

She must have sensed him there because she suddenly turned round looking alarmed. 'Is everything all right?'

He nodded reassurance, too breathless to speak, and she turned back to the keyboard but he'd seen the fear in her green eyes.

He went into the room and stood beside the windows at the far end overlooking the drive. 'Is it all right?' he asked. 'Being back.'

She looked up briefly and nodded.

'It's never easy. Times like these,' he ventured but saw her tense up immediately as she went back to the computer the screen. 'Well,' he concluded, 'At least you've got good friends.'

He looked around the room suddenly wanting to linger. He'd rarely ever been in here over the years and suddenly the place intrigued him, Arthur's private sanctum within the public dwelling he'd built for everyone to scrutinise.

The three narrow windows beside him stretched from floor to ceiling and though the room was small it felt light and spacious. The only furniture was the desk and office chair. The desk was wide but had nothing on it apart from the computer and a silver Montblanc pen case. He supposed Arthur had kept everything in the pedestals at each end, they had drawers all the way down.

The desk stood near the opening to the hall and on the same wall, but close to the windows where William stood, were alcoves and in-built shelves with books of architecture and design, big glossy books with photographs, and a neat row of box files labelled alphabetically.

Halfway along one shelf a space had been cleared for a big photo frame that had five pictures inside carefully positioned and mounted. Arthur's parents were there, Gina too and Esther, about seven years old sipping coke through a straw at a pavement café. Then there was Arthur shaking some dignitary's hand at an awards ceremony and unexpectedly, right at the end, a signed photograph of the wartime pilot, Larry Clifton.

William stepped forward to have a closer look. Clifton's name had often appeared in the local papers but William had never seen his picture. The man was prudish about publicity yet, from his photo, he hardly seemed camera shy.

He was posing slightly sideways, one ear visible at the side of his wing commander's cap and the other hidden behind the gaunt profile of his cheek. His nose was thin and very straight and his eyes deep, dark ovals with fine eyebrows over them. He was clean shaven and would have looked boyish but for the sombre, thoughtful expression. Yet the cap was tilted, almost imperceptibly, nothing rakish, but obviously meant to create a more sympathetic look than the customary straight-set angle. And though the shot finished above the waist, it was clear from the open shoulder and the triangle of white background at the crook of the arm, that Clifton was standing with one hand, quite casually, in his pocket.

It was a showman's stance and though the handwritten message above Clifton's left shoulder was simple; *to my dear friends Arthur and Gina with affection*, the final flamboyant signature completely overshadowed it.

Arthur and Clifton had been old friends, though how they'd met William wasn't sure. Clifton was the county boy turned hero, over thirty kills if you could believe the hearsay and the honoured patron of several charities. Clifton had treated Kimble's Top as something of a personal refuge by all accounts. He'd drunk vodka martinis on the terrace and graced the grander parties but all that was a long time ago now. Larry had moved to Madeira, in search of a milder climate, even before Arthur had died of a heart attack.

The sudden musical flourish of the computer shutting down brought William back with a jolt. Esther had got up from the chair and was standing looking at him.

'I've never really been in here before,' he said.

'I used to sit here all the time when Dad died,' she shrugged. 'Just sitting in his chair made me feel as though he was still around.'

William could picture it: the chair must have engulfed her, she'd been eight years old when Arthur died.

The monitor had turned black except for a green winking light, Esther switched it off and moved towards the hall, then turned back evidently waiting for William to leave with her. He grasped his stick more firmly and followed her slowly out of the room.

Late at night on the last Tuesday in November Gina became worse. William could see something was wrong when Robyn came to pick him up the next morning. He was ready to go as usual but she wanted to come inside for a cup of tea first. She looked as if she hadn't slept much.

'Nearly called you last night,' she said. 'Gina got off to sleep and then all of a sudden she was just really still. Hardly breathing. We couldn't rouse her at all.'

William poured the tea while she talked.

'I was in a right panic. Couldn't find the doctor's file. Or the phone number. It's always in the top drawer of the desk. It had slipped down the back. Me and Tommy: we ended up turning out half the drawers. And there it was all along.'

'Tommy?' queried William.

'He'd stayed on because Gina was so bad. The worst of it is, we didn't even think to call Esther. Just think if something had happened and she hadn't been there.'

William reached across and squeezed her arm. 'You did all the right things. What did the doctor say?'

'Not much. She seemed better by the time he got there.'

'And Tommy?'

She looked at him blankly.

'He was all right with you?' asked William. 'No sharp words?'

'Oh!' she shrugged. 'We got so caught up going through the desk. It was silly. The drawer was overflowing. I should have thought the papers could have slipped down. It's just, I feel so bad about Esther.'

Three days later, on the first Friday in December William sat all through the afternoon listening to Gina's uneven breathing. When evening came they agreed he'd go home, but Robyn phoned after ten o'clock and then Tommy arrived to take him back to Kimble's Top.

They drove in silence round the desolate ring road and it was like a nether world. The bright lights of the retail parks flashed past in the darkness and the succession of roundabouts seemed never ending.

At Hunsbury Hill everything was as it had always been; the sudden windswept feel as William got out of the car, the rhododendrons rustling in the breeze and the familiar white façade with lights shining from the windows.

Robyn must have been looking out for them because she opened the front door straightaway and he was relieved to see she looked composed, even managing a tired smile as she took his coat.

Esther looked up from her usual armchair as he entered the bedroom but said nothing. For once William ignored his own chair and instead lowered himself slowly to sit on the edge of the bed. Gina lay on her side, her breathing painfully slow. He found himself listening anxiously for each new breath, growing tense when the silence between them seemed longer than usual, only to hear the breath come again after all.

He sat that way for some time, his eyes on her frail, wasted cheeks and the dark, shadowy sockets of her eyes. Robyn had put a fresh quilt on the bed and Gina's shoulders barely lifted it as they rose and fell. A single lamp shone from the far corner of the room and its light fell across them both as he watched her.

Eventually he moved to the armchair, glancing at Esther as he got settled, but her face was turned away, half hidden in the shadows.

Tommy had brought an upright chair to the foot of the bed and sat motionless, leaning forward with his elbows on his knees. William couldn't see whether his eyes were on Gina or the floor, or whether they were closed.

He leaned his own head back but was far too wakeful to doze. He was aware of Robyn moving around behind him, occasionally she came and bent over Gina, stroking her forehead and firming the pillows.

He lost track of how long they sat that way but suddenly Robyn's hand was firm on his arm. She moved past him to the bed and he could hear Gina's voice.

Her words were indistinct. A murmur. Robyn turned to look at him. William struggled up and crossed to the bed, his eyes fixed on Gina's face. She had half turned onto her back. Her eyes were open but unfocused, black in the lamplight. She spoke again, indistinctly, repeating something with an incoherent urgency, like a child waking from a dream.

He sat down clumsily on the bed and closed his right hand on Gina's shoulder, reaching across with his left to clasp her thin fingers lying on the quilt. Gina's eyes were on his for a moment and he thought she registered him before they turned drowsy again. She sank back against the pillow with a sigh, eyes closed, but her fingertips moved against his hand.

William covered her hand gently with his own. He couldn't take his eyes off her face. Her brow had cleared suddenly and he thought her cheeks had gained some colour again, almost rose like. Her throat rose and fell with the slightest of breaths.

Robyn was standing at his side and the lamp in the far corner cast her shadow on the wall behind the bed. Tommy's shadow overlaid it as he drew near and William felt his son's hand on his shoulder.

He looked across at Esther but she sat transfixed in the chair opposite her eyes on Gina. William tried to catch her eye, wanting to say something but she neither moved nor lifted her eyes. He was vaguely aware of a sudden change in Gina's breathing, a momentary gasp, as if from a distance. He reached out a hand to draw Esther over but she didn't respond.

And when he looked again at the bed he knew that Gina was gone.

Tommy, behind him, had leaned forward, clasping both arms around William's chest and he could feel his son's tears on the back of his neck. Robyn was crying too but after a few moments she moved across to settle Gina onto her back and fold her hands. Then he heard her on the other side of the room talking softly to Esther but he couldn't make out the words.

It all seemed so distant.

William stayed where he was staring down at the still figure beneath the bedclothes and a loneliness descended on him that no presence on earth could dispel.

Robyn went to make them all a cup of tea and he did doze then, in the armchair, though he wouldn't have thought it was possible. He awoke to see the cup on a little table she'd pulled close to his side but when he reached across for it he found it was already cold.

Esther was lying curled at the bottom of the bed crying. He left the chair and went to sit beside her, taking her hand in his. She locked fingers with his, almost playfully, then pulled his hand close to her chest and lay there alternately quiet and then sobbing, staring at nothing, her auburn hair streaked across her wet cheeks.

He didn't know where Tommy and Robyn were. Once he thought he heard voices raised. He turned his head sharply, listening, but now there was nothing, just the early yowl of a cat in the garden and his granddaughter choking on her tears.

9

The Funeral

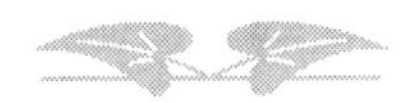

So they buried Gina; where she'd have least expected it, in an unfamiliar cemetery and with a Catholic priest to take the service, though if Gina had been anything it was Baptist, as Doreen made a point of saying to anyone who would listen.

William had closed his ears to it all, dead weary. He'd spent the week in his front room at Hartley Rise while Esther decided the funeral arrangements and everyone else criticised them.

Sitting in Tommy's gold and cream living room after Sunday tea, the rain streaming down the windows and the gardens beyond looking dismal and cold, William stared down at his hands and could feel himself nodding off.

'It's not what Gina would have wanted.' Doreen was saying.

'There's no indication what she wanted,' said Tommy shortly.

It was true. William had heard it from Robyn: '*All Gina ever said was: no dreary music.*'

He closed his eyes and listened to the tinkle of wine being poured into lead crystal: the Riesling Tommy had been persuading Doreen to try.

'Gina had Arthur cremated and kept the ashes. It's obvious she meant them to be scattered together at Kimble's Top. No-one in the family's buried at Doddington Road.'

Doreen again.

His mind was drifting deep and long, her voice distant against the roaring in his ears. Was he snoring?

'And Esther won't be tending any graves. She's flying back to Spain on Friday.'

William's head dropped and jerked him awake. He looked at the family gathered around in the armchairs and on the sofa. Tommy and Bryony were sitting silent, looking nowhere in particular. Doreen was slicing apple strudel with the side of her fork and Richard had walked over to look out of the window.

Outside a fine rain was falling against the dark background of the trees and shrubs. The constant noise of it filled the room and, closer at hand, water cracked intermittently from an overflowing gutter onto the concrete patio.

Why the cemetery? William wondered. And if Esther wasn't scattering her parents' ashes at Kimble's Top, was it because she meant to sell the house?

The day of the funeral was dry and cold. It was the middle of December, the service at two thirty with the young priest none of them knew and nearly two hundred mourners round the grave: friends from Gina's many voluntary groups, the social committees she'd organised, parent governors and uniformed organisations she'd helped out with since Arthur died.

There had been no question of having funeral cars leave from Kimble's Top so the family met at Gilroy & Son's, cramming their vehicles into the tiny back yard and congregating on the pavement outside the genteel windows.

When William arrived the funeral directors were already moving among them all, opening the doors of the three black cars lined up along the kerb. He followed Esther into the back of the first car.

It was quiet in the Bentley. Esther sat with one hand propped against the window and her cheek on her hand, looking out. In her short corduroy jacket and white gypsy shirt she looked thin and frail beside all the heavy winter coats.

At the end of Croyland Road they waited some time for a gap to allow the line of cars to turn right together and climb the hill towards the cemetery. As the hearse finally swung ahead of them across the junction, the light oak coffin came into full view, heavily laden with flowers. William watched it go; saw carnations and roses and, standing up at the back, the beautiful evergreen wreath that Bryony had made herself.

They passed through the ornamental gates of the cemetery where the curved headstones extended in waves on either side and the cars were parked all around. A great tide of people was gathered on the forecourt beside the red brick chapel with teenagers prominent in the dark uniform of the Girls Brigade.

When the cars had pulled up the family stood waiting while the men in black tail coats lifted the coffin out.

William and Esther stood arm in arm, ready to follow immediately behind it.

The priest stepped forward prayer book in hand, surplice rippling in the wind, and William heard a remark behind, caught the word 'Catholic', but if the priest heard he showed no sign of it, just watched the proceedings saying nothing.

As they prepared to enter, he laid one hand momentarily on William's arm and drew Esther forward gently with the other so that they could mount the steps together.

At the graveside they kept it short. The temperature had dropped considerably and an icy wind was picking up, stirring the trees all around them.

For man that is born of woman has but a short time to live . . . earth to earth and ashes to ashes . . . in the sure and certain hope of resurrection to eternal life.

Gina's coffin and Arthur's ashes were lowered together at their feet and as soon as the first handfuls of earth had smattered down William's sons moved swiftly away. The other mourners, who'd stood three and four deep behind them, stepped forward for their own farewells.

William found himself caught up in the crowd, nodding silently at the succession of faces that came towards him with sympathetic smiles and words of condolence. He saw Maurice far ahead on the path glance back for a moment through the dark coats and Richard away to his right, striding through the yew trees, but it was Tommy he wanted.

The crowd was thinning, dispersed along the paths and among the trees but his son was nowhere to be seen, even among the stragglers. A gust of cold air lifted in the trees and gathered pace in the rowans all around. William turned his back against the blast and saw the spindly branches of the trees bow beyond him in a single curve, all the way back to the old brick chapel where suddenly he did see Tommy now. He was standing half-hidden in the shelter of the buttresses with Robyn at his side.

William could see straightaway that they were talking intimately and agreeing on something. Tommy was speaking at length, deliberately, while Robyn listened intently and nodded assent. He saw her blonde head close to Tommy's dark shoulder, her eyes on his face. They were completely engrossed.

William stood transfixed in the cold wind, watching them, wondering what they could be discussing on the quiet like that.

The priest came then offering his arm to William as a support against the wind. A strong gust blew his dark hair on end and he smiled at it: a real smile, full of warmth, and behind it the undaunted air of a man accustomed to gravesides. It comforted William more than words. He leaned hard on the young man's arm and went back with him along the windswept path.

By the time William reached the funeral tea the hall was already filling up. He saw Esther surrounded by a group of her mother's friends, nodding awkwardly at their conversation. Doreen was standing by the long catering tables overseeing a line of people as they made their way along the trays of sandwiches. The caterers were moving among them all offering glasses of sherry from round silver trays.

It was a light, modern hall with a pitched roof and sprung floor marked out for basketball. The Pravasi Mandal Centre; one of the few local venues not booked out for Christmas lunches.

Tommy's daughter Elisabeth, over from Warwickshire for the day, found him a seat by one of the tables at the far end of the hall and brought him a drink.

'When your Dad gets here, tell him I want him, will you?' he said as she went off again to get him some food.

He sat looking through the vista of white shirts and black ties, the new arrivals piling their winter coats in mounds on the stacks of chairs around the walls. Elisabeth was negotiating her way through the crowd. He followed her charcoal grey suit, noticing the turn of her head and the way her silky brown hair swung against her delicate cheekbones. She exchanged a few words here and there but avoided being drawn into conversation as she moved along the table filling a plate for him.

Tommy came in but William lost sight of him straightaway. Robyn arrived too but was immediately caught up in a group of mourners. He shifted in his chair trying to keep her in view but was defeated by the continual flow of people coming in through the double doors.

Soon all the tables around him were occupied. Conversation was subdued but the place was full and the noise echoed up to the metal rafters. Occasional words reached him and some of Gina's friends came over to speak to him but it was Tommy and Robyn he was interested in, wanting to know what they'd been talking about. He scanned the crowd continually hoping to catch sight of them.

Tommy he could see trapped in conversation with an old man in a fair isle sweater. Elisabeth stood beside him and must have seen William looking because she raised her shoulders in a tiny shrug and smiled in mock hopelessness: '*I'll never get him away from here.*'

Robyn was with an opinionated woman of about fifty: big boned, big ear rings and big conversation. William recognised her as the daughter of the woman who used to clean at Kimble's Top. Rita Thomas. He had a feeling the cleaner was in a home somewhere with senile dementia. When he caught Robyn's eye and gestured slightly with his head in hopeful summons she sent Laurel over instead.

'It was really your Mum I wanted,' William said but he reached out an arm to draw the little girl near all the same and she cuddled against him in her new black denim pinafore and knee-high boots.

Laurel was always good company. She chatted on about getting a pet for her birthday and whether it should be a hamster or a guinea pig. 'A guinea pig comes out during the day. But you can let a hamster run down your top.' Her friend had one that did that.

She went off to get him another cup of tea and still Robyn showed no sign of coming over. She'd moved on to a young man in a leather jacket and polo neck sweater. Tommy had broken away too but was sitting down, listening to a man who nursed a whisky glass close and seemed to be pouring out his woes.

In the end it was Esther who joined him. Her conversation with the leader of the Girls Brigade ended and he watched her glance uncertainly round and catch sight of him. Her face was pale and she looked tired as she sat down beside him.

'It's all going on a bit, isn't it?' she said.

He nodded and they sat watching the people milling around, the caterers consolidating trays of sandwiches and collecting up discarded plates.

'Josie Deacon lives on Doddington Road,' she said then. 'Right by the cemetery. We used to go across and put flowers on her Gran's grave. I wanted Mum to be there too. Somewhere friendly that meant something to me.'

'Did you tell the others that?' asked William.

She shook her head. 'They're always so up in arms about everything.'

He knew what she meant. Everything was suddenly too much and, looking round, he knew it was the same for all of them. He saw it in the way his family hardly ate or drank while the guests descended on the buffet; he saw it in Tommy's frozen expression, his eyes constantly straying to Bryony; and in Doreen standing silent by the tables of food when normally she had so much to say.

He wished he could gather them up, draw his own around him and mourn together away from this tide of loose acquaintance, but the guests were well accommodated, sandwiches and drinks still being handed round, and it occurred to him then that if only Gina had been there she'd have known how to manage things.

But Gina was gone and now everything in his life was awry.

10

Lies and Deceit

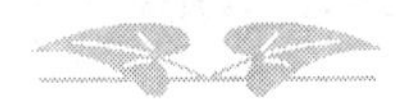

That night William lay awake in the early hours staring at the dark shapes of the furniture round the bedroom and thinking of nothing but the loneliness of being there by himself. It was a relief when morning came: the grey light of another day.

His black suit was still hanging at the front of the wardrobe. He jammed it to the back and pulled out a favourite shirt, worn soft over the years, and a crumpled navy jumper that Gina had given him.

Afterwards he sat on the edge of the bed, sipping his tea, and thought he might just ring Tommy at the office and ask him outright what he'd been talking about with Robyn.

The office number was on the handy list under the phone in the front room There was a mobile too but Tommy didn't like people using it during work hours. *'I don't keep a secretary to have people ring the mobile and get a recorded message.'*

It was barely eight o'clock but he knew Tommy would be there. His secretary was obviously an early bird too; she put him through straightaway.

'Dad?'

'What were you and Robyn talking about at the cemetery?'

'What?'

'I saw you. After everyone had gone. You were talking.'

The silence was momentary but enough for Tommy to gain control, William could hear it in his voice when he replied. 'I daresay she was upset. I was probably trying to comfort her.'

'You haven't had a civil word for Robyn in years.'

'Well I hope even I can behave at a funeral.'

'It was more than that. You two had your heads together over something.'

'Dad, I really haven't got time for this.'

'All right,' said William with sudden inspiration. 'I'll ask Robyn.'

'Okay, she was upset. She's had a lot on her plate. Look, I'll come by tonight and we'll talk about it.'

It was Tommy all over, deliberate and patronising, and it smacked of falsehood.

'You never were a good liar,' said William.

'I didn't have to be!' exploded Tommy. 'For heaven's sake, Dad . . .'

'Tonight,' said William smugly. 'You're busy.' And he clicked the phone down.

It gave him no real satisfaction though. He didn't want to be at odds with Tommy and now his son would have the whole day to get his story straight. *'Idiot!'* said Alice's voice in his head. *'You should have smoked him out. Not stirred up a hornet's nest.'*

'Oh what do I know,' answered William irritably. *'I'm just a tired old man. And now Gina's gone. I might as well just sit around in my dressing gown all day and wait for the end.'*

He slumped in the chair and was still there, lethargic, when the phone began to ring. The clock on the mantelpiece said ten to nine. It rang and rang. In the end he got up and answered it.

'It's me,' said Robyn sounding flat and miserable. 'Let's go out somewhere, Grandad! Yesterday was awful. And today I just don't know what to do with myself.'

He planned what he'd say while he sat waiting but when she arrived at his door with a face like a ghost he didn't want to upset her.

They went to the garden centre at Poddington. William had only ever been there in the summer but now, in December, where the garden furniture usually stood, there were Christmas trees on display and shelves stacked high with boxes of coloured lights. A long aisle stretched away with plastic Santas climbing up rope ladders and reindeer pulling sleighs. Further on, the pond and aquatic stock had been pushed back to make room for inflatable snowmen.

William wandered among the ornaments and scented candles and finally came to a halt beside a fibre optic tree. It glowed purple, blue and red with a soft, pulsating light and he couldn't take his eyes off it.

'Do you like it?' asked Robyn.

He nodded. He'd never seen anything like it.

'Let's buy it!' she said, sounding suddenly enthusiastic.

'Oh, I don't know.'

'Come on! Let me get it for you. I'd like to,' her voice faltered. 'I haven't even thought what to buy anyone for Christmas yet.'

It was less than two weeks away and the thought of it left him cold. Gina had always got his presents for him. She'd suggested things and bought them and usually come up with something unexpected for at least one of the grandchildren, something they'd sit and laugh about together.

He'd made a point of buying her present himself though, always the same; a bottle of martini and one of whisky from the corner shop. Even with Arthur gone she'd had friends who'd drink the whisky. And he knew she'd appreciated it because it was what he'd always given them, ever since they'd first got married.

Robyn had moved away to find the tree he wanted, scanning the piles of boxes, looking for his present.

In the café they sat by the window looking out over the windswept shrubs. They'd both ordered cottage pie and a pot of tea. William was hungry and finished his easily but Robyn gave up halfway and just talked.

'I keep going over and over that last night. The way Gina was. I can't get it out of my mind.'

She'd drunk her tea and sat stroking the handle of the empty cup. Her long, tapered nails were painted cream and she wore silver rings that glistened, one with a big, square stone that matched the pale blue of her jumper.

'When I'm up at the house it feels as though she's still there.'

Outside it had clouded over, dark clouds with a hint of white shining through in patches. Inside a woman in green overalls was moving among the tables, clearing plates onto a big, metal trolley.

'I suppose I'm bound to feel close to her,' said Robyn. 'She always understood me, especially over Laurel. Tommy said that once Gina even talked about leaving Kimble's Top to me.'

The trolley moved closer, crockery rattling.

'In fact we got talking about it yesterday at the grave. I was upset. I suppose it all just washed over me. Tommy probably said it to comfort me.'

William could hear the lie in her voice: her tone gained conviction with every word she said. He hadn't brought four children up not to know when someone was spinning him a line.

He was furious but before he could speak the trolley had come to a noisy halt at his side and the woman was reaching between them to clear the table. She scraped their plates in front of them and stacked them on a tottering pile and Robyn began handing the teapots and cups across, smiling her thanks.

As soon as she'd moved away Robyn picked up her handbag, looking at her watch. 'Well, come on! We'd better make a move. Otherwise I'll be late meeting Laurel from school.'

It was raining now. In the car they had the fan on full blast to clear the steam from the windows and the wipers thumped back and forth smearing the rain in an arc before his eyes. Robyn said nothing more and seemed to be concentrating on the narrow twisting lanes ahead. It wasn't the place for an argument. William sat silent, staring out at the dripping trees and the wooden fences black with wet and wondering what it was that she and Tommy had to hide.

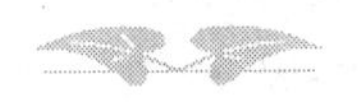

When he got home someone had put the hoover round and there was a casserole in the kitchen with a cross note from Lorraine. He'd completely forgotten she'd been coming to do his lunch. He rang her to apologise, his mind still on Robyn as she castigated him: 'You only had to ring. It's not much to ask, just to pick up the phone.'

He made a cup of tea, sat down in his chair and saw Alice eyeing him with amusement from the photo frame.

'*At least I know when I'm being lied to*,' he said tetchily. '*You weren't always so sharp.*'

He remembered a ten bob note saved up for their nephew's wedding present and stowed away in her mending basket. Richard had begged it off her with a story about a second hand bicycle and blown it instead on a bank holiday outing with the lads to Great Yarmouth.

'I'm ill,' she'd tossed her head. 'I can't be expected to ferret things out.'

The room was fragrant with lilies, part of an exotic bouquet that Larry Clifton had sent and Doreen had rescued from the graveside. The vase stood in the fireplace, filling the space beneath the mantelpiece that would normally have been bright with Christmas cards but instead was crowded with white messages of sympathy.

Still, Robyn had bought him the fibre optic tree. It was leaning in its box against the dining table and perhaps when Tommy came he'd sort it out for him and that might cheer things up a bit.

He nodded off before he'd finished his tea and the bang of the front door woke him. He looked at the clock and saw it was after six and then Tommy was standing in the doorway, one hand raised to show a pair of dark bottles, Old Imperial, he had gripped by the tops. 'Peace offering.'

'It must be bad,' said William, 'If you're drinking as well.'

Tommy gave him a look, put the bottles down on the table and reached into the sideboard for a couple of glasses.

As he poured the thick, black stout, William said, 'You rang Robyn, didn't you? That's why she came to take me out for lunch.'

Tommy looked up and met his eyes but only for an instant. He said nothing as they both watched the beer rise to form an inch of perfect cream then he brought the glass over to William.

'I was worried about you,' he said. 'I thought she might set your mind at rest.'

William had reached out his hand for the glass but Tommy ignored it and put the beer on the table at his side instead: 'Let it settle.'

'I saw you two at the cemetery and you weren't talking about Robyn being upset. You were agreeing on something.'

'I agreed with how she felt. She's bound to miss Gina more being up at Kimble's Top.'

'And you told her Gina once thought of leaving the house to her?' said William.

Tommy shrugged. 'Apparently she was thinking of it once upon a time.'

'Not something you'd have agreed with!'

'No. I've never made any secret of my feelings. Kimble's Top's magnificent. There's a certain heritage there. Robyn doesn't belong in a place like that. But as it happens I'm not so sure Esther does either. She just wants a karaoke bar on the beach somewhere. And since she's probably planning to sell Kimble's Top maybe it wouldn't be such a bad thing if Gina has left the house to Robyn.'

William sat back, confused. The strange thing was, Tommy wasn't lying. He could hear the bedrock of truth behind his words. Yet at the same time he knew he was being deceived. The beer didn't help. He'd taken the first strong mouthful and it was full of sweet flavours that flooded his head with carefree exuberance.

Tommy sat at the dining table opposite calmly sipping his own stout., Anyway,' he said. 'The will's at the solicitor's. Either way, we'll find out tomorrow.'

11

GINA'S WILL

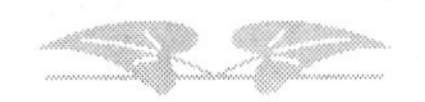

He saw the will for himself the very next morning because Esther brought it round on her way home from the solicitor's in Northampton.

It was in a shiny blue folder with the solicitor's logo on the front and a business card tucked into a slot in the inside flap. Beyond that it was nothing imposing: three sheets of A4 paper, the front one bearing Gina's name and the date, 24 November 1999. William turned to the next page and began to read.

'*I, Georgina Radford . . . revoke all former wills and testamentary dispositions . . . appoint as my Executors and Trustees the Partners at the date of my death in the firm of John Rixon Solicitors . . . I bequeath my house, Kimble's Top, Hunsbury Hill, Northampton to my niece Robyn Lisa Allbright . . . and all my remaining real and personal property whatsoever and wheresoever . . . to my daughter, Esther . . . signed by the Testatrix in our joint presence and by us in her presence . . . Robert Hamilton, Solicitor . . . Eleanor Scott, Legal Assistant.*'

William stared at Gina's signature in bold black ink. There was no disputing it, these were clearly her final wishes. He looked across at Esther sitting quietly on the sofa. She'd tied her hair back for once so he could see her blue-green eyes but could read nothing in them. She seemed completely unconcerned as she looked back at him.

'Don't you mind?' he said at last.

'Actually it's a total relief. Mum obviously knew I'd rather just have the money.'

William looked back at the will wondering what exactly 'all my remaining real and personal property' meant.

'Investments?'

Esther nodded. 'Tommy thought six figures from the shares alone. Plus whatever's in the bank. The solicitor just needs to go through the certificates and work it all out. Anyway the good thing is they don't need me to be here anymore. If there's anything to sign they can send it by DHL. I'm flying back to Spain the day after tomorrow.'

She leaned forward and pulled a gift-wrapped box out of the canvas bag at her feet. It had shiny gold paper, gold ribbons and a bow. 'This is for you. For Christmas.'

She put it under the tree Tommy had set up for him beside the table and inside he thought she was just far too casual about everything but he was too dazed to find the words to challenge her. All he could do was repeat his earlier question: 'Do you really not mind about Kimble's Top?'

'My home's in Spain, Grandad. I just want my life back.'

She pulled on her black corduroy jacket. It was the same one she'd worn to the funeral and her white lacy shirt looked the same too. It unnerved him to see it, to realise it was just normal, every day wear for her.

Her black woolly gloves had shiny sequins on them and brushed softly against his cheek as she reached up to kiss him goodbye. He followed her out to the front door and watched her all the way to the end of the street; a dark little figure in the wide grey of the winter afternoon. At the corner she raised a single hand to him then turned away out of sight.

Back inside he switched the tree on and it glowed cherry red, the light reflecting eerily on the gold paper of the present she'd left for him. He sat watching it, thinking of Gina and trying to remember how it had been back in November 99, when she'd obviously decided to leave Kimble's Top to Robyn.

Laurel had been a year old that September and Robyn had gone back to school under duress, just counting the days until she turned sixteen and could leave. Doreen had changed to part-time hours so she could look after Laurel and the strain was showing in the house at Eastfield Road. The rest of the family had seen it on Sunday afternoons when they gathered for tea.

He remembered one fraught occasion when Laurel had been tired and screaming, refusing to eat, her head turned away from every offered spoonful.

'It's your fault,' Robyn had exploded at her brother Paul. 'Always banging around the house. That's why she never sleeps through. You're just totally inconsiderate.'

'It's your baby!'

'She's a 'she' not an 'it'!'

Robyn's voice had risen high-pitched with fury and in the end Doreen had grabbed the screaming Laurel and disappeared upstairs while Robyn sat incensed and the rest of them breathed a collective sigh of relief.

'Maybe I could arrange for Robyn to get tenancy of one of the flats up by Kimble's Top,' Gina had suggested afterwards to Doreen when they were washing up in the kitchen, but Doreen wouldn't hear of it.

'The last thing Robyn needs is to be stuck in a flat on her own all day. Especially with no money.'

'I could give her some money. An allowance,' Gina had said to William when Doreen stepped outside to throw the scraps out for the birds and Tommy, coming in with an empty teapot in each hand, had overheard and been furious.

'You're effectively rewarding her for bad behaviour!'

'Well it can't be easy, having a baby when she's just a kid herself,' said Gina.

'She should have thought of that! It's what you get for being immoral.'

'Oh, don't be so old fashioned, Tommy! They're all at it these days.'

'No they're not,' said Tommy fiercely with a glance at his own teenage daughter doing the Sunday crossword in the dining room.

William remembered Doreen walking along the garden path, tossing the broken bits of bread onto the grass for the birds. The leaves had been turning orange and they'd had a run of days with blue skies and caterpillar tracks of white cloud.

It had been like that up at Kimble's Top too, soon afterwards, when Gina told him Esther had rung and that she wasn't planning to come home for Christmas, her first since she'd gone out to Spain.

They'd been standing at the French windows watching the lawn dance with copper leaves in the wind. She'd spoken bitterly, galled at being proved wrong about Esther not sticking at bar work, but genuinely hurt as well, he'd thought, despite her dismissive words:

'Oh well, you bring them up the best you can. After that they're on their own.'

There had been a momentous build up to Christmas that year; talk of the new millennium and scaremongering in the news about aeroplanes falling out of the sky and missiles going off unplanned when the clocks reached midnight. They'd been charging silly prices for New Year's Eve parties in the pubs and clubs too. Doreen had told him so, and in the end they'd all shot themselves in the foot because the bookings hadn't come in.

Doreen had somehow got wind of the fact that Gina was thinking of leaving Kimble's Top to Robyn though William had never heard anything specific himself.

'Esther always hated the place,' Lorraine had said that afternoon at Richard's house. That had surprised William yet if truth be told he'd no idea what Esther really felt about anything.

As a little girl she'd been shy in company, retiring after her dad died and positively withdrawn as a teenager.

He'd overheard a row once, long before Esther went to Spain. She must have been about thirteen. He'd been at Kimble's Top in early July and had gone to cut some roses from beside the Peter Pan statue. Coming back to the house he'd taken the narrow paved way that cut alongside the kitchen. The windows had been open and he'd heard Esther and Gina arguing about the holiday bible club

Gina always helped out with at the church. She'd wanted Esther to go along not just for her own week but to help out as well with the other weeks for the younger age groups. Esther had flat refused.

'Well you needn't think you're going to spend the summer sitting round the house all day doing nothing,' Gina had said, her voice carrying out into the sunny afternoon where William made his way slowly with an armful of deep scented roses.

'I'll go and stay at Josie's then,' said Esther.

'That's not what I meant.'

'At least they're not on at me all the time.'

'You'd soon miss your home comforts. You don't know how lucky you are growing up in a house like this.'

'I hate it here,' Esther burst out. 'I'd rather live anywhere but here.'

'Your Dad made his name with this house! He built it for us.'

'So? He wouldn't want me to be miserable.'

'You don't know what miserable is.'

Looking back, William thought there had been quite a few words like that but he'd never felt it was over Kimble's Top. It was just that Gina was such an organiser, never happy unless she was over-committed, whereas Esther just liked to go with the flow.

William sat thinking it all over while he ate the casserole Lorraine had left him the day before. Then he phoned Tommy at the office, the second time in a week.

'Esther came round with the will,' he told his son. 'I can't believe it!'

'It goes back a bit, Dad,' said Tommy. 'Didn't Gina ever talk to you about it?'

'All I remember is her wanting to move Robyn into one of the flats up there.'

'Well, I knew at the time she was thinking that way,' said Tommy. 'She asked me to be Executor. I told her what she could do with that idea. She knew how I felt about Robyn. I didn't see why she should rub my nose in it.'

'She respected you,' said William. 'As a man of business.'

'Gina never talked business with me. I tried once or twice when Arthur died. He used to talk investments sometimes, but not Gina.'

William sat trying to make sense of it all. 'You said Robyn would never manage Kimble's Top on benefits,' he mused aloud.

'She won't have to. Arthur's three flats on Chelmsford Walk go with it. They're all tenanted. Combined rents of about sixteen thousand. She won't be well off but she'll manage if she's careful. And noting to pay in inheritance tax. Gina had the life insurance written in trust to cover it.'

William fell silent, listening to his own breathing amplified by the telephone.

'Look,' said Tommy; 'There's nothing to worry about. Robyn gets the house and Esther gets the shares. They'll both do all right out of it. RSG was turning over hundreds of thousands in the good times and Arthur had nearly ten per cent of the company. The dividends alone were more than a thousand a year and that was a lot of money back then. Whatever Gina put that money into when she pulled out of RSG, it's got to be worth a few hundred thousand.'

'It just doesn't seem right.'

'Gina knew Esther better than any of us. She wouldn't have made a will like that if it prejudiced her, no matter how difficult or distant she could be.'

'She was pretty distant this morning,' said William. 'I thought she must be putting a brave face on things. Was she like that at the solicitor's?'

'She seemed all right.'

'Wasn't she surprised, though, about the house?'

'Perhaps. I don't think Gina had talked to her about it.'

'What about afterwards in the car?' William persisted.

'She didn't say much.'

'But wasn't she shocked? Did she really seem herself?'

'Dad, her mum's died! I'd say she was pretty out of sorts all round. But you know what she's like. All she wants is to get back to Spain.'

William sighed and leaned his head back against the chair. It was all very troubling.

'Come on,' said Tommy. 'Gina knew what she was doing. And she wouldn't have wanted you fretting about it.'

He did fret though. He sat up late with a cup of Horlicks going cold on the table next to him while he turned it over and over in his mind because somehow it just wasn't right.

He thought about Tommy and Robyn talking in depth about something at the cemetery and how they wouldn't tell him what that was about. He thought about Robyn inheriting Kimble's Top and about Esther, desperate to get back to Spain. And while he sat thinking the room glowed with the deep colours of the fibre optic tree: the Christmas present that Robyn had bought him the same afternoon she'd sat and lied to him.

And he thought he'd like to see Robyn again because the more he dwelt on that the more it annoyed him.

12

GHOSTS

The next day it was Doreen's turn to do his lunch and she phoned him first thing to say they'd be going up to Kimble's Top. 'We've all had a rotten time. And I don't want Robyn moping around up there by herself.'

And you can't wait to see the place now it's hers.

It was the last thing he wanted. He hadn't been to the house since the night Gina died and when he did go it wouldn't be like this.

'You go ahead,' he said. 'My chest's a bit off. I'll just have something from the freezer.'

'You've got to go up there sooner or later,' said Doreen. 'I know it's hard but you can't just sit around feeling sorry for yourself. We all know how you feel.'

'I doubt it,' he snapped. 'And I'm not going!'

'All right. Well, I'll just pop in on my way over there and see how you are.'

He put the phone down and went through to the kitchen to shave. They'd no business dragging him out every day. Gina had always eaten lunch with him here. He scraped a trail through the white foam on his cheek and tapped the razor clear against the steel sink. He'd do his own lunches from now on.

Razor in hand, he reached across and opened the freezer; one rock hard loaf of bread, a packet of beef burgers and a bag of mixed vegetables. That would do him for today.

But Doreen wouldn't hear of it.

'We're not having you living on frozen food,' she said when she came over. 'Anyway, you need the company.'

She went on at him and in the end it was easier just to follow her out of the kitchen and put on his coat and gloves.

Her car was parked half on the pavement. She'd taken the back shelf out and the boot was full of cardboard boxes.

'Christmas decorations,' she said, unlocking the car doors. 'For the house.'

At Kimble's Top she swung the car round on the drive and backed it right up to the front steps. By the time William had pushed his door open against the wind and struggled out, Robyn was at the front door, looking tired and dishevelled in tracksuit bottoms and a baggy t-shirt.

We make a matching pair, William thought, feeling pretty faded himself. Doreen in comparison was animated and trim, even in her flat shoes, jeans and a plain top. Her hair was freshly coloured too, he noticed it in the winter sun as she leaned forward to lift something out of the boot; honey-coloured and lighter than before.

'What's all this?' Robyn asked.

'Bits and pieces for the house. Come on then, give me a hand!'

William made his way slowly past them, up the steps and into the hall. He'd last been here in the darkness of that Friday night, with Robyn waiting for him and Gina down the corridor, in bed. There was no time to dwell on it, though, because Doreen was dumping boxes noisily on the tiled floor.

Robyn brought the last one in and crouched beside it to look inside. She took out a large glass Star of Bethlehem, midnight blue with golden angels all around it, blowing trumpets.

'Left over from the hotel,' said Doreen. 'You need ornaments of a certain scale for a house like this.'

William stood catching his breath and watching her, hands on her hips looking round the wide, rectangular hall. It was light and airy with long, narrow windows on either side of the front door.

'I've ordered an eight foot tree,' she said. 'And I think this is going to be just the place for it.'

She delved into one of the boxes then, pulled out a string of coloured lights and dangled them against one of the windows.

'What do you think? We could make it really festive. Bring some chairs through and open the presents in here. I've got that old Turkish rug of my mother's we could put down.'

'No, Mum!' said Robyn.

'You won't have to do a thing. I'll arrange it.'

'It's too soon . . .'

Doreen looked up from folding coloured lights back into the box.

'You won't remember this,' she said to Robyn. 'But when your Uncle Arthur died, Gina absolutely refused to let it get her down. It was a terrible shock to her. But I think Gina did more in those years after Arthur died than she ever did when they were together. She wouldn't expect any of us to sit around moping at Christmas.'

She closed the box lid and stood up, looking round the hallway again.

'And you know what? After Christmas we'll invite Gina's friends round. It'll be a memorial. Drinks. Mince pies. Candles. We'll get a bit of warmth in the place and remember Gina how she used to be. You ought to stay in touch with some of her old friends. That's what Gina would have wanted?'

Galling though it was, William had to admit she had a point. Gina would have smiled to see coloured lights here, a gaudy Christmas tree in the hallway and her friends milling around with a drink in their hands.

He turned away towards the living room.

'You're tired and run down,' he heard Doreen say to Robyn. 'Go and put your feet up. And I'll do the lunch.'

The living room was cold, the midday sun filtered through the blinds on three sides but was too weak to dispel the winter greyness.

William settled in an armchair and tried not to think about how he'd sat here with Gina all last summer. Robyn had followed him in and sank into the nearby sofa, leaning her head back, eyes closed. She'd slipped her shoes off and curled her feet up under her, something he'd never seen her do before.

He looked across at her. Now was his chance. Her lying had infuriated him and he might as well say so.

'About you and Tommy at the funeral,' he began. 'I know you weren't talking about how much you missed Gina. Or about the house.'

Robyn opened her eyes slowly and looked at him without expression. Her blank stare left him cold with aggravation. He sat there, holding her gaze.

'We did talk about that,' she said at last.

'No. You were agreeing on something,' he said. 'Working something out.'

'He was reassuring me.'

She uncurled her foot and moved to sit on the edge of the sofa. In the distance Doreen was laying the table in the dining room, he could hear the clunk of cutlery and the rattle of china plates. Robyn got to her feet.

'Let's have a glass of sherry since we're being all Christmassy.' She moved away from him and called out on her way to the dining room: 'Mum!'

William could hear them talking, banging the heavy door of the sideboard as they looked for the glasses. When Robyn returned Doreen was close behind, she handed William a glass of sherry and raised her own.

'Fernando de Castilla,' she sipped and smiled. 'The taste of things to come.'

At her side Robyn glanced at William calmly as she lifted her own glass to her lips.

'I'll find you out,' he thought with distaste. 'I might be eighty odd. But I'm not past it yet.'

Doreen served lunch and they sat together round one end of the long dining table. It was beef hotpot with roasted vegetables: 'Proper winter food,' as Doreen said, but rich with cream and full of peppers which never had gone down well with him. He chased the chunks of meat round his plate while Doreen talked of Esther.

'She hasn't been up here once since Gina died. Not even to go through her Mum's things. I suppose she's going to leave it all for Robyn to sort out. It's no wonder Gina made her will like that.'

'That will was written years ago,' said William. 'Gina didn't know what was coming. Or how Esther would be.'

But Doreen wasn't listening. 'She's obviously going to take the money and run. Once they've sorted out what the shares are worth, we'll probably never see her again.'

William sat frustrated. Something at the back of his mind, a memory, kept slipping from his grasp. Something Gina had told him.

'We've got to apply for probate,' Robyn was saying. 'It'll be a few months yet.'

He longed to be having lunch with Gina, just the two of them, with Radio Four and the warmth of her across the table, amusement in her green eyes, the exchange of smiles that meant more than words.

He stared down the length of the table at the line of black leather chairs, the sideboard behind with its black enamel cruets and ornaments, and thought of all their shared moments gone forever.

He could feel his heart thudding now, thinking of the three of them sitting like visitors in Gina's house, eating at her table, when all the time Gina wasn't here.

He'd put his knife and fork down on his plate and looked up to see Doreen watching him. Her conversation had halted.

'I'm all right,' he said, pushing back his chair. 'No appetite, that's all. I'll just go outside for some air. Bit of a walk!'

He wandered to the windows in the living room and looked out at the garden. Through the gap in the poplars he could see the familiar shape of the lift tower surrounded by the roofs of the town, the world at the bottom of the hill carrying on untouched by anything up here. He turned away towards the French doors on the other side of the room and stepped out onto the terrace.

It was milder than he'd thought but the wintry afternoon was dull. On the other side of the lawn the trees were dark and still and somewhere among them a solitary bird was chirping.

He was at one end of the terrace where the shrubbery came right up to meet the house. Dark feathery leaves brushed against the balustrade and further along he could see the lighter speckled green of euonymous.

He looked down the length of the terrace at the stone benches and the wall lights and tried to imagine one of Gina's parties: the ripple of silk dresses, the soft glow of the lights, the luminous white of evening gloves and the buzz of conversation. He tried to picture Gina herself looking towards him through the crowd, in a straight-cut evening dress as he'd seen her once in a photograph, but somehow he couldn't conjure her up. He'd seen the pictures but never actually been at the parties and now he felt like an outsider. There was only the long empty space of white stone.

He turned away, miserable, to the edge of the balustrade and stood looking out over the greenery. In the middle of the shrubbery a discarded nest spilled grass over a sawn-off tree stump.

The wind began to stir then in the big trees and the cloud overhead shifted. A hint of warm sunlight fell across his face. He stepped forward to bask in it, caught the scent of winter jasmine from along the wall and suddenly, with it, he thought, the deep fragrant musk of a cigar.

Arthur was there, standing where he had once stood in a memory long forgotten but remembered now. He was drawing on a Cohiba cigar, its silver ash over an inch long, and looking out at the garden, composed and elegant in a grey suit. Smoking in the sunshine, smiling sideways at William. Smoke burst upwards from his mouth, the haze cleared across his face and the sun shone through it.

'I'm afraid I subscribe to the old fashioned notion that a girl's best brought up by her mother,' he was saying and the grey smoke streamed in diaphanous clouds between the two of them, standing talking on a sunny evening.

Esther was a Daddy's girl all the same, William thought. She'd adored Arthur. He remembered the easy-going conversations he'd overheard between father and daughter but as he opened his mouth to speak, Arthur was gone.

Not gone, though, because, turning, William saw him and Gina together then, further along the terrace; Gina leaning back on cushions in a wicker chair and Arthur standing, tie loosened, sleeves rolled up and hands in his pockets. A whisky bottle and single glass stood on the table between them and the liquor had been poured but not yet touched. They were discussing Arthur's plans to take Esther to Switzerland for her birthday.

'She's been asking to come on one of my trips for a long time now.'

'It's just so extravagant. Why not wait? We can all go away in the summer. Have a proper holiday.'

'She's eight. You can't expect her to wait all year for her birthday present.'

'But I'd like to go to Zurich too.'

'Drop some of your commitments then. Come with us.'

But she wouldn't. The school was having an inspection and she was a governor. There was the May Day carnival to plan and the Girls Brigade every week.

'Oh well,' said Arthur smiling, 'If you prefer your committees to us.'

She began to protest but he cut her off, laughing, leaning forward with a kiss. 'I promise I won't spoil her. But it'll be something special for her birthday. And fathers like to treat their daughters sometimes, you know.'

Ghosts, thought William, staring at Gina so close, so familiar, in her stone-coloured satin top and matching cardigan. She wore drop pearl ear rings and the necklace Arthur had bought for their wedding. He stood transfixed, overwhelmed with a sense of utter belonging. Any minute now Gina would turn her head and smile and beckon him close. Yet at the same time he knew that if he turned and walked away beyond the corner of the house and round to the opposite side of Kimble's Top, he could look in at the bedroom window and see himself still there, sitting at Gina's bedside on the night she'd died.

A part of him had stayed there and was lost to him now. Everything that had been vibrant and alive within him seemed gone, just this shadowy part of himself left, standing among the ghosts on the terrace, dreaming in the winter light.

Suddenly a pigeon rose from the trees on the far side of the lawn, flapping noisily with a rustle and snapping of leaves, and as he turned to look, Esther was there; coming along the wooded path from Arthur's workshop.

It was summer and her face was glowing, cheeks shining and rosy in the sunlight, her eyes bright and full of optimism. Two books were tucked under one arm and her pink shirt was dusty from lying in the corner of her Dad's shed where she always went to read.

Then Gina's voice was behind him, echoing from the kitchen door. 'Come on Dolly Daydream! You haven't got time to read. We're meant to be going swimming.'

Esther looked straight through him, unseeing, towards the voice. She dipped her head, stepped out along the path and was gone before she even reached the grass.

Too young, thought William, too full of life, to linger with the ghosts.

13

R S Gypsum

It seemed a long drive home that afternoon. Doreen hardly spoke for whatever reason of her own and William had neither energy nor inclination to break the silence. He sat squinting into the low sun and watched the black scarecrow trees flash past on either side whilst the wet road ahead of them shone silver in the winter light.

Doreen must have rung Richard and said something though because he dropped in to see William on his way home from work that evening. He looked tired, complaining of half-cocked targets and his best people off sick. '*Who do they think's going to do all the work?*' He made the tea, smoked a cigarette at the back door and sat leafing through the evening paper, then announced. 'I'll be off then.'

Only, at the door he turned back for an instant. 'She's in a better place, Dad.'

William nodded, his throat tight, and raised a hand. Richard took it as a farewell salute and left.

He went to bed early and lay thinking of Esther going back to Spain tomorrow, back to the bright young faces in the Spanish bar and the couple in their matching sweatshirts. Except now Gina wouldn't be here to worry about her any more, waiting in tight lipped silence for the phone calls that never came. Only Kimble's Top would still be here with Robyn washed-out and grieving and Doreen festooning the place with coloured lights.

He suddenly felt he was the only one left who cared a damn about Esther and that he was nothing but a tiny thread binding her to that beautiful stone terrace where once Arthur and Gina had sat laughing and talking. And what use were all the thousands Esther had inherited when home and family were gone?

He hadn't the faintest idea how to reach her. Not practically, of course. He had her telephone number and the address she'd left for the solicitor. But even if he did pick up the phone, what would he say?

Esther was drifting away into a distant world and if they didn't do something soon, she'd be lost beyond their reach. He must have drifted himself then, into sleep, because he woke to find it was morning and he could hear doors banging and buggies rattling as the children set off for school.

It was Bryony's turn to do his lunch that day. She brought food for three and shortly afterwards Tommy arrived. William sat watching as his son took his jacket off, arranged it over the arm of the sofa and dropped his inky black scarf on top. Then he wandered over to the table to straighten the cutlery Bryony had laid out on the dark green cloth and stood with his hands in his pockets surveying the room while they waited for Bryony to come through from the kitchen.

They were five days short of the shortest day and even to William's eye the place looked dismal that afternoon: shadows filled every corner and the plants on the windowsill were a dull green. The pulsating glow of the fibre optic tree showed up streaks of dust on the nearby television.

'You ought to get out more,' said Tommy.

'I'm all right as I am.'

Hearing Bryony in the passageway, William began struggling to his feet, one hand on his stick and the other on the tiled edge of the mantelpiece but he leaned in too close to the shelf and sent a flurry of sympathy cards cascading to the floor.

As Tommy bent to retrieve them, Bryony came through the door with a steaming plate in each hand. William sensed their shared glances behind his back as he moved to the table. He could tell they were anxious, weighing him up, but there was no point in protesting. He turned his attention to the sausages and mash.

They talked about Esther and the flight that would have left by now and he wanted to tell them what he'd been thinking, especially Bryony because she'd always seemed sympathetic to Esther, but he sensed Tommy wasn't in the mood for it.

He was in business-like mode, the conversation all about budget airlines and property investments in foreign resorts. So that's how they were, sitting and talking about things that didn't affect them, when suddenly a car door slammed outside and someone pressed the front door bell long and hard.

They'd just about finished eating. Tommy went to answer the door and came back with a young man William recognised: the lad with the pony tail he'd seen up at Kimble's Top once or twice, waiting for Esther.

Gareth, William thought. Esther's friend. Someone who'd made that impossible connection. He stared at him across the table and the lad stared back.

'You're Esther's Granddad, right?'

William nodded:

'Is everything all right?'

'I just dropped her at the airport. She was pretty upset. Something the solicitor said. I wanted her to call you but she wouldn't.' He shrugged; 'I thought you should know.'

'It's two days since we saw the solicitor.' Tommy sounded puzzled.

The young man's eyes were still on William. 'Sounded like he rang her today. First thing.'

Tommy took his mobile phone out of his jacket. 'We'll call her,' he said to Gareth, the phone already at his ear. 'Once I've got hold of the solicitor.'

William leaned forward towards the young man. 'Leave me your number, will you? On that card, there, by the phone.'

Tommy gave him a curious look but then someone at the solicitor's office must have answered because he turned away, frowning, asking to speak to Robert Hamilton.

Gareth wrote his number down and mouthed 'See ya' at William on his way out.

William sat silent, thinking of Esther, upset, sitting on a plane, surrounded by strangers. Tommy was talking to Hamilton now. 'I gather you spoke to my niece this morning.'

She was pretty upset, Gareth had said.

'That can't be right. Your paperwork's out of sync . . . Well, tell me what you've got in front of you.'

I wanted her to call you. But she wouldn't.

'Just tell me exactly what you've got in front of you.'

Tommy's voice was icy. At William's side Bryony had stopped clearing the table and stood watching him. William stared down at the pile of plates and the neat line of cutlery arranged on top but his mind was still on Esther: Esther, with her curtain of auburn hair, sitting curled up in an aeroplane seat among strangers; Esther, with her canvas bag slung across her chest and her little black gloves with the sequins.

'Right,' said Tommy. 'I think I'd better come over there. WELL YOU'RE JUST GOING TO HAVE TO FIT ME IN!'

Sounded like he rang her today. First thing.

Tommy had clicked his phone shut and was slipping on his jacket. 'Something and nothing,' he said. 'But I'd better go and sort it out.'

William got to his feet. 'I'm coming with you.'

Tommy gave him a look of weary annoyance but William was sick of evasions. He went out to the hall.

'Dad!' said Tommy behind him.

'An hour ago you were on at me to get out more!'

William put his coat on, his heart thumping with excitement, for once, not over-exertion. *I'm getting the hang of this.*

Tommy had followed him into the narrow hallway. 'This is completely unnecessary.'

'I've as much right to be there as you have.'

'It's a minor point of clarification.'

Something had upset Esther. Something that had made Tommy angry and impatient. But that wasn't the point. The point was Esther. William pulled the front door open thrilled by his own defiance. 'If you were me, you'd want to know what was going on too.'

Tommy held the car door open for him and his dark eyes were furious but William didn't care. He settled back into the leather seat determined to find out what was going on with Esther.

She was pretty upset. I wanted her to call you.
But Esther wouldn't.

The solicitor's was in Abingdon Vale and Tommy took the back road into Northampton, climbing the hill along the old Wellingborough Road where William and Alice had once ridden the charabanc to work every day.

The cars were much faster along here nowadays, the long country road criss-crossed with white lines against overtaking and his childhood village reduced to a signposted left turn that vanished in seconds from sight.

As they reached Northampton the traffic grew heavier.

'If there's a problem parking I'll drop you at the door and find somewhere,' said Tommy.

William nodded but as it happened there was a bay free opposite the old hospital and they only had a short walk to the solicitor's office.

The receptionist showed them into a meeting room with hard leather chairs round a polished table. A plant with sharp green leaves occupied one corner and blinds hung at the window which overlooked a brick alley.

William sat down, staring at the bottle of water and circle of upturned glasses in the centre of the table. Voices passed in the corridor and a door opened and closed further along.

Then Robert Hamilton entered, carrying a folder of papers under one arm and extending the other to shake Tommy's hand even as he crossed the threshold. He was a pale man with fine grey hair, a light suit and the look of a senior partner.

Hamilton opened the folder and began laying papers out on the table in front of Tommy; a whole line of them, each one carefully turned round for Tommy to read.

'This is all our paperwork. As you can see R S Gypsum went into administration in 2003. All trading has therefore ceased. The interim notice from the administrators advises insufficient residual value in the company to pay even the nominal share value to its members.'

Tommy sat reading the line of documents without saying anything.

William looked at Hamilton. 'Could you explain it to me. I'm a bit in the dark.'

Hamilton slid one of the chairs back and sat down.

'Having reviewed the paperwork and carried out a preliminary evaluation of your daughter's estate, I'm afraid I have to tell you there's almost no monetary value in the property remaining once Kimble's Top is taken out of the equation.'

William looked at Tommy: 'You said the shares were worth thousands.'

His son looked up from the papers but said nothing.

'The vast majority of Gina's investments were in R S Gypsum,' Hamilton went on. 'And that stock, as you know, is effectively worthless. It was a fortune built on asbestos. The company did make some effort to diversify but there was no getting away from the fact that just about every product had once contained asbestos to one degree or another. The liability was immense.'

'I thought the Americans were going to buy them,' said William. 'It was in all the newspapers.'

'It fell through,' said Tommy.

'Gina wasn't the only long-standing shareholder to get caught out,' said Hamilton. 'Some stayed in hoping the shares would recover. Holding out for a profit from the takeover. But I think mostly they were just very loyal to Robert Scholt. No-one wanted to spark a rush in trading.'

'Well then, why didn't Gina change her will?' said William. 'She had plenty of time to do it.'

When Hamilton replied his voice was soft. 'Terminal illness is a funny thing. Sometimes it is the most important concerns, the best intentions that actually get left undone. It's a kind of denial. I said so to Esther this morning.'

'No,' said William. 'Gina wasn't like that.' He looked at Tommy to back him up but his son just shook his head with a doubtful look and said nothing.

Hamilton got up and began collecting the papers he'd laid out on the table. 'I don't want to hurry you,' he said. 'But I do actually have another appointment scheduled for this afternoon.'

'We haven't finished,' said William. 'Obviously we'll want to contest the will.'

Hamilton stopped what he was doing for a moment and looked at him.

'This isn't what Gina would have wanted,' said William. 'The will doesn't express her true intention.'

'It's not a question of intention, Mr Allbright,' said Hamilton. 'It's what the will actually says that counts. And in this case it couldn't be clearer.'

'Well, I think it's up to us whether we want to contest it or not.'

'There is nothing to contest,' said the solicitor gently. 'A will may only be contested on the grounds of invalidity, that is, if there's a suspicion it's not been properly drawn up and witnessed, or on the grounds of undue influence or lack of capacity at the time of writing. In the case of this will, there's no question of that.

If what you're saying is you'd like to make a claim against the provision of the will, then your only possible grounds would be under the Family and Dependents Act, which provides for certain categories of people such as dependent children. But I have to say in the case of a twenty three year old daughter, that claim would be difficult to substantiate.'

'Gina wouldn't have wanted Esther to be left with nothing,' said William. 'There must be some way of dividing things up properly?'

'Where specific assets are named the case is deemed as clear in law. As a general rule we do advise people against naming specific properties and encourage a balance on a percentage basis. In the case of Kimble's Top, of course, it's understandable that Gina wouldn't want the property to be sold and the assets divided.'

William sat back, all the adrenalin of the afternoon fading away.

'What else is in the remainder of the estate?' asked Tommy quietly.

'A minor portfolio,' said Hamilton. 'High street retailers, pharmaceuticals, that sort of thing. The shares are probably worth around four thousand pounds. The life insurance, as you know, is a whole of life assurance policy written in trust and therefore outside the estate and inheritance tax liability. The benefits to be paid to a named Trustee, myself as executor, as provision for inheritance tax and thereafter divided up according to the provision of the will. So that will go to Esther, but only after prior settlement of other expenses; the funeral, any debts, my own fee. Even at the outset you're talking about no more than a few thousand pounds.'

'Well, I don't think there's any more to be said,' Tommy had got to his feet. 'Thank you for your time, Robert. No doubt you'll be in touch.'

It was clear there was no point in arguing. William got up too, shook the solicitor's hand and followed his son out of the room.

'Let's get a drink,' said Tommy. 'The car's good for another half an hour.' He took William's am and steered him towards a nearby side street. 'I think there's a pub somewhere down here.'

It was a shabby old place with brown walls, smoked glass and dimpled bronze panels around an open fire. While Tommy got the drinks William sat down at a little round table, rubbing his hands warm and looking at the line of hardback books on a high-up wooden shelf. Books no-one would ever read.

Tommy came back with two whiskies and a plate of mince pies. 'Special offer. Thought we might as well.'

William bit into the sweet, crumbling pastry. At his side Tommy was clearly preoccupied, he sat with his palm round his glass, swirling the whisky. His black scarf still hung loosely round his neck and even with his angry, troubled expression he looked handsome, younger than his fifty four years, William thought.

'I can't believe Gina kept that stock,' he said to William. 'I was so sure she'd sold it. I talked to her about it a couple of times after Arthur died. Not that she'd ever go into it much. But I honestly thought the last time we spoke that she'd either already dumped it or that she was about to do it.'

Behind them a group of office workers had come in wearing Santa hats and laughing and joking. The pub door closed after them with a bang but Tommy didn't even turn his head.

'Why on earth didn't she sell it?' he said.

William thought hard. 'Well, she never really cared much about money,' he said slowly.

Tommy stared at that: 'Gina loved the high life!'

'Yes, when it came her way. But she wasn't driven by things like that. Not like you. Always wanting to make something out of nothing.'

Tommy smiled at that and lifted the whisky to his lips.

'What Gina cared about was Arthur,' said William. 'And Esther.'

That's why he couldn't believe she'd have left things like this. No matter how bad things might have been at the end.

He looked across at Tommy. 'Are you sure Gina didn't change her will?'

'You saw Hamilton's paperwork,' shrugged Tommy. 'You couldn't fault it.'

It was true. Hamilton's grasp of Gina's affairs had silenced even Tommy.

They'd both finished their whisky. The pub was cold in spite of the open fire and it was getting late.

'Can we go?' said William.

His son gave him a wry smile. 'You shouldn't have come out in the first place. Did you think I wouldn't tell you what was going on?'

14

TRUE NORTH

As soon as Tommy had dropped him at the door and gone, William went inside and phoned Esther on the mobile number she'd left him. The clock on the mantelpiece showed twenty past five but he'd no idea how long her flight was or when she'd reach home. The numbers clicked through, one by one, followed by the sharp buzz of the ring tone. Then he heard her voice; recorded: *Hi, this is Esther; leave me a message and I'll call you back!*

'Esther, it's Granddad. I know you're upset. Your friend came round. And we've been to the solicitor . . .' He was at a loss then what else to say and fell silent, the seconds ticking away while he searched for the words. 'Look, ring me back, will you?' he said at last, hurriedly. 'Just so I know you're all right.'

He was only just in time; his words coincided with a loud beep.

He wondered if she would ring. She'd never rung Gina much by all accounts but everything was different now.

She was pretty upset.

I wanted her to call you.

He turned abruptly away and went to make a cup of tea.

When he'd brought the tray through he put the lamps on and settled down to watch television but it seemed to be all cheerful adverts with Christmas offers and snow scenes. He turned it off and opened The Evening Telegraph instead but his mind was still on Esther and Gina.

He folded the paper and dropped it to the floor and it was then, sitting back drinking tea, that his eye fell on the shiny gold box under the dark branches of the fibre optic tree.

This is for you.

For Christmas.

It had been here all along: a clue, something Esther had bought specifically for him, the possibility of connection.

Christmas was more than a week away but there was no reason why he couldn't open it now. He wasn't a child. He was old by anyone's standards. '*I might not even make it to Christmas Day!*'

'Oh hark at you! Maudlin!'

Alice's voice decided it. She'd have opened the present without a moment's hesitation, just wrapped it up again afterwards and put it back under the tree. '*At least I'm not deceitful*,' he observed sternly and her dark eyes laughed at him from the silver frame.

He fetched the box and sat with it still on his knee for a moment, looking down at the shiny paper and fancy bow. It was oblong and light yet something solid shifted inside when he moved it. He slid his finger between the golden edges, ripped round the sellotape and pushed the paper back.

To his surprise it was a jigsaw. *The Compass* it said in black gothic lettering across the top of the box and the picture was thrilling; a deep orange background with the compass at the centre; sixteen black fleur-de-lis points, the segments between them a colourful chequerboard of yellow and green, and each thin pointing hand containing an elongated mythical figure. In the middle was a circle with an old ship, the sails billowing out from its three tall masts.

When he lifted the lid he found the pieces had been closely packed in a sealed polythene bag which was taped to the base of the box. There was a leaflet too; *seven hundred and fifty years of marine navigation . . . the dry compass of medieval Europe . . . Flavio Giojo . . . the fleur-de-lys in honour of Charles of Anjou . . .*

William stared down at it. He'd never been one for jigsaws but Alice had. It took him back to the days when they'd been young together, younger even than Esther was now, and to Ludlow's Farm on Sunday afternoons when there had always been a jigsaw on the go in the parlour.

He put the box to one side, carefully opened out the end leaf of the dining table and pulled up a chair. When he cut open the polythene bag and emptied the pieces onto the table a fine cloud of shavings descended on the dark wood. He blew them away gently and their dusty cardboard smell filled the back of his throat and set him coughing.

He began the long task of turning all the pieces face up and looking for the edges. His fingers moved methodically as his eyes searched for the straight bits and all the while his mind was wandering, following its own course, until he was back with Alice, the September he was fifteen, and the day they'd gone blackberrying in Grainger's thicket.

A group of them had been planning to go ever since McNee had said the brambles on the furthest side of the woods were still virtually untouched despite the summer forays from Earls Barton and Mears Ashby.

They'd gone straight from work on a Saturday, walking in a line past Ludlow's Farm, their heavy shoes leaving a trail of regular imprints along the muddy track. At the stile they'd climbed past a pile of abandoned bicycles and then split up to cover the little pockets of undergrowth on the deserted south side of the woodland.

For once William had gone after Alice rather than McNee. She'd set off straightaway climbing the steepest route towards the very far corner of the woods and he'd followed her across the uneven field: recently harvested and ploughed with the cream streaks of late summer stubble showing through the furrows.

Alice was small but she'd walked fast even in her long black skirt, swinging her arms with the sleeves of her red and white patterned sweater pushed up to her elbows. William had quickened his pace to catch up and they'd crossed the raw beauty of the ploughed field together in the cold brightness of autumn.

They reached the edge of the trees, clambered over the low fence and followed a path that banked steeply between two great ditches, the trees all around leaning inwards as if to hold their grip. The earth underfoot was dried and cracked like a tortoise shell and the fallen twigs and branches grasped at their feet as they walked.

Crossing a patch of long grass they came across a mass of brambles and set to methodically, blackening their hands as they stripped the treacherous branches of their fruit. They spoke little but voices carried here and occasionally they heard the others' calls and laughter from further along the wood's perimeter.

The briars spread everywhere and they moved on, leaving their filled bowls and baskets in a shady spot to collect on their way back. They turned off the path and cut across the wooded ground where the tree trunks grew close like pillars and pine needles hung like drapery all around. The pools of sunlight on the ground were few and far between now and the noise of branches shifting was closer and more immediate. Once or twice the white heels of a rabbit preceded them through the fallen leaves.

They moved on, picking and eating, following the prickly trail and dropping the ripe blackberries into their pails and, by the time they'd grown tired of it, a stillness had fallen on Grainger's, the birds were silent and the shadows among the tree trunks had turned dark.

They were close to the outer edge again now and emerged beneath a line of horse chestnuts onto rough grassland where the deep bleating of sheep sounded along the hedgerow.

Overhead a deep orange tinge streaked westwards across the glowing sky and in the distance William could see the others on the far side of the lower field, climbing the stile into the farm track.

He and Alice followed the line of the trees back towards the place where they'd left their first lot of blackberries and pushed in through the branches to retrieve the baskets.

It was then that William suddenly had a feeling someone else was there. He sensed a movement among the leaves and there, in the deepening twilight, saw the shape of a man, a vagrant by his ragged jacket and old trousers belted with string, who rose up before them with a look of alarm. In his left hand was a tin bowl full of blackberries and under his right, gripped against his flapping coat, one of the wicker baskets.

William stopped short, sizing up the man's build and noting that he stood awkwardly with his weight on one leg and the other stretched out but, before he could say anything, Alice had stepped calmly between them, picked up one of the pails and said casually. 'Walk down the track with us. We've got a barn to sleep in. And something more than blackberries for tea.'

The man didn't move. His fingers gripped the tin bowl and the lengthening shadows accentuated his gaunt face and William had a sudden unnerving sense of what it was to be hungry; the fierce desperation of it.

'People often sleep in our barn,' said Alice conversationally as she turned towards the field.

The man tailed a good distance behind them, though whether by design or because his impaired walking prevented him keeping pace, William didn't know. It was well after six when they came through the old wooden gate at the back of Ludlow's farm. The yard was wet with mud where the cows had been brought in and the long stone barn was quiet and in shadow. They went on past it towards the great, red brick farmhouse with its gables and turrets and long sash windows.

'Will you stay for tea?' Alice had asked William then, surprising him, and like a fool he'd shaken his head dumbly for no other reason than that she'd caught him unawares.

They took the fruit into the outhouse and divided it between them. When William came out with his share in an old wicker basket Alice's Auntie Maud was leading the vagrant across to the barn.

'There's a bucket in there and soap. And mind you use plenty of it.'

Her voice carried after him through the emptiness of the farmyard as he headed homewards by himself.

The next time he saw the vagrant he was in the farmhouse parlour, sitting at the table with his bandaged foot propped on a stool, helping Alice's mother and sister with their Sunday jigsaw. He'd washed and shaved and was wearing fresh clothes but William could see there was more than hunger to him then; a feverish shine in his eyes and an intermittent jerking of the head, as if he'd suddenly come to and register where he was. Some time later he disappeared without a word to anyone, on his way to no-one knew where.

'Dab hand at a jigsaw, mind,' Maud used to say of him.

Maud, Ludlow's sister, who ran his dairy and whose fiancé had come back from the Great War 'not himself' so nothing more had come of that. Maud; tall and stern in black, even to her straw hat, leaning on the hawthorn stick that was now William's own, leaning on it until her final days when she'd died at the grand old age of seventy nine. Younger then than he was now and yet she'd seemed ancient to him and Alice back then, like someone left over from a distant era.

William sat on at the table searching for the jigsaw's edges and thinking about the vagrant, wondering who he'd been, where he'd gone and whether he'd had a family somewhere worrying about him. The cardboard pieces were smooth and light as he lifted them one by one and his fingers seemed to remember with a whole physical remembering that was quite separate from his mind.

He sensed time passing, vaguely conscious of the clock ticking on the mantelpiece: the carriage clock that had been an anniversary present to him and Alice. Yet part of him fancied it was the old grandmother clock at the foot of Ludlow's stairs. It hadn't the deep sonorous tone but there was the same steady rhythm and the conspicuous beat of metal within fine casing. All the time his eyes were on the colours in front of him, comparing the darker and lighter hues of the orange, looking for the tiny black flecks of the fleur de lys, searching out the vital clues that would make these fragments whole.

The clock hands turned and his shoulders and neck grew stiff and cold without him noticing until the telephone rang, shrill in the silence. He felt it then, as he got up to answer, and it was Esther.

She sounded far away. Her voice was thin and distant and he wished he could see her face, especially her green eyes.

'It's not the money,' she said and he listened silently as she told him about the solicitor, hearing her tears held back. 'Mum knew what she was doing, didn't she? Even right at the end?'

He nodded, unable to speak for a moment, then: 'Did she ever talk to you about the will?'

'We never talked about anything.'

'Might there have been another will? Hidden away somewhere?'

'No,' she said. 'Mum never hid things. Everything was always in the desk.'

And he knew she was right.

'I'm glad you rang me back,' he said at last.

Silence.

'Well,' she said. 'Mum knew I didn't want the house. And it's not as if I've ever been interested in money.'

'Ring me sometimes,' said William. 'Let me know you're all right.'

And she promised she would.

That night he dreamt of the compass. The sickly green and yellow shades of the chequerboard had descended on Kimble's Top, covering everything in sight.

'See?' said Gina, showing it to him.

She spoke as if she'd explained it all to him and he'd see what she meant as soon as he laid eyes on it but he had no idea what it signified. Meanwhile there was a compass wheel spinning in the background. Its arms were curved and grasping like a ship's wheel but full of evil intent and he kept turning sharply to catch it unawares, but he never managed it.

The whole family was up at Kimble's Top, partying on the lawn, and he wanted to tell them about the wheel turning but whenever he tried to say something they made a point of talking loudly among themselves until he realised they were doing it on purpose.

'It's the power of the compass,' said a voice knowingly.

He awoke then in the dark, breathing fast, and the past seemed closer and more lucid than ever before. Only it wasn't the past of his life but just the background to it.

He felt the austere cold space of the farmhouse all around him and saw the tiny details, barely noticed and long forgotten. The heavy silver cutlery laid out in rows on the dresser ready for setting the table, the deep bowl of every spoon and the sharp angle of the handles tilting up and away. The smooth wooden length of the barometer in the hall and the sheen on the beige wallpaper behind it. The stair carpet that changed after the first floor landing from red and blue Wilton to an older grey weave, frayed at the edges.

The scenes passed vividly through his mind in a swift and strange succession but of the people he'd loved and the landmark events of their lives, there was no trace.

He slept again and woke up tired with the worn down hollow of the pillow like iron against his cheek. He felt breathless again but then he always was bad in the mornings and he hadn't slept well.

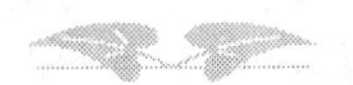

It was a quiet weekend. Richard and Doreen were visiting her family and Tommy and Bryony would be going down to London for some charity dinner.

First thing on Saturday William made his way up to the paper shop to pay his bill.

'How's your grandchildren?' asked the woman in front of him in the queue. He recognised her from somewhere down Knox Road: retired and faded with dyed hair piled up high, big glass beads and earrings. She'd done all her Christmas shopping early, she told him, at the jeweller's in the Arndale. 'That's with having only granddaughters, you see. Easy to buy for. And you can put it all in the post.'

It gave him an idea for Esther and when he got in he rang Bryony who'd offered to get his Christmas presents for him and said he'd sort Esther's out himself.

'But it's the week before Christmas, Dad! It'll be busy in town. And horrendous queues at the post office.'

'I can manage.'

He'd go first thing Monday.

In the meantime Maurice and Lorraine had invited him over for Saturday afternoon and most of Sunday and in between it all he sat at his dining table and got on with the jigsaw. There was something compelling about it now. He'd joined up what he could of the edge and produced a wobbly rectangle that didn't look quite right but the puzzle had a thousand pieces and though he'd spent ages sifting through them, looking for the missing edges, he couldn't find any more.

He gave up and looked instead for some distinctive section to start on, choosing the north west arm of the compass, which was green with a serene figure in a fur coat advancing through a flurry of snowflakes.

On Sunday night the temperature dropped below freezing and when he got up on Monday every surface outside was white with frost. The morning was light and still but the cold air cut like a knife.

He was a fool to go out in it, he knew, especially with his breathing the way it was, but he'd made up his mind to find something special for Esther and the thought spurred him on.

The taxi dropped him at the glass doors to the shopping centre and he took the escalator up to the shops. Christmas music was playing and although it was early the place was already busy with grey-haired couples, young girls with buggies and teenagers talking on mobile phones.

The jeweller's shop was decorated with turquoise ribbons and silver glitter. His own reflection flashed at him from the glass display cabinets all around as he made his way to the counter.

'I wanted something for my granddaughter,' he told the assistant.

'Gold or silver?'

Apparently it was all to do with skin tone and when he described Esther she thought gold would be best, with garnet or amber. Something else had caught William's eye, though: a necklace with a much lighter stone, like tangerine, twinkling in the light.

'Citrine,' said the woman. 'And the little ones are diamonds.'

The necklace was heart-shaped with delicate sections linked together and the stone suspended from loops that swept around each other like angel's wings, shiny and speckled with tiny diamonds. It looked just Esther's kind of thing.

Bryony had been right about the queue in the post office but he reached the counter eventually and posted the gift off in a jiffy bag without any difficulty.

The cold really hit him then. The taxis left from the market square and he'd forgotten what a steady incline it was along there. The freezing air penetrated his wool coat and trousers as though they were thin cotton and all he could think about was getting back in the warm. It was the worst possible thing for his breathing. He felt as though crystals of ice were settling in his chest.

When he reached the taxi rank there were four people ahead of him in the queue and not a car in sight. Specks of rain were falling and his nose and cheeks had gone numb. He pulled his scarf up over his mouth and leaned hard on his stick but within a few minutes he'd begun to feel odd. His head was empty, echoing with the cold, and the backs of his eyes, when he blinked, were stinging.

Finally a single yellow cab pulled in from Church Street but there was no sign of any more behind it. William looked around the old wooden market stalls to see if there was a bench where he could sit down for a few minutes and he must have swayed then because someone gripped him under the arm.

It was a young man with Rastafarian locks tied back who smiled cheerfully at him. 'Where you going, man?'

'Hartley Rise.'

The taxi had reached the head of the line and another youngster had moved forward to take it, pushing a baby in a buggy.

'Hey!' called the Rastafarian. 'Why you don't take the old man with you?'

The other man just shrugged and nodded and the rest of the line agreed despite William's protests.

He began to feel more like himself in the warmth of the car but he'd been home half an hour before his fingers lost their stiffness and every breath still set him coughing.

'You ought to see the doctor,' said Lorraine when she came to do his lunch but he shook his head and waved her away.

'It's just the cold.'

When she'd gone he fetched the phone book and looked up Hamilton's number. The receptionist put him through straightaway and the solicitor was studiously polite and patient in response to his questions.

'We're a small firm, Mr Allbright. And I've been a partner here for fifteen years. If Gina had changed her will we'd have known about it. We handled all her affairs.'

And so that was that.

By the next day he had a rotten cold. He started feeling weary after lunch and his throat hurt. By evening he was shivering and couldn't get warm and on Wednesday he woke up with catarragh and a sick feeling in the pit of his stomach. When he looked in the mirror to shave his face stared back gaunt with tender bags under the eyes, not black from lack of sleep but red-rimmed and sensitive.

As the week wore on his limbs felt heavier every day and he wondered how he'd ever summon the energy to get up, but he couldn't stand the thought of lying in bed all day. He dozed in the front room instead with the hot water bottle on his knee and an old woollen jumper round his neck and shoulders for extra warmth. If he could have slept it off he'd have been all right but his coughing kept him awake half the night.

Doreen and Bryony fussed about with soup and toast but he preferred Tommy's cure-all: a shot of whisky and

Drambuie with hot water. His son dropped by with it on Friday, the night before Christmas Eve.

William caught his breath on the alcohol but it warmed his chest like nothing on earth. He took little sips while Tommy stood at the dining table and surveyed the jigsaw.

'Wasn't this meant to be a Christmas present?' he observed with a cynical smile that William ignored. 'You've got half the bits joined up wrong for a start.'

He sat down and began dismantling it.

'Did you speak to Esther?' asked William from the armchair.

Tommy nodded.

'And'

'I said we'd sort something out.'

'Like what?'

'Well, the obvious choice is to see if we can sell the flats. Arthur put them in trust to fund the running of Kimble's Top, so Robyn doesn't actually own them. But there must be some provision for selling them. They've got to be worth about two hundred and fifty grand.'

'I thought Robyn needed the rents to stay at Kimble's Top.'

'She'll have to find another source of income. She's got some options.'

'Has she?'

Tommy was frowning now, looking for the right edge pieces.

'What options?' asked William.

'Richard and Doreen could sell up and move in.'

William couldn't imagine that for one moment. 'Have you suggested that to Robyn?'

Tommy said nothing, still intent on the jigsaw.

'Have you talked about it?' said William.
Tommy looked up, his dark eyes distracted: 'What?'
'Have you talked about it?'
'Dad,' he sighed. 'It's Christmas.'

15

CHRISTMAS

By the weekend William's cold had gone to his chest. His cough rattled endlessly yet the phlegm never seemed to clear and he couldn't sleep: just as his eyes and head were sinking away his throat would erupt, jerking him awake to cough and spit.

On Saturday morning he felt exhausted, his chest glowed with the effort of his constant hacking but he was supposed to be going to Richard's and they wouldn't let him stay at home.

'You can't spend Christmas Eve on your own, Dad.'

Apparently Laurel had decorated their tree and was dying to show him and the only other option was to have them all come here, which he couldn't face. In the end he swallowed a remedy from the chemist's and got himself ready to go.

Doreen was at work and when he got there only Lee was around, stretched out on the sofa with his eyes closed and the tell-tale black wires of earphones trailing down into his collar.

Robyn and Laurel arrived soon afterwards. William had just settled down with a cup of tea when he heard a car crunching the gravel and looked out to see Gina's blue

Citroen Picasso. Laurel was already climbing down from the passenger seat and running for the front door.

'We're here!'

She came into the living room, her face alight with happiness, darted across to him and threw herself over the wide arm of the chair for a hug.

'Look at my new dress!'

When he'd admired it she led him over to the Christmas tree and he admired that too. Most of the decorations were years old. Her favourite was an old glass bird with a long glittery tail but he preferred the snowman she'd made herself from cardboard and decorated with a white paper doily.

All the while he was aware of Robyn watching them from the doorway. She still looked pale and tired but he noticed she'd put some lipstick on and she was wearing a sheepskin jacket he hadn't seen before, with a fleecy collar and cuffs. She smiled coolly but made no movement to come over and join him and Laurel.

Later on he heard her saying she wanted to pop into town and pick a few things up so it was just himself and Richard with Laurel and the boys for lunch; home-made burgers with oven chips and beans.

'So you're all going up to Kimble's Top tomorrow,' said William at the table.

Lee pulled a face. 'It's miles from anywhere. None of our mates can come round.'

'They won't be coming round anyway,' said Richard passing the plates down. 'Not on Christmas Day.'

'They will when I text to say I've got an Xbox 360.'

Paul laughed loudly with derision and jabbed a finger at his brother. 'You're getting nothing, mate.'

'Yeah,' insisted Lee. 'I asked Santa, didn't I, Laurel? Wrote it on a letter and stuck it up the chimney.'

Laurel nodded but said nothing, preoccupied with draping tomato sauce over her chips.

Afterwards they all sat down in the living room to watch a film. Laurel brought a cushion and settled down comfortably at William's feet, a bowl of mixed nuts and raisins balanced in the lap of her skirt. She was warm and soft against his legs and in the comfort of the room, having just eaten, he slept.

When he woke he was on his own and it felt late. The television had been turned down low and from upstairs he could hear voices and laughter; the boys and Laurel playing a computer game.

He closed his eyes to doze again but then realised there was someone in the dining room behind him. Richard had left the double doors ajar earlier to listen for the dishwasher finishing. Now William heard a chair creak and a teaspoon ringing against the sides of a cup as someone stirred a drink. He wanted to cough but something made him clench his lips tight instead. As he pressed the back of his hand against his mouth, listening, Robyn spoke.

'I'm not being funny, right, but Esther's had money all her life. And what's she ever done with it? Now it's my turn.'

'What exactly was Tommy suggesting?'

Doreen: further away, probably speaking through the open doorway to the kitchen.

'Lodgers,' said Robyn. 'Or all of you moving in. I told him to forget it. It's not my fault Esther's ended up with nothing.'

'Well, I suppose your Dad and I could think about it.'

'Gina wanted me to have Kimble's Top. That's what the will said. And the income from the flats goes with it.'

The desire to sleep vanished. William sat quietly, staring past the twinkling Christmas lights to the blue Citroen parked outside, where once Gina had sat at the wheel and he'd never troubled to think that one day she might not be there.

The next morning he felt hot and light-headed but he couldn't be ill on Christmas Day. He took his time getting up, shaved and then dressed in a new shirt and grey cardigan Bryony had given him: presents she'd put under the tree earlier in the week.

'Open them first thing. Something to cheer you up.'

And feeling the soft bulk of the packages he'd guessed what they were.

At twelve o'clock Tommy came by to pick him up for Christmas lunch. He stood in the hall holding William's dark overcoat out for him.

'Are you sure you're all right?'

William nodded. 'I just need to get going,' his voice was a dry whisper.

In the car he sat breathing heavily, making a mental note of everything they passed to take his mind off the breathlessness.

Ise Avenue. Trees and brick walls on either side; not old red walls but smart new one with honey-coloured bricks. Here and there inlaid with wrought iron, a glimpse of a garden, sweeping woodland and gateways, drives at an angle, so that even if you craned to look through the gates you never saw a house, just once or twice a free standing garage and the gleam of a BMW.

Across the road from Tommy's house: double gates and a flagpole, the round thatch of a summer house and the cry of peacocks.

They turned away from it, the electric gates to Tommy's drive swinging gently inwards and as they drove through it struck William that where Kimble's Top confronted you with hilltop grandeur, Tommy's place was modest and shady. It was a chalet-style house with a sloping roof, big windows and white fascia boards.

Everything here was low and wide, both house and garden, with overhanging trees, designed to draw you in.

The family had been entertaining all morning and there was a line of cars on the drive.

'Old school friends of Chris and Elisabeth,' said Tommy.

Bryony came out to the hall to take his coat but William could see she wanted to get back to the kitchen and Tommy with her so he went on through to the living room. There was quite a gathering of young people. He had an impression of slender long-haired girls in their party finery and well dressed young men. His grandson, Chris, stood out among them all, wearing a bright red poncho with wide sleeves and narrow stripes in yellow and blue.

'Grandad!' he spotted William across the room. 'Come and have a drink.' He looked around for a clean glass, champagne bottle in hand and a linen napkin slung casually over one shoulder.

You've had a few, thought William, and that's all it would take with Chris: a few.

Elisabeth came to take his arm. 'He'd probably rather have a sherry!'

William gestured towards his customary armchair. 'I just need to sit quiet. Get my breath.'

He sank down gratefully into the Queen Anne chair and she set his drink on a side table at his elbow. William sat back comfortably and looked out of the window at the pond and the flowering cherry tree. The tree was bare, its thin branches sketching dismal lines on the grey water beneath. He sipped his sherry and let the young people's conversation wash over him.

'More blinis,' Chris had announced and disappeared off to the kitchen, returning with a plate in each hand. 'Chicken and chilli. Positively the last!'

'So what exactly are you up to these days?' one of the girls asked him.

'Working! R and D. For ChemSed. They funded my Masters.'

Researching and developing hydroclaves. Waste *treatment*, not disposal. Low cost sterilisation and no emissions. The conversation moved on to Elisabeth.

'Wasn't there a promotion?'

Yes. Brand manager now, for core whites. High gloss trade paints.

'Full of emissions,' said Chris smugly. 'Carbon compounds. And formaldehyde. Probably carcinogenic.'

William closed his eyes, the sherry only half finished. From the kitchen he could smell the turkey cooking. Normally it would have been a welcome smell but today it seemed overpowering.

Soon the guests were getting up to leave, opening doors, creating a draught, and the aroma was even stronger: sausages and bacon cooking in the oven.

He had a sudden desire not to move, feeling as though he might suffocate.

'Dad?'

Bryony had come to find him.

'We're just finishing up in the kitchen.'

He nodded, tried to speak but his mouth was dry.

'You don't look very well,' she said, her tone concerned.

'I'm fine. I'll be better when I've eaten.'

He followed her to the kitchen where Tommy was mixing black pepper and lime juice with mayonnaise, Worcester sauce and dill. Chris was in the far corner of the room, perched on the arm of a battered red sofa.

When Tommy and Bryony had first moved here they'd planned a playroom at the front of the house but the children had never warmed to it. They'd brought their toys instead to this corner of the kitchen and in the end Tommy had fitted it out for them with a sofa and bookshelves.

On Sunday afternoons William's grandchildren had played for hours here, drawing and colouring on computer listing paper from Tommy's work. Even now books and magazines were still strewn around and there was a black and white portable television that, amazingly, still worked.

Chris had slipped off his shoes and was sitting with his feet up on the cushions.

'Those guys are just so not clued up about the environment,' he said. 'Kirsty's working for a travel management company whose sole aim is to jet people around the world when they could just talk on the phone. It's obscene.'

'There's no substitute for face to face contact,' said Tommy washing his hands at the sink and drying them meticulously on a towel.

'Oh we wouldn't expect you to agree,' said Chris drunkenly. 'Not with an Audi A8 on the drive.'

Elisabeth was at the fridge, taking out bottles of sparkling water. 'It's got the lowest drag coefficient of anything in its class,' she protested.

Chris sat up tall at that and flung his arms wide. 'Do you have any idea how much energy it takes to manufacture aluminium?'

The dining room was beautiful: the oval table spacious in spite of the evergreen decorations, candelabra, crystal glasses and silver ware. There were big gold crackers with a black velvet pattern; Elisabeth had picked them up in the Harrods sale the previous January and they pulled them in true festive spirit, wore the hats and exchanged jokes.

Why did Captain Hook cross the road? To get to the second hand shop on the other side!

William found he could barely eat anything and as Bryony reached across to clear the plates he could feel her eyes on him. He made an effort to smile and reassure her, to show he was enjoying the warm atmosphere of the table.

With the Christmas pudding they toasted absent friends and it was then that Elisabeth asked her dad. 'So what's Esther doing today?'

Tommy looked surprised.

'I heard you ringing her last night,' she said.

'Again?' Bryony looked up from spooning the pudding into bowls.

'I had a couple of possibilities I wanted to run by her,' said Tommy.

Bryony just looked at him.

'Well no-one else is going to advise her,' said Tommy. 'She needs to know we're working on something for her.'

'We?'

'This is a family problem. We can't just leave her with nothing.'

'Why not?' said Chris loudly, his words slurred. 'Gina did.'

William gripped his spoon tight, the metal pressing into his fingers. Tommy's expression was cold and distant. Chris had picked up his spoon and begun eating the pudding, totally unconcerned. Elisabeth glanced anxiously at Bryony but said nothing.

William's own heart was thumping. Bryony passed the last of the bowls down the table and he raised a spoonful of pudding to his mouth. His head was ringing with voices and memories. Gina, angry, when Esther had first come home before the summer; *'For goodness sake do something with your life.'* Gina, arguing with Tommy over Robyn; *'What I want is someone close.'* Gina over Sunday tea at Kimble's Top, coolly peeling an apple while the rest of them sat uneasily by and no-one mentioned her cancer.

Around him a stilted conversation was going on: Elisabeth and Bryony making an effort to keep things going while Chris seemed oblivious and Tommy sat in angry silence at the far end of the table.

'She wasn't the only long-term shareholder to get caught out.' The words of the pale-faced solicitor came into William's head, and his tone of professional regret, and the more William thought about it, the more it offended him.

It was unthinkable that Gina would have left Esther with nothing.

It was with the coffee that it all went wrong for William.

Bryony brought it to the table on a silver tray with fine white china cups, the silver sugar and milk set, heavy teaspoons with beaded edges.

He rarely drank coffee but it seemed in keeping with the meal.

Within minutes he was fading fast.

When he got up to help clear the table he was already dizzy and his mind was wandering alarmingly. Bryony stopped him as he carried the custard jug into the kitchen. 'You go and sit down!' She took the jug from him.

In the living room Elisabeth had the television on, waiting for the Queen's speech. An old Christmas film was finishing: Meet Me in St Louis. He'd seen it at the pictures with Alice when it first came out. He sat listening to the sound of Hollywood: the breathless interchange of adolescent girls, Judy Garland talking so fast he couldn't make out the words, the sweet crescendo of stringed instruments.

It was the sound of yesteryear and its note of melancholy filled him with regret. It held the ambience of years ago, his years and Alice's. Listening to it he was back there again and yet 'there' had never really existed. There was nothing remotely real about the film. Yet strangely it filled him with a sense of loss, of Christmases come and gone, of . . .

A hand was pressing tight on his arm and Tommy was beside him looking concerned. William smiled widely. He was all right.

He wasn't sitting in his usual chair though. For some reason he'd sat down on one of the regency striped sofas. Silky upholstery in yellow and gold. He felt weary just sitting, utterly fatigued, and his own voice sounded larger than life in his head, uttering disconnected thoughts that had no logic to them. He was off colour today. A bit of a temperature. That's where thoughts like that came from.

Across from him Elisabeth was sipping brandy with tiny proper sips and no expression to show she'd even tasted the cognac. Bryony was there too and they were talking among themselves, the three of them.

It all seemed very far away

The cushions were smooth against his cheek, shining with yellow and gold. There were voices around him and, when he turned his head, a flashing blue light at the window. Flashing and flashing with a gentle turning rhythm.

With the mask over his face the air was sweet. The voices were deliberate and reassuring but he didn't know what they were saying. Sleep was finally coming and perhaps he wouldn't wake. They draped a pink blanket with holes over him and tilted him back in a chair to go outside.

The back doors of the ambulance were open ready, silver metal, and Tommy looked so substantial beside the thin paramedics in their bright green clothes.

16

HOSPITAL

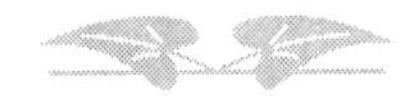

Venetian blinds at a little window and next to it a door to the corridor beyond. The length of the bed stretching out ahead of him. Behind his head a panel with sockets and equipment and the oxygen line from his nose trailed back there. They were forever reaching over him to adjust things and flick switches; the sister in a dark blue dress and younger nurses in dark trousers and white tunics.

They came and went and in between they left him alone with the bulky white pillows, with the narrow sheets that tugged round his legs and the memories.

They were brilliant memories, vivid, dreams some of them; the whole depths of his unconscious mind exposed as if something were reaching into its furthest corners and turning everything out remorselessly.

Alice was more than a face in a frame now. She was warm and lithe and breathing; hanging on his arm on their wedding day in loose fitting white silk with gathered sleeves and dainty buttons, clutching her yellow posy.

Four windswept days in Cromer. The town's third best hotel. Lying in the vast old bed with the curtains at the window drawn right back, wide awake and listening to the sea and watching the dark clouds move across the black night sky. In the morning she sat at the dressing table and he lay sideways on the bed, resting on one arm, watching, until their eyes met, smiling, in the mirror.

He was coming through the back gate, kitbag in hand, to find her reaching up to hang the washing on the line, the collar of her cotton dress blowing up against her face in the wind. At her feet Gina, three years old, clutched the peg bag tight against her chest.

'This is your Daddy,' Alice told her, after the first startled silence.

And Gina had repeated it over and over to him, her face close to his, with her fingers pulling at his cheeks. 'You're my Daddy.'

As though he were in danger of forgetting it.

On and on. Sleeping and dreaming. Waking again. And on the boundaries between, remembering.

Voices came and went. Men and women stood in a group at his bed. Shiny white coats rucked up at the sleeves and the stethoscope handed round, listening to his chest.

Breathe in.

And out.

When he doubled up coughing, his mouth was full of sickly phlegm: a foul yellow substance he spat into the plastic dish they held out for him.

They spoke over him as if he wasn't there.

'Crackles on auscultation but otherwise no sign of pulmonary edema. We'll do some PFTs. The chest X-ray you've seen. Some evidence of strain on the right side of the heart. Amoxicillin in capsules. Should clear the infection.'

Whatever it was, it made him sleep and he dreamed and dreamed of Gina but always as a little girl, her hair as orange as the jigsaw. Never Gina as he'd grown closest to her: Gina the widow who came to do his lunch and sat with him because she knew what loss meant.

Tommy and Bryony. Richard. Doreen. They appeared at the door and sat with him until he lost track of who was there and when. Someone had brought his own blue pyjamas and an array of Christmas cards that looked down on him from the formica tops of his cabinet and bedside tray.

'You hadn't opened them,' said Bryony. 'They were in a pile on the sideboard.'

She read through them for him as she set them out in a colourful display of robins and snowmen. 'And there's a letter, from Larry Clifton.'

He'd closed his eyes to doze again.

'I'll put it here in the drawer. For when you're a bit better.'

Only he opened his eyes to see Tommy reading it. Not aloud, for William to hear, but silently, to himself. The empty envelope lay on the bed with the gold sticker in the top left hand corner proclaiming: *Lawrence R Clifton* and four neat lines of an address in Madeira.

'I thought it might be important,' said his son, seeing he was awake, but he slid the folded sheets back into the envelope without telling William what they said.

He slept again and was back at Tommy's for Christmas dinner, staring at the reflection of the cutlery and glasses in the shiny dark wood of the table, while all around him the family were laughing and joking and pulling crackers,

Why did Captain Hook cross the road?

He dreamt of Peter Pan. Not the wistful cherub of the statue at Kimble's Top but a boy with a conniving resentful face he must have seen in a film. And he knew then he ought to warn Esther. There's something you should know about Kimble's Top.

The children were flying home through the night sky and Tootie was watching for Santa Claus through leaded panes sparkling with frost while Judy Garland sang in tones of tender melancholy.

Someday soon we all will be together

If the fates allow

Until then we'll have to muddle through somehow

So have yourself . . .

A sharp pinch on the finger woke him abruptly.

'Pulse oximeter,' said the nurse fixing the clip. 'Saves us taking more blood.'

He woke again to find the sister setting up a nebuliser on his bedside tray. 'Have you used one of these before, William?'

He hadn't. It was small and curved, made of tough white plastic. She clicked the lid open and lifted it up.

'We put the medicine into the bowl here and it converts the drug into mist. So when you inhale it'll go directly into the lungs. Particularly the blocked airways. We'll try it morning and evening and see how we go.'

She pulled the face mask over his mouth and nose. 'Probably best if you keep your mouth closed and just breathe through the nose.'

He followed her instructions and the relief was immediate. He could hardly believe it. After a few days his breathing was better than it had been in years. Now when he spat into the plastic dish his saliva was all but clear.

'Glutathione,' said the doctor with obvious satisfaction. 'Excellent for respiratory crises. When you go home we'll switch you onto one of the beta agonists. You can use the nebuliser whenever you feel the need.'

They moved him into the main ward then and he lay awake half the night listening to the snoring and night time moans of the men around him.

His bed was closest to the nurses' station and all day long there was a constant coming and going. Ringing telephones. Conversations all around. Visitors at all hours.

He lay on his side with the sheet pulled up over his shoulder and mostly just closed his eyes to it but then came the argument and a commotion it was impossible to ignore.

It started at the next bed where an elderly man wheezed constantly. His niece came to visit, professional looking in black rimmed glasses and a smart overcoat with a high collar. She brought a bouquet wrapped in cellophane.

'I'm afraid we don't allow floral gifts on the wards,' said the nurse in charge when she saw it.

'Oh come on! It's just a few flowers. What harm can it do?'

'Patients in respiratory care can find flowers an irritant.'

'Oh don't be ridiculous,' the niece glared round and William listening to the conversation was too slow to avoid her eye.

'You don't mind, do you?'

The nurse saved him from answering. 'There are a number of hygiene factors,' she said firmly. 'The risk of bacteria, of spilling water on electrical equipment.'

'Oh for goodness sake!' The woman picked up the bouquet and pushed it into the nurse's hands. 'You have them then! Put them in your staff room or something if the patients can't have them.'

She left shortly afterwards and the flowers lay on the counter of the nurses' station. William heard the nurses discussing what to do with them.

'It's a shame to waste them. They are lovely. What does the label say?'

'*Winter Fragrance.* Asiatic lilies. Lonicera; that's honeysuckle, I think. And Nicotiana Sylvestris. Must be from a hot house.'

Nicotiana. Tobacco.

His mind jolted awake then, as clear and alert as his lungs had been when the mist from the nebuliser first hit home.

Now he remembered. Gina, her adult self, solid and real at the end of that August day when they'd been together at Kimble's Top. The onset of dusk had brought the scent of the tobacco plants floating on the air and Gina, satisfied and determined in spite of it all, had made it clear everything was in order.

'It's not a bad legacy,' she'd said. 'The house from Arthur and the garden from me.'

It was Esther she'd been speaking of as she'd gathered up her things to go indoors. Esther not Robyn.

And now he knew with certainty that there must have been another will. And he'd better get home because it was up to him to find it.

17

STEALTH

It was well into January when they finally let him come home, on a Monday morning. He'd had to wait for a doctor to sign the papers, sitting with his bag packed, his overcoat folded on his knees until someone said he could go.

The sky was grey and heavy with the threat of rain. Byrony had picked him up and as they turned into Hartley Rise the red brick facades looked gloomy. The street had contracted, shrunken in on itself in the dull winter light.

His front room was dingy too after the bright spaces of the hospital, empty and still, but at least it was the old familiar place. William lowered himself into the armchair and sat looking round at his own things: the green patterned curtains half pulled across the bay window, the jigsaw pieces all over the table, the faded upholstery of the chairs and sofa.

The faces of his children and grandchildren smiled from the photographs on the windowsill and sideboard whilst Alice regarded him coolly from the silver frame on the mantelpiece, as though he'd never been away.

'Miss me?'

'*Like a hole in the head.*'

It was a retort she'd learned late in life from the grandchildren and used to the full.

Bryony stayed for lunch and afterwards he washed up and then settled down with the Radio Times crossword.

He was still at it when the children came home from school, banging the doors along the street and calling to one another as they passed his window.

A party of teenage lads jostled against the glass shouting at someone out of view. 'Geek! . . . . Oi! . . . GEEK.'

William saw anoraks and backpacks and heard a retort called back, words he couldn't make out, as the group moved on, laughing.

Soon afterwards the doorbell rang, loud and shrill, and he looked up in surprise. The family usually let themselves in.

As he made his way out to the hall the bell rang again, pressed down hard.

'All right. All right.'

He pulled the door open to find Paul there, Richard's oldest boy, towering over him on the front step. Tall and thickset already, there was nothing of the stringy adolescent about Paul. Not normally one for social calls either, William thought.

'I've only got tea,' he said, leading the way inside. 'No coke or anything.'

'That's okay.'

His grandson followed him through to the kitchen and hung at his elbow, dodging left and right as William moved among the cupboards assembling the tea things and looking for a packet of biscuits to open.

The boy clearly had something on his mind. Back in the living room he sat on the sofa with one foot resting on the knee of the other and a hand on his ankle, flicking the laces of his baseball boot backwards and forwards.

'School all right?' asked William. Or should he say college?

'College. Yeah. College was cool.'

'Mum and Dad?'

Paul put his tea cup down carefully on the arm of the chair and leaned forward, hands clasped.

Now they were getting to it. William watched the heavy links of a gold bracelet slip forward against his grandson's thick wrist.

'See that's the thing. Me and Lee. We want to move in here with you.'

William was taken aback. For an instant he had a wild vision of the three of them living here: of youth and vigour, bags of chips and the tomato sauce bottle permanently on the table. The thought of it made him smile.

'Seriously,' said Paul, looking agitated. 'There's this whole BIG PLAN. We're all supposed to be moving up to Kimble's Top. Miles away from anywhere.' He gave William a determined look. 'We're not going.'

'I wouldn't worry about it,' said William. 'There's a lot of sorting out to do around the will. I doubt it'll come to that.'

He could see his grandson wasn't convinced but William was suddenly full of energy and purpose. 'Speaking of which,' he said briskly. 'I need to get up to Kimble's Top as soon as possible. I don't suppose your mum's going anytime soon?'

'Tonight,' said Paul. 'Laurel still comes to ours after school. Mum's taking her home later.'

'Tell her I want to go with them, will you?'

'What on earth for?' Doreen sounded appalled on the phone.

'Does there have to be a reason?'

'Well yes there does, given you've only just come out of hospital. You can't possibly go out in the cold and wet.'

'I miss Gina,' said William. 'I dreamt about her in hospital. All the time. I want to go up there where I feel close to her. I want to go today.'

For the first time in his life he played the emotional card and from her silence he knew she was at a loss. He was never normally difficult or emotional.

Finally she said she'd pick him up on the way.

'*I've turned wily,*' he told Alice. '*Now let's sort this thing out.*'

Laurel was in the back of the car, bundled up in her bright blue school sweatshirt with a silver puffa jacket over the top and talking non-stop.

Although she'd moved up to Kimble's Top she wasn't changing schools till next term so Robyn drove her over to Wellingborough every morning. Laurel liked that. It was much more fun than walking the same old boring route to school every day.

'It takes twenty five minutes. So we have to leave by twenty past eight at the latest. Above all, she loved Kimble's Top. 'It's got blinds instead of curtains and the garden's like a whole park and famous people came for parties.'

She was writing stories about them. 'Robert Scholt was a rich businessman and his wife was an heiress who fell in love with his charm and didn't mind about him being short and ugly. James Stowey was an engineer. He had his engagement party on the terrace but ended up not getting married . . .'

William smiled and nodded in response as she rode roughshod over his grief, naming names and recalling scenes that turned like a knife in his wounds but he hadn't the heart to stop her. It was right that she should be happy at Kimble's Top. The house deserved a child's love and Gina wouldn't have begrudged her happiness. Gina had loved Laurel.

Doreen cut her off sharply though when she began talking about the separate garden full of roses where Peter Pan lived.

'I think that's enough about Kimble's Top. Why don't you choose one of your CDs to put on?'

It reminded him, though, he really must talk to Esther about Kimble's Top. He gazed out at the line of scarlet tail lights that filled the dual carriageway ahead of them and thought perhaps he'd ring her tomorrow.

The lights were on as they approached the house and a couple of dazzling beams shone out, triggered by sensors, as they pulled in to the final sweep of the drive and parked close to the front door.

When he got out of the car the trees seemed more dominant than ever in the dusk and there was the smell of wet leaves all around.

If Robyn was surprised to see him she didn't show it, calmly holding the front door open and looking now as if she'd always belonged here. She was smartly dressed, in a long cherry coloured skirt, embroidered top and a cardigan with deep pockets. Her hair was different too: shorter than the girlish bob, it framed her face in a messed up fashion and had lighter streaks running through it. A grown up sophisticated style, he thought, all trace of the washed-out tearful girl had gone.

They sat in the kitchen which they'd never have done in Gina's time but Robyn had made it her own place. There was no table, just the high counters with stools, but she'd arranged a couple of wicker chairs next to the glazed back door and he sat looking out at the floodlit garden with its herbaceous borders and the winding path set in the grass all along this side of the house.

Robyn brought him a cup of tea. 'I've got jacket potatoes in the oven, if you'd like one. Cheese and salad as well.'

'Thanks.'

He sipped his tea and watched her at work at the central counter, lifting chalky white camembert out of its waxed paper. A collection of fine cheeses stood nearby and a container of fresh olives.

Laurel looked across from where she sat colouring and wrinkled her nose. 'Not that funny cheese again. Can't I have fish fingers?'

'You don't eat fast food in a place like this,' said Doreen fiddling around in one of the cupboards, looking for herbs to make a salad dressing and rearranging things as she went. 'There's no logic at all to these cupboards. I don't know how Gina kept track of things.'

Robyn was getting annoyed. William noticed her glance across at Doreen a couple of times with an impatient look.

He sat silent, watching and waiting.

Robyn had removed the green rind from a vintage cheddar and was preparing to grate the cheese, Doreen was measuring oil and vinegar in a glass container, Laurel was busy with her rainbow pack of felt tip pens.

William muttered something about going to the bathroom and made his way out of the room and across the hall towards the study.

Nothing had changed since the last time he was here: the wide desk at the end near the hall and the thin room beyond it with the wall of in-built shelves and three narrow windows like the slits in a fortress to defend against arrows.

He pulled the high backed office chair away from the desk and slid into its buttoned green leather seat where once Esther had sat, curled up, tapping away on the computer keyboard to her friends in Spain. Now the computer stood unused, the screen silent and dark.

Each end of the desk rested on a pedestal with four drawers. He opened the top right hand drawer first, pulling it gently. The drawer slid noiselessly out and he looked in, expecting to see papers, pens and the usual office paraphernalia, but it was empty.

Surprised, he leaned down and looked to the very back of the drawer.

Nothing at all.

He pulled the others open, one by one, and found nothing but empty drawers.

William sat back defeated, his head sunk low in his shoulders. Now what?

Outside it was raining fast. He listened to it falling in fits and starts on leaves and bushes as the wind blew it back and forth in sheets.

Of course, if something had been lost it might still be trapped at the back of one of the drawers. He pulled the top one open again but it wouldn't come all the way out, something metallic and heavy on the runners resisted even when he lifted and pulled at the same time. Undeterred, he closed it again and opened the next one down, then knelt carefully on the floor and put his arm in as far as he could towards the back of the desk, feeling for a tell tale rustle of paper or any sign of something lodged there.

'Looking for something?'

He jumped, twisted round and looked up to see Robyn.

He got up stiffly, feeling utterly ridiculous. He must have been so engrossed in the matter at hand he hadn't even heard her footsteps in the hall.

She'd moved across to one of the shelves and taken down a couple of box files which she laid on the desk. 'All Gina's papers are in here. We thought it made sense to re-file them as we went along. Tommy had everything out. For the solicitor and the banks.'

'Right,' William nodded. 'I don't suppose there was any sign at all of another will?'

No point now in trying to hide what he was about.

'I thought you'd been through all that with the solicitor,' said Robyn crossly.

William sat back down in the chair. 'Was everything always handled by Hamilton's firm?' he wondered aloud, lifting the lid of the nearest box file and staring at the pile of documents. 'Did Gina ever use another solicitor for anything?'

'No, Granddad! I don't think so.'

Robyn's voice was sharp, her old brash self. She turned abruptly and left the room and he sat alone staring at the papers with their bright logos of banks and building societies. He had no desire whatsoever to go through them.

He put the files back on their shelf and went to find Robyn instead. She was in the dining room laying the table.

'Sorry,' he said.

She said nothing but went on laying Gina's heavy silver cutlery beside the place mats on the polished wood and, when she'd finished, rested her arms on the back of a chair and looked at him.

'I do know half the family doesn't actually want me here.'

'It's not that.'

'Esther doesn't even want Kimble's Top. And she's not that interested in money either by the sound of it. Ask Tommy! He's been trying to ring her about finding some kind of solution to all this.'

'It's the principle,' said William. 'The thought that Gina would have left her with nothing.'

'So?'

He was taken aback by her aggressiveness.

'Where was she?' said Robyn. 'Where the hell was she? Gina was dying. All those months and she didn't even bother to come. Even at the end.'

She broke off at that and turned away towards the kitchen.

Not everyone can cope with illness thought William desperately but he knew she wouldn't understand. He felt stupid at how naive he'd been. He'd got nowhere with his silly plan. Everything was just as snarled up as ever.

'Heard you had a run in with Robyn,' said Tommy with evident amusement when he dropped in to Hartley Rise the next evening.

'It soon got back to you,' said William.

'We are in communication.'

'About Doreen and Richard moving up to Kimble's Top?'

'No,' said Tommy. 'That one hit the buffers weeks ago. Robyn won't see sense. Doesn't want the family up there, apparently. And she won't take lodgers either to raise some income. Not what Gina would have wanted.'

He was standing at the dining table where he'd deposited the tray, swirling the tea in the pot as he talked.

'What did Gina want?' asked William.

'Esther to have the money and Robyn to have the house,' Tommy said straightaway. 'That much is obvious.'

'Unless there was another will?'

Tommy shook his head.

'Gina did talk about it,' said William. 'I remembered in hospital. She was talking about their legacy, hers and Arthur's. The house and garden together. She spoke as if she was leaving both to Esther.'

Tommy looked up at that.

William stared at him, waiting for an answer, but Tommy just shrugged and poured the tea. 'I don't know what to say, Dad. She was ill. Not herself.'

Oh! William groaned inwardly. It was useless.

That night Esther rang. 'You're home,' she said 'I was worried about you.'

Her voice was low. He thought she sounded very down.

'Listen, I remembered something,' he said. 'It proves your mum didn't mean to leave you with nothing.'

He told her what Gina had said but she didn't seem convinced.

'Did she actually mention me? By name?'

'It was you she meant.'

'Right.'

She was silent after that.

'You sound a bit down,' said William.

'It's not what I thought, coming back.'

He could tell she was on the verge of tears.

'I thought I'd just pick up where I left off. But nothing's the same any more.'

He wanted to say, 'Come home!' but he was afraid: afraid of losing her to the distance already between them.

'It takes time,' he said instead and even as he spoke the words sounded worthless and empty.

He couldn't prolong the conversation either. She rang off and he sat at the dining table feeling utterly miserable.

It was all so stupid. He pulled a brown envelope from the pile of unopened mail on the sideboard and began writing his thoughts on the back in his spidery hand.

Gina. Esther. Robyn. He wrote them in a triangle then added Tommy with a line to Robyn.

At the cemetery they agreed something between them.

Now they don't agree.

He stared at it for a while but it made no sense. He got up to turn the lights off and climbed the stairs to bed, making his way slowly, one at a time, to go and lie alone in the bedroom, surrounded by the heavy furniture that Alice's parents had given them.

18

REMEMBERING

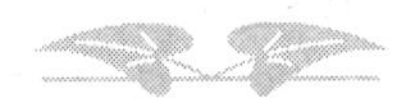

It was only in the morning that he realised he hadn't told Esther what he'd wanted to about Kimble's Top. He thought about ringing her straightaway but, on reflection, decided he'd be better off writing it down and went to fetch some flimsy blue airmail paper from the hall bureau.

He sat down at the dining table to gather his thoughts while the clock ticked on the mantelpiece and the rattle of letter boxes further along the street marked the progress of the postman.

He thought a cup of tea might help and went through to boil the kettle and, since the breakfast things were draining by the sink, he dried them up and put them away then ran a cloth along the work top and stove while he was at it. After that he noticed the bin needed emptying too.

Finally he came back to the table with his tea and a couple of biscuits balanced on the saucer.

He needed to tell her about that day: bank holiday Monday two years before she was born.

He sat there sipping his tea and cast his mind back into the days when they'd all been a lot younger but his thoughts wouldn't go where he directed them. They settled instead on another bank holiday: August 1977.

Not the year of the drought, he recalled, but a run of hot days all the same and street parties for the Queen's Silver Jubilee. The family had been gathered at Kimble's Top. Tommy's daughter, Elisabeth, had been a baby then, asleep in the carry cot, in the study at the front of the house, where it was cool and quiet.

Everyone else was at the back of the house: Tommy and Arthur in the living room with the pink financial pages, talking Jim Callaghan and the Lib-Lab pact. Maurice had been nearby, on his knees on the parquet floor, arranging wooden train tracks and engines.

That should have been his line of thought but somehow he couldn't follow it and found himself remembering Gina instead. She'd been in the kitchen with Alice and Maurice's wife, Lorraine, demonstrating her brand new percolator. There had been laughter and exclamations, the smell of ground coffee in the air.

William had been standing at the French windows looking out into bright sunshine and Gina's new garden with its half planted borders: young shrubs at intervals and baby perennials in wide plots. Only the trees at Kimble's Top had been mature then, last year's fallen needles spread out in a bright orange carpet below the firs while the birds and squirrels moved busily overhead.

William had stepped outside and strolled across the grass heading nowhere in particular. He remembered clouds in the distance, grey and ominous underneath but white and shining at the top.

Then, from beyond the garden he'd heard a throaty roar, like an old banger in need of attention. Rather out of place in the polite housing estate that now covered the slopes of Hunsbury Hill.

The noise was coming nearer.

He took the path round the side of the house towards the drive, curious to see what it was, and by then the noise was deafening and two men on a great black motorbike came careering down the drive of Kimble's Top. The bike came to a halt right outside the front door of the house, its engine throbbing and cracking in the still afternoon.

William's youngest, Richard, clambered off the back struggling to undo the strap of his crash helmet just as the front door was flung open and Gina emerged with Alice close behind holding a screaming Elisabeth, her face as pink as the folds of baby blanket wrapped around her.

'Either switch it off or go!' shouted Gina over the noise of the bike.

The rider gave a cheery thumbs up, pulled the heavy bike round and prepared to make his exit.

'Did you have to wake the baby?' Gina said, exasperated, as Richard, unkempt and the worse for wear, tried to kiss her cheek.

'Ah, she's all right!'

And the next minute he'd dumped his knapsack on the drive, seized the screaming bundle from Alice and snuggled her against his filthy t-shirt.

Gina looked appalled at that but Alice intervened. 'Oh come on in and have some tea,' she said, pulling Richard away towards the living room where he slumped on the cream leather settee still clutching Elisabeth to his chest.

'Yarmouth?' asked Tommy, looking up from the newspapers.

'Buxton,' said Richard jiggling the baby on his knee and provoking hiccups.

'They have spa waters there, don't they?' said Alice.

'Not that I noticed,' grinned Richard and indeed he smelt of good old fashioned beer.

William remembered how Gina had stood and laughed then in spite of herself. He could see her in his mind's eye, the set mouth widening into a reluctant smile and finally a full blown laugh accompanied by a shake of the head. Their eyes had met and she'd raised hers heavenward, full of sisterly exasperation, so that he'd laughed too.

Sister and brothers, himself and Alice, all together. His Gina laughing, Richard young and carefree and Tommy, unruffled, his mind on making money as usual.

William closed his eyes, remembering summer, the bank holiday feeling and a time when everything in the family had been right.

He left the writing paper untouched and went to sit in his armchair, conscious of his own breathing as rough as the breeze on that exposed hill top where he and his children had spent happy days together through so many uncounted, easy years.

When he woke, his head was pressed against the wing of the chair and his pulse resounded in his ear. He sat listening to the beat of his heart. There was a strain, they'd told him, on the right side. He could hear no sound of it but the little sticky patches had revealed it, stuck on his arms, legs and chest and connected to a machine that had printed out wild graphics.

Not uncommon, they'd said, the heart labouring to pump his blood through all the little vessels of his torn bronchial tubes.

At least he had the nebuliser. He looked across at it, carefully packed in the square blue bag on the sideboard and thought it was about the best thing going for him. He was more confident of his breathing than he had been for a long time, just knowing the nebuliser was there and if he needed to he could put the mask over his face and feel the sudden ease in his chest and lungs.

If only everything else could be solved so easily.

He mustn't think about it. The key was to keep busy. He'd tidy up before Bryony came to do his lunch.

He put the writing paper back in the bureau for another time, filled the kettle for some more tea and decided to tackle the pile of Christmas cards that had come home with him from the hospital. He flicked through them, assembling a pile for recycling, glancing only briefly at them so as not to think too much about Christmas come and gone.

Halfway through the pile he came across Larry Clifton's letter again. He'd forgotten all about it. He pulled the letter out of its long white envelope with the little gold address sticker in the corner.

My deepest condolences to you, Gina's father on this tragic loss . . . so many memorable times at Kimble's Top, so many treasured memories . . .

Pompous, but the sentiment was right.

. . . *As fortune would have it I shall be paying a rare, and possibly final, visit to the area for the launch of my autobiography. If you would be agreeable to some sort of memorial gathering at Kimble's Top, perhaps even a fund or a school prize to commemorate Gina and Arthur, I would be more than happy to raise some of the 'old crowd' on Gina's behalf. My telephone number is below . . .*

The man was tedious but William didn't want to refuse. Clifton had his own memories, his own need to grieve. He'd better talk to Tommy about it.

In fact, he had a feeling Tommy had read the letter, unless he'd imagined it, dreamt it. It had all been so confused.

Anyway his son would know what to do. What arrangements to make.

In the kitchen the kettle was whistling, he left the pile of cards and the letter on the sideboard and went to make the tea. They were all still there when Tommy dropped in to see him that evening.

'By the way,' said William. 'Larry Clifton wrote about a memorial for Gina.'

'I know,' said Tommy. 'I rang him. Thought it best to let him know straightaway we weren't up to it.'

William looked at him, surprised. 'Why?' he asked.

'It was hardly the time, Dad. You were at death's door. And the way things are with Esther.'

'You could have asked me,' said William.

Tommy shrugged: 'We're not hosting some big jamboree just to suit Larry Clifton.'

'You had no business ringing him,' William said, needled by his son's dismissiveness. 'I'll talk to him myself. See what he's got in mind.'

But later on, when he came to look for the letter among the things on the sideboard, it was gone.

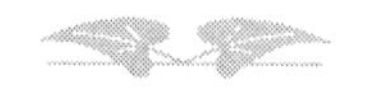

19

TOMMY

William hadn't seen Tommy for weeks.

It was his season for trade shows, William knew; big fashion and footwear events in Italy, then Germany, and again in Italy, coming up soon, he thought, but it was more than that. There had been evenings and weekends working, long distance phone calls at all hours and a transatlantic trip, though Tommy didn't normally visit his North American customers this early in the year.

William had a feeling Tommy was avoiding them all. He had put in a brief appearance, looking weary and out of sorts, one Sunday afternoon in the middle of February. His son working all hours was nothing new in William's experience but there had always been energy and enthusiasm behind the tiredness. Now, looking at Tommy's face across the table, he seemed worn out and anxious.

There was no opportunity to say anything, though, because as soon as they'd finished eating, Tommy got up from the table. 'Sorry,' he said to Doreen. 'I'm expecting a business call from the States.'

'On a Sunday?'

'It's an offline project. Everyone's working in their own time.'

He raised a hand in farewell to the rest of them at the table and left.

'I always thought Sundays were sacrosanct for Tommy,' Doreen commented to William afterwards.

They were. William remembered raised voices when Tommy's children had been hard at it revising for 'A'Levels and he'd insisted on them leaving their books to join the family on a Sunday afternoon.

'Is everything all right with Tommy?' he asked Bryony when she drove him home but she just smiled:

'What, long hours, impossible deadlines? He's in his element!'

It made him smile as he looked back at her; she was as elegant as ever, wrapped up against the cold in a blue cable knit sweater and matching cap. 'You could have had Alex Whitby,' he said. 'Victorian heirlooms and a Bentley on the drive.'

'Oh, but I preferred my market trader.'

She swung her BMW effortlessly round the narrow turning into Hartley Rise.

'Well,' shrugged William. 'He did all right in the end.'

'Even if he hadn't,' said Bryony. 'It was only ever him I wanted.'

She pulled up outside number fourteen and he climbed slowly out of the car, back to his dark front room, the solitary days and the jigsaw.

The puzzle was well advanced now. The mass of unrelated pieces had receded and even the unfinished bits seemed familiar. Within the edge that Tommy had re-done for him was the yellow and green chequerboard, now complete, then a series of black gothic letters: the designation at the end of each compass point. William had worked painstakingly through them, looking again and again at the letters on the box and comparing them to the fragments in front of him: N, NE, E, SE and so on, all the way round the flame coloured circle. He'd finished the little Santa Maria ship too, sailing gaily in its central spyglass.

He sat for long hours at the jigsaw, not bothering with the television or radio, just listening to the occasional banging of pots and pans in next door's kitchen and the sounds of the children coming and going in the street outside.

Of all the family it was Bryony he saw most these days, when she came to do his lunch, and Richard, dropping by after work. Richard, it turned out, had seen quite a bit of Tommy back in January and early February.

'He took to drinking at the Coach and Horses all of a sudden. A mate of mine saw him there. So I dropped by myself and managed to catch up with him once or twice.'

William knew the place: an old Georgian ale house with whitewashed walls, black casements and window boxes full of flowers. Tommy had probably drunk there in his market days but that was a long time ago now.

'Does he go there to meet someone?' William asked, puzzled.

Richard shook his head. 'Thinking time he says. Somewhere to mull things over.'

Tommy had a whole house to mull things over in, William thought. A study with state of the art technology and all the latest computer equipment.

'It's this hostile takeover stuff,' said Richard. 'The big offline project. His US distributor's under threat from some big corporate. Their chairman rang Tommy on the quiet for a bit of advice and now there's this whole working group trying to head it off. Sounds like he's doing most of the running though. They seem to think he's some kind of whizz kid.'

William could believe it. Tommy would be good at it too. Just his kind of thing.

He remembered the town carnival one year when Tommy was about eighteen, watching the parade with his mother on his arm.

They'd all ended up at the Golden Lion and he and Tommy had manoeuvred their way through the crowd to get drinks at the bar, William jingling the coins in his pocket, trying to catch the eye of the landlord and Tommy at his shoulder to help carry the glasses.

It had been a long wait but the jostling was good humoured and then, just as they'd reached the counter, William had noticed a smart young man, away to his left, leaning forward among the faces to catch Tommy's attention.

'Allbright!' he'd called to Tommy. 'Allbright! I'll get yours.'

He'd been as fresh faced as any of the youngsters around him but older in style with his open necked shirt and tweed jacket.

Tommy had glanced across and lifted the pint William had just bought him. 'Got it,' he'd said. 'Thanks all the same.'

William remembered following Tommy back through the crowd, clutching the handful of cold glasses against his chest.

'Alex Whitby,' he'd said to Alice. 'Falling over himself to buy Tommy a drink!'

Needless to say, that had been before Tommy had brought Bryony Richardson home for Sunday tea. William never did know exactly how he'd managed to woo her away from Whitby, son and heir to the town's leading manufacturing family.

He knew about their engagement though. Half the town knew about that because George Richardson hadn't the manners to invite Tommy into the front room properly as the occasion demanded. He'd led him instead into their old conservatory at the back, where the Richardson's char lady was down on her hands and knees behind the tables, cleaning mildew off the wall where the pipes leaked.

She'd heard everything and relayed it word for word to all the regulars afterwards at The Swan & Nest.

'We don't heed gossip in this house,' Alice had said, but in the end it had been impossible to avoid as the story spread third and fourth hand.

'I'm not in favour of it,' George Richardson had said as soon as Tommy had followed him in and closed the door. 'I don't know what you make out of that tatty little shop of yours. A good deal more than you should, probably. But whatever it is, it's not enough and it never will be. You're nothing more than a shop boy. What's worse: you've got quite a name for yourself.'

He'd struck a match then and made hard work of lighting his pipe while Tommy Allbright stood watching and said nothing.

Richards had finally waved the match out and dropped it on the floor, puffing the sweet aroma of Golden Virginia as he spoke.

'Oh nothing specific, I know. Nothing anyone can say is actually untoward. But you're talked about all the same and I don't like it. You've got no qualifications, no profession and no security at all to offer my girl.'

'I'll have her all the same,' Tommy had said then. 'With or without your permission.'

And that's all he had said, and done it too, no matter what the old man thought about it.

Richardson had been right about the talk, though, William reflected and things had got worse after that. Orton had been in hospital with a hernia and Tommy had started changing things wholesale at the old ironmongers backed, everyone said, by James Wilcox who'd funded all Tommy's earlier buying for the markets.

William had tried to talk to Tommy about it one Saturday night when his son was getting ready to go out.

All the other youngsters had been growing their hair out in those days, dressing in bright colours, but Tommy had stood there in the front room with his short hair neatly combed, brushing his dark jacket to put on over a plain tank top and straight trousers.

'You know,' said William; 'I gather Orton's hearing all kinds of rumours down at the hospital and it's not doing him any good. His shop's getting a reputation for undercutting the traditional stores. And they say it's all new fancy stuff on the shelves now, not proper hardware.'

'That's because there's money in electricals, Dad. Mangles and stove blacking are a thing of the past.'

'But that's what people go to Orton's for. If they want a television they'll go to a specialist place.'

'Not if their prices are too high, they won't. Things are changing, Dad. No-one has a right to own the market. Not if they can't give people what they want.'

Soon after that Tommy and James Wilcox had visited Orton on the hospital ward and presented him with a set of papers, bought his shop off him outright.

That had been Tommy all over: knowing exactly what he wanted and taking it without an apology to anyone.

The more he thought about it, the more William missed him: his volatile, mercurial son. He wanted to talk to him, to ask him why on earth he'd taken Clifton's letter and what was going on with him, but something held him back.

Alice had gone quiet on him too when he tried to talk to her about it.

'*Nothing to say to me, eh?*'

Now March was nearly here and he still hadn't broached it.

Sitting alone one morning he picked up the phone in a moment of sudden resolve and dialled Tommy's mobile, rehearsing the conversation in his mind as he waited for the connection.

You took my letter from Larry Clifton!

Of course I didn't. I've no idea what you're talking about.

He put the phone down again. He didn't want to hear his son lie and if it weren't lies it'd be avoidance.

Dad, you're upset. You've probably misplaced it.

There again, he might be misjudging Tommy. He picked the phone up again and dialled.

I need Clifton's number.

Dad, I only rang him that once. Why would I keep the number?

It was no good. He hung up and went back to his jigsaw.

A few minutes later the phone rang.

'Are you all right?' Tommy's voice sounded far away.

'Yes, fine.'

'You rang me.'

'I didn't,' said William.

'Just now. I've got two missed calls.'

'I changed my mind.'

'So, you're okay?'

'Where are you?' said William. 'I never see you.'

'I'm in the US, Dad. It's four thirty a.m.'

'Oh.'

Back at the table William sat moving the last few pieces around the gaps of the jigsaw. Above the central spyglass was a full sun with a smiling face, followed round the circle by clouds, stars, a thunder storm and finally the sun again, emerging from rain clouds. This was the final section and it came together all of a sudden, the bits fitting easily one after another. He patted the rough edges down and sat back for some time admiring his finished work.

The house was quiet all around him and shafts of light fell into the room where the sun shone thinly through patches of grey cloud outside.

Everything that ever mattered had happened to him here. Even at work he'd been close by. Some people wouldn't have liked Hartley Rise, it being so close to the railway, but it had done for them and his children weren't too proud to come back even though they'd risen so high. He'd never heard any of them complain about their childhood home even among themselves.

Esther had liked it too. What was it she'd said?

'I always wanted to live on the way to somewhere.'

Funny when she'd grown up somewhere so much nicer.

It struck him then, so forcefully he sat up straight, staring. All along it had been right there in front of him. He was the one person who could put things right. The one person who actually had something Esther wanted, something she desired despite all that withdrawn reticence.

The house wasn't worth much, not compared to Kimble's Top but there was no mortgage to pay and it was a real home, full of family memories, somewhere she belonged. No-one could take that away from her.

He went into the hall and fished his will out of the bureau. He'd made it years ago, when Alice had died and his old will had become invalid. Made it without a second thought; everything to be divided equally between his children, knowing it wouldn't amount to much that way but then they hadn't needed much.

He thought about his grandchildren. Robyn was well set up now. Tommy's children wanted for nothing. He could leave Paul and Lee whatever was in the savings account and Esther could have the house.

The solicitor's card was in the envelope with the will. He rang for an appointment.

He knew what he wanted and the changes were straightforward so they offered to draft it for him and then all he'd have to do would be to go in and sign it. He made an appointment for the following week.

'I'll take a taxi,' he said grandly.

He thought about ringing Esther to tell her straightaway but decided it would sound morbid talking about his death and he wasn't sure how she'd take it. Better to wait until she rang and then see if it came up. Maybe then he'd tell her about Kimble's Top as well.

Signing the will was all very simple. The solicitor and a legal assistant witnessed his signature and then gave him a copy to take away in a glossy folder.

Afterwards they telephoned for a taxi to take him home and he sat in the reception area until it arrived.

That was how he came to see it; glancing down at all the leaflets on the coffee table advertising local events, he noticed the name Larry Clifton in bold print on a yellow flier. There was a lunchtime do at the library to celebrate Clifton's autobiography. The local hero was too frail for readings or book signings but there would be an opportunity for photos and his nephew, Ian, would share reminiscences and answer questions. It was he who had organised the event, in association with the Royal British Legion and there was a number to phone for tickets.

William slipped the leaflet into his pocket and, when he got home, phoned the number.

'I'm trying to contact Ian Clifton.'

'Oh, he's not here. This number's for buying tickets.

'My name's William Allbright.'

He asked them to take his number and get Ian Clifton to ring him.

'It's about Kimble's Top. And Gina Radford. Larry Clifton wrote to me.'

He went through it all a couple of times and got the lady to repeat it back to him so he knew she had it straight. She sounded dubious but Clifton's nephew would make something of it.

20

Larry Clifton

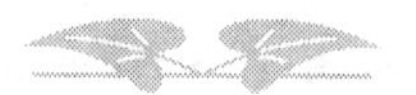

'Mr Allbright? Ian Clifton. You've been unwell. Hospital wasn't it? Larry mentioned it. Your son rang him. How are you?'

William followed the refined tones through the jumble of words. 'I'm fine,' he said. 'I wanted to talk to your uncle. He wrote to me about doing something for Gina at Kimble's Top. A memorial.'

'That's right. But he quite understands. Not entirely appropriate under the circumstances.'

'Well, I think there might have been a misunderstanding about that.'

'Oh no! Not at all. We absolutely understand. And Larry's more than happy with what we've arranged. To tell you the truth, I am too. My uncle's rather given to his little soirées but he's not always a hundred per cent up to it. I much prefer a quiet affair.'

'Oh?'

'Ah! Your son hasn't had a chance to fill you in. Abroad a lot on business, I gather. Well, I'm afraid Larry can be rather insistent and he did particularly want to pay his respects at Kimble's Top. Not that the ashes are there of course, we know that, but it's the place as much as anything, isn't it? Shared memories and all that. I think just going up to Kimble's Top will mean a lot to him. Let him say goodbye in his own way. Sort of spirit of the place, if you know what I mean.'

William didn't. He was too busy imagining Tommy on the receiving end of Larry Clifton being 'rather insistent'.

'Anyway, it'll just be the two of us coming over,' the nephew was saying. 'Nothing too exciteable.'

'When?'

'Afternoon of March 10$^{th.}$ After three. Once we've got all this book launch stuff out of the way.'

March 10th. Today was Thursday the second. So: a week on Friday.

'Right. Well, that's fine then,' said William.

The next Sunday, tea was at Tommy's house and he was just back from Milan, looking tired.

William looked at him, sitting in his favourite armchair, a scroll-backed colonial chair with cream upholstery and dark wooden arms. He had a folded newspaper on his knee and a pen in hand, Bryony having got as far as she could with the Sunday crossword and passed it to him to finish.

Robyn had settled herself nearby, in one corner of the gold striped sofa, her head back against the deep cushions. William thought she looked tense, for all the studied relaxation of her pose, the glossy make-up and her fetching green top with the big jewellery to match. She was sitting back watching Richard and Doreen and the others, kneeling round a big marble coffee table, playing a riotous game of Uno with Laurel.

Only once, when a particularly loud burst of laughter rang out among the general banter and cries of protest, did William notice Tommy glance up from the paper and, as he took in the scene, his eyes met Robyn's briefly so that it seemed a look was exchanged, but nothing William could read.

Larry Clifton was coming to Kimble's Top on Friday and neither of them was going to mention it. For a moment, watching the rapid sequence of cards slapping down on the table top, William wondered if the others already knew about it. But it was impossible. Doreen for one would have been talking about it.

They couldn't know and, sitting there among the laughter, an idea formed in William's mind that he at least was going to go up there and find out just what was going on.

When the day came he booked a taxi for half past three and got himself ready in a thick winter jumper, his woollen overcoat and best leather gloves.

The taxi was twenty minutes late.

'Sorry, mate,' said the driver. 'Hospital pick-up at two o'clock. They always keep you waiting around.'

On the ring road the Friday traffic had already built up and it was after four thirty when he reached Kimble's Top.

The house looked strange as they drew near and he realised the blinds were closed at all the front windows though the spring sunshine couldn't have been that penetrating. He wondered if it was some old fashioned mark of respect for Larry but it seemed odd all the same.

A gold Jaguar was parked on the drive beside Tommy's black Audi and his son was there with the two visitors, obviously in the act of saying goodbye.

Clifton was instantly recognisable, tall and elderly in a cream suit with a matching waistcoat and a handkerchief in his top pocket. He was very grey now, his hair receding and thin, his cheeks gaunt.

The younger man in the tweed jacket and cravat was obviously the nephew.

Tommy in his immaculately pressed jeans and a dark rugby shirt had presumably taken the day off work. He'd turned to watch the taxi as it approached and came to a halt beside the other cars, but as William leaned forward to pay the driver it was Clifton's nephew who came over and opened the door to help him out.

Tommy's expression was blank but William could tell he was on edge as he stepped forward to make the introductions.

'My father, William Allbright. Larry Clifton. Ian.' He looked at William: 'We're all finished here. They've got an evening engagement over in Polebrook.'

'My uncle's old squadron, I'm afraid,' said the nephew. 'We really mustn't get caught in the rush hour.'

'Nonsense,' Larry intervened. 'There's always time for old friends.'

He seized William's arm and waved dismissively at the others. 'When you get to our age you'll find there's always time to do what we're here to do. Isn't that right, William?' He began leading the way towards the garden at the side of the house. 'All right if we walk? Supposed to be good for you, so the Easterns say: massages the energy points on the feet.'

He was seven or eight years older than William but still walked with an enviable stride, effortless and long-legged. His manner was easy too despite the air of command.

William struggled on beside him as they walked along past the kitchen window, stopping frequently so he could get his breath.

'I always imagined Gina grieving for me,' said Larry as they stood at the corner of the terrace. 'Something incongruous about the older generation outliving the younger. Not quite right, is it?'

William breathed in hard, staring across at the shrubbery where the virburnum was white with flowers and the forsythia made bright yellow patches among the evergreen shrubs.

After a while Clifton took the lead again and they went on past the living room to the far side of the house and the sheltered space where the dining room wall made a triangle as it met the adjacent wall of the bedrooms.

Clifton stopped and gestured at the white lines of the building all around them.

'This is where you have to come to understand Arthur. It's actually the best facet of the house whatever the critics say. They never got past the open plan interiors and living room quadrangle overlooking Northampton. But this is what Arthur's genius is really all about. Overwhelming regularity and complete freedom combined.'

The dining room was lit by a succession of tall windows while the adjacent bedrooms had a complex arrangement of small rectangular windows over larger square ones with white frames dividing the panes in a mesmerising geometric pattern. William stood wondering about the blinds, closed all along here too, while Clifton talked on at his side.

'Big windows, little windows. Tall and thin, square and flat, all in one place. Total freedom to choose, unconstrained by any norms. But you can see how it's all carefully spaced. Designed and planned, specifically, with the wellbeing of the inhabitants in mind. Not built to impress like the old grand houses. Rather more innovative: a prime architectural space designed purely to meet the needs of the people who live in it.

Of course to really appreciate it you have to remember what went before. Now we take all this for granted. The clean lines. Open space. Back then it was a new concept. A total departure from all those awful streets of red brick houses. Cramped. Dirty. Faceless streets for the faceless masses. Here things were visionary. A bright new world away from those dingy little towns full of dingy little people.'

Behind them the trees were lifting and swaying in the breeze. William could tell from the shadows moving on the grass at his feet.

'What a loss!' said Clifton. 'Arthur Radford. Still young. Talented and forward thinking. And now Gina.'

William no longer knew why he'd come. He thought wistfully of the crowd of mourners at Gina's graveside. The Girls Brigade who'd turned out in the freezing cold, the do-gooders of Gina's committees, who helped out at primary schools and ran the volunteers' shop at the hospital. People like Gina who rubbed shoulders with the real world and had stood alongside him with a grief he understood.

Over by the croquet lawn there was a wooden bench. He turned away from the house and began walking towards it, the standing too much for him.

Clifton followed and stood upright at his side, while William propped himself, wheezing, against the high wooden back, the bench seat too low for him to sit on.

'What you need is your second wind,' said Clifton. 'And to accept your limitations. That's the secret of a good old age. Lean on other people whenever you can. Let them do all the running around for a change. After all, we've earned it. Where would they be without the sacrifices we made?'

On this side of the garden the ground was uneven. Beyond the level green of the croquet lawn the heavy trees stood among great banks of red earth and in the distance the roof tops of the town could be glimpsed, long and far, on the horizon.

'Danes Camp,' pronounced Clifton in a tone of satisfaction as he looked around. 'And the wildness is still here. Hilltop and woodland. The wind always blowing. And history. The cataclysm. The great Celt over run by Cymbeline himself. Cunobelinus Rex. King of Britain. He of the troublesome sons. Defiant to the end. There's a spirit to this place. That's what inspired Arthur.'

It was all so depressingly predictable, thought William: Clifton spouting common knowledge as if it were something new. The iron age homestead. Grain pits so big the tribute must have come from far afield. The great collection of unused whernstones no-one could explain, brought from long distances. He'd seen them in Northampton Museum: a brown humped stone with traces of white: that was millstone grit from Derbyshire, and a smaller flatter one, like a round cheese: greensand from Folkestone. As for Cymbeline, though, the jury was out. No-one really knew for sure why Hunsbury Hill had been so suddenly abandoned.

He felt suddenly sorry for Clifton with his grandiose statements and unfounded stories.

Over in the trees the sunshine dappled on the leaves in a thousand different facets and couldn't be captured. The old trees were shaggy and windswept, the leaves hanging in tatters at all angles, in springtime abundance, some curled, others flattened out and the sun met them all, caught each one differently. The flat outer leaves were bright, those further in a darker green and nearer the trunk they disappeared into a black mass. He stared across silently at the cracked bark and shifting branches that would outlive them both.

Tommy appeared then round the corner of the house, raised his left arm from a distance indicating his watch.

Clifton raised his hand in acknowledgement and took a last look round. 'I should have liked to have seen Esther,' he said. 'I missed her when I was last here. Do you remember it? 2003. That unbearably hot summer.'

William did remember but hadn't known Clifton had been here. Now was the moment he ought to seize to talk about Gina, to ask about inheritance, share his worries, but he couldn't. He was numb with cold, his heart hammering alarmingly within the tight band of his chest and there was just no talking to this man. No means of broaching anything so sensitive.

Clifton had finished anyway. He was reaching out to shake William's hand. 'I'm glad we talked. Don't worry about seeing me off.'

He stepped away, leaving William at the bench, then turned back as if on a whim, waving a hand to the walls behind them. 'I think it's criminal, by the way: leaving a house like this shut up!'

William stared after him.

The wind was too cold for lingering. He got to his feet and set off slowly, back round the house towards the drive.

On the terrace was a window where the blinds didn't close properly. They stood a little way out from the edge of the frame. He made his way there, stepped close to peer into the living room and saw white dustsheets everywhere. He was still there looking when Tommy returned from seeing the Cliftons off.

William watched his son approach, his face tense and wary, and asked: 'What's going on?'

'We closed the blinds as a mark of respect.'

William pointed to the gap in the blinds. 'And the dust sheets?'

Tommy sighed and ran a hand through his hair. 'We told him the house was shut up. Thought it might upset him to know Gina hadn't left it to Esther.'

'You lied to him!'

'Not in so many words,' said Tommy. 'He didn't ask outright. Anyway, he's an old man. He's frail.'

'I'm an old man,' said William. 'And I'm not too feeble for the truth.'

He stared perplexed into his son's dark eyes and Tommy returned his gaze stubbornly. It was impossible to read anything in his face but William knew there was much more than this apparent deception.

'Where's Robyn?' he asked at last.

'She went out for the day,' said Tommy. 'She felt out of her depth.'

'I'll bet she did,' muttered William.

They drove home without speaking.

When Tommy pulled up outside fourteen Hartley Rise, William sat for a moment before attempting to get out of the car. 'I've never questioned you,' he said to Tommy. 'All these years, I've never asked about your business affairs. Never doubted you.'

He turned to look at his son but Tommy just sat silent, staring out of the windscreen.

'I know you,' said William. 'I know when you're not right within yourself. Whatever you did all those years ago when you bought Orton's. Then with Lister's. All the things people said, I never really worried because I knew you were right within yourself. But this. You haven't been right since Gina died.'

Tommy turned to face him then. 'She was my sister, Dad. What do you expect?'

'It's not that. I thought it was. But it's not. It's you and Robyn. It's this deceit over Clifton. Taking his letter. Lying to him.'

'We didn't lie!'

William opened the car door. 'There's something going on. I'd be a fool not to know it.'

He climbed out and made his way to the house without looking back and for once Tommy made no move to come and help him.

21

Riding the Ellipse

William went straight through to the living room, still in his heavy winter coat, and plugged in the nebuliser. With the soft mask over his nose and mouth, inhaling, he felt better by the minute as his chest opened up and his breathing eased.

Afterwards he sat at the dining table gathering his strength. He was cold through and through, his skin prickling with chilly shivers even under his vest and woolly layers.

He went into the kitchen and opened a tin of soup, stirring it in a pan on the stove until the steam rose, the smell of oxtail filled the room and the windows fogged up. Then he carried the saucepan back to the front room, poured the soup into a bowl there and sat at the table, tearing up pieces of bread and dropping them in, nudging them back and forth with his spoon.

When he'd eaten he finally took his coat off and sat thinking about that afternoon.

'Our boy's not right.'

He fetched Alice's picture from the mantelpiece and stared into her dark eyes, willing a response. It was her birthday portrait, twenty-one today! She stood upright for the camera, her shoulders narrow in the neatly buttoned blouse, head held high.

'Happy birthday, darling.'

She seemed a lifetime away. He closed his eyes and summoned his most treasured remembrances. The sound of her washing her hair on a Saturday morning while he lay in bed, listening along the length of the corridor to the water pouring from the jug and into the bath. The two of them laughing with friends and Alice, a hand over her mouth, eyes wide, always turning to him first to share the joke. Purposeful and serious with her new-born babies, leaning over to tie ribbons on baby bonnets and button the knitted clothes.

'Talk to me!'

He tried to picture her with Tommy as a little boy but couldn't. She'd been laid up for weeks after he was born. It was always Gina he saw when he thought of Tommy's childhood.

Tommy had grown close to his mother later, though, always treating her like a lady: flowers and chocolates for her birthday, never the household things the others bought, the tea cosies and aprons. Tommy had had his own ways, more and more so over time.

'Time. Yes, give him time.'

William started. Was it her voice? Or just his own, wanting it to be her?

He leaned an elbow on the table and rested his forehead on his hand.

It was true, time had healed Tommy once before.

The next morning he was chesty again and by evening had a cough that really hurt.

'You shouldn't have come out to Kimble's Top in the cold,' Tommy said in a brief moment alone together at Sunday tea the following afternoon.

'Yes, I am aware of that,' William began, but there was no time to talk about what had happened on Friday with the family all around.

'Drop by and see me, will you?' he said instead. 'This week.'

Tommy nodded but Monday and Tuesday passed and he still hadn't come. Then, on Wednesday, a red and white card landed on William's doormat with the morning post. There was a parcel too big for his letterbox, to be collected from the sorting office on Midland Road.

He slipped the card into a drawer so Bryony wouldn't see it when she came to do his lunch and rang Tommy at work that afternoon.

'Why didn't you give it to Bryony?' said his son. 'The sorting office closes at six. It's pushing it to get there after work.'

'It doesn't matter. Just come and get the card and pick the parcel up another day.'

'What is it anyway?'

'No idea.'

He didn't really care.

As it was, Tommy came round at ten to six, collected the card and went straight down Midland Road to get the parcel. It was a thick package in a jiffy bag with a handwritten address and Northamptonshire postmark.

'Did you order something?' asked Tommy.

'No.'

'Well, it feels like a book. You must have bought it from somewhere.'

'Just leave it on the side,' said William. 'And make us some tea.'

He sat in the armchair feeling utterly weary until Tommy came back with the tea things and a plate of shortbread he'd picked up on his way back from the depot. 'You looked as though you could do with the sugar.'

William watched him pour the tea. 'It's nearly a year since we went to the doctor's that day and heard about Gina,' he said.

Tommy nodded, adding milk to the tea then spooning sugar into William's cup.

The wind rattled in the chimney and a shower of dirt fell into the disused grate.

'I remember Gina teaching you to lay that fire,' said William. 'Twisting the newspaper tight, putting the kindling twigs underneath. You used to like trailing your fingers through the cold ash. You must have only been about five.'

'Six,' said Tommy. 'She was fifteen. The year after she started at the bakery.'

He brought the tea cup over and a china plate with petticoat tails arranged in a circle.

'You two always were the early birds,' said William. 'First up, every day. Busy about your own things.'

He talked on about her, couldn't help it. He was supposed to be resolving things with Tommy but now it came to it all he could think about was Gina.

'Always tut-tutting about me going to the corner shop!'

'It's overpriced and the food's not as fresh,' she'd say.

'I like choosing my own things.'

'Well let me take you down to the supermarket then.'

But it was too big. Too far to walk. Too many people. And he could never find anything.

'You two ganged up on us,' he said aloud to Tommy. 'You and Gina. Always on at us to get central heating.'

'Well it wasn't doing mother any good in the cold.'

'You turned up here together,' said William. 'With your brochures and quotations. You already had it all worked out.'

'Waste of money,' Alice had said. 'It'll breed germs.'

They'd had their way over it, though, Tommy and Gina. William still kept the top vents of the bay window permanently open in protest at the stuffiness.

'You two never agreed on anything but that bloody heating!'

'We did sometimes,' said Tommy. 'After she was married.' He'd sat down in the chair opposite, one leg crossed casually over the other with the tea cup balanced on his knee. 'I should have liked to have known Arthur better, though,' he remarked.

'Yes.' William knew what he meant. 'He was a private man, was Arthur. Even when he'd had a few.' He tapped his forehead. 'Kept it all up here.'

'Unlike Gina,' smiled Tommy.

And so they talked on until the pot was empty and the shortbread half gone. Tommy looked at his watch then and began collecting the tea things back on the tray.

William listened to him out in the kitchen, rinsing the cups under a running tap. They hadn't talked at all about Friday and Kimble's Top but he was too tired now and, anyway, what could he say?

'Don't forget your mystery parcel!'

Tommy was standing in the doorway smiling, brandishing a pair of scissors he'd brought through from the kitchen. He lay them down on the jiffy bag and came over to the armchair. William caught the faint musk of expensive aftershave as his son leaned down to kiss him.

'See you then, Dad.'

'Bye.'

The parcel did indeed feel like a book. William snipped carefully through the flap of the padded envelope and drew out a thick hardback tome.

The name, Larry Clifton, met his eyes first and, above it, the yellow block letters of the title: Riding The Ellipse.

Below it was the evocative picture of a MKII Spitfire in flight across Dover cliffs. The plane was in sharp focus: its propeller a silver blur indicative of speed and the stark white letters of the squadron and aircraft codes prominent on the fuselage, with the RAF's coloured roundel between them. The background was in softer focus but easily recognisable: the chalk cliffs with their flat green top and the distant bumps of the waves far below with a hint of surf along the beach.

Opening the cover, William saw Clifton's signature, dipping and looping across the width of the page. There was no personal message with it and no card or note in the envelope. It was typical of Clifton. A flamboyant gesture and the unquestioning assumption that William would want to sit and read this man's account of his life.

He put the book down on the table at his side, leaned his head back and closed his eyes. It was getting late and his cough was always worse at night. He sat with his teeth clamped shut, trying to suppress it and listening to the whistle of his breathing through his nose.

Sleep came, a dreamless doze, and when he woke it was after midnight.

He made a cup of Horlicks, returned to the armchair and, feeling quite awake now, picked up Clifton's book again for want of anything better to do.

He was mildly curious about Clifton's early years, roughly contemporary with his own and lived out in the same rural Northamptonshire of his youth.

He lifted the cover and scanned the opening pages. There was a lengthy foreward on the various individuals *"both influential and prominent, who, for reasons of privacy I shall not name, notwithstanding the modern obsession with over-exposure . . . these have prevailed on me for some years to record and publish my own account of what has been a most singular and remarkable period of our island history."*

William flicked ahead to the first chapter but found almost nothing of Clifton's childhood. There was a whole section dedicated instead to the historic derivation of the family name: not the Nottinghamshire Gervases and Roberts of the manors of Clifton and Wilford, descendants rather of Henri de Clyf, seigneur de Glénan. His coat of arms, a black stag leaping across a silver shield, was reproduced in colour print and blazoned in the accompanying narrative.

"Argent, a stag salient sable between three ermine spots sable . . . the motto, 'Ex Umbris', 'out of the shadows', entirely fitting for this refined contingent from Brittany who crossed the channel only in the wake of the Conqueror and his thrusting Norman barons . . . the family name eventually

anglicised with the acquisition of their own Saxon 'tun' . . . a sizeable estate in the Rockingham Forest."

William looked with interest though at the photographs. There were several of the sixteenth century manor house: pale limestone with an immense gatehouse, enclosed courtyards and oriel windows.

"I must, however, decline to name either house or village. Suffice it to say they lie within striking distance of Fotheringhay, whose ill-fated royal connections included the Plantagenet Dukes of York and the persecuted Queen of Scots. A place once bound up with national destinies and political intrigue of the highest order but blessed, now, rather by seclusion . . . an unspoilt high street of sixteenth century limestone cottages mercifully undiscovered by the relentless modern day tripper and ubiquitous motorist . . ."

The middle of the book covered Clifton's wartime exploits and the spitfire: the *"Lady of Castle Bromwich"*, the elliptical wings and life-saving turns in combat, the Merlin engine and heart-stopping precipitous dives. Clifton had fought in the Battle of Britain, the rapid early engagements of August 1940, the dogfights and all-out raids of September, and in low level offensives against military targets in France.

"Thank God Winnie put a stop to all that!"

Then Malta, the glory days, real fighting again at last.

After the war he developed a passion for motor cars, driving an Aston Martin DB4, *"aluminium panels and a tubeframe . . . Italian designs, but anyone who'd seen Signor Castoldi's work in the air over Malta knew better than to turn their nose up at that."* There was a Bristol 403 for the wife, *"aluminium again, limited production and more than a whiff of the aeronautical."*

William flipped through the remaining pages, letting them fall in twos and threes, glancing at them as they dropped. Clifton talked of his move to Madeira, of the mild climate and horticulture. There were colour prints of Funchal, white houses and red tiled roofs, views of the bay and surrounding crags, the botanical garden and annual flower festival.

He reached the back of the book and, noticing the index, looked through it for *"Arthur Radford"*.

He'd been mentioned in one of the later chapters in Clifton's diatribe against the decline of standards in modern Britain, *"a systematic destruction of every norm of common decency, of public morality, industrial endeavour and national aspiration . . . left to a handful of undaunted individuals to uphold our time-honoured values and traditions . . . Arthur Radford, architect of Kimble's Top and self-confessed disciple of Wells Coates, the unashamed product of an age when learning and apprenticeship were still considered an essential, and sometimes lengthy, preliminary to creativity and innovation."*

Something of a eulogy followed then Clifton's views on the design of the house and his personal memories of the place. Going back to the index he found no references to Gina but towards the end of the book there was a second mention of Kimble's Top.

"A rare visit home in the July of 2003 . . . the hottest summer in five hundred years . . . unbearable." Clifton had been going to the Cambridge Folk Festival to see his great niece perform alongside the likes of Steve Earle and Roddy Frame but the weekend before had come *"my first unexpected and utterly depressing encounter with the world wide web . . ."*.

At Kimble's Top again, with an old friend, long widowed. There had been a discussion about the state of the markets, falling investments. A snap decision made in the family living room on a blistering Saturday afternoon and, without further ado, her will had been changed.

"Nothing more to do than switch on the home computer, print a template straight off the internet, fill it in and sign in the presence of two witnesses . . . the family gardener and myself, a chance visitor . . . witness both to the signature on the will and to the termination of centuries-old patterns of human interaction . . . what was once the sacred preserve of the family solicitor, his credentials established in bricks and mortar, a brass door plate, a sense of standing steadily acquired in the local community, had given way to the arbitrary and unsubstantiated authority of the internet . . . and so, a last will and testament, written, signed, dated in a matter of minutes and consigned to the desk drawer with no more ceremony or solemnity than if it had been the weekly shopping list."

William set the book down on his lap, heart pounding.

2003. The year RSG had gone into receivership and Gina had realised the shares were finally worth nothing. Four years after the will Esther had shown him, leaving the house to Robyn and the investments to Esther.

A last will and testament, consigned to the desk drawer.

He thought again of Gina, satisfied, looking round the garden, *'It's not a bad legacy . . . '*, and of her final weeks when she'd been silenced by pain, fading before them while the tumours just grew and grew, yet all the time untroubled, because she knew everything had been settled.

Robyn had been there with him, every day, in the dark of the bedroom. Patient. Calm. Only that once, right near the end, that night when Gina had turned suddenly bad, and now he remembered her words with lightning clarity.

She'd told him about it the next morning.

'I couldn't find the doctor's file. It's always in the desk . . . me and Tommy, we ended up turning out half the drawers.'

Together they must have found the later will and destroyed it, leaving only the earlier one that the solicitor had written.

William knew why too. Looking back at the way things had been with Robyn and Esther, it all became clear.

It was nearly one in the morning. His heart was pounding and his hands trembling but he had to do something straightaway. He struggled out of the chair, went to the phone and dialled Tommy's mobile number.

The voice mail cut in straightaway. The phone was switched off.

William talked as calmly as he could to the message service, hampered only by the breathing that made his words seem like gasps.

'I know what you've done, Tommy. I know about the will Clifton witnessed. You and Robyn found it going through the desk. You just couldn't let Esther have the house, could you? Couldn't risk it.'

The beep of the voice mail cut him off but he'd said enough. He set the phone down clumsily and stumbled back to the armchair, feeling light-headed and sick.

His joints cracked as he dropped shaking into the seat. He pushed his stick towards the wall but it slipped and fell to the carpet instead. He sat back in the chair, mouth open, searching desperately for each new breath.

Now Alice, from her picture, seemed to reach out to him. Or was it that his head was swimming?

'It's not surprising,' he gasped. 'That house . . .'

She nodded agreement: 'It's more to Tommy than bricks and mortar.'

'You always understood things.'

He was whispering but the words barely crossed his lips. He was aware of them moving but it felt strange and distant. Not that it mattered anymore because Alice was near him now, nearer than she'd seemed in years so that he felt her presence, a togetherness that was more than his imagination.

'Oh!' he mouthed and for an instant his voice seemed full of breath and volume.

Yet at the same time he knew he hadn't actually spoken it in quite that way and, at the back of his mind, he was conscious of a pain ripping through his chest with a sharpness that snatched his breath and left it suspended on his lips, dry as a desert wind.

Alice's face was turned towards him and she was laughing, her features lit with a brightness, a glowing delight that radiated and warmed him so that he laughed too, a glorious rushing laugh that sounded like a waterfall in his ears, a summer torrent that drenched them both, falling and falling, while he reached out to take her hand and the great cascade swept every last struggling breath away.

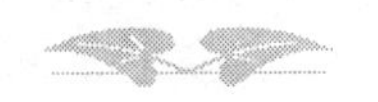

22

FOURTEEN HARTLEY RISE

In the front room of fourteen Hartley Rise only the inanimate moves; the clock ticks on the mantelpiece, the curtains shift in the draught from the window and the shadows flit across the walls but the body of the old man in the armchair is lifeless and still.

His head is tilted back and his lined brow turned in against the chair. His cheeks are colourless and his mouth is partly open, the folds of his throat visible within the open-necked shirt.

One hand lies curled on a book and his sleeve is hitched up away from the wrist, showing a smooth length of arm. The other hand hangs over the side of the chair.

His long legs are stretched out, one knee slightly twisted in towards the other and narrow ankles in grey socks show beneath the dark hem of the trousers.

The door to the room is closed and everything within is waiting. Now the familiar contents will assume a new significance: the spidery numbers listed on a square of cardboard by the phone; the jigsaw recently tidied away in its box on the dining table; the mug of Horlicks, half drunk, on the side table; the hawthorn stick fallen at his feet.

Memories are all around, poised to overwhelm those who will come here and push the door open, wanting just to love him again.

23

Halfway Home

The dollar was still losing value and the euro had dipped slightly to one point four but stayed buoyant. Bad news for his US retailers, fifty fifty when it came to selling brogues to the Germans and buying calf skin from Italy.

Meanwhile, London retail had seen a 71% uplift in sales over the previous three months, last summer's terrorist attacks having receded in the public memory, but the UK footwear market as a whole wasn't doing well: a double whammy of cost inflation and price deflation.

Tommy sat back and peeled a banana. It was half past five in the morning and he was sitting in his study, dressed for work, with a glass of orange juice beside him, scanning a series of online reports on the markets and economy.

On the desk was a pile of papers for two days of uninterrupted business meetings, beginning at 08:30 today. Annual meetings that had always been carefully timed to follow one another at a week's interval, until Tommy had taken last Friday off to meet Clifton up at Kimble's Top.

His secretary, Jayne Gardiner, had looked aghast when he'd told her he wouldn't be coming in that day. 'And the Quarter Three Sales Meeting?'

Q3SM at Lister's happened without fail on the second Friday of March: a three line whip for the Operations Manager, Sales Executives, Head of Production and Brand Manger with no absence tolerated.

'Put it back a week,' Tommy had said. 'We'll do quarter three results to date and quarter four forecasts next Thursday then pick up Friday as planned with budgeting and planning for next year.'

'All together? They won't like that.'

'They know where I am if they want to complain.'

True: it wasn't ideal. If the Q3 and 4 figures weren't spot on today there wouldn't be enough time to adjust the assumptions for tomorrow's planning meeting. It put the heat on, too, for getting the Business Plan out to the Board next week.

The figures should be spot on, though. They'd no business presenting half cocked figures this late in the quarter. They ought to know that by now.

Tommy lifted the top wadge of papers from the pile and pulled out Anacleto's spreadsheets.

Anacleto Sapatos, Portuguese manufacturers of low cost, high fashion footwear for which Lister's was the sole UK distributor. Anacleto was Lister's cash cow thanks to the deal Tommy had cut himself when he first came on board as Managing Director in Spring 1980.

Lister's had been going downhill fast back then. A traditional shoe works 'since 1881', employer of four hundred skilled locals and the company hadn't paid a dividend for ten years. Profits had plummeted, costs were through the roof and the trends on every product line were abysmal. It was a story that had been repeated across the whole footwear industry: rising costs, falling consumption and an unstoppable tide of cheap imports, first from the EEC and then the far east.

In the north, K Shoes had closed its Workington factory with over four hundred redundancies. In Norwich, the heartland of women's shoe production, the old names had closed in quick succession: Pell, Trimfoot and Sexton, then Norvic. Start-Rite had only held on by ditching its adult range and specialising in children's shoes, with significant redundancies.

There had been nothing to distinguish Lister's from any of these. The company had been so debt ridden, Tommy had had to visit the suppliers in person, paying the outstanding bills with cash from a briefcase to convince them Lister's was still a going concern.

There had only been one way to guarantee the company's survival long enough to rationalise the traditional shoemaking operation. He'd gone cap in hand to the Portuguese, planted both feet firmly on the bandwagon of cheap foreign imports and secured exclusive distribution rights for Anacleto, buying at a reduced price based on agreed volume of sales with a premium thrown in for advertising. Then he'd traded on Lister's name and credibility to get the Portuguese product into every possible high street stockist in the south of England.

The market hadn't disappointed him. Anacleto was just the kind of business Tommy loved: cheap volume sales and the gamble of the populist trends.

Now a key part of the forthcoming Board meeting would be to agree the distribution deal with Anacleto for the next eighteen months. He wanted to offer significantly higher volume on a couple of lines for a lower unit price overall but to do that he'd need to be absolutely sure of what Lister's could realistically deliver in the retail market.

He lost himself in the spreadsheets. Assumptions for next year were confident and the promotional strategy carefully ambitious. It was just the competitor analysis he needed to review now. He flicked through the rest of the papers to find it, pulled out a couple of names from the charts and went online to do some googling.

The rest of the Operations Plan was conservative, as expected: tight margins on the transport contract with scenario planning around rising fuel prices and one or two increases in back office headcount. Anacleto was expecting to hold its own, but he needed to talk through with the sales guys how that might change if he raised the sales commitment on the distribution deal.

Tommy leaned back in his chair and sipped his orange juice, thinking hard.

Steady performance on the import side would be fundamental for the other, more traditional arm, of Lister's operations. Hand-making shoes was a tricky business at the best of times. The margins were horrendous with little room for manoeuvre in an operation that involved over 160 individual processes to produce a single shoe. One mistake at any point could jeopardise a whole order. A hundred shoes might be progressing through Lister's rooms, clicking, closing, lasting, finishing, but a single error at any point would reduce the final output to ninety nine, then ninety eight, ninety seven. Starting again on a whole new shoe would have significant cost implications.

Not that his staff made many mistakes. They were highly trained, very experienced and totally committed to the Lister's brand. Second, third and fourth generation shoe workers some of them, often in the same factory as their ancestors. Their trade was something they'd learnt from their own fathers and grandfathers.

Not the kind of people to look favourably on cheap mass-produced imports as he'd found out back in '81. They'd accused him then of selling out to the competition and he hadn't denied it. They'd accused him of not knowing the first thing about shoemaking and he hadn't denied that either. He had known about the markets though and the fact was, commercial success in shoemaking today lay in the cheap replacement market. His ability to recognise that was the only reason they were all still here doing business.

The clock on the computer showed nearly seven o'clock. He decided to look through the rest of the paperwork in the office.

In the kitchen he made toast and coffee and stood at the window looking across the garden. Despite the early morning grey, the sky was light enough to show the green stalks of irises around the pond and the bowed heads of daffodils going over.

He'd unplugged his mobile from the recharger on the kitchen unit and switched the phone on. Now it was vibrating noisily on the counter, spinning under the impetus.

'You have one new message. Message received today at 00:54am.'

'I know what you've done, Tommy. I know about the will Clifton witnessed. You and Robyn found it . . .'

He stiffened at his dad's voice, barely registering the words, struck by the gasping struggle to speak. He'd never known the old man so out of breath.

At the end of the message he waited impatiently for the menu options and pressed two to listen again, leaned a hand on the work top and stared frowning out of the window.

Why on earth couldn't they leave him to sort things out? He was halfway home resolving this mess with Esther and now here was his dad again blowing things up out of all proportion.

Tommy clicked the phone off without bothering to delete the message and picked up his jacket to go. His slice of toast was unfinished on the plate; he slid it into the bin and stacked the plate in the empty dishwasher on his way out.

In the hall he left a note for Bryony, who wouldn't be up for at least another hour. She'd be going over to Hartley Rise to do lunch that day.

Tell Dad—got his message. Will see him tonight. No need to worry.

He was in his office by 07:20 with an hour to look through all the spreadsheets on Lister's hand-made shoes. Production was on line for the Spring 07 range to meet the existing order book and all the signs were good for next year's Autumn and Winter orders which would start production in the first half of the new financial year.

By the time they started the sales meeting he'd got a clear idea of where he wanted the discussion to focus.

They opened with the designer's report from Pitti Uomo, PSO and MICAM: the recent trade shows in Florence, Frankfurt and Milan. After that came the details of quarter three and four performance with a digression into aged debtors and credit control round some old accounts so that by late morning they were running behind schedule.

Tommy suggested putting lunch back to one o'clock. 'I want to get absolute clarity on this year's performance before we look at next year's planning assumptions this afternoon. So let's press on with that.'

The energy round the table was wearing thin but if he didn't keep them at it they'd never get things finished for the Board Meeting.

Jim McKenna, his Brand Manager, had finished a presentation on the forty-five per cent of Lister's hand-made sales in the north American markets and was just beginning on performance in the UK and Germany when Jayne Gardiner slipped into the room and laid a note in front of Tommy.

Wife on phone. Imperative speak now.

Tommy cut McKenna off in mid-sentence. 'Apologies. Two minutes.' He went straight out and picked up the phone in his office. 'Darling?'

There was a single instant of silence then her voice: choked, trying to be calm. 'I'm sorry. I know it's not a good time. I'm at your dad's. Tommy, I don't know how to tell you this but he must have died in the night. I found him. Just sitting in the chair.'

Nothing could be clearer. Her words sent a surge of adrenalin through him and he was sharply conscious of the fear in her voice, the fear of causing him pain.

He pressed his hand close round the telephone. 'I'd better come straightaway.'

Even as he said it his mind was on his business schedule. The sales meeting was only halfway through. Next year's plan hadn't been finalised and the budget still had to be agreed, the papers sent to the Board.

There was absolutely no leeway. The Board had to meet before the end of March to agree terms and meet the due date for renegotiating the Anacleto deal.

He stared out through the glazed partition at the familiar view of the office beyond his own, at JG's desk and computer, the roll-top cupboards and the bank of spare desks where the sales guys sat when they were in the office.

They'd just have to work late tomorrow night and maybe some of Saturday.

He told Bryony he'd be with her in ten minutes, replaced the receiver and sat down at his desk. Reaching inside his jacket, he took out his mobile phone and listened again to the message from his dad, to the sound of his hoarse gasping voice.

JG had returned to her own desk now, he saw her glance in at him and then come, hesitant, to the half-open door. 'Everything all right?'

'My father's died. His heart probably.' Where were the words coming from? 'I'll have to go over there. See if the guys will work late tomorrow night. That'll give us an extra three or four hours.'

She nodded, her face, after the initial shock, displaying only the usual professionalism.

'That'll just leave the Board stuff,' said Tommy. 'Any chance you could come in on Saturday?'

He didn't even have to ask. The company had always come first with her. As he picked up his car key she was already on her way to arrange things with the colleagues he'd left in the meeting room.

At Hartley Rise he unlocked the front door and found Bryony already in the hall, alerted by the sound of his car and coming to meet him. 'I'm so sorry, darling.' Her voice again, broken with tears.

He reached out to her. 'Don't worry.'

His dad was sitting in the chair as he always was when Tommy arrived at the house and let himself in. Tommy stood looking down at him, taking in the familiar features, the whiteness around the cheeks and lips, the stillness of the face and chest. He touched the hand curled on the knee and the skin felt cold and smooth.

'We should ring the GP,' he said.

He found the number, dialled and she offered to come out as soon as the morning rush was over.

After that he rang his brothers, Richard first, on his direct line at the council. 'Hey, Richard.'

His voice, unintentionally soft, alerted his brother straightaway: 'What is it?'

'Dad.'

'Oh no! I'm coming over.'

'He's dead, Richard.'

'I'm coming. I'm coming now.'

'Get someone to drive you . . .' Tommy began but his brother had already hung up.

He cursed inwardly. *Should have gone over there. Broken it face to face.*

Maurice was in Cambridgeshire on some new build contract, his mobile on voicemail, halfway up a ladder, probably, plastering a ceiling. Tommy left a message telling him to call.

Bryony had gone to put the kettle on for tea.

On the table at his dad's side was a book Tommy had never seen before, presumably yesterday's parcel since the discarded wrapping was still lying on the dining table with the scissors. He picked it up, glanced at the cover and understood everything.

'I know about the will Clifton witnessed.'

He put the book next to Bryony's things on the sideboard to take home.

When Richard arrived he was tearful and shocked. 'I just can't believe it. He was over at ours all day Saturday. He was fine. And Sunday. He was all right then.'

'It was only ever a matter of time,' said Tommy. 'They said at the hospital his heart was weak.'

'But he was better than he had been for ages. Not like at Christmas.'

Maurice rang then and he explained things briefly and handed the phone to Richard who talked at length. His brother was still shaking his head when he came off the phone. 'I just can't believe it.'

At half past twelve the GP arrived. 'I am so very sorry,' she said, extending a hand to each of them in turn. 'Obviously, given your dad's age and his pulmonary disease, it's not altogether a surprise. But without being absolutely sure of the cause of death, I won't be able to issue a medical certificate.'

She examined the body anyway, her hands moving gently around his dad's face and arms. 'Yes, it may well have been his heart, but it could also have been a clot or even a stroke. We won't know without a post mortem.'

They stood around in silence while she called the coroner's office for them and made arrangements for the body to be collected.

'He'll ring you to confirm the circumstances surrounding your dad's death,' she told Tommy. 'And he'll let you know what the PM shows. If you've got a funeral director in mind you can go ahead and make preliminary arrangements but obviously they won't be able to finalise anything until the death certificate's been issued.'

Tommy showed her to the door and, while Bryony and Richard stood talking in the front room, he went through the hall bureau for his Dad's things: the bank details, pension book, medical card and birth and marriage certificates.

It was all where he'd expected it to be, only the updated will surprised him. He opened the folder and read the contents, noting it was only a few weeks old.

Well, that resolves things.

The house wasn't worth a lot by property standards, probably about eighty grand, but it was a damn sight more than Esther had at the moment.

She'd probably want them just to sell it on her behalf but that shouldn't be difficult and the thought of it didn't trouble him. He'd grown up here but the happy memories went with you, it was only the bad stuff that pinned you down.

He gathered up all the papers and went through to the front room.

'I've got all the official stuff,' he said. 'No point leaving it in an empty house.'

Richard still looked dazed with grief, so Tommy said nothing about the will.

Plenty of time for that later. He had enough on his mind with work.

24

Lister's Board

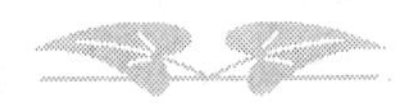

The next morning he was back in Lister's meeting room by 08:30.

McKenna finished the remainder of his presentation and by 09:30 they were ready to look at the draft Business Plan for the next financial year.

Tommy cut straight to the distribution deal with the Portuguese.

'Your plans are well thought through from what I've seen but looking at them and at the offer on the table I suggest a rethink. I want to propose an 80-95% increase in volume on the Ines, Graca and Candela lines in return for a much lower unit price overall. And, given promotional spend hasn't gone up beyond inflation for a couple of years now, I'd expect to see a real increase there as well.'

It was a cool call but Anacleto needed Lister's. They'd struggle to match their current output through any other distributor and all the signs were they'd been asking around and hadn't found a better offer.

The discussion took most of the day. He made them revisit the return on investment on all their proposed promotional activity and revise the 07 forecasts on the basis of his proposals.

He was conscious of Jim Mckenna, whose domain was purely the hand-made side of the business, sitting patiently at his side, listening. He'd tipped him off by phone before the meeting started that it would be a long wait.

'Getting clarity on the distribution deal's going to take a bit of work. But if we can achieve that there'll be more in the pot for experimentation on hand-made. So have a think about where we might take that in our own discussions later. It still needs to be a seamless plan.'

Not that he needed to explain things. McKenna was Tommy's best player, an ex-Harrods buyer who knew top-end retail inside out. When he'd grown tired of shop hours, Tommy had persuaded him to join Lister's. Now he brought all the well-bred conviction of Knightsbridge to the promotion of Lister's hand-made shoes.

By late afternoon they were ready to explore that.

'So, Jim, let's talk bespoke,' said Tommy.

The most obvious development was in Made to Order. Lister's already made shoes in conjunction with a couple of successful fashion designers. Now a third name was in the offing, a big name. Serious interest had been expressed at the trade show in Milan with designs out on the table but McKenna was understandably reserved.

It was business that kept the order book going but did nothing to build Lister's own name. The end product retailed under the fashion designer's label. Besides which production could be difficult.

There again it was a substantial order and would build Lister's credibility within the fashion trade. Tommy mused over McKenna's arguments. It was one route to go. All the projections suggested real growth was in the luxury market. People with a weakness for fashion and a thousand quid to spend on a pair of shoes usually had many more thousands to spend the same way without too much hesitation.

'I'd say we're definitely interested,' he told McKenna. 'But we need to keep a close eye on volume and lead times. Let's get some hard figures in as soon as possible. I don't want the production schedule up to the hilt with no room to manoeuvre on the standard order book.'

Which brought him to the next big issue.

'Where do you see the most potential for growth?'

'Well, it's a tough market,' said McKenna.

Lister's had lost ground in the fifties and sixties when other traditional shoemakers had been establishing their retail empires. Now everyone had been reduced to concessions in the smarter department stores but it was still the old high street names, like Church's and Barkers, that endured in the public memory. Lister's was at best a minor player.

'We're seeing growth in the secondary European cities,' said McKenna. 'And the Far East, of course. But that's another story.'

'Yes, let's talk about that.'

Again, in Tokyo and Osaka Lister's had lost out to the long-standing names but in Milan Tommy had fallen in with a venture capitalist looking to establish retail outlets on a couple of new Japanese cruise liners. He had an eye to the up and coming cities of Kyoto and Naha too.

'This guy, Tokanaga, reckons if we can lower the spec on some of the traditional designs and come up with something distinctive for a competitive price, we'd make a killing,' he told McKenna. 'Obviously it needs investigation and I don't want the Board getting wind of it. But keep some leeway in the production schedule.

And tone the US projections down a bit, would you? There's not nearly enough hard evidence for what they're promising.'

Their US distributor was full of enthusiasm since he'd helped stave off the hostile takeover bid. They were determined to do their utmost for Lister's in the coming year but the last thing he needed was the Board getting over excited. They already seemed to think Lister's was still operating in the heyday of Victorian shoemaking.

It was seven in the evening by the time they'd finalised the plan.

'Email the spreadsheets to JG,' Tommy told the sales guys. 'And then let's get a bite to eat.'

On Saturday morning he was back in before eight with JG close behind. He had all the spreadsheets to double check and his own quarterly report to write and it took until mid afternoon to get the Board papers collated. Way too late for the lunchtime post.

JG offered to drive round and hand deliver them and he didn't argue. His fellow directors were sticklers for having the papers to read the weekend before the meeting. In truth they should have door-matted that morning.

'Make sure you claim the petrol though,' he told her on the way out to the car park.

It was late afternoon when he got home. Elisabeth's silver Volkswagen Beetle was on the drive and Chris was home for the weekend too, Tommy heard his laughter in the living room as he came into the kitchen through the back door.

Byrony was at the stove frying onion and mushrooms for coq au vin. 'Richard's here,' she said quietly. 'He's been here all afternoon.'

Tommy cursed his own callousness. Saturday would have been his dad's day for going over to Richard's and he hadn't even thought about it.

He found his brother sitting on the living room sofa looking through photos Chris had brought on his laptop. He stood up as soon as Tommy came in, the emotion evident on his face.

'Beer!' said Tommy and turned back towards the kitchen.

Richard followed him and sat on the arm of the old red sofa, drinking straight from the bottle, while Tommy leaned against the central counter.

Bryony had finished her preparations, put the chicken in the oven and disappeared off to the living room.

'I just can't believe it,' said Richard yet again, his eyes wet with tears as he talked. 'This time last week, Dad was fine. We'd got the old dart board out of the garage. The boys are really into it all of a sudden. They were all for Dad having a go.'

He couldn't say any more for crying.

Tommy went to put an arm round him. Normally Richard would have made a joke of that, pulled away or hugged back with mock ferocity, but now he made no response at all. Eventually, though, he made an effort to pull himself together. 'Oh well! End of an era.' He reached into his shirt pocket for his cigarettes. 'Think I'll step outside.'

'Come into the study,' said Tommy. Normally he didn't like smoking in the house but it was cold out and dark. He brought an old saucer through for an ashtray, pulled the study door closed and opened the window.

Richard had sat himself down on the flat surface of the baby filing cabinet. He lit a cigarette and drew deeply on it. 'What a year! Unbelievable!'

It was Gina he was talking about now, Tommy thought. He sat in the leather chair at his desk and swung it round to face Richard.

Elisabeth had brought him a clock for Christmas, it projected the time onto a wall or ceiling and its segmented red digits were shining on the plaster above Richard's head: 18:43.

He thought of JG out delivering the Board papers. She'd probably be at Pitsford by now, where Penelope Leys lived in a five bedroom detached with views of the reservoir. Leys would be haughty, complaining about the late arrival of the papers, as if she had anything better to do than polish her nails and flick through the weekend travel supplement.

Richard wouldn't stay for dinner. When he'd gone Tommy sat on in the study thinking about the Board. Twenty six years ago he'd stood in this room and watched Lister's Chairman and one of the directors walk down the drive to his front door: David Lister and Robert Hartman; he'd known them by sight.

Ise Avenue had only been half built then.

'Nice place you've got here', they'd commented. 'We're thinking of investing, mind if we have a look around? Developers treated you all right? What about the noise from the railway?'

Hartman the solicitor, with his hearty laugh and wispy grey hair off a receding forehead. Lister, the Chairman, straight backed as a general but he'd needed Hartman to boost his courage that afternoon.

'So what are you doing these days?' they'd asked him.

It had been a year since he'd sold Orton's. Something he never dwelt on: a time in his life never to be revisited.

'I'm considering my options,' he'd said.

'Care to throw something into the mix?'

It was Lister who'd done the talking then.

'We're at an impasse, so to speak, in our line of business. Trade doesn't favour the traditional shoe industry. Unlike your own recent line of work. Not in Great Britain anyway.'

He could tell from what followed where it had all gone wrong. Lister had glossed over it, blamed everyone except himself but his conclusion had been straight enough when it came.

'If we don't do something radical, the signs are, there won't be a Lister's in the next three to five years.'

'What are you proposing?' Tommy had asked, more to end the conversation than out of interest in what they might have to offer him.

'The current MD's got to go,' Lister had said. 'The Board's of one mind on that. What isn't so clear is: what next?'

He'd stared at Tommy then, as if expecting him to say something. In the end Hartman had had to step in: 'We're here to find out if you'd be interested.'

'On what terms?'

They'd exchanged sheepish glances at that and he'd wanted to laugh in their faces. They'd actually come to his door with no concrete terms in mind at all. As if he'd be grateful just for a chance to join their hundred year old company.

'I won't come for anything less than a stake in the business.'

He'd said it to put them out of their misery.

'But it's a family business,' Lister had sounded horrified.

'I'm a self made man, Lister. I need the stake. The taste of blood.'

He'd shown them out expecting to hear nothing more of it but they'd obviously been desperate.

Desperate enough to take on Penelope Leys.

Leys was David Lister's cousin. She'd inherited her shares in the company from their grandfather, one of the two founding brothers, and she and her own brother, Stephen, together owned twenty five per cent of it. David Lister likewise. Hartman, grandson of the other founding brother, owned fifty per cent.

Hartman had strong views about the company but the sense to leave its operations to David Lister who at least knew shoemaking. Stephen Leys took no interest whatsoever and that left Penelope Leys: opinionated, high handed and thoroughly out of touch with the commercial world. Penelope Leys wasn't about to let anyone outside the family get a share in their precious family business, least of all a jumped up market trader like Tommy Allbright with a name for cut-throat dealing.

Lister had had his work cut out by all accounts but then he'd been driven by a strong personal interest. He hadn't wanted to go down in family history as the Chairman who'd presided over the company's demise.

It was JG who'd told Tommy how it was: eighteen months into the job when he'd finally gained her trust and taken her out for lunch to celebrate the Anacleto contract on which she'd done so much of the background work for him.

They'd had gravad lax in dill sauce, he remembered, and a bottle of Chablis.

'I think David hoped he could buy the Leys out and offer you their share,' she told Tommy. 'But of course Penelope wouldn't hear of it. I don't think at that stage she even realised it was you he had in mind. She just wouldn't countenance an MD who'd demand a share in the business. In the end, David over-ruled her. He passed a resolution to increase the authorised share capital and insisted on a poll vote proportionate to stock held. Of course it devalued all the shares, but it meant he and Hartman had the deciding votes. Leys was spitting feathers.'

Tommy could imagine it. He'd ended up with twenty five per cent of the company and a seat at the Board table so he could sit and watch Penelope Leys oppose every single business decision he ever proposed there.

Things had moved on with the Board since then. David Lister had retired, leaving Hartman as Chair, and his shares had gone to his grandson, Andy Lister, who'd also inherited from Stephen Leys. Andy was polite enough, an accountant with at least some sense of commercial reality, but as far as the Lister family was concerned, Tommy would always be the outsider.

Which was why, this week of all weeks, he needed his wits about him and the minimum of distractions.

25

SUNDAY

Tommy sat at the desk in his study, pulled the top drawer open and took out Clifton's book.

It was five a.m. His favourite time of the day, the hour of the market trader and manual labourer. The house around him was quiet; no-one else would be up for at least a couple of hours.

He thumbed to the index at the back of the book. Kimble's Top came halfway down with two page numbers referenced. He turned to the first and found a conceited endorsement of Arthur Radford's innovative design for the house, as if Clifton's views on modern architecture carried any weight.

The second reference was the one he was looking for: July 2003, a will template printed off the internet, the document written and signed, then witnessed by one David Matthews, aka 'Stan'. He'd been Gina's gardener and was living in a distant care home now up near Carlisle. The second witness had been Clifton himself, also distant, reclusive even, in Madeira, at least until a few weeks ago. Little danger of the truth coming to light through either of them, or so it had seemed.

Tommy lay the book down on the desk and stared idly at the front cover. Not a bad picture, in fact: the Spit crossing Dover cliffs, iconic outlines of both plane and landscape, beautiful even with the spinning propeller and curved wings.

Not really his dad's thing though. He'd always given short shrift to anyone who started up about the war.

'Yes, we know all about that,' he'd say. 'We don't want to hear about that.'

His dad would never have gone out and bought a book like this. It was utterly galling that Clifton should have sent it on the fly and upset everything.

Still, now we know where we stand.

He linked his arms back behind his head, thinking about Gina's will. The reference here was too oblique for anyone outside the family to make anything of it. Except for Clifton and he wasn't likely to come over again any time soon, if at all.

All the same, he'd better look into the legal situation and it wasn't one for his usual solicitor.

He went online and found a host of options with one credible-looking firm in Oxford inviting questions by email. He clicked on the window and began typing then thought better of it.

Nothing in writing!

He stored the number in his mobile phone instead so he could call in the week, shut Clifton's book away in the drawer and turned to the online sports news. It was full of France's Six Nations win at the Millennium Stadium, and, in Mumbai, England had closed at 272 for 3 on the first day of the Test. He trawled through the coverage then moved on to the football scores and by half past seven could hear movement upstairs, switched the PC off and wandered into the living room to open the curtains.

The room was as they'd left it last night. The fragrance of scented candles lingered and his son's laptop was still open on the coffee table with all his other things strewn around it: a soft grey sweater, trainers, canvas bag with contents spilling onto the floor. A wallet had fallen out and a mobile phone lay alongside, left on overnight when it should have been recharging.

'Just walk on by,' Bryony would have warned him but he picked it up instead and took it through to the kitchen to plug into his own recharger.

Outside, traces of the sun's red fingers were still groping across the sky. He unlocked the back door and went for a breath of fresh air before breakfast.

Neither he nor Bryony went in for gardening, everything here was left to a local landscaper apart from the few glazed pots and wooden planters on the patio. Tommy picked his way through them, past the heavy beech wood furniture covered with tarpaulin and stepped out onto the lawn, skirting the pond and passing the windows of the living room that ran the whole length of the house on this side.

The beds all around were full of mature greenery and sturdy shrubs and at the far end of the plot, near the road, was an orchard. The word made him wince, as though they'd moved into some grand estate but it was the children who'd christened it. In reality it was just a big space where the grass grew long and ornamental fruit trees had been planted; almond and cherry trees, laden now with pink and white blossom.

He ducked under their low branches as he made his way across to the drive and followed it back up to the house.

In the kitchen Bryony and the children had obviously been talking about his dad. The conversation stopped as he entered and Elisabeth left off folding linen napkins to come and slip her arm through his in a sideways hug, typical of her. Christopher, less confident, just nodded from where he stood awkwardly in his socked feet half-leaning against the fridge.

Was I ever so vulnerable? thought Tommy.

It struck him suddenly that Christopher was just like his dad in that respect.

Strange I never noticed!

He'd always assumed his son's gentle side came from Bryony but, thinking about it now, he realised his wife wasn't vulnerable like that at all. It was his dad who'd been gentle in the way Chris was: uncertain and sensitive.

The realisation of it jolted him. He'd never noticed it before and now it was too late.

Too late for what?

Bryony was laying out slices of smoked salmon on plates to go with bagels and scrambled eggs. He slipped a hand against the small of her back as he kissed her, then took the box of eggs, fetched a bowl from the cupboard and assembled mayonnaise, Worcester sauce and black pepper to mix together.

'Don't say I never do anything around here!'

That afternoon they gathered for tea at Kimble's Top and now his dad seemed to be all around him: on the gravel drive where he'd shown up that Friday, looking determined and grim as he struggled out of the taxi while Clifton's nephew held the door for him; in the hallway where they'd arrived together late at night: the night Gina had died; in the living room where his favourite arm chair stood empty beside the window.

As Tommy entered the house, Robyn was in the dining room setting out the joint of ham, the bowls of salad and baskets of sliced baguette, exactly as Gina would have done; and in the kitchen Doreen was supervising the dessert offerings everyone had brought.

He went on to the living room and found Richard and Maurice sitting silent where normally they'd have been chatting and even Paul and Lee had nothing to say for themselves, their heads buried in the Sunday sports pages.

Tommy sat down with one of the business supplements and glanced through it. The Euro was at 1.44 which reminded him he hadn't thought through his forex strategy for the Anacleto deal yet. Things had calmed down a bit recently, they'd seen nothing like the fluctuations of two or three years ago: exchange rates as low as 1.39 then up to 1.53 within a matter of months. Still, he needed to think about it. Lister's was facing significant expenditure in Euros over the next eighteen months and the phasing was crucial.

In July 04 he'd managed to hedge at 1.49 and that had paid dividends into the first six months of 05. There had been nothing comparable since then, though.

The question was: would the exchange rate keep falling or rise again and if so, by how much?

'Tea? Tommy? You will be joining us?'

Doreen's voice jerked him back to the present and he looked up to see that the others were already on their way to the dining room.

'About the funeral,' she said as he got up. 'I gather you've taken all your dad's papers. Does that mean you're making all the arrangements?'

'Not necessarily. I just didn't want to leave things in an empty house,' said Tommy. 'Why, are you offering?'

'It ought to be shared. It's good for people to do something constructive.'

He realised she was talking about Richard.

'I'm more than happy for you to do as much as you want,' he said. 'I can easily drop the paperwork round. You just need to wait for the post mortem and the coroner to issue a death certificate. Then he'll release the body.'

When they were all seated at the table, eating, he thought he'd better broach the subject of the will. 'Now's probably the time to tell you Dad's left the house to Esther.'

Their response took him completely by surprise. Doreen put her knife and fork down straightaway with a bang. 'Why on earth would he do that?'

Too late it occurred to him she'd probably been counting on Richard's share. He'd written it all off as not worth very much, which it wasn't to him and Bryony, or in property terms, but to Richard and Doreen, even divided threeways with himself and Maurice, it would no doubt have constituted a fair amount.

For a moment he actually felt sorry for Doreen, she looked furious.

'What did Esther ever do for him? When did she even spend time with him? Our lads had him round every

Saturday.' She looked at Bryony: 'And it was us doing his lunches every day!'

'Doreen!' began Richard.

'Well, come on! It's hardly fair.'

'It's what he wanted,' said Richard fiercely. 'It doesn't have to be fair. It's just . . . what he wanted.'

Doreen picked her knife and fork up again, her mouth tight.

Tommy leaned across to her and spoke quietly. 'Dad felt very bad about the business with Gina's will. It was on his mind. All tied up with losing Gina.'

He could see that it mollified her. She nodded and the conversation moved on to funeral arrangements.

After tea he stayed on in the dining room, waiting for Robyn. She'd thrown him a couple of glances during the meal and he suspected she wanted to talk. He was right, she came back through from clearing the plates away in the kitchen.

'Granddad knew, didn't he?' she said. 'About Gina's will?'

'He suspected. I suppose he felt for Esther because of the shares.'

He could still hardly believe it himself: that Gina had held onto those shares in RSG. And for what? Out of loyalty to a man like Scholt? He hadn't exactly been beggared by it. All Scholt's property had turned out to be in his wife's name. But then he'd have seen it coming; RSG had been settling medical claims out of court long before the lobbying groups had got it together.

Robyn was shaking her head with a cynical look. 'It's amazing! Esther goes through life doing nothing for anyone. And everyone feels sorry for her.'

Tommy pushed his chair back to leave the table.

'So, is Esther coming back for Grandad's funeral?' asked Robyn.

'Apparently.'

'Well, I don't suppose she'll stay long.'

She moved along the table, pushing the black leather chairs back into their places and collecting up the discarded napkins.

'You should still think about lodgers,' he told her. 'Even with the flats it'll take more money than you've got to keep a place like this going in the long run.'

He'd pretty much accepted the fact that selling the flats and giving the capital to Esther to compensate for the worthless shares was a non-starter. The property was held in a fixed trust with rental income used to cover liabilities and thereafter paid to the owner of Kimble's Top. There was simply no option for the corporate Trustee to sell the properties unless the liabilities exceeded a fixed proportion of their value. Robyn had never been amenable to the suggestion anyway and she certainly wasn't in the mood to discuss it now.

'I've got plans,' she told him ominously and left the room before he had a chance to enquire further.

It was about the time he and Bryony normally went to visit the rose garden statue of Peter Pan. He went to look for her in Laurel's room; she'd gone with Elisabeth to see the new colour scheme where Richard had redecorated.

She was sitting beside Laurel's desk watching her cut round a drawing of a Victorian lady and looked up to shake her head at him, almost imperceptibly.

Not today.

Too emotional he supposed.

He went outside debating whether or not to visit the garden by himself then spotted Richard and Maurice coming back from the greenhouses, Richard's favoured location for a smoke, so he leaned on the balustrade of the terrace instead and waited for his brothers to join him.

All across the hill top the air was fresh and the lawns and shrubs had been recently trimmed, Richard's work he assumed since Robyn couldn't afford to keep a gardener. Richard nodded when he commented on it.

'Takes a bit of doing,' he said, looking out across the grass. 'Got most of the beds mulched down. The earlier the better with that but the lawn needs re-seeding, you can see the bare patches.'

The perennials wanted stakes in too before the year's growth really took off and there were a load of weeds to hoe out.

'Dig out, I should think,' Maurice remarked, 'Place this size. They get really established.'

Richard had swung his legs over the balustrade and jumped down into the shrubbery below. He grabbed a handful of downcast cream petals. 'Hellebore. See!' he lifted them upwards to show the intricate centres. 'I told Robyn to bring a handful in and float them in a bowl. It's the best way to enjoy them. Gina always did that.'

'Oh yes. Very Gina,' nodded Maurice.

Tommy folded his arms and stared out across the hilltop.

One point four the currency report had said. The rates had dipped as low as 1.43 earlier this month but all the signs were that it'd go up again. The question was when and by how much?

If it hits 1.48 again before the autumn I'll buy options for six months' time.

26

ULTRA VIRES

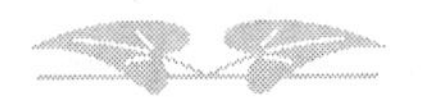

When he got back to the office on Monday morning Hartman rang him first thing.

'I've had a look through the Board papers and a bit of a chat with the others and there are one or two changes to the agenda. We want more on Lister's end of the business. Anacleto dominates in terms of volume; we understand that but the heart of Lister's business is hand-made shoes and the 06 results aren't exactly earth-shattering, Tommy. We'd like a little more detail, please, to show we are doing everything possible to build the brand.'

'I'll ask McKenna to extend his presentation,' said Tommy. 'And perhaps you'd like to hear more from the designer. He's got a fresh eye and made some good contacts at the trade shows.'

It was the perfect sop. The kid was good. He'd talk the talk and get them excited without being in a position to reveal anything of substance or make commitments.

'Good!' said Hartman. 'Well then, I suggest we make McKenna's twenty minutes into thirty five and have a full length discussion with the designer. If we cut the Anacleto section right back it should give us the extra time. Say, fifteen minutes for that?'

Fifteen minutes!

'Robert, the single most important decision facing the Board is the terms of the distribution deal,' said Tommy. 'We're committing the company to a significant liability.'

'Yes. The Board is aware of its fiduciary responsibilities, Tommy. However there is also the question of strategic priorities and the long-term success of Lister's brand is paramount in that. Oh, and ask the Americans to join us by conference call, will you? We feel there's some optimism behind those proposed targets that we'd like to explore.'

Tommy put the phone down, frustrated. They really hadn't got the first idea when it came to business.

He arranged for the Americans to dial into the meeting on Friday afternoon and then had their lead guy on the phone all week checking and re-checking his presentation, wanting to know what Tommy thought of it.

'Just give them the essence,' he said repeatedly after wading through pages of analysis and ambitious scenarios.

In between it all he rang the solicitors in Oxford about Clifton's book. They were reluctant at first to hold a telephone consultation but he made it clear he wasn't up for a drive over there, offered money on account and finally got a call back from one of their senior people.

'It's an enquiry about a family will,' he explained. 'My sister died in December leaving a will dated November 1999. It's since come to light that she probably made a later will in July of 2003 but no-one's got a copy of it.'

'How exactly did this come to light?'

'Family correspondence,' he lied. 'Our uncle. Also dead. We found a letter he'd written mentioning that he witnessed a will in the summer of 2003.

'And there's definitely no copy of this will anywhere? Nothing with your sister's solicitor?'

'No. It sounds like it was done on the spur of the moment. Our uncle witnessed it and the gardener. Unfortunately neither of them is around now. The thing is, we're pretty sure the later will would have been different from the earlier one. Back in '99 my sister left her house to a niece and a lot of valuable investments to her daughter. By 2003 those investments had lost value so it seems likely she redid the will in the light of that, leaving her daughter the house.'

'Does your uncle's letter actually mention the provisions of the will?'

'No.'

'Is there even any indication that he saw the contents of the later will?'

'No.'

'Well, I'm afraid unless you can actually find a copy of the will, or a clear reference to its provisions and with it, ideally, some indication that it was both valid and complied with Section 9 of the Wills Act, there's really not very much you can do about it. From what you're saying, this letter only establishes that there was a will and that your uncle and a gardener witnessed the signature.'

'I see,' said Tommy. 'Well that's very helpful. Incidentally, just as a matter of interest, suppose this later will had been deliberately destroyed? Presumably there'd be some sort of legal case against that?'

'A will is proved in good faith; the law protects the executors and beneficiaries. So, yes, it is a criminal offence to destroy a will. However the question of proof would be essential for a court to reach a decision on that. Do you have any grounds to believe the will was destroyed? The word of a credible witness, for example?'

'No. It's just obvious there was a later will.'

'As I say, the question of proof would be essential in a court of law.'

'Well, thank you very much then. I appreciate your calling me back.'

He sat back, satisfied: so much for that then.

On Tuesday night he dropped his dad's documents off to Doreen: a modest bundle of official papers.

Is this all we amount to in the end?

The next evening she rang him with the post mortem results.

'Congestive cardiac failure, according to the Pathologist's report. That's the cause of death. And COPD as secondary.'

Chronic Obstructive Pulmonary Disease. Emphysema as his dad had always called it. No surprises there then.

'Gilroy's have collected the body,' she went on. 'We just have to ring if we want a viewing. Otherwise we're all set for next Tuesday. Eleven thirty a.m.'

On Thursday he went through the extended presentation with McKenna, briefed the designer for the open discussion and had a last attempt at getting the Americans to tone their material down.

'We just want you all to know we're planning on doing everything we can for Lister's in the year ahead. It's the least we can do after all your help on the takeover bid,' Rich Dubrowski, their Chief Executive told him.

'The best thing you can offer this Board is a reality check,' said Tommy. 'No-one doubts your commitment to the product.'

It was all getting out of hand. He went back to the Board agenda and made some last minute changes himself, bringing the Anacleto discussion forward to mid morning and pushing the designer's item to the afternoon, right before the American call. Once they got talking trade shows and hand-made design concepts they'd never come back to sales targets and scenarios for Portuguese imports.

The next morning he was in early as usual and wandered along to the meeting room where JG was setting up for the board meeting.

The boardroom, or lack thereof, was a bone of contention with every one of his fellow directors and they'd be reminded of it the minute they walked through the door but at least it was a contention Tommy had won.

Back in '83 when cash flow had been a daily crisis and he'd been running the Victorian factory and looking for warehouse space to accommodate 15,000 boxes of imported shoes, he'd proposed selling the original red brick Lister's building and moving the whole operation into a low cost unit on one of the town's new industrial estates.

The Board had been violently opposed to it. Leys in particular had raised a whole series of objections concerning the disposal of company assets, but there had been no disputing the financial arguments for it. She'd continued her opposition in the public domain, he was sure of it, igniting the barrage of local publicity: a press campaign that had reared its head again later with accusations that Lister's relocation had forced the closure of a pre-war café that had long catered for the factory's work force.

It was laughable. The only reason Lister's actually had a workforce to cater for was due to the release of capital and the reduction in operating costs generated by the relocation.

Nevertheless, the long-serving workforce had lamented the demise of the rabbit-warren building with its Victorian shoe-making rooms and barred windows and the directors had been positively beside themselves at losing the wood-panelled inner sanctum that had been Lister's board room.

When they discovered he'd even sold off the furniture they'd been livid.

'That table was solid walnut,' Leys had fumed.

And much good it did you for all the sense any of you ever talked around it!

He'd refused outright to reconstruct the room at Dennington Road. 'The building hardly lends itself. And anyway, there's no budget.'

They met now in a plain meeting room on the first floor, round a flimsy metal table with functional modern chairs.

Tommy watched JG setting out pads of paper and a pencil for every seat. It was a far cry from the sacred hush of Lister's old board room and if the older members didn't like it they only had themselves to blame. It had been a situation entirely of their own making.

As nine o'clock drew near, Hartman arrived, old-fashioned in Harris tweed with a handkerchief in his top pocket, and Andy Lister followed: a young man in a hurry with a heavy laptop bag and a folder of loose papers tucked under one arm.

Leys walked through the door on the dot of nine. Her blonde hair was back combed in true fifties style and she wore a cerise jacket with a matching scarf over a dark top and trousers. She was peremptory towards JG who was offering drinks and Tommy despised her for that. He took the jug and went to pour her coffee himself.

The early part of the day was slow going. Only Andy Lister seemed interested in the financial updates with Hartman venturing a few minor points of clarification and of Tommy's own quarterly report they had nothing whatsoever to say.

He brought McKenna in to charm them when they broke for coffee but he could sense their impatience when they sat down again and he raised the Anacleto deal.

Again, Andy Lister was the most engaged.' What if we don't make the additional volume you're proposing?' he asked, barely waiting for Tommy to conclude his introductory remarks.

Tommy made reference to the projections he'd provided and began explaining the assumptions behind them, meaning to lead on to the increased investment in promotional activity, but Hartman interrupted him. 'I don't see any point in reiterating what we've already seen in the Board papers. Andy, do you have a material objection to this proposal?'

'I'd like more time to discuss it,' said Lister.

Hartman looked at Leys but she just shook her head.

'Well,' said Hartman. 'In the interests of time, I suggest the Board agrees the proposed terms, subject to resolution of Andy's reservations offline. You can confirm by the middle of next week. The due date's not until the first of April so, if necessary, we can always convene an emergency meeting before then.' He looked across at JG who was taking minutes:

'Got that?'

She nodded.

'Right! Let's bring Jim McKenna in and move on to the hand-made market.'

It was after that, in the discussions over the American business, that they really cut up rough and Tommy never even saw it coming.

Dubrowski's report on the American market for capped Oxfords and Burford and Derby boots was glowing and the discussion that followed it fuelled by the Board's own optimism about Lister's superior brand and the projected rise in top end footwear for the outdoor market.

Tommy finally leaned on Hartman to draw the call to a close well after the allotted hour had elapsed but the ideas were still flowing thick and fast even with Dubrowski off the line.

In the end he cut in to remind them that the Americans' optimism lay in their gratitude for the work he'd done to stave off the takeover bid:

'Dubrowski as good as said so himself. They're wildly enthusiastic to promote the brand but it doesn't mean the market's there and last year's return on investment certainly doesn't suggest an easy ride.'

Leys was frowning. 'This work you did for them on the hostile bid? I don't remember it coming to the Board.' She looked at Hartman. 'Is this really the first we're hearing about it? Three months after the event?'

'It wasn't a Board matter,' said Tommy before Hartman even had a chance to answer.

'Lister's Managing Director putting company resource and man hours into warding off a takeover of its US distributor? If that's not a Board matter, I'd like to know what is,' said Leys.

'It was an off line project. They approached me personally at home and I did the work in my own time.'

'You had no business doing it,' said Leys. 'For all we know it might have been in Lister's best interests for the takeover to go ahead.'

'Being swallowed up by a big impersonal corporate would hardly be in the interests of promoting a niche product like Lister's,' said Tommy.

'All the same, it should have been a Board decision.'

Tommy was furious. Hartman was looking at him for an apology now and he was damned if he'd give it when they'd just wasted the best part of the afternoon on peripherals.

Penelope Leys was sitting back, though, with a cool smile, twisting a pencil between her fingers. 'I don't know that your work on that takeover bid wasn't ultra vires.'

'Rubbish!'

Tommy hadn't crossed swords with her all these years not to know where he stood in relation to the Companies Act. 'In the first place I was acting without recompense in my own time and not on behalf of Lister's,' he stormed. 'And secondly, the ultimate outcome was without a doubt conducive to the objects of this Company.'

'Not without a Board decision it wasn't!' snapped Leys.

So sack me then!

Even Andy Lister was looking uncertain now and JG had looked up from her shorthand pad with a frown.

'I'd like us to review our legal position,' Leys told Hartman. 'Take some advice.'

'Well, I suppose it wouldn't hurt,' he murmured.

Tommy sat back in his chair with a humourless laugh: 'Whatever you think best!'

Really it was the limit and if he'd thought about it he'd have seen it coming but then he'd had a lot going on this week.

When the others had gone he stayed behind to help JG clear away the half-empty coffee cups.

'Are you all right?' she asked.

'It's nothing,' he shrugged.

All the same. He should have seen it coming.

27

Family

When he got home Bryony was in the kitchen. He sat on one of the high stools at the central counter and watched her squeeze fresh lemon juice onto tuna steaks, ready for grilling.

'Bad day?' she asked.

'Unbelievable! They haven't got the first bloody idea!'

She dropped the squeezed-out lemon into the compost tub and went to wash her hands at the sink. 'We could have a martini: talk about it!'

'I wouldn't ruin a good martini!'

She laughed and it made him smile. She was beautiful, stylish and immaculately turned-out yet never manufactured. It was what he'd loved about her when they'd first met, that and her raw intelligence, the damn-it-all look in her eyes.

'You're the best thing that ever happened to me,' he said and she just looked back into his eyes and smiled, let the words linger between them without needing to shrug them off or reassure him it was mutual.

'So how was your day?' he asked.

'You'll wish you'd gone for the martini!'

'Oh?'

'Esther's people rang from Spain. The couple she works for. They're flying her home. Everything in excess baggage. Just a couple of boxes to follow by train.'

'Why?'

'Not herself, apparently. Hasn't been right since she went back. They think she needs to be with her family.'

'She won't want that,' said Tommy.

'She's coming all the same. Five o'clock tomorrow at Heathrow. I said she could stay with us.'

He sat there, taking it in. 'Looks like we're braving the M25 on a Saturday afternoon then.'

'I am,' she said. 'You're cooking, remember?'

It was something he liked to do; Chris and Elisabeth were coming for the weekend, staying through to the funeral on Tuesday, and he'd planned one of his special dishes. Now, though, he wasn't so sure.

'You'll never get all her stuff in the Z3,' he said.

'So, I'll take the Audi.'

Early the next morning he drove up to Oakham. It was a sixty mile round trip but he was in the mood for it and the old A-road was pretty clear at that time on a Saturday.

He'd planned a sausage risotto, one of his favourite dishes, with celeriac cut up small, oregano and Gran Padano. In Oakham there was a traditional butcher with a name for speciality sausages and an independent wine importer who specialised in the Veneto region, dealing directly with the growers.

Tommy had first got to know the wines visiting a leather supplier just outside Arzignano in the north of Italy: a tough old guy who'd wined and dined him at an old family restaurant. He could still remember his first taste of their bigoli co l'anara: duck's liver with herbs and vegetables, washed down with a smoky red Refosco.

He'd tracked the Oakham importer down on the internet soon afterwards and shown up at the little industrial unit on the outskirts of the town.

'Yes, they've got some original grapes in that region,' the guy had told him. 'Limestone mountains, tight coastal plain and the upper reaches of those big rivers with a lot of vineyards in the gravel banks. Best vines are in the foothills though. Lovely sharp whites as well as the reds.'

He'd poured Tommy a sample from a bottle of Schioppettino. 'Brick and smoke. Comes right off the nose!'

Tommy had developed a taste for the strong enduring flavour and it was always worth the trip to see what the importer had on the shelves.

He drove at a leisurely pace. The sky overhead was a dull humid blue and there was nothing else about, just a couple of horse boxes that he overtook easily enough. The road dipped and climbed between green fields, curving back on itself past a water-logged meadow covered with birds and isolated old houses with great chimney stacks.

When he reached the town he made his way straight to the butcher. A tray of fresh pork pies was just coming out of the oven and the whole place smelt sweet with them. He bought pork sausages made with stilton and thyme and then drove out beyond the level crossing to the wine importer and spent a pleasant hour browsing the list and selecting bottles.

When he'd finished it was still only mid morning so he wandered round the shops and had a coffee at the Whipper-In.

By the time he got home Elisabeth had arrived and was upstairs helping Bryony get the spare bedroom ready for Esther.

It was a large room with a sloping roof and a picture window low enough to sit beside and look out over the garden. Bry had put a wicker chair beside it with a cream and turquoise throw that matched the hand-woven Soumak rug on the floor with its exotic pattern of birds and flowers.

She set off for Heathrow around two thirty and he settled down in the living room with The Financial Times to catch up on the longer articles he hadn't had time for during the week.

He was well into L'Oréal's takeover of Body Shop when Elisabeth came in with an armful of photo albums and sat herself down on the sofa.

'Are you disturbable?'

She opened the first of the albums; it was dog-eared with dark porous pages and little black and white snaps in diagonal corner settings: their oldest family photographs.

Tommy looked down at a stout little boy poised sideways on the rush seat of a kitchen chair, holding on to the wooden back and staring intently at the camera. He was fair haired, about two years old, and wearing hard shoes and an embroidered cotton smock.

His mother's brother, Paul.

More pictures of the Ludlows followed. Shots of the farm and the whole family, on a summer's day, sitting on a bench in the garden at the front of the farmhouse. His mother: a young woman, in a long cotton dress with short sleeves and high heeled sandals, had her arms around her own mother who was looking wistful in her thick stockings and heavy shoes, her dress with a wide collar and buttons up the front. The three boys, hair neatly combed, were arranged round them. Their dad stood at the back in his formal suit with a waistcoat, collar and tie, arms spread to either side along the bench.

'What happened to them all?' asked Elisabeth.

'The younger two boys went out to Australia on assisted passage and Paul followed after their dad died. It was getting more and more difficult to keep the farm going. He sold the land off and divided the money between them.'

The later pages were of his dad's family, starting with his grandfather, George Allbright, on a day at the seaside, reclining on a pebbly beach in his best suit and tie. He had trousers with turn-ups, thick socks and shoes and wore a wide flat cap on his head. He smiled with clenched teeth round the pipe he was smoking and in the background the beach rose up behind him to a skyline filled with cottage roofs and chimneys.

Tommy watched the family scenes as Elisabeth moved on through the pages, asking questions about his dad's sisters and their remaining cousins over in Coventry.

It's information, that's all. Just information.

Typical of Elisabeth, though, to address her grief methodically like this: turning the pages on an orderly set of pictures.

There were some loose colour snaps slipped into the back of the album for safe-keeping, and he picked up a late picture of his grandfather Ludlow by the old stone barn. The old man was glancing up from caressing a sheep dog, his face sunburnt and surprised, caught unawares by the photographer. He'd treated children with the same rough affection as his and animals, Tommy remembered.

He thought of Esther coming home, troubled reticent Esther, and wondered what her great grandfather would have made of her.

Chris arrived just in time for dinner and he and Elisabeth were on good form at the table, picking up where they'd left off on the environment and her alleged sell-out to the corporate machine.

'You're in a prime position to make a difference,' Chris started up. 'It's every middle management decision in every environmentally unsustainable industry across the country. If you don't do something, who will?'

'We've got an environmental policy,' said Elisabeth. 'There's a whole working group on it.'

'That's precisely the problem! The environment's got to be mainstream. Not some special interest thing.'

Tommy just listened, savouring the Refosco, his eyes straying now and again to Esther who sat eating silently beside Chris, her eyes on her plate.

When she'd first walked through the front door he'd been struck by how altered she was: she'd looked vulnerable, bruised somehow. Now she was sitting huddled in a thick-knit blue sweater that didn't suit her and he wondered what had happened to the lacy shirts and fashionable t-shirts she'd worn all last winter.

Once or twice he was aware of Bryony's eyes on him as he glanced at Esther and finally he looked across and met her eyes. He expression was calm and appraising.

What?

She half-smiled at his querying look.

Elisabeth had tried without success to draw Esther into the conversation, asking about the environmental movement in Spain and what she thought of climate change, but in the end it was Chris who cut to the chase. 'So what exactly are you going to do now?' he asked.

'I have absolutely no idea,' she said and, as Chris looked nonplussed at that: 'Why? Does it matter?'

'I don't know,' she said. 'Does it matter?'

Tommy sensed Elisabeth next to him was similarly taken aback by that but Bryony stepped in unperturbed. 'There's plenty of time,' she said calmly. 'Things have a habit of working themselves out.'

Do they? It wasn't a philosophy he'd ever heard her espouse before.

'Since when . . . ?'

'They would have done,' Bry cut him off. 'If we'd ever just let them.'

At breakfast the next morning Elisabeth and Chris invited her to join them in a get-together with some old school friends but Esther declined and Tommy assumed she'd gone out shopping with Bryony until she appeared at the open door of his study.

'Can I ask you something?'

His heart sank but he pulled a spare chair across from the wall for her. 'Of course.'

'You know all about stocks and shares,' she said sitting down. 'Why do you think Mum left all her money in RSG?'

It was exactly the question that haunted him.

'Scholt was a very charismatic guy,' he told her. 'He and your dad went back a long way and shares in RSG were a big deal at the time. High dividends. Your parents socialised with Scholt too, and the other directors: cocktail parties, dinners, that kind of thing. It was a whole way of life. I think perhaps your mum couldn't bring herself to cut and run, even when it all went wrong.'

'The others did.'

'Not all of them.'

He watched her musing it over, wondering if he should add his other idea, something he kept coming back to even though he had no evidence for it.

She must have read it in his face, though, because her blue-green eyes fixed themselves on him, expectantly.

'Your dad was old school when it came to investments,' said Tommy. 'Things were different then. Stocks and shares were a closed shop. I think for Arthur, at least, it was about putting money into the country. Manufacturing. Construction. Refurbishment. It's possible that if he'd said something like that to your mum: about taking the lows with the highs, not just making a fast buck, it might have stayed with her. Even after he was gone.'

It was the only conceivable solution he'd been able to find and he steeled himself now for the question that must surely follow: so why didn't Gina change her will?

But Esther just sat frowning into the middle distance and when she finally spoke her question took him by surprise.

'Did you like my dad?'

He looked at her, perplexed. 'Yes,' he said. 'I liked him very much.'

'Everything went wrong when he died,' said Esther. 'I remember him really well in some ways. The stuff we did together. Things he said. But it was just such a tiny part of him. There's so much I never got to know.'

'You can't remake the past, Esther.'

'I just want some idea. What he was like.'

'He was clever,' said Tommy. 'In all the right ways. Clear sighted and visionary. Everything he envisaged was about excellence; technical things he'd learnt from scratch and developed. And he was a quiet man. Unassuming.'

He knew it wasn't what she wanted: Arthur Radford, architect, the text book eulogy. But he couldn't help it. His best memories of Arthur belonged to a time he couldn't ever revisit.

She wasn't just disappointed, he could tell, she was hurt: rebuffed by his refusal to acknowledge her loss.

He watched her go and hoped she'd move on soon, take up with Josie Deacon again or some of those other friends she'd been so desperate to escape to last winter. They'd probably sympathise with her: *Families!*

It was their turn to host Sunday tea that afternoon and the family started arriving from three o'clock.

Chris had appointed himself the welcoming committee, opening the front door, taking coats and relaying drinks orders through to the kitchen while Tommy stood in the living room making small talk, aware all the time of Esther slouched silently in a corner of the sofa while her aunts and uncles chatted around her.

It's probably her worst nightmare. Stuck here with all of us.

Robyn wasn't happy either He saw her give Esther a cold look then keep her distance.

'It complicates things,' she said when he asked her about it on the way into the dining room.

'I don't see why.'

But she didn't elaborate.

After tea Bryony suggested a walk by the river and most of the family took her up on it but he stayed behind and Doreen came to find him in the kitchen where he'd just finished loading the dishwasher. She wanted to talk about the order of service for the funeral. 'Laurel's written a poem she'd like to read. We've had it printed as well in case it's too much for her on the day.'

They went into the dining room and he sat down at the table and looked through the service booklet she handed him: thick cream stationery with a solemn black line and heavy type on the front cover:

William George Allbright
died
16th March 2006
"Precious in the eyes of the Lord
is the death of his saints."

'The minister chose the quote. We weren't sure about hymns but Richard thought your dad liked Jerusalem the Golden. And the twenty third psalm, that's traditional.'

'Right.'

'Everything's arranged with the hotel. It'll be a finger buffet with one or two extras, hot potato wedges and samosas. And an open bar. It's only family and maybe one or two from the church but they won't take advantage. Is there anything I've missed?'

She hadn't of course but he answered politely, waiting to hear what was really on her mind. He handed the order of service back to her but she made no move to leave the table, put the booklet carefully back in the folder she had with her and finally asked:

'Is it true Esther's planning to stay?'

'It looks like it,' said Tommy.

'I really can't understand your dad leaving her the house. I know it was up to him what he did. But honestly, why should Esther get it?'

'Because it resolves things?'

She looked surprised.

'Kimble's Top,' Tommy reminded her. 'Esther's family home? That's now Robyn's.'

'Robyn was there for Gina,' said Doreen. 'Every hour of every day. The whole time she was ill. And for all the right reasons. She never expected to get the house.'

'But she did get it,' said Tommy. 'And Esther ended up with nothing.'

'Well whose fault's that?'

Mine!

She must have read the shock in his face and thought she'd upset him, talking like this with his dad gone because she reached out a hand straightaway and squeezed his wrist.

'Sorry, Tommy, my fault. I shouldn't have mentioned it at a time like this!'

28

Lisbon

It was a relief to get back to work on Monday notwithstanding the debacle with the Board.

JG asked him about it first thing. 'This ultra vires business: should we be worried?'

'Hardly. Leys hasn't got a case against me.'

'It doesn't mean she won't try!'

It was true Leys had tried more than once to bring a resolution to remove him from the Board but she'd never managed it yet.

'That's why we have a Shareholder Agreement!' he smiled.

Lister's gave him two votes per share in any attempt to remove him. So even if Hartman backed Leys, which was highly unlikely, Tommy would only need Andy Lister's support to even things out.

He had a call scheduled with Andy that morning to resolve his concerns about the Anacleto contract. It was a long conversation that would have been better face-to-face but Andy was away on business, in the final stages of an audit at some godforsaken meat packer's in Lincolnshire.

They went through the penalties should Lister's fail to meet the increased sales targets and Tommy reiterated the risk assessments and scenario planning.

'We can always hold the stock and sell on into the following season. The three high volume lines are all classics. They never go out of fashion. And we're selling through mainstream stockists with a stable customer base.'

In the end Andy seemed reassured that there were no hidden costs or unforeseen contingencies.

'And don't forget the figures will be front-ended,' said Tommy. 'The Q1 results should give an early indication on all three lines so we'll still have time to reforecast.'

'Okay. Fine,' said Andy. 'You've obviously considered all the eventualities. So, yes, I think, go ahead.'

'I'll have JG draft an addendum to the Board minutes,' said Tommy. 'We'll get it off to you straight away. If you could sign and return it first thing? For the record.'

He wasn't taking any chances with this one.

He stepped out of his office to update JG.

'Mr Lapuente rang from Anacleto,' she said. 'They're anxious to know what the Board decided about the contract.'

'Tell him they want a couple of days to reflect. I'll call him first thing Wednesday. And schedule that in for us, would you?'

He was flying to Lisbon anyway on Thursday to finalise the deal and a briefing the day before was all they needed. Anacleto's accountants had had months to devise the original terms, he didn't want them picking over his return offer and turning it to their advantage. By the time they met on Thursday they'd be keen to close the deal and run it by their lawyers on Friday morning so they could all sign before the weekend.

After lunch he was in a meeting with his finance team when JG put her head round the door. 'Sorry, Tommy: Mr Hartman's here.'

It was the kind of thing that really annoyed him. Only Hartman would show up without an appointment and expect to find Lister's MD sitting in his office with time to spare.

'Get him a coffee,' he said to JG. 'I'll be half an hour.'

He ignored the looks between the finance guys; they'd been on the point of finishing the meeting. Tommy didn't care, he suspected everyone at Lister's knew how things stood between him and the Board.

'I suggest we go ahead and look at the audit timetable while we're all here,' he said.

When he returned to his office he found Hartman sitting at the round table by the window flicking through the latest trade journals. He looked up as Tommy came in. 'You should be aware that Penelope's very concerned about this business with the takeover, Tommy. It's not good. You've exposed the company to a potential legal situation and, quite apart from that, and whatever the outcome . . . we are taking advice . . . the fact is: you acted unilaterally and that's a matter of concern for your fellow directors. So I thought you ought to know that.' He got up then: 'Well, I don't think there's anything more to say at this stage.'

Tommy opened the door for him, furious. In the outer office JG half rose from her desk as if to accompany Hartman to reception but Tommy caught her eye and shook his head slightly and she stayed where she was.

'He found his own way in,' he said as the door to the corridor closed behind the Chairman. 'And make sure

Andy Lister signs that addendum, will you. I want it on file before we finalise the contract on Friday.'

In between it all his dad's funeral came and went like the inevitability that it was.

Tommy stood in the Garden Room at the hotel where Doreen worked and watched her preside over the reception in her new black suit and glittering brooch. It was an old fashioned place, all creaking floorboards and faded chintz. Behind him the sunlight fell through leaded panes into a room that must have hosted decades worth of family weddings, christenings and funerals.

He felt utterly detached from it all: the sight of the coffin, the traditional hymns, his brothers grim-faced around him and yet none of it seemed connected to his dad.

As he sipped his sherry he kept an eye on the antique clock in the corner, trying to estimate when he could acceptably leave and get on with his week, his trip to Lisbon on Thursday.

He flew out first thing in the morning and took Jayne Gardiner with him. Hartman would have raised his eyebrows at that but she deserved the trip. Anacleto was a key relationship she'd done a lot to maintain over the years.

The factory was north of Lisbon, in Aveiro, but for the purposes of renewing the contract they were meeting in the capital at the auditors' offices. It was more convenient for flights and Anacleto's Chairman, Fabio Oliveira, liked a visit to the city to meet his friends and business contacts.

It was just before ten as they began their descent over the wide sweep of the bay with the straight lines of the harbour beneath them and breathtaking views of the suspension bridge.

Oliveira was at the airport to meet them and as they drove into the city in his Mercedes a seaside breeze was rippling the palm trees and the sun shone on the grey cobbles of the older narrow streets. They made their way past ornate apartment blocks with wrought iron balconies to the auditors' offices in Duque de Palmela.

It was the one modern building on a traditional square with parking bays at the centre full of cars and motorcyles. Oliveira pulled sharp right past them and the car dipped down a steep slope beneath plate glass windows and into an underground car park.

Once inside they got straight down to business. Tommy talked through his proposed terms and fielded a host of questions and by lunchtime Anacleto's MD, Senhor Lapuente, had heard enough.

'Com permissão, Tommy,' he said. 'The team here needs some time, I think, to discuss your proposal. While you and Senhor Oliveira can take a break together.'

It was the usual format. The Chairman would take him out for an extended lunch while Lapuente and his senior managers talked through scenarios and the implications of the deal.

Lapuente's PA, Adriana, was taking JG out shopping and Oliveira dropped them off en route at a cervejaria in an old convent, a fashionable place for a light lunch close to the Baixa.

The Chairman's tastes were more ornate: an exclusive restaurant in an old palazzo. The dining room heavily decorated in gold and white with a vaulted ceiling, chandeliers and mirrors. The tables were covered with thick white cloths and the waiters wore white jackets. There were no waitresses, Tommy noticed. He'd been here before. Oliveira liked its after-dinner cigars and smoking room.

Before the menus had even been brought, Oliveira ordered Codorníu, a sparkling rosado cava, and raised his glass. 'More than twenty five years of profitable business. Quite a track record!'

Tommy smiled and raised his own glass. He liked Oliveira, the man had a genuine warmth. He was elegant too, with his silver hair swept back, swathes of it still dark, as were his eyebrows and the traces of a moustache, two halves closely trimmed above his upper lip. He wore a large signet ring on his little finger and a tie pin with a curious lumpy stone that had the lustre of a pearl.

'It is a barroco,' he'd said the first time Tommy remarked on it. 'An irregular pearl. The origin of the term Baroque. Misshapen. Grotesque. And yet still beautiful.'

To Tommy it epitomised Oliveira: expensive and high class with more than a touch of the exotic.

His family had been *retornados*, among the thousands who'd returned destitute from the overseas provinces in the wake of Portugal's Colonial War.

Fabio Oliveira had spent his childhood roaming the coffee plantations of Cazengo until Angola's independence had crumbled into civil war and the family had headed back to Portugal with all the capital they could muster and bought a share in their cousins' footwear company.

The waiter had brought the menus. Tommy ordered bacalao to start, with tomatoes and peppers, and chanfana to follow, a slow-roasted lamb dish.

'And, what shall we have . . . a Douro . . . . Reserva?' Oliveira looked enquiringly at Tommy. 'Yes, a Quinta do Crasto. 2000.' He handed the wine list back to the waiter.

The bottle was still a third full by the time they'd finished eating and Oliveira had noted it.

'Business and pleasure,' he commented. 'For you, I think, they are quite separate.'

'Just different kinds of pleasure,' said Tommy. 'For different occasions.'

Business and drinking never mixed in his view, not unless the other guy was doing all the drinking.

They moved on to delicate rice puddings streaked with cinnamon and then went through to the leather armchairs for coffee, brandy and cigars.

Fabio Oliveira leaned back comfortably and swirled the cognac in his glass. 'You know, it is a surprise to me that you never bring your Chairman to Lisbon,' he said. 'After all our years of partnership. I should like to be his host here. Aveiro, I know is too provincial. But Lisbon,' he leaned forward almost conspiratorially, 'Why don't you bring him?'

Tommy smiled but said nothing, just inclined his head slightly, a hint of acceptance, as he thought of Hartman and his dismissive views on Portuguese imports.

He's not worthy of you.

Back in the foyer of the office his mobile bleeped. He'd switched it off during the morning's meeting and through lunch but turned it on momentarily to check for messages while Oliveira went ahead of him into the meeting room to assess the state of play.

A series of missed calls from Andy Lister flashed up on the screen and there was an urgent voicemail from him too.

'Tommy, we need to talk! I've been trying to reach you all morning and Jayne Gardiner's not in the office. Hartman's been on the phone about this business with Leys and, it's not just the takeover. The thing is, Tommy, they think you're more interested in Anacleto than you are in Lister's. Everyone knows you've done a great job turning the company around. But Leys and Hartman . . . well now, we're finally in a position to boost the brand with the Americans and . . . frankly . . . they think your heart's not in it. That you're not the best man for the job any more.'

Tommy stood listening to Andy's voice and heard everything: the line of argument that smacked of Hartman and the urgency that was Andy's, which meant he thought Hartman was serious.

Andy Lister, desperate to get hold of him, before he signed the deal with Anacleto, because Andy was the only one of them with the sense to see that if Lister's was thinking of getting rid of Tommy, they couldn't afford to sign up to an ambitious new contract with Anacleto.

Nothing was certain though.

He looked down for a moment at the LED screen, deleted the message and clicked the phone off just as Senhor Lapuente, full of smiles, emerged from the meeting room. 'Tommy!' he extended a hand.

With a single stride, Tommy stepped forward to meet him and shook his hand warmly. 'I take it we have a deal.'

In the meeting room Oliveira had a bottle of champagne at the ready and Adriana stood beside him with a tray of glasses. Tommy shook hands all round and made his way over to JG. She was smiling and he thought it must have been a good lunch, judging by the pile of shopping bags in the corner.

'Ask Adriana to book me into a hotel for the night, would you?' he said. 'I'll stay on and sign the contract here tomorrow. Save us messing around with Fedex.'

29

EXPENDABLE

Tommy flew home on Friday evening from an airport crowded with commuters and long-weekenders heading for the Algarve. Switching his mobile on briefly in the departure lounge, he found a single text from JG who'd flown home the night before: *Andy Lister anxious to talk.* He knew. She'd left a message earlier on Adriana's landline: 'Have Tommy call me, would you?'

His flight arrived at Luton just after seven thirty and he'd been home for a good half hour when Andy called: a single call, well timed. He'd obviously asked JG when the flight got in and estimated from that. His successful timing had done nothing for his temper though.

'You're a bloody maverick, Tommy. I've been trying to get hold of you for the last two days! Please tell me you haven't gone ahead and signed that deal.'

'The deal the Board authorised me to sign?'

'Like I said in my message. Things have changed. The Board don't think you're necessarily the best person to take Lister's to the next level.'

'Oh come on, Andy. You may not have been around that long but I've certainly been here before.'

'It's different this time. Hartman's talking about not renewing your contract at year-end.'

'And who else does he think is going to run Lister's?'

Silence.

'I can promise you, Andy, there isn't anyone else. I'm in all the retail and footwear networks. Even if there were people out there who'd be up to the job, they wouldn't see Lister's as their next big career move.'

'Things have changed,' Andy repeated. 'You should have returned my calls.'

Tommy put the phone down and dismissed the conversation from his mind. There wasn't anyone externally who'd be interested in running Lister's and internally the operation was too divided. Jim McKenna was a great salesman for bespoke but knew nothing at all about the distribution side of the business and Tim Salter, his Head of Operations, was an excellent general manager for Anacleto's but had no idea about sales and marketing.

It was something and nothing: Leys stirring up trouble as usual, trying to set the rest of the Board against him, and Hartman, for once, seemed to have got sucked in. Even so, it'd come to nothing.

The claim that he'd acted ultra vires had no basis. JG had established that before he even went to Lisbon. Without even asking him, she'd called a solicitor on his behalf.

'You acted in good faith,' she paraphrased, handing him her notes from the conversation. 'In what you believed were the best interests of the company. It's not as though you did anything reckless or dishonest.'

As for building Lister's brand, he was doing his level best given all the ground they'd lost in the post-war years.

He made a mental note to dig out the file on Tokanaga, the Japanese investor he'd met in Milan, to see what potential there was for growth in the far eastern markets. That ought to get the Board off his back.

It was a good weekend. The beginning of April and after months of grey days everything was suddenly colourful beneath a blue sky, the trees white with blossom or already in green leaf. Even the bare fields on the distant horizon shone a warm tone of brown in the sunshine.

It was the time of year when Bryony picked up some freelance PR work from old family contacts and on Saturday the two of them went out for lunch with one of her clients: a budding young equestrian for whom she was trying to get sponsorship from local companies. The family lived closed to Deene Park, historic home of the Brudenells of Lord Cardigan fame and the parents were semi-retired with investments in France, 'property development, holiday lets, that kind of thing.'

It transpired that Bryony had brought Esther along to an appointment with them earlier in the week.

'Did she enjoy it?' Tommy asked in the car on the way home.

'Oh heavens, no! I don't think she enjoys anything much. I just didn't want to leave her on her own all day.'

They'd left her that Saturday, though, up in her room, just lying on her bed staring at the ceiling, Tommy suspected. It was all she seemed to do.

Still, she'd be gone soon. Bryony had heard from Doreen who'd been to see the solicitor dealing with his dad's will and reported as much to Tommy.

'Everything's in hand apparently. Probate shouldn't take more than a couple of months and in the meantime he doesn't see why Esther shouldn't move into Hartley

Rise. Obviously she won't get the deeds until it's all finalised but the will's in place and everything's clear.'

'Is that what she wants?' Tommy had asked.

'I think so.'

Good luck to her then!

When he got back into the office on Monday morning, Hartman rang. 'I know in theory the Board signed off on the Business Plan but on reflection we'd like a rethink on one or two areas.'

'We?'

'Your fellow Directors, Tommy. We feel the plan's not ambitious enough around the American market.'

'Robert, I gave you a thorough analysis at the Board meeting and in the supporting papers. And the Board approved the plan. There's no 'in theory' about it.'

'Yes, well in the light of subsequent events . . .'

'What events?'

Had they called Dubrowski behind his back?

'I am the Chairman of this company, Tommy.'

'And I'm the Managing Director.'

'There's clearly potential in the market that you're not prepared to explore. If there wasn't time to discuss it fully at the Board meeting it's because you cut the call with Dubrowski short.'

'It was way over the scheduled time and adding no value.'

'Well, if you're not prepared to take their market analysis seriously . . .' said Hartman.

'There is no market analysis,' fumed Tommy. 'It's sheer unfounded optimism!'

'Please review the plan,' said Hartman smoothly. 'And let's talk again in a week. Next Tuesday.'

It wouldn't take a week. Tommy spent all afternoon and the following morning going through his original assumptions, downloading the latest report from an online analyst he subscribed to and updating his competitor files. None of the long-standing British manufacturers was seeing the kind of growth Dubrowski was predicting, even with thirty years of sustained investment behind them.

By Wednesday he was impatient to resolve things and called Hartman at home late morning. Mrs Hartman answered. 'Oh, Tommy, yes. But I'm afraid Robert's in America.'

He frowned. 'Rockford?' It was the town in Illinois where Dubrowski was based.

'No,' said Mrs Hartman. 'They're meeting in West Virginia to fit in with Daniel Roper. Shall I ask Robert to ring you? He'll be back at the weekend.'

'No,' said Tommy. 'Thank you.'

He put the phone down and sat dumbfounded.

JG put her head round the door of his office. 'Everything all right? You look odd.'

'Know anything about a Daniel Roper?' he asked. 'Some connection with Dubrowski?'

She shook her head.

'Have a look through the files, would you? Anything at all.'

He went online but after forty five minutes of searching he'd found no reference at all to a Daniel Roper with a potential connection to the footwear industry or Dubrowski.

He went about subscribing to a couple of US footwear journals and began trawling through their archives, until finally he found what he was looking for in a five-year old edition of one of the weeklies.

"With a Bachelor's degree in Business Administration from California State University and his sights on Stanford's Sloan Masters Program, Dan Roper cuts an innovative dash in the traditional heartland of America's top-end footwear industry.

Roper joined his own family's retail business straight out of CSU back in '92, transforming their traditional trek and trail stores into the west coast's leading outdoor footwear outlet with a focus of their initial multi-range offering down to nothing more nor less than the newest and best quality footwear for outdoor pursuits. By '94 Red Creek Traders had assembled the most comprehensive range of high quality boots and trail shoes on the market: a combination of known brands with the best and most innovative of the rubber-soled products from Asia. Add to that a reputation for unparalleled service and a Northridge appreciation for virtual opportunities and it's no surprise that Red Creek had emerged as one of the most profitable retail businesses in the sector by the end of the decade.

Now Roper's bringing his sales agility to bear in the heavy-weight world of wholesale and distribution. Head hunted by Rich Dubrowski back in '98, Roper's clearly learned a thing or two about supply chain and federal distribution without losing his edge on segmentation and alternative routes to market. This week Dubrowski unveils plans for an integrated online facility that will unite its top ten retailers in a single rewards program and offer the company's upwardly mobile consumer base all the top quality brands with the added benefits of competitive pricing and the best in service delivery.

Watch this space for more on Daniel J Roper destined no doubt for the Fedra shortlist and industry halls of fame."

Tommy scoured his memory for any trace of Roper on his visits to the US. He had no recollection of him at all but then perhaps Roper had moved on from the distributor, gone off to do his Masters degree. Besides, Dubrowski always monopolised Tommy when he visited.

It looked as though he'd set Hartman up to interview Roper, though.

Tommy picked the phone up and rang Andy Lister.

'What's going on with Daniel Roper?' he demanded as soon as Andy answered.

'I'm not in a position to comment.'

'You better had comment. Hartman's out there interviewing him for Lister's, isn't he?'

'Look, Tommy, I warned you what's in the offing.'

'And you're worried if Roper takes over he won't be able to deliver on the terms of the Anacleto deal, right?'

'I certainly don't think it's a good time to be committing to something quite as ambitious as those targets, no.'

'Well you'd damn well better start backing me to the rest of the Board, then.'

'It's not as simple as that. I have a minority share in this company, remember.'

'Not if you're voting with me you don't.'

Things had progressed far more seriously than he'd realised. If he was due to speak to Hartman next Tuesday, he'd better have something concrete to offer, something substantial to compete with the growth Dubrowski was promising.

Tommy went back to the file on Tokanaga and the figures Jim McKenna had provided on existing Japanese sales. Tokanaga had talked with enthusiasm of South East Asia's growing economies and emerging middle class and was looking to fund retail outlets in Kyoto, a fashionable international summit venue and home to Nintendo. Naha was also high on his agenda, the commercial capital of Okinawa, and he had plans to open exclusive boutiques on Japanese cruise liners, another expanding market.

Tommy sat looking through the market intelligence report he'd commissioned. It showed an increase in foreign companies entering Japan's retail industry and a significant rise in profits among the country's leading department stores. He scanned the competitor analysis and industry comment but it wasn't enough. If he was to come up with a winning plan to build Lister's brand, he needed primary research: something first-hand, convincing and irrevocably linked to a relationship of his own making.

There was no time to commission what he needed by Tuesday and he was in no position to make a trip to Japan himself. If he absented himself from the office now he'd be even more out of touch with whatever Hartman was cooking up behind his back.

He sat back and thought about it. Jim McKenna could go. McKenna was seasoned in shop floor retail, he could get alongside Lister's existing buyers in Tokyo and sound them out about Tokanaga's proposals. He'd seen enough of the technical side of shoe-making too and could make a preliminary assessment of Tokanaga's initial designs for a lower-cost hand-made shoe aimed exclusively at the far-eastern consumer.

He rang McKenna's mobile and caught him in the middle of a busy London street en route to a sales call.

'I need to talk to you,' said Tommy. 'Face-to-face and preferably today. I'll come to you. Wherever works best.'

They met that evening at the Edwardian Berkshire off Oxford Street.

Tommy sat silent while the waiter set their drinks out on the low coffee table then handed the print-out of Roper's profile to McKenna. 'Fancy working for this guy?'

McKenna stirred his gin and tonic, a long double, and sipped it while he read the report, then handed the paper back to Tommy without comment, obviously aware it was a loaded question.

'Hartman's over in the US interviewing him as we speak,' said Tommy. 'The Board thinks I'm not doing enough to promote hand-made sales.'

'He took the folder on Tokanaga out of his briefcase and gave it to McKenna. 'It's a lot to ask, I know. Busy time of year. But I need you out there fast.'

McKenna would do it too. He was a lone operator, no significant other, besides which, he loved Lister's and was grateful to Tommy for giving him an alternative to west-end shop hours.

'I need you to find out what the stockists think,' said Tommy. 'And what Tokanaga's not telling us. I'll arrange for you to meet him in Kyoto. Get sight of any research he's got. Everything he knows about those markets. And get a sense of the place for yourself as well: how the retail looks. Then make sure you get time with our Tokyo guys again on the way out, even if it's only a phone call from the hotel.'

'So, flying out when?' said McKenna.

'Saturday,' said Tommy. 'And back Wednesday. If you're up for it. I'll get JG to reschedule your appointments here. It's not ideal, I know, but she'll make it work somehow. Ring me from the hotel Tuesday night with the lowdown. That'll be Tuesday morning over here. In time for me to present something to Hartman.'

McKenna asked a few more questions, finished his drink and left.

It took no more than a couple of hours to set up the arrangements for McKenna's visit. The Tokyo stockists were polite and accommodating as always, Tokanaga delighted at the prospect of a visit from Lister's Brand Manager.

After that the rest of the week dragged for Tommy. He should have been reviewing production schedules for Spring 07 and going through the latest made-to-order designs but he wasn't in the mood. He stood instead at the window of his office looking out at the car park that stretched alongside the building and brooding over Hartman's meeting with Daniel J Roper.

'Even if it's an interview,' said JG, bringing him a cup of coffee. 'It doesn't mean Hartman will like what he sees. Or that Roper will want to come. Would you swap California for Wellingborough?'

Tommy wasn't convinced. He was restless all weekend. Bryony was going over to his dad's place to finish cleaning and sorting out the personal effects and wanted him to come; the family had agreed they'd each choose something personal they wanted to keep, but he pleaded errands of his own.

'You choose for me,' he said and spent most of Saturday sitting in his study doing nothing productive, aware, at the back of his mind, of Esther, upstairs, doing much the same. A thought that annoyed him.

She came with them, though, on Sunday to see Elisabeth's new flat in Alcester where they'd been invited for Sunday lunch. To Tommy she seemed like a pale shadow: sitting behind him in the car, trailing after him on their walk through the old town, like a sad reflection of his own vibrant children.

On Monday he couldn't settle to anything for wondering how things were going with McKenna in Tokyo.

In the end he went out to walk the floor.

They took little notice of him in the Lister's rooms, the highly skilled workforce labouring side-by-side but often in a solitary fashion, each focused on their own processes, surrounded by heavy machinery and piles of work.

On the first floor he lingered for a while in the quiet environment of the design room and then moved on through the skins room with its metal racks stacked high with rolls of calfskin, into the clicking room where men in aprons worked alone in the midst of long metal benches with bright lights overhead. All around was the constant noise of mechanical cutters and occasional snatches of a radio playing in the background.

He made his way between plastic bins full of leather shapes, sixteen or so per brogue, hand-cut and bundled together with elastic bands then down to the closing room where women sat at big grey sewing machines, three or four deep across the room. They were hard at it, production schedules tight, and trolleys everywhere with crates full of leather bundles and blue and pink work ticket marked 'URGENT and 'VERY URGENT.

Tommy stood for a while and watched them, expert hands moving the leather swiftly around as the machines operated, single stitching, double stitching, stopping and starting, all of them working to diagrams they could interpret without a single error.

He followed each of the different processes, trying to identify the designs he knew best from their characteristic stitching and decorative medallions.

The way back to his office lay through the finishing room, another male preserve and the most like a factory floor, it was noisy and full of big machines, some with spinning wheels, and smelt of a shoe-mender's, a mixture of adhesive, rubber and oil. Again the men worked apart here, surrounded by racks of leather shoes, each with a yellow plastic last inside.

It was therapeutic, a taste at least of pressure and activity when he himself felt caught like a sailing boat in a deadly calm.

After lunch he got up, meaning to walk round again, but JG stopped him at the door. 'Don't! They'll scent trouble.'

She was right. Besides, he'd never really been welcome in the rooms except as someone passing through and to be treated with respect. It was an unwritten agreement: they left him to his spreadsheets and his sales targets and he left them to their craftsmanship.

On Tuesday morning he was sitting at his desk by seven thirty waiting for McKenna, even though Jim wasn't scheduled to call until at least nine.

When he did ring it wasn't good news.

'The analysis is right in that the main department stores are growing,' he told Tommy. 'But basically it's the big stores expanding and restructuring while a whole lot of others are closing. There's been a shake-up, that's all. Sales are growing in volume but not value. So pricing's of the essence. Which is bad news for Lister's. We'd have to be really competitive to see any kind of cut-through.'

'What about Tokanaga's new outlets?'

'He's going into Naha: Shintoshin, the smart new commercial district, but it's all fashion boutiques, western brands for the youngsters. Kyoto's got glossy new retail developments too but it's traditional crafts aimed at tourists. So, overall, yes, there's retail expansion but nothing to suggest a major opportunity for British hand-made shoes.'

'And the cruise liners?'

'Cruise lines are on the up. Japanese passengers at around 160,000 a year with money to spend and plenty of time to spend it. But it's a global market. The Caribbean routes are saturated, everyone's looking east and there's significant investment coming in from outside, which means North American and European passengers with western tastes in footwear and high expectations of the Lister's brand.'

'And the designs he's proposing will devalue that?'

'Absolutely. He wants a two-tone loafer in beige and brown. A cream or two-tone Derby. All well and good for the east. But to meet the cost price he's asking you'd be looking at dropping from full grain to top grain skins, hopefully retaining the leather insole but only a half leather lining. Even if the eastern markets were utterly self-contained it'd still be a drop too far in terms of quality. Disastrous in a global market. I'm sorry, Tommy. But it's a no-go on every front.'

There was no arguing with it. By a quarter to ten he was agitated, impatient to talk to Hartman. He couldn't make a case for building the brand in the Far East but he'd challenge Hartman all the same. Think on his feet. That was his forte. Anyway, as JG had said, Roper in the flesh might not have been all that Hartman had in mind.

He asked her to get the Chairman on the line. 'Tell him I want to bring the call forward.'

She returned within minutes. 'He's happy to bring it forward. But he wants face-to-face. He's coming in and he's bringing Andy Lister.'

They arrived at eleven, Lister looking on edge and Hartman still dark-eyed from his transatlantic crossing.

It took them less than ten minutes, sitting at the table by the window in Tommy's office, to serve him 21 day's notice of an Extraordinary General Meeting with a single resolution on the agenda, his removal from the Board, followed by the offer of a compromise agreement: his resignation with immediate effect in return for a generous price on the compulsory purchase of his shares and nine months' salary; three times the period outstanding on his contract. There were the usual clauses restricting his right to set himself up in direct competition within a defined period and he had 15 days in which to sign and return it.

'That's everything, I think,' said Hartman. 'In view of the circumstances we'd obviously like you to take extended leave. You'll need time to review your options.'

'So you like the look of this Daniel Roper, then?' said Tommy still sitting though Hartman had got to his feet. 'You're making a mistake, Robert. He'll need more than a knack for internet sales to run an operation like Lister's. Never mind achieve the kind of market growth you're looking for.'

Hartman said nothing.

Tommy turned to Lister. 'Think about it, Andy! You're an accountant. You were prudent enough when I was pushing for revised terms on Anacleto. Are you really going to be wowed now by a set of half-baked projections?'

Andy just frowned down at the table.

'Your fellow directors are of one mind in calling an EGM, Tommy,' said Hartman. 'That's the time and place to make a case, if you feel you're got one.'

'We're not even matching the other British brands in the American market,' insisted Tommy. 'Roper's track record in sales growth was based on multiple brands. And half of those were innovative rubber-based products from Asia.'

He could feel his blood pressure rising as he spoke but Andy Lister had got to his feet as well now. Both he and Hartman were standing there looking down at him and Tommy realised, with sudden humiliation, that they were actually standing there waiting to escort him out of his own office.

Stunned, he collected a few personal items from his desk and went ahead of them to the door where JG had got up from her computer and stood tongue-tied at his departure.

30

FABIO OLIVEIRA

At home Tommy went into his study and shut the door, conscious of Esther upstairs, then sat down to ring Bryony who was over in Northampton catching up with her local press contacts.

'Trouble?' she asked.

'Hartman and Lister. They've effectively sacked me. Three weeks' notice to fight it out at an EGM or they'll pay me to go quietly within fifteen days.'

'You'd better ring Theo!'

Theo Laine was an out-of-town legal friend who went way back, a specialist in employment law and industrial relations who'd advised Tommy in his early days at Lister's, the days of redundancies and rationalisation.

Theo was old-school, a dour Presbyterian with a face like a glacial loch and a manner to match. He had an unparalleled reputation for mediation, though; a reputation that had bought him a well appointed family home in an exclusive Hertfordshire village and membership of the golf club at Denham.

Tommy met him the following afternoon in the sixteenth century clubhouse beneath the stags' heads that lined the brick dining room. Theo's advice, over the lunchtime grill and a bottle of Marsannay, was brief and to the point.

'Take the money and run! A resolution like that's cut and dried. If you can't win it in the board room, you can't win.'

Tommy wouldn't go without a fight, though. He just needed Andy Lister to back him, phoned the accountant first thing the next morning.

'Andy, we need to talk. You have to support me at the EGM. You know as well as I do, there's no substance to Dubrowski's forecasts. And however good this guy Roper is, he's not going to deliver that kind of growth.'

'I'm really not in a position to discuss this, Tommy.'

'You're in every position to discuss it. You're a director of the company.'

'Well then let's say I don't want to discuss it. At least, not right now. I'm about to go into a meeting.'

The line went dead.

He thought about ringing Jim McKenna. Jim had called him within an hour or so of Tommy leaving the office on Tuesday, no doubt tipped off by JG. But there'd been little he could say then and it wouldn't be any different now. It was Lister he needed.

He searched again through the latest online reports and market analysis on the US and far eastern footwear industries but found nothing new to add to his case.

Meanwhile the Easter weekend stretched frustratingly ahead of him. The next day was Good Friday and he spent most of it sitting in his study, mulling over his prospects for the EGM until Bryony came looking for him.

'How about doing something constructive?'

She had a project for him: choosing the menus and wine for a fundraising dinner she was planning for Diana, the young equestrian, but even that only whiled away a couple of hours.

On Saturday they were due at a Rotarians' barbecue, the first of the season that some optimist organised every year. It was at a former president's house, beside the swimming pool with patio heaters to take the April chill off things and a marquee in case it rained.

He rang Andy twice before they set off, left messages on his voicemail and decided that if he hadn't heard back by the evening he'd drive over to Northampton and catch him at home.

In the meantime he and Bryony went to the barbecue early to help set up, arranging bowls of salad and bottles of wine on a long trestle table.

The weather was almost warm enough. He hung around drinking Chardonnay and listening to the usual tales of parental angst: unsuitable boyfriends, offspring dropping out of college and revelations of unimagined debts.

One of the group had just come back from a long break in Florida and talked at length about property prices over there and waterfront apartments going for a song.

'You're over in the States a fair bit, Tommy. You should think about it.'

'Too far south,' said Tommy. 'My trips are all Midwest.'

'It's about now you usually go out there, isn't it?' said one of the others.

Tommy shrugged noncommittally but now, as he stood there, the cold wine set his teeth on edge, it was exactly what he should have been doing at this time of the year: planning his annual visit to the American stockists, squeezing it in between the strategy sessions for Anacleto's promotional spend, meetings with the PR and creative agencies and blue-sky thinking with his buyers to dream up Lister's next bold move in the volume market. Instead of which he was cast adrift, stranded while he waited for the likes of Andy Lister to see sense.

It was intolerable!

He stepped away from the group and headed for the table as if going to top-up his drink but dumped his wine glass and, carrying on towards the stretch of lawn behind the marquee, he took his mobile phone out and rang Lister again.

The call went straight to voicemail and when he tried Lister's home number there was no answer.

Frustrated, he scrolled down his contacts list to Hartman and hit the call button, rehearsing what he'd say while the numbers dialled: *I want a full and frank discussion. You owe me that at least.*

Hartman's phone just rang and rang.

Over by the swimming pool there was laughter and clapping; a surprise cake had been brought out for someone's birthday and, looking across, he saw Bryony giving him the evil eye. Tommy pocketed the phone and went to join her. 'Sorry!'

Around six o'clock he dropped Bryony home and drove over to Andy Lister's house but the place was clearly empty. No lights shone in the dusk, the curtains were open at every window and there were no cars on the drive. He wondered if they'd gone away for the week. It was the school holidays and Lister had a couple of kids. He hadn't said anything about it at the Board, though, and JG usually kept a record of when the directors were away.

He slept badly and on Sunday morning drafted a long email to Fabio Oliveira, with Roper's profile attached, then phoned the Portuguese Chairman to discuss it.

Voicemail again: a long message in Fabio's warm tones. Tommy picked out a few words: 'desculpas . . . somos de férias . . . Braga'. It sounded as though Oliveira was away for Easter too.

He left a short message asking Fabio to call him and spent the rest of the day trying to keep the lid on his frustration; they were driving down to Kingston to see Chris and his girlfriend. At least this time he was spared Esther's company. She'd come home from a trip to town in the week and announced she'd taken a job at The Mail Room, a basement bar in the dilapidated building that had once been part of Wellingborough's main post office.

'Couldn't she have found somewhere a bit more salubrious?' Tommy had asked Bryony on the quiet but Esther liked it apparently: 'a good craic'.

Chris had cooked an elaborate lunch with Moroccan tagine and afterwards they walked in Richmond Park. Tommy was agitated, wondering when Fabio might call and fiddling with the mobile phone in his pocket as he strode ahead through the tufts of spring grass and baby nettles while Bryony brought up the rear with the others and kept the conversation going.

'Is this going to go on for some time?' she asked as they sped home along the M40, his preferred route before cutting north east through Aylesbury and Buckingham.

'It's just that it's Easter,' he said. 'And I can't get hold of anyone.'

She put a hand on his arm. 'Patience, then.'

He managed a smile.

Patience was one thing. This was sheer provocation.

The following day, bank holiday Monday, he cleared his study out, shredding old bills and filling the car with bags of rubbish to take to the household tip then, at five o'clock, Oliveira rang.

'Tommy! I am sorry to be out of contact. Semana Santa. We have historic processions, you know, in Braga.'

'Did you read my email?'

'This must be some kind of joke, yes? To appoint an American who knows nothing of Europe or our business. But we have commitments to one another. We have a contract. Don't worry. I will ring your chairman. This cannot go ahead.'

He must have rung Hartman soon afterwards because first thing the next morning Tommy had a call from JG.

'Mr Hartman's asked me to remind you that you're on leave from Lister's and that you had no business ringing Fabio Oliveira.'

'Is Hartman there?' asked Tommy.

'Yes. He's sitting at the desk in your office.'

'Put me through then.'

'I'm afraid he's not taking any calls.'

'Okay. I'll come down there.'

'He won't see you, Tommy. They're having a pow-wow this afternoon. The contract for Roper's all ready to go.'

'What about Andy Lister? Is he on holiday?'

'No. We're expecting him at two. As far as I know he's at his office in Northampton this morning.'

'Thanks!'

Tommy got in his car and drove over to the accountancy firm where Lister worked.

'I'm sorry,' said the receptionist. 'Andy's got a client with him all morning.'

'Tell him I'll wait.'

Lister came down about ten minutes later and showed him into a meeting room on the ground floor. 'This has to stop, Tommy! Everything I have to say is in the compromise agreement.'

'What about what I have to say? I talked to Fabio Oliveira yesterday.'

'Yes, I'm aware of that.'

'Well then you'll know how he feels about what's happening. We just signed the most ambitious deal we've ever had with them. He wants to know our end of it's in the hands of someone with the experience to deliver. Look, we're not in the days of foreign quotas anymore. Just because Fabio's old fashioned and likes to use a distributor, it doesn't mean he couldn't cut out the middle man if he wanted to.'

Lister stood silent at that, chewing his lip.

'This is serious, Andy,' urged Tommy. 'Okay, so you can't talk now. Fine! But don't leave it to the EGM. I need to know I can count on your support before we come to that.'

He left the office and walked back to his car. He'd ring Lister again in a couple of days. Give it time to sink in. Andy was naturally cautious, he'd taken a lot of convincing about the Anacleto deal and panicked when he thought Tommy might not be around to see it through. Once the reality of the situation hit him, he'd be more amenable to taking a stand against Hartman.

The weekend had been horrendous, though. He needed to get some order back into his life. The next couple of days he made a point of sitting down first thing to look at the financial markets and news online and, when he'd stretched that out as long as he could, filled his afternoons with errands, seeing his accountant and pension adviser and ringing old business contacts.

When Thursday came he planned to ring Andy Lister in the late afternoon but at lunchtime Fabio Oliveira rang him from Portugal.

'You should know, Tommy, that your Mr Lister has been here today. With Daniel Roper.'

What?

'This morning, Tommy. What could I do? They gave me no notice. Simply arrived.'

Tommy gripped the phone: 'What did they want?'

'To introduce Mr Roper. Show him the workshops. All very charming. He talks of a new sales strategy to support the contract. An online catalogue. You know, Tommy, your Mr Lister, tells me this is an opportunity that was already being considered at your Board meeting back in March. Before we even signed the deal.'

'That's simply not true, Fabio.'

'Well, I believe you. But, their minds are made up. That is clear. I don't know what else I can do.'

Bryony was in the dining room working on a press article about Diana's hopes for the forthcoming show-jumping championships at the South of England Show.

Tommy chilled a couple of glasses in the refrigerator, mixed gin and vermouth over ice, twisted a slice of lemon in and took the drinks through to join her.

She put her pen down and sat back to look at him as he set the two glasses down.

'That devious little swine, Andy Lister, is out in Aveiro giving Roper the tour of Anacleto,' said Tommy as he sat down. He savoured a mouthful of ice-cold martini. 'Well, he listened. I'll give him that. He certainly listened to what I told him.'

'He's not going to back you at the EGM?'

Tommy shook his head and drank again.

'You know,' said Bryony. 'Even if he had, wouldn't that just have made the votes even? Doesn't the chairman still have the deciding vote?'

'Yes, but Hartman wouldn't want to split the Board,' said Tommy. 'I was relying on him to see sense if Lister backed me.'

'Take the pay-off,' said Bryony. 'You could do anything. You don't need Lister's!'

Tommy sighed and sat back, looking at her notepad and papers scattered across the polished veneer of the table, at the line of chairs opposite and the windows behind them, white with the glare of the sun.

He thought of Lister's walnut board table, of Hartman, Penelope Leys and old David Lister sitting around it the day they'd formally appointed him. Hartman and Lister who'd come cap-in-hand, uninvited down the drive to this very house, with their tale of woe about the mess at Lister's. Hartman, with his pompous bloody attitude, sitting now at his, Tommy's own desk, in the MD's office at Dennington Road, ordering JG to ring and warn him off talking to Oliveira.

He took another sip of the icy spirits. 'God!' he said. 'I can't stand to lose like this!'

31

LOSING

He had lost, though.

The next day the weather was fine. He abandoned his study, left the house and walked.

The River Nene ran south of the town and he followed its dusty tow path, through the sudden smell of damp meadows, away from the wooden benches and formal embankment and into the rough grassland of the angling club.

There were flooded gravel pits all around here, the blue water alive with ripples on every side and a series of grey metal footbridges with rails you could lean on to watch the black-headed geese and the swathes of grass stirring in the breeze.

He did lean and did watch but his mind was embroiled in angry scenarios, imagined conversations in which Hartman finally saw sense and interlinked fantasies building to a single conclusion: Lister's Board bitterly regretting its decision. Roper would fail, JG and all their best operatives would leave. The buyers, alienated, would contact Hartman: 'It's not working. Your American's no use to us.'

His phone would ring and he'd pick it up to hear Andy Lister, tentative: 'Tommy? Can we talk?'

'Fine by me,' he'd be coolly objective.

A blue and green train snaked its way through woodland towards Wellingborough station. Trees dominated the skyline here, bordering the fields rising to his right and screening the town on his left. The dark crenellated tower of St Mary's church with its handsome white lintels peeped through the greenery like a fairy castle.

Tommy walked on, dismissing his angry thoughts, but within minutes his mind was at it again.

He envisaged Oliveira, disgusted with the contract, pulling out of the distribution deal. Without the import sales Lister's would struggle financially and the American hopes would turn sour: growth, but nothing radical, incremental at best. When the company went into receivership the gossip would start: 'Shame about Lister's eh?' 'They never should have let Allbright go.' 'Didn't know a good thing when they had it.'

His heart pounded with resentment and the walking gave it rhythm but nothing could dissipate his nervous energy.

Still, it kept him out of the house, out of Bryony's way.

Andy Lister rang. 'I guess you know I took Roper to meet Oliveira. As you said, the situation needed stabilising. Anyway . . . '; swallowing hard. 'You must know by now, Tommy. I can't back you at the EGM.'

Tommy heard him out without comment.

Hartman rang and his tone was comfortable, all trace of antagonism gone, and that was the worst of all because it meant he knew he'd won and had nothing more to fear. 'Well now, Tommy. Any thoughts? About your future?'

They'd want him to sign the compromise and take the pay-off. To go quietly. A seamless transition, nothing to unsettle the buyers. The sooner the better so they could appoint Roper, issue the press releases, establish control.

'I'll let you know,' Tommy said shortly.

When he got tired of walking by the river there was always the town itself. He avoided the shops, though, not wanting anyone he knew to see him at a loose end.

Thirty odd years ago the area around the council offices had housed the zoopark. It had been the standard treat when he was a child, queuing on the steps of the big slide and watching the chimps' tea party.

Now it was all modern buildings, sloping lawns strewn with daisies and uncut circular patches of bluebells and dandelion clocks.

He followed the line of the Swanspool Brook, once a central feature of the zoopark but now obscured by weeds, the little ironstone bridge almost impassable. The grassy spaces stretched away from what had once been Croyland

Abbey, the estate farm of a much bigger monastery in medieval Lincolnshire.

In Croyland Park, with its willow trees, the brook was less overgrown and the tarmac path stretched on and on to the farthest edges of town. He could have walked practically all the way to Wilby.

At the weekend he'd found himself at odds with Richard.

The family had met for Sunday tea at Richard and Doreen's, all of them sitting shoulder to shoulder round the dining table. When they'd arrived, Tommy had thought his brother looked low in spirits and then there had been sharp words between husband and wife over Richard's plans to redecorate at Hartley Rise.

'I don't see why you should use up your annual leave,' Doreen had complained.

'It needs doing before Esther moves in,' said Richard.

'Do it at the weekends then! Or in the evenings.'

'I'm getting past that, Doreen!'

Esther hadn't been there, of course, off working in her basement bar but Richard had got all the stuff together, discussing the colour scheme with Maurice and showing the pots of lilac and yellow paint he'd bought.

When he went outside for his usual smoke, Tommy followed him.

Richard had gone to sit in his usual place behind the greenhouse.

'What's up?' Tommy leaned against the metal frame, hands in his pockets.

Richard drew on his cigarette: 'With me? Nothing! Our dad's died. Gina's gone. It's all just a barrel of laughs.'

Tommy nodded slowly.

'And you're distant,' said Richard. 'Nothing to say. Nowhere to be seen. Have you even been over to Dad's?' He was looking up at Tommy, accusingly. 'No, I thought not. Too busy cutting your next big deal!'

Now was the time to say something about Lister's but Tommy didn't, for reasons he couldn't even begin to work out.

'You ought to go over there,' Richard leaned back where he sat, face to the sun, and closed his eyes. 'Pay your respects at the very least.'

'It's a house!' said Tommy.

'It's our dad's house. Where we grew up.'

'It'll still be there.'

And Richard had just laughed softly at that and shaken his head, eyes still closed.

He never should have got Dubrowski on the phone at the Board meeting. That's where it had all gone wrong and he might have known it would. He'd tried to make him tone the sales projections down but, of course, the Board had latched straight onto them.

Dubrowski with his bushy grey hair, either side of a bald patch, and a moustache to match, bubbling with enthusiasm over the phone to Lister's Board.

'We just know we can hit those targets, gentlemen. Trust me: we're aiming high!'

His words echoed in Tommy's head along the quiet streets, the long lines of inter-war semis where he could walk unremarked, crossing between the parked cars that lined every kerb despite the spacious drives in front of every house. It was because of the new build, he supposed, executive flats crammed in all around, smart designs, appealing but for their miniature proportions, and every one adding half a dozen parked cars to the neighbourhood.

He passed a line of eight houses with matching gables and porches, occupying the space where once a terrace of three had stood, and now he'd reached the town centre again, was heading for the market that had been such familiar territory for him, but nothing here was as it had been.

Once the place had been full of stalls, their pitched tarpaulin roofs stretched across the Market Square in the shadow of the great Norman church, the tethering rings still visible in the churchyard wall from the days when this had also been a cattle market. People had been coming here to trade every week for eight hundred years.

The market had drawn him from early childhood. When his sister and brothers had been chalking hopscotch squares and squabbling in back alleys he'd hung around here doing odd jobs for an apple off the stall or an old ha'penny if he was lucky.

Greengrocers' stalls had been everywhere and everything fresh. He remembered the smell of it. Wooden crates of fruit and vegetables piled high, prices handwritten in marker pen, the big weighing scale like a quarter slice of dairylea. The market had been the preserve of formidable women, ladies with shopping bags, hats and sturdy shoes, who liked to pick things up, handle everything before they bought it.

People had come from miles around. If you couldn't get it in Rothwell or Kettering, they'd said, you could get it in Wellingborough. So everyone had shopped here and everyone had known everyone else.

They'd known him too. It had been an easy step from hanging around helping to selling a few things of his own. 'Oh it's you! Come on then: let's have a look. What have you got?'

He'd loved it. Money changing hands. And nothing had really changed in that respect. It was all still going on: just, not here. The money was in the big supermarkets now, the retail parks or online, while the old Market Square had become little more now than a cut-through for the bus stops in Church Street and a convenient place for a taxi rank.

JG brought another copy of the compromise agreement round and he knew he had to sign it, for Bryony's sake if nothing else, for the family and for money. Bry wouldn't insist, of course, though she'd made her feelings clear: 'Do something different, Tommy. Walk away!'

He already had: walked away under coercion, escorted off the premises, but he refrained from pointing it out.

It wasn't just the money, though. It was a matter of good sense.

Face the facts. You're finished at Lister's. Make the best of it!

That was JG's line too. 'You owe it to yourself, Tommy. Don't walk away with nothing. Not after all these years!'

She'd dropped by in her lunch-hour on Wednesday, the deadline date, in fact, for signing it.

He made fresh coffee and brought it through to the living room where she was sitting.

'What's he like then? Mr Daniel J Roper?' he couldn't resist asking.

'Oh I suspect he finds me very last century.'

'And that would be his mistake!'

He stopped there, though, could see she wasn't in a position to discuss it even though his mind seethed with questions.

So what's he into? Who's he seeing and what questions does he ask them? What decisions is he making?

JG handed him a pristine white copy of the proposed agreement. 'Just sign it and forget about it. I'll do the rest.'

And he had signed it. He'd gone into the study for his fountain pen and put his name to the damn thing in a matter of seconds, his hand passing swiftly over the paper just as he'd signed countless scores of documents under her gaze over the years.

'You're a hundred grand richer,' he told Bryony when she got in that evening.

She was fully occupied with her freelance PR work now that summer was approaching: writing regional adverts and feature articles for the local craft fairs and food festivals at nearby stately homes: Lamport Hall, Boughton

House, Holdenby, Houghton, Deene Park. She was involved with a recruitment drive too for the Chamber of Commerce and working on some big promotional deal between the town's fitness club and a sports retailer.

Her face lit up at his news: 'You've signed!' and she came to kiss him.

She probably hoped it would be the end of his late night fretting. It had always been at night that it seemed to get to him most: the two of them getting undressed and he, sitting on the edge of the bed, going over it all again and again.

'How can they do this to me? Why can't they see it! Have they no idea?'

Now he just lay awake in the darkness. A resigned weariness had replaced his continual rehearsing of what had happened and his conclusions had become philosophical.

Oh well, that's it then! There you have it. What can you do?

32

The Delinquent

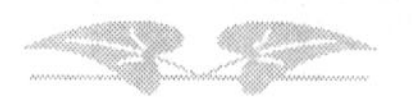

Halfway along Midland Road, behind a metal fence with a yellow sign proclaiming 'Construction Site', stood what was left of the house in which James Wilcox and his family had lived.

Tommy stood looking through the mesh at the cement mixers and coils of industrial cable. Tarpaulin flapped across the scaffolding where the house had once stood.

It had been a handsome villa, standing in its own grounds with outhouses for the servants and a front lawn planted with lilacs. Victorian redbrick with finials on the gables, a blue slate roof and decorative patterns of blue brick across the façade. He remembered sash windows that rattled and a black front door wider than any he'd ever seen. You had to walk through it to appreciate that, the depth of it swinging inwards as you passed.

He had walked through it, had known the house well: the shining red tiles of the passage, the echoing tick of the grandfather clock, the black weighing scales on the kitchen table with a brass pan on one side and a platform for the weights on the other, sitting and watching Mrs Wilcox roll brown biscuit mix on a floury surface.

A big house for solid self-assured people: James Wilcox and children of whom the oldest son had brought Tommy here in the autumn of '66.

Tommy had become interested in car radios and pocket transistors, saw money in them. He'd heard about an amateur repair club that was meeting in the evenings at the new technical college and thought it might give him a way in, a contact for business. Instead he'd found a roomful of schoolboys building four valve superhets from mail order kits.

'My Dad's got a car radio,' Ronny Wilcox had suggested, helpfully. 'He knows about that kind of thing.'

So he'd gone home with the boy, walked in through the black front door and met the man who, it turned out, knew about a damn sight more than car radios.

'Tommy Allbright! Seen you on the market. Hey, if I give you a tanner can you make it a shilling? If I give you a crown will you bring me a pound?'

Wilcox had made his fortune selling boot polish and he didn't care who knew it.

'Late 1920s,' he told Tommy. 'New formulas on the market, big names on the high street. Kiwi, Cherry, Hampton. Still around today. Leather ware was everything back then. Boots and shoes made to last. You looked after them. Big domestic market but that's not where the money was. Oh no! Fancy two ounce tins with pretty names! Who uses more of that stuff than anyone, eh? Shoe menders. Cobblers. Manufacturers. Hundreds of pairs a week, all polished up before they go. That was the way in. Plain tins. Unbranded. Six ounces a time and tuppence off for the refill.'

He'd taken a pound note out of his wallet and tucked it into Tommy's top pocket. 'Make it a tenner and we'll split the difference.'

'What about me?' Ronny had said.

'Never mind about you. It's not for spending. Not the way you spend, eh, Tommy?'

A wink and a nod, a pound note, that's how it had started: buying for the market and then for Orton's; anything that would sell.

Tommy had spent half his adolescence in that front room, now a construction site, the big room Wilcox had made his domain. It had always been dark, not because the window was small, the bay had been wide enough, but because of the velvet drapes, dark wall paper and heavy furniture. Furniture just for looking at, not using, and Tommy had never seen that before: a Jacobean chair with a woven seat too fragile to sit on, antique wash stand with a basin and pitcher, polished library steps though there was no library.

Wilcox had sat among it all in his cracked leather armchair, teaching Tommy how to make money, while his wife sat drinking tea in the kitchen like the working class girl she'd always be.

Tommy turned away from the site and walked on down Midland Road, built by a Victorian railway company to transport its passengers from the old town out to the bright new station.

He'd been into town, perusing the magazines in Smith's. He'd taken to buying Dalton's Weekly, scanning the businesses for sale, though he knew they were too small to interest him. He could occupy himself for a while with What car? or Autosport, too, had even thought about reading up on classic cars, but common sense had intervened: it wouldn't be enough to hold his interest for long.

He'd browsed as long as he could then wandered aimlessly round the shops, no longer concerned about bumping into people he knew. Lister's had issued their press release. The Evening Telegraph had run a feature on the young American taking over one of the town's long-established shoe companies.

He'd let Bryony break it to the family, casually, in her phone calls to them about clearing out Hartley Rise. 'Just the clothes to do now. So if you do still want anything . . . Our situation's changed a bit, by the way. New developments at Lister's. Tommy got a pay-off. He's looking around for the next big thing.'

They'd accepted it without question. No doubt in their minds that Tommy was anything other than master of his own destiny. Easily impressed by the mention of a pay-off.

Richard had seen it as a move towards early retirement. 'Don't blame you, mate. Wish I could do the same. You're a long time dead!'

They'd been sitting round the table at Kimble's Top on Sunday afternoon.

'About Hartley Rise,' Tommy had offered. 'I could give you a hand with the decorating.'

'No thanks!'

'I mean it.'

'Come off it, Tommy! You don't know one end of a paintbrush from the other. And frankly I don't need the distraction.'

So there had been nothing for it but to go back to his walking. Setting out early in the mornings as he had done today, browsing through magazines, but it was mid-morning now and he'd already run out of things to do, could no longer delay the inevitable. Bryony had insisted he drop by Hartley Rise.

'You don't have to come for long but it's your last chance to see the place before everything changes and you ought at least to do that!'

He hadn't the heart to argue. She was concerned about him and that nettled him, making him feel out of the ordinary, out of control.

At his dad's place there was a step ladder in the narrow hall and a line of paint pots with brushes and rags. Tommy had let himself in and called a greeting to Bryony, heard her moving around upstairs.

There was a smell of disinfectant. Up in the front bedroom the wardrobe door was open and Bryony was taking his dad's clothes out and folding them on the bed.

He leaned a shoulder on the door frame, watching, with a sense of unreality. His dad was gone and here was Bryony folding the old man's shirts and jumpers. It was the strange familiarity, the intimacy and care with which she took each item from its hanger and lay it flat on the bed, gently smoothing and folding.

'They're all rather worn,' she said. 'Still, I suppose . . . the charity shop . . .'

'I'll get some bags.'

He turned abruptly and went downstairs.

His dad had always kept a store of plastic bags in the sideboard but when he went into the front room to look, they'd gone: the sideboard was empty, the drawers dusted and polished.

Looking round the room it hit him then that he hadn't been here since the day his dad had died. The day of the quarterly sales meeting when he'd been finalising the business plan for the Board. His mind had been on Lister's and the deal he'd been pushing and the big plans he'd had for next year's imports.

Tommy sat down absently in the armchair, finding the seat sooner than expected, remembering too late that the chair had been raised to make it easier for his dad to get in and out. Stuck up at an awkward height, an odd angle, he had a sudden sense of what it was to be immobile, stiff and, for one appalling instant, he felt how it must have been for his dad, sitting here alone with the long empty days stretching ahead of him. The same emptiness that stretched ahead of Tommy now.

A sense of loss swept over him. He missed his dad.

The last time Tommy had seen him had been that Wednesday night. He'd picked up the parcel from the post office and they'd sat here and talked about Gina.

And after he'd gone, the old man had opened the package, long after Tommy had gone home, and he'd rung and left the voicemail.

I know what you've done.

He'd long since deleted the message, erased it with straightforward efficiency in the days when all that mattered had been Lister's and Anacleto. Now he tried to recall it, conjure up his dad's tone. Had it been reproach? Accusation?

They'd had that awful conversation the week before. That damn-fool Friday with the whole charade of Clifton at Kimble's Top, bringing his dad home, total silence in the car. His dad had been anxious, puzzled.

You're not right within yourself.

He hadn't even helped his dad out of the car. He'd just sat there and let him struggle, watched him go into the house without a word. Furious at being found out.

He tried to banish it all from his mind but it was impossible, sitting here in this room, the hollow echoes of his dad's life all around him.

He got up suddenly and headed for the front door, calling an incoherent farewell up the stairs to Bryony.

Outside he set off along the street without a thought to where he was going, back along Midland Road, past the site where Wilcox had once lived and on towards town.

A group youths was ahead of him, laughing and joking. He turned into a side street to avoid them, passed the tarmac playground of a primary school and found himself in Castle Road with its square fronted Victorian houses.

The colonnade of the old cattle market lay ahead, it was part of the theatre now, and there were more teenagers: a group of girls in school uniform.

Glancing around, he spotted the gate of the disused cemetery that bordered the street and pushed it open, making his way along the mud-strewn path until there was nothing but graves and trees all around him.

He'd never been in here before, had only ever walked past the fence, and it was bigger than he'd realised. The place had been completely neglected, there were crumbling headstones on every side with weathered letters and streaks of lichen. He made out old-fashioned names . . . 'George' . . . 'Frederick' . . . and the remnants of inscriptions . . . 'sacred to the memory of' . . . 'affectionately remembered'.

The older monuments were all in disrepair, their tumbled blocks lying within the foot-high walls of the family plots, and there were broken crosses, corbels and engraved stones piled in ivy-covered heaps, sprouting green holly.

Further along the path were twin chapels, old stone buildings like toy churches with gothic windows, buttresses and blue slate spires that rose, tall and slender, among the cedars and fir trees. If he carried on that way he'd reach the main gate onto London Road, close to Denington Industry and Lister's shoe factory.

He turned away diagonally and crossed the grass to his left, making for a park bench on the far side of an overgrown stretch where the graves were spread out and the yew trees grew, bulbous.

It was only as he made his way between the dark scaly trunks and extended lower boughs of the conifers, that he realised someone else was there ahead of him: a young man hard at work clearing the weeds. He was down on his knees beside a fallen headstone that had been propped up against its own plinth. The graves all around were thick with moss and brambles.

To Tommy the man's clothes had the look of a coarse uniform; his light blue shirt sleeves were rolled up to the elbows and he wore plain black trousers. His dark hair had been roughly shorn in an old fashioned style: short back and sides.

Juvenile delinquent, thought Tommy: had his hair cut for court and now it's a hundred hours of community service.

A waste of time it was too! The young man was working alone. As soon as he moved on to the next patch this one would be completely overgrown again.

'You'd be better off painting community centres,' Tommy told him, loudly.

The man looked up enquiringly at that and Tommy saw straightaway that he was older than he'd first appeared. Early thirties probably, by his face, but short and wiry which was why he'd looked younger from a distance.

Tommy had a vague feeling that he'd seen him before but the young man showed no sign of recognition, just sat back on his haunches and looked up at him.

'They ought to have a strategy for this kind of thing,' Tommy told him. 'If they really want to clear this place up they need a gang of you on it. Presumably there's enough of you for a gang? I gather this community sentencing is the big way forward.'

The young man got to his feet with a smile. 'No gang,' he said, holding out his hand as if to shake Tommy's. 'Actually I'm a priest. Dominic Palmer.'

Tommy stared at him. 'I thought you were a delinquent!'

'I guess you found me out then!'

The young man was still smiling and, as he stared at him, dumbfounded, Tommy was sure again that he knew him from somewhere and it wasn't church.

He stood trying to recall the memory. He wasn't normally bad with names and faces. Meanwhile the young man had dropped back to his knees and was weeding again, digging away with his trowel at a prickly stem.

He stopped for a moment, his dark hair dishevelled, and brushed the sweat from his forehead with the back of his hand and now Tommy saw the similarity.

'You took my sister's funeral,' he said. 'December of last year.'

He was the young Roman Catholic none of them had known. Esther had wanted the funeral before Christmas so she could go back to Spain and none of the other ministers had been available when the cemetery could offer them a booking.

The young man was looking up at him again and as Tommy took in the dark eyes and unkempt hair he was back in that December cold; in the growing darkness of the afternoon, his dad beside him, hollow-eyed with grief.

'My dad's dead too, now,' he said without knowing why.

'I'm sorry,' said the priest. 'I remember him. He stayed behind at the grave.'

He'd stayed behind because they'd all left him there. Tommy had left him to it without even thinking because Robyn had turned panicky on him, what with Esther looking forlorn and all those worthy mourners gathering round the grave; Gina's oldest friends.

'What if they know?' she'd hissed at him. 'What if they know about the will?'

'No-one knows,' he'd said. 'And even if they do, they can't prove it.'

He'd leaned on her to keep her mouth shut and trust him. The last thing he'd needed then was Robyn blurting it all out in remorse.

He'd had everything all worked out back then: the house for Robyn and the money for Esther. It had all seemed straightforward. Keep Kimble's Top in the family.

Give Esther the shares. Only they'd turned out to be worthless. And the whole damn mess had started. The problem he just couldn't solve and his dad fretting and fussing over it.

By February he'd been desperate for a diversion. Something to occupy his brain and let the solution emerge of itself the way it always did. So he'd got involved with Dubrowski's fight against the takeover bid. An energising battle. The diversion Leys had proclaimed ultra vires.

It struck him then with utter clarity that the whole debacle at Lister's came back to that. He'd needed a diversion and Dubrowski had been eager to return the favour, talking up the U.S. sales figures to the Board, making overblown promises they couldn't resist.

The insoluble issue of the will and the last few weeks at Lister's: it was all just one big bloody mess. A problem entirely of his own making.

He stood there with his heart thumping, while it flashed through his mind in full colour. The will. Dubrowski. The fiasco with the Board. His dad left alone at Gina's grave.

The priest was still kneeling there, silent, watching him. Tommy swallowed hard. 'I'd better be going!'

He turned away without another word, set off through the trees and across the grass towards the boarded up chapels.

Better be going!

What a joke! He of all people, who had nothing to go to, not a single call on his time, apart from the almighty cock-up he'd made and could never put right.

33

A Moment of Clarity

The night they found the wills he'd arrived at Kimble's Top straight from work while Robyn was taking his dad home from an afternoon with Gina. It had been the end of November, everything wretched by then, Gina bedridden, mostly asleep.

He'd gone down the corridor to her room to sit with her, listening to her breathing as she lay there and, somehow, something had changed. Her slumber had become more than deep. There was a stillness to it and when he'd touched her face with the back of his hand and spoken her name there had been no hint of a response.

Normally he'd have left the house before Robyn was due back to avoid the antagonism of seeing her there but now he sat and waited for her.

Like him, she'd leaned over Gina, called her name and then she'd panicked. 'I'd better phone the doctor.'

From where he'd sat at Gina's bedside he'd heard her getting flustered in the study, banging the desk drawers, until finally he'd gone to help, pulling Gina's bedroom door to softly behind him.

'I can't find the out-of-hours number.' Robyn's voice had been high with frustration. 'It's not here.'

She'd been rifling through Gina's papers: consultants' letters, appointment cards and pamphlets from the Macmillan nurses.

'Calm down.'

He'd gone through the desk himself, emptied the remaining contents of the top drawer and pulled it right out. Then the other drawers, one by one. The doctor's leaflet had fallen down the back of the drawers and was stuck behind the bottom one.

While Robyn went to make the call he'd replaced the contents of the desk, methodically ordering things as he went, and that was how he'd found them: two wills, one on top of the other, and he'd stood and read through them both without even thinking about it.

It was exactly what the family had been speculating about six months earlier, at Sunday tea, the week Esther had come home in June, only to leave for Spain again a few days later.

They'd all been up in arms about that. Lorraine had started on about Esther never being happy at Kimble's Top and Doreen had talked about Gina leaving the house to Robyn.

Tommy had dismissed it out of hand.

He'd known for a fact that Gina had once been thinking that way because she'd told him, asked if he'd be executor, and he'd told her what she could do with that idea.

It had been a difficult time, Robyn at fifteen with a six-month old baby and the whole family at Eastfield Road under pressure: Richard and Doreen, the two lads barely into their teenage years and Robyn with her baby, all crammed into a three bedroomed semi.

Meanwhile Gina was alone at Kimble's Top. Esther had gone off to Spain for Easter and announced she wasn't coming back to take her 'A'Levels.

Gina had been angry and disappointed over Esther, sympathetic towards Robyn, but he'd argued against her leaving the house to Robyn, impressed it on her that she wouldn't be doing the girl any favours: running Kimble's Top was far more responsibility than Robyn could ever handle.

He'd always assumed he'd convinced Gina. She'd never said any more about it to anyone.

Yet here it was in front of him: Gina's last will and testament of 24th November 1999:

'*I, Georgina Radford . . . appoint as my Executors and Trustees the Partners at the date of my death in the firm of John Rixon Solicitors . . . I bequeath my home, Kimble's Top . . . to my niece Robyn Lisa Allbright . . . and all my remaining real and personal property whatsoever and wheresoever . . . to my daughter, Esther . . .*'

She'd done it after all in spite of what he'd said, but then thought better of it because here was a different will four years later, revoking all former wills and testamentary dispositions:

'*I give, devise and bequeath all my real and personal property to my daughter, Esther Radford . . . in witness whereof I have hereunto set my hand this twenty sixth day of July two thousand and three . . . signed by the Testatrix in our joint presence and by us in her presence, Laurence E Clifton and David Matthews.*'

In 2003 she'd left everything, including the house, to Esther.

As he'd stood looking down at the words, thinking about it, Robyn had come back from phoning the doctor:

'He's coming. I told him we can't wake her and he's coming out. I think this might be it.'

She'd been tearful but Tommy's mind had been on the papers. He'd already absorbed the prospect of Gina's death while he'd sat beside her, waiting for Robyn. Now his mind was on the future.

'Have you seen these?' he asked her.

He showed her the wills and she shrugged, frowning. He handed them to her to read.

'Did Gina ever talk about leaving you Kimble's Top?'

She shook her head, looking confused.

'What about Esther?' he asked. 'Did she talk to Esther about it?'

'I don't think so.'

He could see she wasn't taking it in so he spoke slowly and deliberately:

'Do you want Kimble's Top? If it was yours, would you come and live here?'

She stared up at him, perplexed. 'If it's what Gina wants . . .'

'It's what she originally wanted,' he'd said it firmly and slipped the second of the two wills into his pocket, put the earlier one, leaving the house to Robyn, back in the desk. 'The last thing Esther wants is to be saddled with this house,' he'd told Robyn. 'This way you get Kimble's Top and she goes back to Spain with a couple of hundred grand in cash. Which is all she wants.'

Robyn had grasped that. Esther hadn't been there of course, she'd been over at whichever friend's house she was staying in, never around when they'd needed her.

So Robyn had just watched while he'd pocketed the will. As far as he could tell it had never been passed by the solicitors and it didn't look as though any copies had been made. Even if one did come to light, he and Robyn could always feign ignorance. No-one would ever know what they'd done.

He'd taken the second will into work the following day and put it through the shredder by JG's desk, disposed of it as though it were nothing more than a sheet of outdated sales figures, and his decision to do that had been on a par with all such decisions over the years, clear-headed, business-like and logical.

Inheriting Kimble's Top was the last thing Esther had wanted. She'd told him so herself two months earlier when he'd driven south on Spain's A66 to see her.

It was September. Gina had been due for a scan and all their hopes were pinned on the results. The family had talked about it constantly and there had been murmuring about Esther and why she hadn't come home over the summer. Some of them were beginning to question whether Gina had really told Esther how things stood.

For Tommy the solution was simple. He'd been due to visit Oliveira to set up next winter's order book and it was an easy matter to pick up a car afterwards in Lisbon, cross the border and drive down to Spain's Costa del Sol to visit Esther.

He'd known the name of the English bar where she worked and it hadn't been difficult to find it, climbing the steep mountains into Bénalmadena and the old pueblo of white washed houses, palm trees and cobbled squares.

Tommy had parked up, strolled through the old town and spotted the white façade of Esther's bar with its aluminium tables and chairs on the other side of a quiet plaza. An English couple had been sitting out front, smoking cigarettes, with empty plates and coffee cups in front of them.

Inside the landlady had smiled a welcome as his eyes got used to the dark and then he'd seen Esther staring at him from the far end of the counter, linen cloth in hand as she polished the wine glasses. She'd put her cloth down and come to meet him, looking anxious. 'Has something happened?'

'Yes,' he said shortly. 'I've been trying to call you and all I ever get is that blasted answerphone.'

'Well if you'd left me a message I'd have called you back.'

'Is there somewhere we can talk?'

She'd taken him out through the narrow streets to a taverna that had a private patio with expensive wicker chairs and soft red cushions.

He suggested lunch but she shook her head so he settled for beer and a slice of tortilla while she sipped a coke.

When he'd talked to Bryony about his planned trip, she'd urged him to be gentle with Esther, but now it came to it he felt no compunction at all.

'When did you last speak to Gina?' he asked her.

'A couple of days ago.'

'And how much time do you think she's got, Esther?'

'I don't know,' her voice was indignant. 'Neither does she. No-one does.'

'Precisely. So what the hell are you doing still here?'

'Look, I am coming back. Mum knows that. She doesn't expect me just to jack everything in.'

'You can't run away from it, Esther. If you don't come home soon, you'll always regret it.'

'I am home.'

And that had been typical Esther: offbeam. He'd made an effort to be patient then:

'I'm talking about your family home. And if you don't come soon, you'll find Kimble's Top's all you've got left.'

She'd laughed abruptly at that. 'Well I won't be hanging onto it! I'm not interested in all that hilltop splendour.'

'You can't mean that.'

She'd just shrugged.

'Your dad created Kimble's Top!' he'd said.

'Oh, don't!' She'd mimicked the journalists with exaggerated weariness: '"*The ground breaking design. The innovation*" . . .'

'Your dad designed that house to be a family home,' he'd cut in, exasperated. 'He built it for you.'

'He built it for Mum,' she said.' That's what Kimble's Top was all about. Him and Mum. It was never about me! And it can go to the highest bidder. My life's here.'

He should have told her then, why Kimble's Top was about more than just Arthur and Gina. But he couldn't. She'd been too harsh, too angry and he only had himself to blame for that because he'd set the tone.

He'd struggled to believe she really meant it, though. He'd sat there in the dazzling sunshine and stared at her, perplexed as to how she'd ended up in such a frame of mind and she'd just looked back at him, squinting in the bright light and offering no clues, nothing at all to help him make sense of it all.

He'd told himself she'd feel differently when it came to it, that she'd never sell Kimble's Top once it was all she had left, but when she finally did come back in October he wasn't so sure. She seemed to have an aversion to being at Kimble's Top, that much was evident, but he couldn't tell whether it was the house itself or the painful reality playing out within its walls.

When he'd found the wills, though, the way forward had been obvious. His decision had been made in a moment of complete clarity.

All his reluctance to see Robyn inherit Kimble's Top had gone. Robyn had changed. She'd done well looking after Gina. And she'd keep Kimble's Top in the family.

He sat in the garden at Ise Avenue now thinking back over it all. At the foot of his chair discarded copies of the *Daily Telegraph* and *Financial Times* rustled in the fresh air; the kind of newspapers whose analysis had appealed to him and shaped his own thinking over the years: clear-headed, rational analysis.

He'd never been rash or impulsive. Sharp and decisive, yes; foolhardy: no. He'd prided himself on that: Tommy Allbright: the man with an eye for an opportunity.

Hey, Tommy! If I give you a tanner can you make it a shilling?

He could and he had. And his decision in Gina's study the night he'd found the wills had been of that ilk. The house for Robyn, to keep it in the family, and the investments for Esther who wanted her own life in Spain.

Just that one fatal flaw. He'd never stopped to ask why Gina had changed her will. He'd even seen the date, 2003, and never thought to connect it with RS Gypsum.

He'd always assumed Gina had sold her shares and invested her money elsewhere. He'd been so blinded by his own interests that he'd never stopped to question what was right in front of him.

He never made mistakes like that.

Never.

But he'd made one hell of a mistake that day.

He remembered the meeting at the solicitor's office. His dad insisting on coming too and he, Tommy, sitting there, reading the paperwork with the horrible realisation that Gina had never pulled out of RSG.

He still couldn't believe it.

He'd followed the company's decline with the same detached curiosity as everyone else. Everyone in the county knew RSG just as everyone knew Robert Scholt, always good for a donation and one of the best local employers: apprenticeships for the disadvantaged and staff benefits that kept whole families loyal for decades.

RSG had employed thousands in asbestos processing, turning out fibres, fireproof paint, pipe lagging and wall panels. Even when asbestos had been banned the company had still kept going, diversifying all the time.

It had been ten years or so before the court cases started: personal injury claims for asbestosis and mesothelioma. Even then it had still looked as though RSG would pull through, they'd estimated the liability on the balance sheet, bought insurance and courted private equity, come close to a deal with the American asset strippers.

Then suddenly everything had changed. 2001. The action groups and lobbyists mobilised. Litigation went through the roof. Thousands of claims were filed and the investors vanished. RSG's shares went into free fall.

Tommy had read the headlines without concern, assuming Gina had sold her shares long before. Even if she'd been slow off the mark and left it until the takeover was in the offing: RSG had still been trading at around 152p a time, more than enough for a decent return.

But Gina never had sold. Arthur's investments were gone and so she'd changed her will in 2003, the year RSG had called in the administrators.

'The residual value in the company insufficient to pay even the nominal share value.'

The solicitor's words still echoed in Tommy's mind.

With nothing but Kimble's Top to leave, Gina had thought of her daughter first, leaving the house to Esther despite her antipathy towards the place and he, Tommy, had taken it away from her because, for once in his life, he hadn't stopped to think things through.

As if privy to his secret guilt, Esther was moving out from under his roof. Within the next couple of weeks she'd be moving into Fourteen Hartley Rise, not that he saw much of her, anyway, working pub hours as she did and generally eating her meals at work because it was a good place to hang out with its trendy sofas, pool tables and Sky TV.

Bryony, meanwhile, had a project for him. There was a shopping list of things for his dad's house that needed picking up from Argos, Marks & Spencer and the new IKEA in Milton Keynes.

Tommy stood in the kitchen reading it through. 'Do we really need all this?'

He could understand the new sideboard, beech with glazed doors; the steel bed and freestanding clothes rail. His dad's furniture had all gone to the auction house. When it came to it, none of the family had wanted the old wardrobe and dressing table, the sideboard or bureau.

Heirlooms they might have been, from the grandparent's farmhouse, but they'd have had to be real aficionados to accommodate such big old piece in any of their modern houses and so they'd let them go.

There were a lot of additional things, though, on Bryony's list. Tommy raised his eyebrows at the economy dinner service, bright yellow toaster and kettle set, new storage canisters. 'Aren't half these things already there?'

'Esther won't want an old man's stuff!' said Bryony. 'She's got her own taste.'

'Are we paying?'

'I said we'd go halves with Richard. Is that a problem?'

'No . . .' he stood looking at the list. It was all such cheap, bargain-basement stuff. 'It's just not exactly Fratelli Toso, is it?' he said. 'Portmeirion Malachite?'

They'd been Gina's favourites up at Kimble's Top: millefiori glass vases, a Portmeirion coffee set in green with gold leaf; McCoy jardinières and white glazed basketweave.

'All very 1960s,' said Bryony. 'Gina wanted Kimble's Top to be a showcase. Esther likes girlie, fun things.'

'Kimble's Top all about them? Never her?'

It was still on his mind, what Esther had told him out in Spain. He'd mentioned it to Bryony at the time but she'd shaken her head then and did so now:

'No-one's house was child focused in those days. Our tastes prevailed here too. The toys came out during the day and got put away before you came home. No computers, no play station. Kimble's Top wasn't any less about Esther than any other house would have been,' she shrugged. 'If she felt excluded it was just circumstance. Arthur out at work all day. Not exactly a hands-on dad even when he was at home. Then he died and after that Gina did everything her way.'

'We never noticed a rift,' said Tommy.

'*Dolly daydream?* quoted Bryony. '*If they had lessons in lazing around she'd be top of the class!* We all heard the things Gina said.'

'Everyone says things like that,' said Tommy. 'We were pretty sharp with our two on occasion. They're not holding it against us.'

'People respond differently,' said Bryony. 'And our two had each other. Esther only had Gina.'

'Well there's nothing we can do about it now,' said Tommy, folding the shopping list and putting it in his wallet.

And if things worked out for Esther at Hartley Rise they could put the past behind them.

He collected all the shopping and arranged to take it over to Hartley Rise in one trip.

Richard was at work in the house, tiling round the bath where they'd had a shower put in. He came downstairs when Tommy arrived.

On the ground floor the carpet had been taken up from the hall, stairs and front room and the wooden floor boards sanded and painted cream with a lilac border. The walls were lilac too.

In the front room there were two cream tub sofas and a glass and chrome dining table with four chairs stood by the bay window. The curtains had been replaced with venetian blinds and there was a painting of tulips over the mantelpiece, three long mirrors in a line on the wall opposite.

'Bit of a change, eh?' said Richard.

'Does Esther like it?'

'She chose the colours. Painted all the borders herself.' He followed Tommy out to the car to help him bring all the boxes through to the front room. 'Dad would have enjoyed it, anyway. A breath of fresh air in the old place. And at least it reassured Esther, having dad leave her the house.'

He gathered up an armful of bed linen in slippery packets to take upstairs. 'I have to say, though, Gina could be hard as nails but I never thought she'd leave Esther with nothing.'

'Esther didn't want Kimble's Top,' said Tommy.

'That's not the point. The fact is, Gina knew those shares were worthless and she just left it. Knowing Esther would end up penniless.' He turned to the door, 'I'd never have thought she could be that callous.'

'She wasn't,' protested Tommy but Richard had gone.

He grabbed a load of bathroom towels and went after his brother. 'Is that what Esther thinks?' he demanded.

'Wouldn't you?' said Richard.

'But Esther's never been bothered about money . . .'

Richard stared at him: 'It's not about money. It's about knowing your mum gave a damn.' He dumped his packages in the back bedroom. 'Tea?'

'Thanks!' said Tommy.

He watched his brother go downstairs then stood alone by the window in the bedroom he and Richard had shared as boys.

The walls had been painted yellow, there was a roll of carpet waiting to be laid and smart new blinds at the window. The view into the backyard was the same though, the same brick alleyway at the end and the succession of neighbours' houses to right and left: some with plain yards and others prettified with terracotta pots and hanging baskets.

His earliest memory of Gina was of the two of them right here at this window.

She'd been nine years older than him, broad-shouldered and freckled with distinctive red hair.

It had been a winter's morning, he three or four years old and the ice thick on the bedroom window. He remembered kneeling on the bed and tracing the lacy fan-shaped pattern with his fingers, craning his neck to see the chickens in the backyard at number ten.

'Come away from there,' Gina had said. 'You'll catch cold.'

Three. Four. Five. Six. He'd counted the chickens off under his breath.

She'd grabbed his arm. 'I said come away!'

'Why can't we have chickens?'

'Because they need looking after. We've got enough of that in this house.'

'I don't need looking after,' he'd said proudly and she'd looked down at him for a moment with an expression he couldn't read.

'No,' she'd said. 'You've always been one on your own, you have.'

The memory of her came back to him, vivid and powerful. His big sister. She'd taken his hand to lead him down the stairs. He was filled then with the realisation of what he'd done, taking her will, destroying her last wishes.

A sick guilt flooded through him, a distaste for his own self that he'd never felt before in his life.

34

JAMES

He'd completed Bryony's project, delivered all the shopping to Hartley Rise, and Esther had moved out the following Saturday: an easy move with just the single car-load of her belongings that Richard had come and collected.

His own children came home briefly. Chris stayed for a couple of nights en route for a hiking trip with friends to bag half a dozen Munros and Elisabeth came over for dinner while he was there. She was busy planning a holiday in Cuba with friends. Bry's PR work was in full swing with photo shoots and feature articles to arrange for the different county events she'd been promoting.

With nothing at all to do, Tommy retreated to the garden.

It was mid-July, the schools hadn't quite broken up for the summer and everything was quiet and enclosed, not even the sound of children playing out in neighbours' gardens.

He reclined back in his wooden chair, arms cushioning his head, and looked at the clouds. They'd had a run of hazy days, the sky a low shining white with the sun evident somewhere behind it all. The clouds had more shape to them today, they were curved and billowing with a dark grey tinge to the edges.

The garden around him stirred; sharp pointed leaves of crocosmia shifted in the currents of air, pink cascades of fuschia hoods dangled and the smaller leaves on the shrubs rustled while the branches of the trees in the background moved gently.

He was supposed to be looking at a business proposition from an acquaintance, a proposal for online gourmet hampers with jámon serrano, rillettes and terrines from the continent. The acquaintance was looking for a partner and thought it might be of interest to Tommy.

It wasn't. He'd read the opening paragraph twice and couldn't remember any of it.

Down by the pond a blackbird was fluttering and preening itself in a shallow puddle, the rocks around it so moss covered they seemed embedded in the ground. They reminded Tommy of the old fallen headstones in the cemetery where the priest had been working: they'd lain flat and deep in the soil as if emerging from the earth itself. There were traces of groundsel too in the flowerbeds around the pond, though nothing on a par with the weeds overtaking those graves.

Tommy frowned. He never had got to the bottom of what the priest had been about. Tidying up a family plot? But his work had been larger scale than that and he'd had an air of detachment to him.

Now Tommy came to think about it, he felt as if he'd been wrong-footed somehow by that young man. An awkward encounter altogether. He vaguely recalled Dominic Palmer offering his hand as he'd introduced himself. Had he ignored it?

He ought to wander back up there sometime and sort it out. Now, in fact.

Tommy picked up his papers, packed the garden chair away and set off along Ise Avenue. He crossed the railway line near the old engine sheds and followed a dog-leg route through the narrow terraced streets that backed onto the cutting. Coming out onto Elsden Road, he headed past Hartley Rise towards town.

These were the streets he'd inhabited all his life and yet everything had changed now. The memory of his dad confronted him at every turn, the sense of him indelible in every sight and sound of the landscape, a landscape familiar but one he'd never known without his dad being a part of it.

He pushed the thought from his mind as he passed the Victorian houses along Midland Road then turned towards Castle Street and the old cattle market. As he pushed back the wooden gate of the cemetery and made his way up through the graves, it struck him that here was a world apart, unconnected with anything in his life so far. He could walk easily among the yews and conifers, the crumbling memorials to lives of which he knew nothing.

Once again the priest was there ahead of him, at work in the same far corner, tackling a mass of great thorny branches that stuck out unashamedly through the air, extending at all angles from the weeds and long grass around the headstones.

Tommy watched him handling the branches gingerly, snipping them off in sections and depositing them in a wheelbarrow. The priest must have heard Tommy's approach because he glanced round suddenly and smiled, stopping work for a moment.

'Tommy Allbright, said Tommy, offering his hand. 'Don't think I actually said so when we first met.'

Dominic Palmer smiled and shook his hand.

'So what are you doing here?' asked Tommy. 'If it's not community service.'

The priest shrugged. 'It's downtime. Keeps the hands busy, frees the mind.'

Tommy sat down on the nearby bench and Dominic went back to tearing the brambles free of the long grass and weeds. Tommy watched as the grass came away in strands, spilling across the path, and scattering little yellow flowers of wild parsnip everywhere.

'So, how about you?' said Dominic Palmer after a while. 'It it somewhere to think?'

'Hardly!' said Tommy. 'I came here to escape thinking.'

The priest looked at him enquiringly.

'Oh, nothing specific,' Tommy shrugged. 'Just life, you know.'

The words sounded hollow even to his own ears.

He leaned forward, resting his elbows on his knees, and stared at the branches stacked up in the wheelbarrow. Some were as thick as his thumb, terrific segmented stems with thorns that curved like arcs, red at the base. The brambles were thinner and purple with much closer spikes, their leaves on flimsy stalks with fine thorns of their own. There was bindweed too, a softer stem with delicate curling tendrils impossible to trace to a single source.

Gradually the pile in the wheelbarrow became a tottering mound and the sweet smell of grass and mulched leaves wafted on the air from the disturbed undergrowth.

To the left of the bench a patch was clearing, a mere indent in the great tangle of briers and weeds but a break from them nevertheless, a hint of clarity and space. Where the weeds had been cut back, fresh growth was evident, the deep green blades of young grass and a little purple flower he didn't recognise.

He looked down at its satin petals, not purple he realised but lilac, the same shade as the walls at Hartley Rise and the decorative border that Esther had painted herself on the stairs.

'Did you ever do something really stupid?' he mused. 'Really screw up?'

The priest looked across from what he was doing and nodded slowly, not acquiescence, Tommy realised, but an invitation to say more.

'My sister, Gina,' he went on, thinking aloud. 'The one you buried. She made two wills. The later one invalidated the first. Should have done. But I got rid of it. Told the family there was just the earlier one. It seemed the obvious thing to do at the time.'

It sounded so unremarkable now he put it like this.

'The trouble is: it's all gone hopelessly wrong. And I just can't seem to put it right.'

'That's usually the way of it with sin,' said Dominic.

Tommy laughed at that. *Religion!*

'I don't believe in sin,' he said.

'Not even your own?'

'I did what I thought was right at the time,' said Tommy.

'Lying? Breaking the law?'

Tommy got to his feet. 'I don't need a priest to tell me right from wrong.'

He turned to go.

Dominic Palmer, still looking up at him from where he crouched among the brambles, was nodding again, nodding in agreement this time. 'No,' he said. 'You don't.'

It irked him that the priest had judged him but then that's what religious people did. They focused on everyone else's shortcomings and pronounced judgement.

Lying? Breaking the law?

Of course, from a purely factual point of view, that was what he'd done and therein lay his problem. Not breaking the law, that was a technicality with no bearing on anything, but he had lied, perpetrated a deceit. That was the heart of the matter. He'd initiated the lie that Gina hadn't changed her will and now the only conclusion the family could draw, faced as they were with the final outcome of it all, was that Gina hadn't cared enough to provide for Esther.

He was sitting at the PC in his study, trawling the internet to investigate this wretched gourmet hamper business. Competitors abounded: all the long-established companies had known brands and a myriad of lone entrepeneurs filled every niche in between.

Bored, he looked up the Oakham wine importer instead. He had an interesting Bianco di Custoza in stock, a blend of Garganega with Cortese and Chardonnay, partly oak aged: *fresh and creamy with overtones of citrus.* It would be just the thing to go with the sea trout Bryony had brought home from one of the food fairs she'd been promoting and he might as well drive over there and buy a few bottles.

In Oakham the pavements were busy, the swifter pedestrians ducking onto the road to pass the pushchairs and elderly couples. Tommy took a short cut through the market place, past the low-hanging timbers of the old butter market and along by the church. He'd picked up his wine and was heading now for a social enterprise outlet that sold home-grown produce.

On the way he noticed the church was advertising organic fair trade foods and stepped inside to take a look. Long tables had been set up near the door and in the nave beyond he glimpsed a sea of pews, gothic windows and thin stone columns.

He browsed the packets of Ethiopian coffee and aduki beans and exchanged a few remarks with the ladies in attendance, pleasant churchy types with gracious smiles. A gentleman in a dog collar, retired apparently, not the regular vicar, nodded a genteel blessing.

This was how religious people ought to be: polite, useful, not passing judgement on other people's lives.

He paid for some fresh coffee beans, picked up spinach, chives and dill at the social enterprise store and set off for home.

The main road opened up straight and clear ahead of him and the Audi handled like a dream, without the rev counter he'd barely have known he was moving. There was no more than a whisper from outside, just the flash of hedges and fields as he accelerated, the clarity of the dashboard before him and the leather seat at his back. It was a feeling he loved, just him and the car.

He drove in silence, absorbed in his thoughts and a sense of speed and adrenalin. The more he thought about those church people in Oakham, the more he felt he should go back and see Dominic Palmer.

After all, what did he have to be afraid of? He'd had good reasons for taking the will. He'd had to do it because of Kimble's Top. He couldn't explain that to anyone else but he didn't want to fall out with Dominic Palmer.

No doubt he'd felt it was his duty to point out Tommy's sin.

Tommy Allbright wasn't a man to be intimidated by someone else's religion. He'd always prided himself on being broad-minded and since he'd been the one to walk away he'd have to be the one to go back and show the guy's puritanical streak hadn't phased him.

It had been a minor impasse that was all. It was his own fault for getting up and walking away.

It was the second time he'd done that.

Why?

Tommy set off for the cemetery the next morning.

It was a couple of weeks since he'd been there and the priest had clearly been busy. The area all around the bench was free of brambles and it was just the swathes of ivy and stinging nettles obscuring the graves now.

The bench was a good place to sit, secluded yet still in touch with the world. From the other side of the hedge he caught the occasional slam of a car door, the sound of children's voices as they moved between lessons at Wellingborough School and, from the far side of the cemetery, the drone of traffic on the main road. Yet with all that going on, Tommy could still sit here unremarked.

The school clock had just struck half past twelve when he spotted Dominic pushing his wheelbarrow along the path through the trees. He brought it to a halt nearby and smiled. 'Hello, Tommy.'

'Hi.'

Tommy was relaxed, his arms stretched along the back of the bench as he sat watching the priest attack a clump of dark velvety nettles, depositing the stalks into the wheelbarrow where the sun glistened on the tiny sharp hairs of every stem, making a glittering fuzz.

'What you said last time,' he ventured after a while. 'I just want you to know, it's okay. I mean, there's no offence.'

Dominic looked up from cutting back the nettles.

'Religion's obviously your thing,' said Tommy. 'I'm more your scientific type. Evolution. Big bang. All that kind of thing. The things that disprove religion.'

'Do they?' the priest looked genuinely surprised.

'Pretty much,' Tommy nodded.

Dominic nodded too, slowly, as if thinking about that.

'And the meaning of life?' he asked Tommy after a moment or two.

'We all find our own meaning,' said Tommy with a shrug. 'Whatever makes sense to us.'

'And the basis for morality?'

No morality without God, that's what he was driving at, Tommy knew. The answer was meant to be enlightened self interest, the social contract, but he didn't actually buy any of that.

'I believe in right and wrong,' he told the priest.

Dominic Palmer looked at him.

'I know what I did was wrong,' said Tommy. 'I'm not denying that. But I had my reasons.'

He was getting, defensive, conscious of the young man's eyes on him. This was where he'd left off last time. He'd talked himself into a corner.

The fact was it all came down to Kimble's Top and he couldn't explain that, not to anyone. If he could he'd simply have told Esther why she mustn't ever sell the house. But he couldn't.

'There's some things you can't talk about,' he told Dominic. 'Some things you just don't . . .' he tailed off.

'Too painful?' asked the priest.

Tommy got to his feet without thinking and turned to go but then saw a look cross the priest's face, a fleeting expression of recognition.

He was doing it again: walking out on the conversation. He stopped himself and sat down abruptly again on the bench, his mind in turmoil.

Beyond the hedge the sixth formers were coming out for lunch. He could hear their voices, the squeal of bicycle brakes and somewhere out on the main road a lorry thundered over a loose manhole cover with a terrific crack.

Suddenly everything he didn't want to talk about swept over him. The smell of freshly cut grass hung in the air and his head was full of memories, of the August bank holiday in 1979.

James, his boy.

The feel of him, his infant warmth. Soft to the touch but always kicking and struggling, wanting to get down, thrusting his way out of the encircling arms to hurtle forwards on his own path.

It had seemed only a moment since he'd been a laughing toddler posting the door keys down the back of the storage heater in the lounge; jamming his fingers into the cassette player and pushing the buttons on the washing machine mid-cycle.

Now he was nearly six: in possession of a new pair of roller skates he couldn't wait to try out on the drive at Aunty Gina's house.

'You be very careful,' Bryony had warned him.

They'd watched for a bit as he'd made awkward progress backwards and forwards along the concrete, the skates heavy and cumbersome to his young feet but always looking up in the midst of his exertions, flushed with excitement.

'Watch me! Watch this,' he'd held his arms wide and picked up speed down the slope to the garage, using the thin metal door to bring himself to a crashing halt.

'Stay on the drive, won't you?' Bryony had called as he'd set off then in the other direction. There had been older children playing out with bikes and she hadn't wanted him going off with them.

Had he looked back and smiled then? Had he answered: 'okay'? Sometimes Tommy thought so but the scene was always elusive.

They'd left him to it, joining the rest of the family by the terrace at the side of the house: Arthur mixing a volatile fruit punch that his mum had developed a taste for and Gina and his dad had been laughing over that. The others had been stretched out on sun beds on the grass, Lorraine and Doreen anyway, Richard somewhere about.

Tommy had gone up onto the terrace for a drink and then into the house to fetch a jug of ice Arthur had left in the kitchen. He'd left Bryony down on the lawn, still near the drive, looking at Gina's new pampas grass.

In the summer stillness they'd all heard the engine start up further along Hunsbury Hill, tracked the rattle of it approaching: an articulated lorry, lower gears working hard as it rounded the bend by Kimble's Top.

He'd been conscious of it as he'd crossed the living room, jug in hand, caught the piercing whistle of brakes through the open French windows and looked up at the desperate screech of tyres as he'd stepped out onto the terrace. They'd all looked round, braced themselves for the crash of impact but none came. Yet the engine had throbbed on and on, surprisingly loud, too close at hand.

Across the lawn he saw Bryony had gone, driven by a mother's instinct, she'd already been halfway along the drive.

The others had sat up, looking after her, uncertain, then looking back at him.

As he crossed the grass his wife's cries had torn the air and he was running, running fast at her rising hysteria. When he'd rounded the drive, he'd found her down on her knees on the white concrete, the incongruous orange bulk of the lorry above her, filling the gateway.

He'd seen it all in an instant. Senseless with shock, every detail had impressed itself on him: the black stream of blood, the twisted feet lying sideways in the red straps of the roller skates and the fragile crushed figure against the great double treads of the tyres. Out in the road two fair haired girls were shrieking and their mother was running towards them, arms wide, straight through the flower beds of the front garden. A shiny blue bicycle lay discarded in the road where the truck had swerved to avoid it.

His knees hit the hard surface of the drive beside Bryony. He grabbed her with one hand and reached for the driver with the other, pulling the man away so he could lean over his boy himself, do what had to be done. But there was nothing to be done. The driver's tears had splashed onto the bare legs of his son and there was no movement, no cry, no hope of response.

'He was nearly six.'

Gina had dug a rose garden for him, where he died. The lorry had brought the gatepost down and half the wall with it when they'd reversed it out. They'd had to rebuild it. So she'd moved the gates and changed the entrance altogether so he and Bryony wouldn't have to remember, wouldn't ever have to drive through there and be reminded.

'We put his ashes among the roses.'

Soft speckled ash in the dark brown soil. The memory of it flitted across his mind like an ash trail deep within him.

'That's why we could never let the house go. Esther didn't know of course. None of the others, the children . . . it was before their time, just Elisabeth and she was a baby. We never talked about it. Never said. But the house . . . not that he's there. I know that . . .'

Tears were blurring his eyes and his thoughts were jumping like a nervous rabbit.

'Where is he, my boy?' he sat shaking his head.

'Romping through paradise?' the priest's tone was gentle, a suggestion: 'Surveying the universe in the company of angels?'

He'd come to sit beside Tommy on the bench and turned now to face him. 'Truly,' he said. 'With all my heart, I believe your boy is in the arms of love.'

'God?' Tommy sat back with a bitter laugh. 'If there is a god he took my son.'

'Death took your son,' said Dominic. 'The mortality of a fallen world. For myself, I believe God received him with joy.'

'But he'll never grow up. Never live his life.'

'In that place he's all that he could ever be. As you will be too one day.'

'Oh!' Tommy shook his head. 'Religion! Myths and fables. It's just what you say to comfort people.'

'Well then,' said the priest. 'Be comforted!'

35

Death

He walked home from the cemetery utterly drained, the conversation a blur but the images in his mind still vivid.

For once he walked directly along London Road, past Denington Industry and Lister's but that no longer troubled him. The scenes in his mind belonged to a worse grief than any of that.

He'd just sold his two shops to an aggressive retail chain when James died, finalised the deal that had paid for the house on Ise Avenue. He could still remember the exhilaration they'd felt over that.

When he'd first seen Ise Avenue it had been a summer's day like this one: the new development all marked out in plots, along a line of Ash trees that had stretched ahead of him, oval leaves fluttering in the breeze. The new road had curved westwards as he'd stared along it and to his left the wind had swept across the river and the open fields to sting his cheeks.

The salesman had been waiting for him, briefcase in hand and a fleeting look on his face as he'd registered Tommy's youth. It was a look Tommy had seen more than once, on the faces of wholesalers and agents, even his bank manager, as small electricals had taken off and his old ironmonger's shop had turned into two successful outlets.

The man had shown him the plans for a modern family home: chalet-style with a galleried landing, a living room that ran the length of the house, dining room, study and five bedrooms.

Tommy had listened attentively, nodded and smiled as required and ended the meeting with a simple handshake.

Everything had been favourable: he and Bryony poised with their lives about to take off. Whatever Tommy ended up doing next, they'd agreed there'd be no more shop hours, no more evenings at the wholesalers or weekends stock-taking.

A stone's throw from the brick alleyways where he'd grown up, his own children would play in a comfortable oasis they could call their own.

Then, the unthinkable!

He'd walked the length of Ise Avenue by now and the automatic gates to number fifteen swung inwards at his key. He walked up the drive and let himself into the house.

Bryony was out.

Tommy left his keys on the hall table and went upstairs to the galleried landing, looked down on the hall with its reproduction table and gilt mirrors. Up here the bedroom doors were all ajar: the door to the guest room that had been Esther's, his children's rooms and, beyond them, his and Bryony's bedroom at the front of the house.

Opposite that, on the far side of the gallery, was the small room at the front of the house, the one they never used. It was a third the size of the main bedroom, a little corner room in which the roof sloped almost to the floor and there were windows on two sides. That's why James had wanted it for his own.

They never came in here. Never even passed it, lying as it did at this far end of the landing. Sometimes he'd glance across at it from the top of the stairs, or coming out of the bathroom, and imagine that all the pain of his life was hidden behind its closed door but now that he pushed it open and crossed the threshold, he saw it was just an empty room.

They'd painted the walls and ceiling white and meant to use it for something else but nothing had ever presented itself. Even Elisabeth and Christopher had never really played here, preferring their adopted corner of the kitchen or each other's bedrooms.

Tommy stepped across to the wooden cupboard, built-in under the eaves and opened the door. Out of sight, pushed to the back of the top shelf were the sealed boxes: three of toys and two of clothes. He pulled out the nearest one and took it over to the window, sat down on the floor with his back to the wall and broke through the tape with his thumb nail.

The last time he'd sat here like this had been twenty six years ago. He and Bryony had spent a grim Easter weekend doing what they had to do, stripping off the childish wallpaper, repainting and putting everything into boxes.

Stopping occasionally for a break, they'd sat side by side on the floor like this, Bryony utterly distracted in her grief and he sick with it, alternately tearful and silent as each day wore on and the evening shadows spread across the room.

It had been a turning point.

A nightmare eight months had preceded it, their only common ground ending up in the same bed at the close of each heartbroken day. Even that had been short-lived. Tommy had woken frequently to find Bryony's side of the bed empty and had come down early in the mornings to find her sitting in the living room, staring at nothing.

'I wish you'd wake me if you can't sleep,' he'd remonstrated but she wouldn't.

'You need your sleep.'

Preoccupied as they were, they had never even explored the wider grief within the family. He remembered his mum and dad had seemed struck down as if by a physical blow though few words had been exchanged, just their arms around him, a tighter hug than usual. His brothers had become tongue-tied in his presence and it was as if an implicit understanding had been reached never to mention what had happened.

Tommy reached into the box and pulled out the bright red fire engine Gina had given James on his second birthday.

The memory of her face that August afternoon still chilled him. He saw her again in the mêlée on the drive, her head held up amidst the crying and the one trembling hand that clung to Arthur.

He'd been afraid she might feel responsible, grow to hate the house Arthur had built for her but that hadn't been her way.

She'd gone to work swiftly, getting the fallen bricks of the wall removed, digging over the ground herself and she hadn't said anything to them until it was finished and they'd found a whole new garden freshly planted with rose bushes. Afterwards she'd bought the statue, the beautiful white marble of Peter Pan: an innocent, light hearted figure watching over the spot where his little boy had last played.

He put the fire engine down on the floor and rifled through the box, taking out the matchbox cars and arranging them around him: a little red Volkswagen with doors that opened, an orange Lamborghini, a blue Lancia and a black London taxi. The half-familiar, well worn surfaces that his little boy had grasped and played with.

Sitting there, remembering, he lost track of time until a car pulled up outside and then Bryony had let herself in through the front door and was calling his name.

'Up here!'

She looked stunned as she appeared in the doorway. 'What on earth are you doing?'

He said nothing, beckoning her over.

'Tommy,' she said in a warning tone but he beckoned again until she finally came to sit awkwardly beside him.

He reached an arm around her and she sat rigid against him.

'Please,' she said. 'Put it away.'

He picked up the little red Volkswagen instead and held it out in front of him. 'He'd have had his own children by now.'

'Stop it, Tommy!'

She took the toy from him and began gathering the others up, packing them swiftly away in the box while he watched.

'You're scaring me,' she said shortly, turning to look at him and he leaned forward to help her then, closed the box lid for her and laughed softly:

'Oh well,' he said. 'We can't have that.'

Death was on his mind, though, for all that he'd laughed it off to reassure her.

It was the second half of July and the roses were in full bloom: the big frilly Albertines he'd taken up to Kimble's Top to comfort Gina this time last year. Now she was gone.

Her memory plagued him. She who'd seemed strong as an oak brought down in a matter of months. His dad too, nothing to complain of given his age but there had been no real warning and Tommy would have given anything to sit down and have one final conversation with him.

He moped around the garden, full of inexplicable feelings, things that made no sense and wouldn't be dispelled.

It had all started with Dominic. He went back in search of him.

The cemetery was deserted.

Tommy sat on the usual bench and waited. All around him was a sea of ivy. The hedge and fence posts were shaggy with it: dark green luscious leaves, white-veined like stars. The woody stems at the top of the fence, finding nothing to cling to, waved experimentally in the breeze.

The growth was thickest of all, though, in among the graves, dripping from the boughs of a nearby yew tree, extending along the ground and creeping upwards over every headstone. The long tendrils, sometimes leafless, snaked over the worn inscriptions.

The priest had his work cut out if he was planning to clear the graves completely. He arrived shortly after midday, bringing his wheelbarrow to a halt beside the bench with a smile.

'How are you, Tommy?'

'Fine,' shrugged Tommy and said no more, sitting back to watch as Dominic knelt down to examine the thick mass of stems covering a nearby headstone, pulling the ivy aside and following the different trails to establish where best to start cutting it back.

As he began pulling the twining branches away and depositing them in the wheelbarrow, fragments of broken masonry and ornaments emerged from the undergrowth.

Tommy gazed idly down at the bas relief of an angel on a stone medallion, half worn away, and made out the remains of an inscription . . . 'at rest'.

'Death,' he said thoughtfully. 'What's the answer?'

Dominic glanced up at him.

'Well, you're a priest!' said Tommy. 'You're supposed to know about these things.'

'There is no answer,' said Dominic. 'Death's not a question. It's a certainty. The question is life: given the fact that we die, how shall we live?'

He reached for his scissors and began snipping away again at the woody stems.

How shall I live?

Tommy had never stopped to think about it before. Never been in doubt about what he wanted. Even after James he hadn't been unsure of the way forward. After James there had been Lister's.

He didn't want to dwell on that. The humiliation of being ousted still rankled. The business with the will was even more humiliating but, thankfully, no-one knew about it.

'Suppose I don't know how to live?' he said at last. 'Suppose I'm at a loss?'

'Well, what do you most want?' asked Dominic.

Not to have destroyed the will.

Not to have lied.

The remedy, of course, was appallingly simple.

He'd have to tell the truth.

It meant telling Bryony first and she wasn't going to like it. He called her mobile as he walked home. She was at the printer's in Milton Keynes, arranging leaflets for autumn events at Cottesbrooke.

'Thought I'd cook tonight,' he said. 'There's something I need to tell you.'

'Oh?' Her tone was wary.

'Don't worry,' he said, trying to sound more confident than he felt. 'I'll see you tonight. It'll be duck.'

Their courtship had been this way: a partnership of experimentation in the kitchen. Her parents had been big theatre goers, provincial repertory at the Royal in Northampton, opera and ballet in London. Always out on Saturday nights. Her mother had turned a blind eye to the culinary projects that went on in her kitchen.

He'd been nineteen the first time he'd walked through the door of the Richardson home, could remember even now the way Bryony had set the dining table for him, not just one candle but three or four grouped together round a silver rose bowl, the perfume of the roses wafting in the heat from the flames.

They'd laughed over her parent's tastes, the heavy furniture and old-fashioned dinner service. Bryony had been studying textile and furniture restoration, working on the Mortlake tapestries at Boughton House. It was a pastime her mother thought worth while before marriage but what Bryony had loved was the people she'd met, the new places she'd seen, the excitement of driving around the county on her own, not the painstaking labour of conservation.

He'd told her about the market, about all the new things coming up from London, about James Wilcox and his plan for Orton's.

When it came to the food, though, they'd mostly sat silent, comparing it all. They'd tried oefs en cocotte, veal escalopes and coq au vin, followed on with chocolate soufflé or home baked meringues. Whatever it was, they'd sat and savoured it, exchanging mute glances over the rim of their wine glasses while they ate.

He'd loved her appetite for trying new things, her enthusiasm for those she liked and her equal ability to reserve judgement without embarrassment: *'No, I don't know. I don't know about that one. No idea!'*

She'd know about this one tonight, it was an old favourite.

He cooked a crown of duck covered in plums, thinly sliced and mixed with cranberries soaked in cassis, roasted it slowly in the oven. Then he parboiled mini courgettes and baby carrots to go with it, turned them with a squeeze of orange juice, honey and chopped chives and left them in the oven with a touch of butter.

The smell at least was mouth-watering and he hoped it boded well.

The wine was his final touch to surprise her. He'd picked up a Faugeres, not particularly expensive but a good one: a blend of Mourvedre and Grenache, fruity like the duck but crunchy too, a wine you could bite on.

He poured it in the kitchen, left the bottle concealed and watched her drink it with an inquisitive look, conscious in his play-acting that he was delaying the inevitable.

'French?' she ventured. 'Chateauneuf du Pape? No, not quite.'

He let her drink some more then fetched the bottle and showed her the label.

'Faugeres! South west.'

She laughed and took another mouthful, savoured it, but her eyes were on his face now and when she'd swallowed and put the glass down her approach was forthright:

'So, what's on your mind?'

He'd sat down adjacent to her and reached across to put a hand over hers on the table.

'I've done something I shouldn't have,' he said.

'More than usual?'

He nodded.

Her expression grew worried and he steeled himself as he broke it to her. 'Gina left Kimble's Top to Esther not Robyn. There was another will.'

'Right.' She looked at him, waiting for the rest.

'I took it,' said Tommy. 'Shredded it. Esther would have sold the house. We could never let that happen.'

Her look of disgust shook him.

'She had the shares,' he said in defence. 'At least, I thought she did.'

'How could you be so dishonest?' She was staring at him in cold wonder. 'Is that why you've been so uptight? I thought it was grief. I thought, just give it time: he's grieving. And all along it was . . .'

He tightened his hand on hers. 'I was afraid. Because of the house . . .'

'You destroyed a will, Tommy!' she slipped her hand out from under his and pressed it to her forehead looking bewildered. 'What were you thinking?'

'I was thinking about Kimble's Top,' said Tommy. 'And how Esther mustn't be allowed to sell it.'

He looked at her hard, concerned that she wasn't grasping it.

'Don't you understand, Bryony? I did it because of the house. And now, if I tell Esther the truth, which I need to do: I've got to tell her what happened there.'

His wife's expression froze. Her eyes flooded with pain. 'I don't want all that raking up,' she said.

'I can't help it,' said Tommy gently. 'We should have told them years ago. Especially Chris and Elisabeth.'

She was shaking her head, her eyes looking down at the table. 'They don't need to know,' she said. 'It's pointless. Pointless pain.'

'They do need to know,' argued Tommy. 'Because look where it's got us.'

'Look where it's got you,' she snapped. Her eyes, dark with fury, were on him now. 'This was you. Not us.'

Panic gripped him. He took a deep breath and reached for her hand again but she withheld it. 'All I'm saying is . . . I've got to tell Esther.'

'Tell her then!' said Bryony. 'But I'm not having everyone picking over the past.'

36

Telling Esther

Now that he'd made up his mind he just wanted to get on with it. He lay awake half the night full of dread. If he was going to be wound up about anything it should have been the thought of telling Esther he'd lied about her mother's will but in fact it was the prospect of talking about James that made his stomach churn. A dismal realisation that did nothing for his sense of moral stature.

He got up well before five and went to sit in his study, weary at the whole damn mess. Even if Robyn agreed to give up Kimble's Top he'd only be right back where he'd started because Esther would sell the house, sell it for the money that was rightfully hers, and strangers would own the ground where his son had died. They'd dig up the garden, rearrange everything. Above all, he and Bryony would never again be able to stand where their boy had last been alive.

In his mind's eye he saw the marble figure of Peter Pan glancing up, looking for him, reassured as James had been reassured, busy with his roller skates but always glancing up to see if they were watching him.

'Stay on the drive!' Bryony had called and had he smiled back? Called back 'yes, okay' in his clear boyish tone?

Where would his boy be without the knowledge of them being there, never forgetting him?

As the clock moved on towards six, he tried to conjure up some sympathy for Esther but all he felt was an irritated guilt, irritated that her negative, passive indifference towards Kimble's Top had put him in this situation in the first place.

He wondered how Gina could have produced such offspring. She who'd been as strong as an oak and deep rooted, extending herself for everyone around, while Esther seemed no more than a fallen leaf, skittering along the ground, barely audible, leaving neither trace nor impression.

He sighed and checked again that her mobile number was close at hand, sitting on in his study, waiting for an acceptable hour to call.

Just after seven he heard Bryony moving around upstairs. She'd gone to bed ahead of him; given up on the meal and left him to clear the dishes. He'd heard her on the phone chasing RSVPs for a golden wedding party they were hosting for friends and come into the study to check his emails. Then, for want of anything better to do, he'd flicked through Christopher's online photos from his hiking trip in Scotland, assuming she'd come and find him and they'd talk further. It was only when he'd come out to make their usual night time drinks that he'd realised she'd already gone to bed.

Lying awake in the darkness, he'd fancied more than once that she was awake too but she'd given him no indication of it and he'd been afraid to reach out and draw her close.

Now as he heard the shower running he wandered through the downstairs rooms, tidying up bits and pieces, then on into the kitchen to make some coffee. She was due at a meeting in Watford around nine to sort out polo shirts and umbrellas for the golf club.

When she came downstairs she was dressed and ready to go. He offered her the cup of black coffee, which she took without saying anything, and stood watching her pour muesli into a bowl, willing her to speak first, until eventually she glanced up at him. 'So you're going to tell Esther today?'

He nodded.

'And then?'

'I don't know,' he said. 'It all depends on Robyn.'

She was staring at him, waiting for more, but all he could do was shrug. 'One thing at a time!'

She sipped the remainder of her coffee in silence, finished her breakfast and went to put her bowl and cup in the dishwasher, ignoring his outstretched hand to take them from her.

'How to needlessly complicate your life,' was her parting shot as she left the kitchen and he stayed at the counter listening to her gathering her bag and keys in the hall, pulling the front door closed and starting up the BMW, the noise of its engine receding down the drive.

At eight thirty he could wait no longer and dialled Esther's mobile but it was switched off. He ignored the voicemail service, and whiled away an impatient half an hour, then another and another, calling her repeatedly to no avail until by mid-morning he'd had enough.

The last thing he'd wanted was to go to Hartley Rise, to ring the doorbell at his dad's old house and sit in that front room to make his confession, but there seemed nothing else for it.

He slipped his jacket on and set off, suppressing his feelings of trepidation, but there was no answer at the front door of fourteen Hartley Rise and when he tried the mobile again it was still turned off.

Thoroughly agitated now, he headed for her work place, The Sorting Room, hoping to find her there or at least discover when she was due in.

The bar was cavernous and empty. The young manager, stick-thin in his black shirt and trousers, was playing pool in a far corner while wide screen televisions blasted out a music channel on every side.

'Esther Radford?' enquired Tommy. 'Is she due in any time? She's my niece. Not answering her mobile.'

'Esther?' the guy shook his head. 'She's only here weekends now. Got herself a job at Ariadne's in Kettering.'

'A bar?' asked Tommy.

'Shop. In Market Place.'

'Right,' said Tommy. 'Thanks!'

He walked home, got straight in the car and drove over to Kettering, parked by the Council Offices and made his way to Market Place where he spotted the shop front between a bookmaker's and a tanning studio. Ariadne's window was full of dreamcatchers, crystals and dolphin posters. As Tommy pushed the door open a collection of miniature windchimes tinkled by his ear and the rich aroma of sandalwood caught his throat.

Esther looked across from the counter and was clearly startled to see him.

'We need to talk,' he said.

'I'm working, Tommy.'

She was wearing an embroidered turquoise top with matching beads and it was the first time in ages he'd seen her looking so colourful:

'Don't you get a lunch break?' he asked.

She shrugged. 'The manager's at the bank. I suppose, when she gets back . . .'

'I'll wait,' he said, knowing from her expression and the reluctance in her voice that she wouldn't welcome that but he couldn't turn back now.

He turned away from her to browse among the amber jewellery and semi-precious stones.

Was there much of a market for this kind of thing?

Esther was folding multi-coloured scarves with glittering threads and knotted tassels. He glanced across surreptitiously now and then but neither of them spoke.

Not one customer came into the shop all the while he was waiting and he'd give it three months with footfall like that. Even when people did come in he doubted they'd spend much.

Finally the wind chimes at the door tinkled and he looked across to see a woman entering, clearly the manager by her tie-dye skirt and beaded top. She wore a young person's glasses with narrow tortoiseshell frames but the thick plait of grey hair pulled over one shoulder gave the game away.

Typical of Esther to fall in with a washed-up hippy, he thought. Meanwhile his niece had exchanged a few words with her and was reaching under the counter for her handbag.

'Twenty minutes,' she told Tommy. 'Then I'm coming back.'

He followed her up to the old horsemarket café and they sat at a plain wooden table beside the square panes of the bow window.

'If this is about my so-called inheritance,' she said: 'I'm not interested in your schemes. So, Mum left me with nothing? Let's just leave it at that.'

'She didn't,' said Tommy, looking her in the eye. 'She left you Kimble's Top. There was another will. Written in 2003 when RSG went under.'

'What?' she was visibly shocked.

'Your mum made a later will,' he put the facts to her again, slowly, as he'd rehearsed them. 'It was in the desk at Kimble's Top. I found it, along with the earlier one. And I shredded it.'

His heart was pounding now as he faced the outrage in her green eyes.

'You bastard!' Her words were barely more than a whisper: 'Why?'

This was it. The first part had been easy but this was the moment. Even sitting down, his knees were trembling and he felt suddenly short of breath. He tried to fix on something concrete, a way in.

'I was afraid you'd sell the house. You would have, wouldn't you?'

She laughed contemptuously and swung her head slowly from side to side with an expression of consternation. 'So?'

'Esther . . .' He leaned forward, resting his arms on the table but her thoughts had run on and she was speaking again, full of contempt. 'You know, you're unbelievable! You've known this for months. And now I've got a new job, something I really like, and you come and find me here . . . and you just . . . dump it on me.'

She pushed her chair back from the table and for a moment he was afraid she was going to leave but she carried on talking. 'Why can't you just leave me alone? All of you? Every time I find somewhere I feel good about myself, somewhere I'm okay . . . you all just trash it.'

He stared at her, caught completely unawares by her response.

'Look,' he said. 'We have to talk about Kimble's Top.'

'Fine: talk about it! So Mum left me the house and you thought better. Obviously.' Her tone was heavy with sarcasm.

'My son died there,' the words were big, unmanageable even as he forced them out of his mouth. 'He died there and I was afraid you'd sell the house.'

'What son?'

'James. Our eldest. It was a long time ago.'

She was silent, transfixed, and he just kept on talking. 'I wasn't thinking straight. When I saw the will. All I could think about was Kimble's Top. I didn't realise about the shares. Truly, Esther. I thought you'd still get an awful lot of money.'

The waiter arrived with their coffees and they sat motionless while he set them down. Tommy nodded a thank-you, conscious of the man's curious glance and of the shoppers at the tables all around them.

'So that's it, is it?' said Esther. 'That's everything?'

Her expression was impenetrable. He sat numb and silent and finally she gave a cold shrug. 'Well I don't know what you expect me to do. I'm twenty five. And all I've had is death. First dad then mum, Granddad. And now this.' She got to her feet and picked up her bag. 'I don't know what you expect me to do.'

'Esther: we need to resolve things. There's the house. The money.'

'Money!' she laughed then, a low contemptuous laugh. 'Well you're the one who's good with money, Tommy. So you sort it out!'

And with that she stepped away and pushed her chair roughly back under the table. 'And don't ever come to the shop again. It's where I go to get away from all your crap!'

Back home he sat in his study without even bothering to take his coat off, sat and stared at the blank computer screen until Bryony's car pulled up on the drive outside.

He watched her from the window, heard her key in the front door and her movements as she took her coat off in the hall. She stopped by the open door and looked in on him.

'How did it go?'

'Don't ask,' he said without even turning his head.

She hesitated and he swung the chair round to look at her, saw her face tight with anger. She stared at him silently for a moment then went off to the kitchen without a word.

37

LIMBO

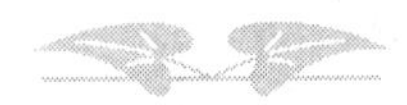

He was in limbo. Purgatory. Whatever the official state was. He gave Esther a day to get over the shock then phoned her mobile again.

'Hi it's Esther. Sorry I'm not around. Leave a message!'

We need to talk. We need to resolve this.

He repeated it several times that day and on the days that followed, his messages increasingly curt and angry. He wanted to go to the shop again but didn't dare and when he rang the bell at Hartley Rise there was no answer, though he suspected more than once that she was in.

Bloody ridiculous!

Then there was Bryony: angry, cold and hostile.

When Saturday came she was going out all day, doing PR at one of the country craft fairs she'd been working on. He offered to go with her, they'd have stalls with outdoor clothing and hiking gear, they'd talked about getting Chris something for his birthday, but she wouldn't have it.

'Not today. I'm not in the mood.'

'Come on, Bry! The only way we're going to get beyond this is to face it.'

'Face it!' she turned on him angrily, in the middle of assembling keys, business cards and promotional fliers for the event.

'Look, I know what I did was wrong!'

She slipped her jacket on and picked up her bag.

'For goodness sake, Bryony. What do you want me to do? Just say . . . and I'll do it.'

'I want you not to have done what you did. I want you not to be the person you appear to be. Just leave all that!' he'd picked up her camera bag and flask of tea. 'You're not coming. Can't you see, I'm going there to work? The least you can do is leave me in peace.'

He walked up to the cemetery instead, sat alone on the bench and stared at the monuments to the dead, wondering if any of them had screwed up their lives as spectacularly as he'd done. Or had they all been exemplary, flawless people?

The next day the family was meeting for Sunday tea at Kimble's Top and, for the first time, he felt the precariousness of the situation around him. Robyn had broken with tradition and set the table outside on the terrace, though the food was Gina's traditional fare: baguettes, bowls of salad, cold ham and the elegant white crockery exactly as she'd have liked it.

Tommy looked along the length of the stone terrace: at Richard and Maurice sitting on the curved benches, heads bent over their plates; at his sisters-in-law helping themselves to food with Robyn presiding; while Laurel and the boys gingerly handed round the cups and saucers.

It all seemed so solid and well-founded but one word from Esther, had she been here, one word from Bryony and the whole façade would be shattered, everything shown up for the sham that it was.

Bryony, however, wasn't speaking, at least not to him. She'd gone to sit some distance away, elegant in her thin pink cardigan with black checks, a black silk top and knee-length pink skirt. She'd gathered her blonde hair back loosely into a pink ribbon, pulling it away from her face so everyone could see the lines of tension round her mouth and the dangerous look in her eyes.

He caught enough glances between the others to know they'd registered the conflict between them but no-one said anything. They sat in silent collusion, the real issue unacknowledged while Robyn and Paul squabbled noisily over trivialities.

Robyn was wearing a striking necklace of long amber beads with a soft grey cardigan buttoned across her chest and wide silk trousers in bright blue. 'They were Gina's,' she said, fingering the beads when her aunts remarked on them. 'The trousers too, I had them cut to size.'

Richard looked taken aback by that but Robyn just shrugged. 'Esther had her chance. She could have taken them at Christmas.'

'Oh they wouldn't suit Esther,' said Doreen. 'Not her style at all.'

There was a question about the wisdom of bringing the china serving plates out onto the folding picnic tables but Robyn was insistent. 'Gina always liked to use them. Otherwise what's the point of having nice things. That's what she always said.'

And the shortbread she'd made with grains of lavender from the garden was Gina's recipe. 'I found it written on a card in one of her books.'

'Oh well, as long as it's what Gina liked,' mimicked Paul.

'So what?' retorted Robyn. 'If she had taste . . .'

'Or you could just think for yourself . . .'

It went on all afternoon while Tommy sat listening and staring out across the mown stripes of the lawn, wishing he could just close his eyes and be free of it all.

Esther's name was mentioned more than once, her absence put down to her working at the bar, and no-one seemed to know she'd got a new job. Neither he nor Bryony mentioned it.

He could hardly bear to think of her, here at the house he'd put out of her reach, but she was on his mind all afternoon. His dad too; Tommy pictured him, leaning on his stick, breathing hard, watching them all, and it reminded him of last summer: Gina here with his dad, day after day, waiting for Esther to come home to what was rightfully hers.

As soon as they'd finished tea he left the terrace and wandered away through the long grass under the trees where the foxgloves grew tall, their translucent pink hoods as delicate as Bryony's skirt, then followed the path beyond the shrubbery and along the perimeter fence towards the rose garden.

He'd hoped Bryony would join him but she didn't. He stood there alone instead, his shadow engulfing the little marble boy, and for the first time ever he imagined James as a young man, shoulder to shoulder with him.

If you'd lived would things have been different?

Might Esther have been a different person with you as her cousin?

God knows!

In the week that followed, Bryony avoided him. She worked long hours, combining several meetings in a single day and travelling some distance for them. From the names and places he could tell it wasn't current business. She was either drumming up trade, keeping old contacts warm or just plain avoiding him. She ate lunch out and once or twice that extended to evening meals too.

His own days were uneasy. Memories of James came back vividly now. When he strolled into town, he was conscious of every thirty-something youngster he passed: young men the age his son would have been today.

James William Allbright, what would you have done with your life?

He went in search of the priest, found the wheelbarrow abandoned by the bench in the usual corner of the cemetery and, strolling through the trees, spotted Dominic down near the gate. A black bin liner trailed from his hand and he was standing half bent over, looking intently at a clump of flowers.

'Some sort of hybrid Echium,' he said as Tommy drew near. 'See how the bees love it!'

Tommy stared down at the frond-like plant with its long clusters of blue and white flowers. The honey bees were all over it, crawling deep into the petals.

'I like the way they tip themselves right up to get inside,' said Dominic. 'Imagine a lifetime spent in the gentle places. The taste of nectar!'

'Hmm,' Tommy moved away from the plant, hoping to initiate a serious conversation. 'Can we talk about real things?'

'Such as?'

'The meaning of life? And just what is the point when we're all going to die anyway?'

The priest followed him along the path, stopping now and again to pick up litter and drop it into his bin liner.

'The meaning of life?' he mused, considering Tommy's words. 'I suppose it's to love and be loved?'

And what if you lose that love?

He kept it hypothetical. 'Supposing no-one loves you?'

'No-one's completely unloved,' said Dominic. 'God's love is always there.'

Religion again!

'It's just a myth,' said Tommy. 'A load of fables. And completely intangible. God's a philosophical concept.'

'God's a person,' said the priest. 'And his love's not intangible. It's in your every breath. Embedded in the fabric of the universe. The very fact that you exist is an expression of his love for you individually.'

'Okay,' shrugged Tommy. 'Supposing it's true. So, what then? You psyche yourself up to feel something? To love this god?'

'No,' said Dominic. 'You realise how much God loves you and, bit by bit, you respond.'

'How?'

'With love,' laughed the priest as though it were obvious. 'With the desire he puts in our hearts, we desire to desire him more.

'Isn't that rather circular?' said Tommy.

'Oh yes. It's all of him.'

They'd walked some way among the graves, Tommy pointing out the crisp packets and foil wrappers ensnared in the ivy for Dominic to pick up.

Ahead of them a fallen cross lay spread-eagled on the ground, its double plinth carpeted with moss. The priest reached down to retrieve an empty beer can lodged in the angle behind it. 'The human and the divine, Tommy. Our lives are inextricably linked. Whatever our response to him, it is that: a response.'

Tommy tried a half-hearted prayer on the way home: *If you exist, get me out of this mess!* That night Bryony told him she was going away for a few days. Her equestrian client was competing up in Yorkshire and she wanted to get some decent photographs for a sponsorship deal they'd set up through the regional Business Link.

'Four days should give me time to get some real action shots.'

He wasn't invited to join her and when she'd gone the week stretched ahead, empty.

After a couple of days he wrote a letter to Esther, put it through the door at Hartley Rise and sent her a text: This has gone on long enough. I WANT a response.

In the letter he admitted again that what he'd done was wrong and gave her three options: either we lean on Robyn to give up Kimble's Top entirely; or we find a financial compromise that allows you to realise some of the value of the house; or you think of something else altogether and we discuss it.

Her text came the following day: Option 3 Hartley Rise 6:30 2nite 2 discuss.

His spirits soared. She'd finally seen sense. He had no idea what she had in mind but, whatever it was, he was sure they could work it out. He was a businessman and if he couldn't arrange things himself he'd have contacts who could do so.

His euphoria lasted for all of half an hour then a dull oppression descended. What if she came up with something totally outlandish? This was Esther after all.

He rang Bryony in Yorkshire. 'Things seem to be moving forward. Esther has something in mind she wants to talk about.'

'Great,' her tone was cold, unimpressed.

'I miss you,' he said.

Silence.

'Look Bry, please . . .'

'Tommy, I'm taking photos in the middle of a dressage ring. This isn't the time.'

'Ring me later then,' he said. 'When you can talk.'

She didn't.

At six fifteen he set off for Hartley Rise.

Esther opened the door looking white faced, on edge, and said nothing as she led the way inside.

Tommy followed her into the front room and was taken aback to find the manager from Ariadne's there. She smiled up at him serenely from one of the sofas.

He nodded cautiously, expecting her to get up and announce she was going, but she didn't move.

He sat down awkwardly on the adjacent sofa.

'Fleur's from the shop,' said Esther, taking a seat next to the woman, so that they sat there, shoulder to shoulder, observing him. 'We've been talking and she agreed to be here.'

'Why?'

His anger was rising and they hadn't even started yet.

'Fleur's here for me,' said Esther. 'It's what I want.'

She looked up at him for a moment:

'What you told me was quite upsetting. And I was already upset over mum.'

It had all been rehearsed, he could tell from her words. He clenched his teeth, furious at having his guilt paraded before this stranger.

'I've been thinking about what you told me,' said Esther. 'And you want a response. But I'm not ready to talk about it. It's too overwhelming. So that's my response. I'm not ready to deal with it.'

You are dealing with it! We're here, aren't we? Let's just talk.

She raised a hand as if sensing he was about to speak. 'When I'm ready to talk about it, Tommy. I'll let you know.'

'And do you have any idea when that might be?' he spoke with forced civility.

Esther shook her head but from his peripheral vision he could have sworn he saw triumph on her companion's face. It took him back to his office. Hartman and Lister, standing, waiting to escort him from the premises.

He got to his feet, hot with humiliation, and, to his fury, the washed-up hippy of a manager followed him out to the hall.

'Esther was very upset when she came back from your meeting,' she said. 'There's a lot of grief there.'

'It's a family matter,' said Tommy curtly.

'Oh, it's not about you,' she said matter of factly. 'Or the will. Money, houses. No, it goes much deeper than that.'

'Really?'

He'd opened the front door but couldn't pull it inwards with her standing there.

'Losing her dad at a young age,' she was saying. 'Not being able to grieve in the way she needed to. Her mum didn't really accept her for who she was, did she? It's very damaging.'

'And what are you?' he snapped. 'Some kind of therapist? Feeding off other people's misery!'

She just smiled quietly and said nothing but at least their session was finished. She moved away and he yanked the door wide open and left the house.

He was livid, dialling Bryony's mobile even as he reached the end of the terraced street and entered the alley over the railway.

'It's bloody useless,' he raged as soon as she answered. 'She's hooked up with some do-gooder. All very alternative. Therapy. Counselling. Apparently she isn't ready to deal with it. Can you believe it! I've admitted the truth, I'm doing my everything I can to put things right and she won't meet me halfway!'

'Darling, you can't write the script for everyone else!' said Bryony. 'You made a choice, Tommy. You chose to do something and how people respond is up to them. You can't dictate it. You made your choice. Now they're making theirs.'

'She's not making a choice! She's doing nothing.'

'Well she gave you a response. And you're just going to have to live with it.'

'Thanks!'

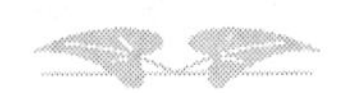

It was no better when she came home at the end of the week.

'Good trip?' he asked, out in the hall with the front door open as soon as he heard her car on the drive.

'Not really,' she dumped her overnight bag on the floor. 'It turns out I'm not like you. I thought I could lose myself in my work. But it just doesn't do it for me.'

'So where does that leave us?'

'I don't know, Tommy.'

He closed the front door and stood leaning against it, looking at her.

'I'm sorry,' she said. 'But you're going to have to accept that what you did has consequences for all of us, not just Esther. And it's not just the will. I'm talking about us.'

'That's exactly why we need to resolve it,' he said.

'We do,' she agreed. 'But I'm afraid I'm like Esther. I'm not ready.'

38

Another Sunday

Another Sunday and still it felt as if everything were hanging by a thread. The family was together at Richard and Doreen's house and he was afraid of every last thing that perpetuated his lie; everything that reinforced the falsehood that was going to come to light.

It was all Esther's fault. She was holding him back, refusing to let things reach their conclusion.

He sat in relative isolation, at one end of the dining table beside the patio door, while the others had gravitated with their plates to the lounge.

Bryony was filling them in on her trip to Yorkshire, the equestrian world and show-jumping, or the 'hunting, shooting, fishing crowd' as the others liked to call it.

'There's money there,' she said. 'It may not make the front pages like the celebrities. But it's the same old families, the same public schools. Directorships. Nothing's changed.'

'Well we can't complain,' said Maurice. 'Gina and Arthur did all right for themselves. That was all company shares. Big fat dividends.'

‘They were part of it,’ agreed Bryony. ‘Though not on a grand scale. Arthur wasn’t one for spending, either, except on Kimble’s Top.’

Keep it general, thought Tommy, willing the conversation to move on. He sensed the others waiting for his contribution. It was just the kind of thing he’d have taken an authoritative view on once but now he stared down at his salad and wished to God they’d leave Kimble’s Top alone.

He glanced surreptitiously at his watch. Not even three o’clock yet.

Out on the patio a scattering of breadcrumbs had attracted the birds and a blue tit clung precariously to a strand of ivy hanging from the garden fence.

It reminded him of the ivy in the graveyard and he wondered idly what Dominic was doing this afternoon. He’d have been at church this morning, of course, but that must have finished ages ago and where your average vicar had a wife and family, Sunday lunch at home, it must be different for these Catholic guys, Tommy realised. He sat frowning over it, wondering if Dominic spent all day praying like some kind of monk.

The priest smiled when Tommy suggested it two days later.

The worst of the ivy had been gone now and he was touching up the iron railings round one of the big graves. It was a double memorial: two long stone caskets side by side with a decorative knotted border along the edges. The rectangular space around them was bounded by rusty railings, wrought iron arches complete with gothic tracery and topped with trefoils.

Tommy sat watching the red flakes of rust scatter on the ground as the priest brushed the loose bits away and answered his question.

'Well, Sunday's my quietest day. Two, maybe three masses if I'm lucky. Sometimes there's a baptism in the afternoon. But other than that, yes, I do actually get to stop and pray.'

'What do you pray about?'

'Life,' said Dominic. 'The things I do. People I meet.'

'Like me?'

'Yes. I pray for you.'

He said it so simply Tommy was dumbstruck. 'What do you pray?' he asked.

'That you'll find God. His grace and love. His forgiveness.'

Tommy laughed. 'You've got some kind of faith!'

'I've got some kind of God.'

It was ridiculous, this belief in God, but the thought of Dominic praying for him was intriguing beyond belief.

The rusty flakes were falling again, peppering the grass, and as Dominic leaned forward, a line of inscription on the headstone behind him came into view:

~angels to beckon thee nearer to God~

'Supposing I did want to go for it?' said Tommy suddenly. 'This whole God thing? What then?'

Dominic looked up at him. 'I think if you're at all interested in meeting God he'll come and find you.'

'What if he doesn't?'

'Make a rendezvous,' suggested the priest. 'Choose somewhere.'

Church was the obvious place but he wouldn't go locally, not where people might recognise him.

He drove sixty miles, the following Sunday, and that was Bryony's fault. He hadn't intended to do anything about it so soon but she went away for the weekend. He'd forgotten it was in the diary: a spa break at a country hotel, the hen weekend and pre-wedding celebration for the daughter of some not very good friends of theirs.

'Don't go,' Tommy urged her. 'You were away all last week.'

'I know,' she conceded with a pained look. 'But I did have my reasons, Tommy. And this date's been in the diary for ages.'

He picked up the embossed invitation that lay on the kitchen counter. 'We don't even like these people,' he said.

'That's not true,' she protested with a wry smile but they both knew he was right.

The hosts were domineering people, friends of some rotary friends. Tommy and Bryony would have dropped them years ago except Chris had been a big mate of their son, so it had been shared lifts to the rugby and long chats at parents' evenings. By the time they'd been talked into accepting a social invitation and then felt obliged to return it, they'd found themselves unable to break the connection.

'I can't pull out now,' said Bryony taking the invitation from him. 'Anyway, it's their big event and they want me to be there.'

'You won't be back until Monday lunchtime,' he pointed out but she wouldn't be dissuaded.

When she'd gone he phoned Chris, thinking he might go down to Kingston, but his son was going away for the weekend with friends, and when he tried Elisabeth he got the answerphone, then realised she was on her Cuban holiday.

By Saturday afternoon he'd done all the possible household chores and found himself looking online at Catholic churches.

There was one about an hour's drive away, just into Suffolk. It was modern, like so many of them, but looked tasteful; a half-timbered building with latticed windows. Sunday mass was at ten thirty.

He set off early and arrived with plenty of time to park the car and wander round the little market town beforehand.

He'd never been inside a Catholic church before, apart from sightseeing in foreign cathedrals, and this one was nothing like he'd imagined. There were no images or statues, just a crucifix hanging over the altar steps. The cross was very slender, the young strong arms of Christ almost obscuring the thin horizontal beam. His dark head was bowed, feet elegantly crossed with a trace of red for blood.

Beyond the crucifix everything was highly decorated. The ceiling was blue with gold stars and the end wall had a line of gilded columns topped with crowns and alternating panels of red and green painted with lilies.

The main body of the church was plain, though, with white walls and the wooden roof pitched high above them.

He was one of the first to arrive and sat at the very back to avoid attention. By ten twenty five the church was full. He estimated about a hundred people, totting up the heads in front of him and multiplying by the number of rows beyond. About a third of them were children and there was a mix of nationalities.

He found he didn't know the responses or the hymns and the bible readings seemed unfamiliar too. The priest talked on about divine light and the glory of God but Tommy wasn't really taking it in, overwhelmed instead by the closeness of people all around and a sense of being caught up in something to which he clearly didn't belong.

Afterwards he avoided the throng, stepping firmly away from the drift towards coffee in the adjoining hall and bypassing the priest at the main door.

As he drove home he thought back on it all, probing for something meaningful, but there was nothing, just the unfamiliarity of it all: sitting, standing, the line of people taking communion. He'd stayed where he was for that, glanced at one or two of them making their way back, wondering what it meant, what it did for them.

He'd been driving for about twenty minutes when he ran into congestion on the motorway. He pulled off at the next exit and took the back roads, stopping on impulse at a village pub with a carvery and a nice line in cask ales.

It was a beautiful day so he sat on after lunch with a pint of Woodforde's Wherry, enjoying the pub garden and it was nearly six o'clock by the time he finally got home.

To his surprise Bryony's car was on the drive.

He found her curled up on the living room sofa and she looked up at him with obvious relief. 'Where have you been? Your phone was off!'

'Sorry.'

He'd switched it off going in to church and not thought to turn it on again. He leaned down to kiss her. 'I wasn't expecting you back.'

'Well, you were right!' she said. 'I don't know why I went. We've never liked those people. All they talk about is manicures, body wraps and the latest designer handbag. Don't ever let me agree to a weekend like that again!'

He laughed and sat down beside her. 'You prefer your old market trader then?'

She nodded and got up. 'You stay there. Wait til you see what I picked up on the way home!'

He relaxed on the sofa while she went to the kitchen and returned with two tall glasses of Campari and soda: a throw-back to their courting days.

'Remember these?' she handed him a glass. 'We thought we were so sophisticated!'

As he raised his glass to drink, she reached across to clink hers to it.

'You do still want me then?' he said. 'In spite of everything?'

'You know, Tommy,' she said. 'I never did think you were perfect!'

39

In Memoriam

'Where were you, anyway?' Bryony asked later when they were getting ready for bed.

'Sixty miles away,' he said. 'I went to church.'

'There's one just down the road!'

'I didn't want anyone to see me.'

She stopped massaging her cheeks with moisturiser for a moment and glanced at him. 'Are you getting all religious on me?'

He laughed. 'Don't worry. It did nothing for me.'

He told Dominic as much the following day.

The little railings round the double grave were shiny and black now and the priest was re-gilding the trefoils, tracing each raised outline and the central indents with gold paint.

Tommy sat on the bench enjoying the August sunshine.

'Your rendezvous didn't work, by the way,' he said. 'I went to church. Should have known it wasn't my thing.'

He leaned back comfortably and gazed across the densely packed graves to the blue spire of the chapel framed by fir trees. All around them the graveyard was quiet except for occasional birdsong.

'If anything,' he mused: 'I've felt closer to God sitting here talking to you.'

Dominic just nodded at that and smiled.

'So?' said Tommy.

'So you've found your answer,' said the priest: 'The rendezvous was here all along?'

'Oh!' Tommy had to laugh. You just can't lose, can you? You religious types! You have this whole different logic.'

Dominic shrugged, dipped his narrow brush into the oily paint and resumed the rhythmic brush strokes.

Tommy was done with religion anyway. There was a new business opportunity on the horizon. He'd been emailing his old retail contacts and come up with something much more to his taste than gourmet hampers. This was all about up and coming technology. He couldn't think why it hadn't occurred to him before.

One of his contacts was in the mobile phone market, looking to develop an online product around designer ringtones that could be uploaded directly from a website. Another was exploring the market in digital decoders and thought it was about to take off. According to the article he'd sent Tommy, analogue television sales were still way above sales of digital receivers. Set-top boxes were clearly going to be the top consumer option for the proposed switch-over.

Both contacts were interested in having Tommy as a partner.

He spent hours online looking through the technical commentary on audio editing software and investigating the figures for Top-Up TV subscriptions and BSkyB's plans for FreeSat.

When he needed a break he went up to the graveyard and sat with a takeaway coffee waiting for Dominic. The priest had finished the railings now and was scraping lichen and bird mess off the enclosed headstones and their matching caskets.

'Now that is a complete waste of time,' pronounced Tommy. 'It's only going to come straight back.'

Dominic just smiled, lifted a soaking sponge from his bucket and carried on wetting the old stone.

'And even if it looks good for a while, who's going to see it? No-one ever comes here.'

'You came,' said Dominic.

Tommy watched him drop the sponge back into the bucket and pick up a soft brush, cleaning the stone with a gentle upwards stroke.

'You know, you could have done anything,' he said. 'Really made something of your life.'

He was determined at any rate.

Dominic looked up enquiringly.

'That's all,' shrugged Tommy. 'I'm just saying . . .'

Dominic nodded and went back to his brushing.

Tommy sat back and breathed in the fresh air. It was good to be outside after a morning at the computer. He'd found out all he could about sales of set-top boxes and now, with the benefit of distance, he realised that was the proposal he was the most interested in fleshing out: the one that held real commercial interest.

'You know, I've got a new deal in the offing,' he told Dominic. 'So, if you ever wanted to do something different, I could always give you a start.'

'Well, thank you, Tommy,' said the priest. 'That's very kind of you.'

Yes, it was definitely the one to go for. When he got home he rang his contact and found there was a Taiwanese supplier on board now with a real investment opportunity on offer.

'They're working on something that's a step beyond your basic decoder,' said his friend. 'A next generation model that records onto a hard drive. Forget videos and DVDs! This is going to be the next big thing.'

'Okay. I'm definitely interested,' said Tommy. 'Let's see if we can meet this guy.'

After that there was nothing he could do but daydream about the opportunity and browse the eastern websites in search of a potential tie-in with other retail offerings.

Meanwhile Sunday came round with appalling speed. He'd managed to avoid it last week with Bryony away but they couldn't hide for ever.

It should have been their turn to host but Robyn had rung to say there were potatoes to harvest at Kimble's Top, and fruit to pick, and since the gardens were at their best they might as well all enjoy them.

Driving up through the winding estate took him back this time last year: early evenings with Gina while Robyn took his dad home. Now they were both gone and he was felt trapped in the aftermath of it all.

Still, at least Bryony was on his side again. She sat beside him on the terrace, their chairs pulled into the shady angle of the house and he sensed her listening to the conversation as he did, ready to steer it away from dangerous waters.

The conversation was on work and initially Doreen did all the talking. She'd been pushing for a promotion to the sales team at the hotel, and had managed to get a few hours a week to try it out, but now there were rumours of a sell-out to one of the big chains.

'They say it'll be a total rebrand. Foreign managers coming in. It doesn't look good for the old timers.'

The others were looking to him for an opinion.

'Rumours,' shrugged Tommy. 'Speculation. It could be something or nothing.'

That was when Robyn cut in with her big announcement. 'Since we're on the work front; you might as well know: I've applied to do nursing at De Montfort. It'll be an access course and then there's a degree.'

Tommy sat up with elation. 'That's great!'

'Yes!' Maurice had raised his tea cup by way of a toast. 'Good on you!'

Robyn reclined against the cushions of her wicker chair with an air of triumph:

'I never did much good at school but this is different. There's a point to it now.'

'You seem very pleased,' said Bryony in a low voice when tea was finished.

'Don't you see?' he said softly. 'She'll have a whole new focus in life now. New horizons. She won't want to keep this place up. Not on a nurse's salary. Finally, things are coming together!'

With a bit of luck it would prompt Esther to make a decision as well and he'd actually be free of the whole damn mess.

Tommy got to his feet, combined all the abandoned tea cups into a single tottering stack and carried them to the kitchen where the others were stacking the dishwasher and dividing up the leftover food.

He was brimming with optimism, suddenly ready to congratulate Richard on his daughter's career prospects.

His brother was at the back door, changing into a pair of muddy trainers en route to the vegetable garden.

'Going for a smoke?' asked Tommy.

'Among other things,' said Richard. 'Come anyway. I want to talk to you.'

He picked up a brown envelope from the counter and led the way outside.

'Great news about Robyn!' said Tommy as they crossed the lawn. 'Things are really coming together for her.'

At the greenhouses Richard stopped by a line of grow-bags thick with leafy stems that were wilting slightly. He grabbed a couple of wooden sieves propped against a nearby cold frame and dropped them beside the bags, then handed Tommy the envelope he'd brought from the kitchen.

'The thing is: it's going to cost a bit, this plan of Robyn's. She doesn't want to give this place up for a start and why should she? It's what Gina wanted for her so I suppose we've got to accept that. Anyway she's found something she really wants to do and we've got to support her. We've been looking at different options,' he nodded towards the envelope in Tommy's hand. 'That's the one we've decided on. Thought I'd run it by you first though.'

Tommy sat down on the edge of a brick cold frame and pulled a wadge of papers out of the envelope. They were for an equity release scheme with schedules calculated against Richard and Doreen's house on Eastfield Road. Tommy was shaking his head before he'd even finished the first paragraph.

He looked at his brother who was down on his knees now, reaching deep into the grow bag and lifting out pale shiny potato tubers, brushing the dirt off and laying them in the wooden sieve to dry.

'Richard, don't do it,' said Tommy. 'You'd be better off re-mortgaging.'

'We don't want the monthly payments,' said his brother. 'Not at our time of life. Anyway we're only releasing twenty five per cent.'

'Yes but they'll pay you a fraction of the market rate. And you're talking about fifteen hundred in set-up fees. You'll still be liable for all the maintenance, you know. And it won't even be your property. It's not worth it! Look, get a low interest loan against the value of the house.'

Richard wasn't convinced, Tommy could see it. His brother wiped his hands down his trousers and came to sit beside him on the cold frame, reaching into his shirt pocket for a cigarette.

'Don't give up your house,' Tommy urged him. 'Not for this.'

'You've always had it in for Robyn.'

'It's not about Robyn,' said Tommy. 'I think she'll be a great nurse. She was there with Gina right to the end. This is about money. It doesn't make sense.'

Richard didn't argue. He just took the papers back, folded them neatly together and sat quietly smoking, his fingers curled round the cigarette while the white smoke rose in wisps and vanished into the summer air.

Tommy was perplexed. He wanted to tell Richard what a mistake he was making, jeopardising his investment to help Robyn keep a house that wasn't hers, that Esther would claim for her own any day now, but he couldn't say anything.

'Maybe it's because of Doreen's job,' suggested Bryony when they were back at home. 'She's worried about that. Perhaps they've got other debts. It might seem the obvious choice to release some capital.'

They were in the kitchen, he sitting on a stool at the counter while she picked through a bowl of raspberries they'd brought back from Kimble's Top. The glass jars were boiling on the stove ready for making jam.

He watched her whisk sugar into the fruit it became a fragrant red mass. Then she took a thermometer out of the drawer and went to heat the pan on the stove. The air turned sickly with the scent.

'It's just hopeless,' Tommy shook his head and went out to walk in the garden.

He was restless despite the calm of early evening, unable to resolve any of the things that troubled him.

On impulse he took out his phone and tried Esther's number but there was no reply and he couldn't be bothered to leave a voicemail.

The garden seemed sparse and undeveloped compared to the grandeur of Kimble's Top. The roses were eye-catching among the greenery around the pond, glimpses of deep and light pink, but nothing like the colourful shrubberies at Kimble's Top or the rose garden round the memorial to his boy there.

He didn't want to think about that though.

He turned away and headed for the rough grass of the orchard, dipping his head under the lower boughs of the trees where sturdy red apples lodged among the curling green leaves.

He reached up to pick one, twisting the fruit hard from its stem and biting into the sharp flavour. As a boy an apple like this would have been a treat yet here was an abundance and he hadn't even thought to come and pick them.

It reminded him of an afternoon with Gina and Maurice when he'd been young enough to be dragged along by the hand. They had gone foraging for windfall from the trees that overhung the back fences around Hatton Hall. They'd ended up with pockets full of crab apples; Maurice with several over-ripe ones that he'd aimed expertly at the garden walls on the way home, splattering them against the neat brick work.

'Stop wasting them!' Gina had said.

'They're only rotten anyway.'

'Waste not want not!' she'd retorted.

One of her standard refrains. End of discussion. Tommy could hear her saying it even as he stepped over his own apples, lying unharvested in the grass. When had he grown so careless of good fortune?

He didn't often walk here, that was the trouble. They had a gardener to keep it all under control. His garden was as much a reflection of himself as Kimble's Top was of Gina. Every flowering shrub, every bush and perennial, she had chosen and planted herself, every last ornament and piece of furniture she had placed in the house.

Kimble's Top breathed Gina yet Esther had buried her in that unknown cemetery, interring Arthur's ashes with her. Tommy never had fathomed that out. In fact, he'd never even been back there since the funeral and it came to him then that he might walk over there right now and confront things: the memory of that strong big sister, confide in her all the truth of his mistakes and his misery.

He turned swiftly back towards the house.

'Think I'll go for a walk,' he announced from the back door. Beside it was the utility room where long stems of chrysanthemums had been propped temporarily in the sink, brought here from Kimble's Top. He grabbed a handful of them, lifted them dripping from the water:

'Can I have these?'

'What on earth for?' said Bryony.

'Gina.'

He was already halfway to the front door as he said it, grabbing his keys and wallet on the way out.

Up at the cemetery the sky was an early evening blue and the trees still cast shadows on the red brick walls of the chapel.

He wandered in through the ornamental gates and took the main avenue towards the building where the cars had drawn up at Gina's funeral and the crowd of well-wishers had swelled like a tide across the tarmac.

Looking back he realised it had been his first meeting with Dominic. The priest had stood here waiting for them, though Tommy could barely recall the scene, and here, on the far side of the building, was the arched doorway where he'd stood talking to Robyn, unaware of his dad, watching from a distance.

He'd picked his dad up that morning from Hartley Rise, collected the thick overcoat from its peg on his way down the hall and held it ready while his dad stood motionless, gathering his strength, a selection of loose change spread out on the shiny wood of the sideboard as always, ready to slip into his trouser pocket on the way out. But his dad hadn't picked it up, he'd just stood there breathing hard, while the seconds ticked away into minutes and eventually Tommy had had to step forward and lift his arms into the sleeves of the coat so he could go out to his daughter's funeral.

And then, in spite of it all, Tommy had left him alone, standing at the graveside, because he'd been afraid Robyn might drop him in it.

I saw you, Tommy. You were talking.

He made his way now along the path between the rowans, glancing at the headstones as he passed. They were black and grey, some embossed with gold or engraved with the outline of a church window, a cross, with hearts and flowers.

Gina was somewhere here but it was all so impersonal. He began to wish he hadn't come. How could Esther have wanted her so contained?

He was about the right distance from the chapel now and stepped off the path, moving among the gravestones to look for hers, and when he saw it away to his right, he knew straightaway that it was hers and that only Esther could have chosen it.

It stood in contrast to the shiny black headstones, midway along the line: a low semi-circular arc, neither old nor weathered but not shiny either, rising out of the ground. As he drew level he saw that its surface was chiselled with the circular outline of the sun and, emanating from it, bold pointed rays in regular succession. The sun or a sunflower, it could have been either and, if a sun, either rising or setting though Tommy thought it looked too bold to be on the wane.

He liked it with its simple statement of names and dates. Gina Mary Radford, neé Allbright and Arthur David Radford.

He still held the dripping chrysanthemums he'd brought from the kitchen. A heavy vase stood beside the stone. It held a collection of wildflowers, all but dead, but he didn't want to remove them. He laid his own offering lengthways along the grave instead. They'd die more quickly that way but so what? Quickly or slowly, they'd die anyway.

He stood up directing his thoughts towards Gina.

I'm sorry. I screwed up. It's all such a mess.

There was no response. Just the silence and the evening air, chill now and stinging his cheeks as the wind lifted across the open space. He felt more at peace though and stood for a while gazing over at the prison in the distance and the new housing estate covering the slopes above it.

There was the sound of traffic now from somewhere, not from the road behind, he thought, but further away: a grating murmur borne on the wind. Unless it was the wind, the roar of it filling his ears.

He lingered on, feeling a quietness of sorts and the freshness of the breeze until, turning to go, he found himself face to face with Esther.

She was watching him silently from a few feet away, clasping a collection of greenery with meadowsweet and buttercups.

Numb with cold, he wondered how long she'd been there.

'I came to say sorry,' he stammered out. 'To Gina.'

She just nodded, bent down to tip the stale water sideways from the vase, replacing the flowers with her fresh new posy while he stood motionless in the evening breeze and watched her.

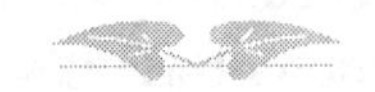

40

ESTHER'S RESPONSE

Tommy wondered if he should go.

She'd reached into her pocket for a water bottle to top up the vase and it was uncanny to see her kneeling beside the chiselled stone with Gina and Arthur's names and dates.

As he hesitated she got to her feet and turned to face him, her gaze unflinching but with no trace of antagonism. He found himself blurting out the first thing that came to mind. 'Why did you bury them here? Why not at Kimble's Top? Or with your nan and granddad?'

His parents' ashes had been scattered in handfuls, spread surreptitiously over the old Ludlow and Allbright graves in the village where they'd grown up.

'I like it here,' said Esther.

She gathered the dead flowers into a tight bundle and went to put them in the bin further along the path. He wandered after her and stood watching while she rinsed her hands under the cold tap fixed to a nearby post.

'I used to come here with a school friend,' she said. 'We put flowers on her Gran's grave. It's very free here. You can sit and think or you can cry. No-one minds. There are kids running around.' She glanced at him. 'You've never come here before.'

'No.'

'Why now?'

'Gina,' he said. 'Kimble's Top. The mess I've made of it all.'

She shook her head. 'You and that bloody house!'

There was a bench nearby, overlooking the line of graves. She went and sat down on it, pulling her jacket tightly round her against the breeze. After a moment he joined her.

'Shall I tell you about Kimble's Top?' said Esther. 'I sat in that house after dad died. Every day. Sitting in his study. And all I wanted was to have him back. But I couldn't. All that money, all those ornaments and paintings and fine things. None of it could give me the one thing that really mattered.'

He wanted to argue, to say that money did matter, that it gave you a future, and that the things had been Arthur's things but the words wouldn't come.

She pulled a knee to her chest, resting one foot on the seat:

'And then there was mum. She wouldn't talk about him. And everything I did was wrong. *Always lazing around! Never wants to do anything!* I didn't. I didn't want to do anything. I just wanted dad back. But she couldn't get it, could she? You wouldn't talk about him either. I came and I asked you. And you wouldn't.'

Guilt pierced him like a knife.

'We can talk,' he said. 'Whenever you want. Just say . . .'

She shrugged and looked away from him.

'Look, whatever you feel about that house,' said Tommy. 'Your mum did want you to have it.'

'No, she didn't,' said Esther. 'She wanted Robyn to have it. It's just that the shares crashed and it was all she had to leave me. And that's the whole problem. I don't want Kimble's Top but deep down I know she wouldn't want me it sold. So she's got me trapped even now.'

Tommy sighed wearily. 'All the same, Esther, things are moving on. People need to know where they stand.'

'Not til I'm ready.'

The sky had darkened and a municipal van had arrived up at the chapel. Tommy saw the driver getting out, looking their way, obviously waiting to lock up.

Esther had seen him too. She got to her feet. 'Talk to me about dad,' she said. 'Come over to Hartley Rise sometime and talk to me about him.'

Tommy sat in his study thinking about Arthur, remembering Gina, at twenty nine, about to get married. He'd been twenty when she left Hartley Rise, selling transistor radios on the markets and preparing to buy Orton's.

On her wedding day he'd sat at the top table and watched Gina and Arthur dance a quickstep on the crowded dance floor. Lorraine had come and flopped down beside him, flushed from dancing with Maurice who took the chair opposite.

'You're next,' she'd said to Tommy. 'Got your eye on anyone?'

He'd looked her full in the face, brazened it out. 'Why? Who do you recommend?'

She'd named a few girls, pretty inoffensive types, and he'd listened with his eyes still on the dance floor, relieved that she didn't mention Bryony Richardson. Or perhaps she'd heard the rumours but didn't dare ask him outright.

Gina and Arthur had danced all afternoon and it was a side to Arthur he'd never really understood: his passion for parties behind that reserved exterior.

There was so little he could tell Esther. Only fleeting impressions: broad shoulders, medium stature, lightly oiled hair without a hint of grey. Arthur had been handsome in his way, clean shaven with a thoughtful expression in his grey eyes.

Beyond that Tommy's memories were piecemeal: Arthur poised midway, pouring whisky from a crystal decanter and looking up to laugh at something Gina had said; standing out on the terrace in the autumn just watching the rain fall; seeing them off from Kimble's Top on a Sunday, at the top of the drive, no wave but standing there magnanimously, watching the cars out of sight.

His vivid memories involved James and he couldn't share those. James had been the first of the younger generation, the first grandchild for his mum and dad, and a boy. Arthur had valued that, he'd harboured the old fashioned preference.

Tommy remembered James in light blue shorts, small against the Arthur's legs, reaching up to show him the red fire engine he'd had for his birthday. Barely more than a toddler, he'd lifted the toy up with both hands while Arthur feigned surprise: *'A fire engine, is it? Well I never did!'*

He pushed the thought away and took Clifton's autobiography out of his desk drawer. It should be of interest to Esther. Irritating though Clifton was, he had after all been one of Arthur's oldest friends.

He slipped the book into a jiffy bag with some photos from their own album and wrote a note offering to get together and talk whenever Esther liked. He put it through the front door at Hartley Rise the next morning and she rang him back the same day. 'Does Bryony know about mum's will?'

'Yes,' said Tommy. 'Why?'

'You could both come over. I'll cook. How about Wednesday?'

They took wine and argued about it beforehand.

'You should have asked what she'd be cooking,' said Bryony. 'Then we'd have known. Now it'll just have to be Chardonnay.'

'New Zealand then,' said Tommy. 'At least it'll have teeth.'

When Esther opened the front door the aroma of fresh curry and coconut milk wafted out.

'We brought wine,' said Bryony with a grimace. 'But it's probably not the thing. Keep it for another time!'

'Oh, I don't know,' said Esther. 'Wine's always good!'

She'd just taken papadum parcels with spiced apples out of the oven so they sat down to eat straightaway.

The dining table was covered with a pink and purple cloth, twinkling with silver thread, and the crockery was the bright set Tommy had picked up with all the shopping when she'd first moved in.

He helped himself to a papadum and found it was delicious.

'Fleur's been giving me a crash course in Indian cuisine,' said Esther. 'She's lived all over the place. She spent six months at an ashram in Kerala.'

Tommy could just imagine it.

When they moved onto curry and naan bread Esther opened the Chardonnay.

Tommy swallowed his down quickly while it was still cold and held enough of its gooseberry flavour to balance the curry powder.

By then their small talk was waning and Esther broached the subject of Kimble's Top with a tentative glance at Bryony. 'So who actually knows about the will? Presumably just the three of us?'

'Why?' asked Tommy.

'I don't want a load of hassle,' she said. 'Couldn't we just say that another will's come to light without going into all the details? I could say I came across it going through mum's things.'

'But we haven't got a copy,' said Bryony.

'We could make a draft,' said Esther. 'Then use the autobiography to prove it got signed.' She turned to Tommy, 'What do you think?'

'You really do take me for quite a liar, don't you?' he said cynically. 'Apart from that one instance, I do actually like to think that I have some integrity.'

'But there'll be the most horrendous scene!' said Esther.

'Yes, but I have to tell the truth,' said Tommy. 'Anyway it's academic. What you're proposing wouldn't work in legal terms. And besides, we're not the only people who know. Robyn was in on it too.'

He heard Bryony on his right take a sharp intake of breath and Esther was staring at him, shocked. 'You're joking!'

'No.'

'Wow,' she looked appalled. 'Robyn really doesn't like me, does she?'

'She was angry,' said Tommy gently.

'Because I wasn't there for mum?'

He nodded. 'All the same. I made her go along with it. The night we found the will, she wasn't really taking it in. And afterwards, at the funeral, she wanted to back out but I wouldn't let her.'

'She's carried on with it, though,' said Bryony. 'She's been lying to us all along.'

'I think she's convinced herself that she somehow deserves Kimble's Top,' said Tommy.

'Maybe she's right,' said Esther. 'If I'd been there that night none of this would have happened.'

'No,' said Tommy. 'This was my fault. Not yours. It was me.'

'It was everything,' said Esther. 'The whole damn mess.'

'So what are we going to do about Kimble's Top?' said Bryony.

'I don't know,' said Esther. 'I've never wanted it. If Robyn wants to live there I'm happy with that. But you've done me out of a lot of money and at some point I want it back.'

'Let's just start with telling everyone about the will,' said Bryony. 'We can work the rest of it out later.'

'Okay,' nodded Esther. 'When and where?'

'When everyone's together,' said Bryony. 'Sunday tea. We're hosting this weekend.'

Esther shook her head. 'It needs to be at Kimble's Top.'

'All right, we'll ask Robyn to host us again,' said Bryony.

'You're joking!' said Tommy. 'Not this weekend! Not at Kimble's Top.'

She was staring back at him while Esther looked from one to the other of them, confused.

'It's the August bank holiday,' he said. 'How can you have forgotten?'

His wife looked at him, coldly. 'I hadn't forgotten. The date's irrelevant, Tommy. It's in the past.'

An uneasy silence fell. She went to the kitchen to refill the water jug and it was left to him to explain to Esther that Sunday was the anniversary of their boy's death up at Kimble's Top.

She told him she was sorry then, that she'd meant to say so before: how sorry she was about their son and when Bryony returned talked about Arthur which had, after all, been the whole point of the evening.

Tommy sat at the table and listened to them talk, his own snippets of memories had been quickly shared. Now Bryony was filling in all the right details, the personal touches she remembered, and drawing out of Esther her own treasured recollections.

Her dad had liked the black and white films on a Saturday afternoon, had always watered the greenhouses at the weekend, the hosepipe in coils along the path and a sprinkler for the grass that twisted and turned.

'He'd put it on for me to play in when it was hot . . . and he used to buy me badges from the market in Northampton.'

Tommy listened while inwardly his mind baulked at what lay ahead: the date they'd agreed in four days' time when everyone would hear what he'd done.

He'd been caught out in a lie, a lie that hadn't delivered, and that irked him more than anything. It went against his morals to lie. He'd always thought it unnecessary. If you used your head and got things right you didn't need to resort to subterfuge. But he hadn't used his head. He'd screwed up in every respect, embroiled Esther and Robyn in an unholy mess and on Sunday afternoon everyone would know it.

Everyone that is except Chris and Elisabeth.

On that he was adamant.

41

Done with Lying

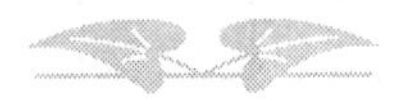

Bryony didn't agree. They argued more ferociously on the way home than they had done coming.

It started over Robyn.

'I can't believe you didn't tell me she was involved all along!'

'I know,' he said. 'I'm sorry.'

'Sorry? For God's sake, Tommy! How much more is there?'

'There's no more. Truly. I just didn't think it was relevant. She didn't want to go along with it. I made her do it.'

'Exactly! You made her an accomplice to something she'd never have done on her own. And now she's up to her neck in fraud.'

'It's not fraud,' he said. 'Technically speaking . . . .'

'I'm not interested in technicalities!'

The night sky was black and heavy with cloud. They were just short of the jitty across the railway, the last of the terraced houses around them with curtains drawn.

He reached out and grasped her arm. 'Honestly, Bry! There isn't anything more. There's nothing I haven't told you. I've done with lying.'

She looked at him long and hard then finally shrugged. 'If you say so.'

They crossed the bridge over the railway and turned into Ise Avenue, walking together under the line of trees, with the dark canopy of leaves overhead blocking out the sky and the garden hedges, fences and walls to their right broken occasionally by gateways.

It was then that he raised what was on his mind. 'We need to make sure Chris and Elisabeth don't come home for the weekend. I don't want them caught up in this.'

Bryony stopped and stared. 'We can't exclude them. The whole point is that everyone hears it together.'

'Not them,' said Tommy.

'Why?'

'Because we don't want them finding out about James in the middle of a row.'

He did it deliberately, used the boy's name to provoke a reaction and sure enough she flinched at it.

'Don't you see?' he said. 'It's all going to come out.'

'This isn't about . . . that. It's about the will.'

'The whole reason for taking the will was to stop Kimble's Top being sold. It's bound to come out, Bryony. And I'm not having Chris and Elisabeth there. We don't know what might get said.'

'You just don't want them hearing what you did! You're a coward!'

'And you wouldn't be? Look, Bry, I'm doing the best I can to make up for all this. But I reserve the right to tell my own children in my own way and my own time. I'm not having them there on Sunday.'

'But it's the bank holiday,' she said. 'They're bound to come home.'

'Put them off then. Tell them we've got the plumbers in.'

'Oh!' she said, tight lipped. 'And I thought you'd done with lying!'

They carried on in silence after that, no sound between them but the rhythm of their own footsteps. The air was damp, fragrant with mown grass and the sharpness of newly trimmed conifers, and he wondered as they walked how they were going to make it through the next week.

It was twenty six years since James had died. He'd like to say not a day had gone by without thinking of his boy but it wasn't true. The time had been so painful, the glaring image of that August day so potent, they'd both done everything in their power to erase it.

By the time he'd joined Lister's his days had been absorbed with business plans, foreign imports and driving the company back into profit. At home he'd deliberately focused on the children who lived and breathed: Elisabeth still taking her first baby steps and Chris, newly born a year or so later.

He'd never allowed the memory of James to surface, the hint of a dark mischievous look, that gleeful smile and irrepressible energy. Nothing could be allowed to reawaken the pain of it.

Their only acknowledgment had been the statue of Peter Pan and he hadn't really allowed that to be about James if he were honest. It had been the symbol of him and Bryony joined in a loss no-one else could understand.

When they'd stood arm in arm beside it, the statue had been a testimony to the bond between them. He'd heard of marriages breaking up over the death of a child, but not theirs. They'd weathered the storm.

Or had they? Now he wondered whether they hadn't rather made an unconscious decision to stay out of it altogether, to take shelter behind their shared denial.

Bryony had removed every trace of James from the house. They had repainted his bedroom and packed away his toys and Tommy had known it was so she could protect herself, not just from the pain but from her terrible fear.

'I can't dwell on it. I can't think about it. Otherwise how will I cope? Every time Elisabeth's out of my sight I'll be afraid, worrying about what could happen.'

And so they'd slipped into silence. As nieces and nephews arrived one by one, nothing was said about the boy who'd been lost. He'd questioned it once with Bryony, when Elisabeth was starting school and he'd thought someone might mention James to her, but Elisabeth was going to a different school where no-one had known her brother and Bryony wouldn't hear of them telling Elisabeth or Christopher anything.

'Why should we tell them what they can't understand?'

'He's their brother.'

'No he isn't, not really,' she'd said. 'A brother's someone you grow up with. Share your memories with. That's what makes a family. Not photos in an album. You look at a photo of your great grandparents and you feel disconnected because you never even met them. It's meaningless and I won't have him made meaningless. We're the ones who lost him. It's nothing to do with anyone else.'

He'd believed her at the time, trusted in her maternal sensibility but now he wasn't so sure. He felt uneasy at the prospect of trying to justify it to Chris and Elisabeth.

'I am going to tell Chris and Elisabeth about James,' he said later that night when they were back home. 'We should have told them before. Look at Esther. How she needed to talk about losing Arthur.'

'That's because Esther knew Arthur. He was a part of her life for eight years. She had an experience of grief to work through.'

'So did we,' said Tommy.

'We talked,' said Bryony. 'At the time.'

It wasn't true. Looking back he remembered it as a time of silence. Shared tears. Shared pain but no words. He couldn't contradict her, though. They were sitting together in the living room, having a night cap. In the soft light of the nearby lamp he could see her face was tense, her mouth set in a hard line, and he wouldn't force it, wouldn't prise the feelings out of her. He only hoped she'd be able to forgive him for what lay ahead.

Telling Chris and Elisabeth about James was a future problem, for now he had enough on his mind planning Sunday's revelation about the will to the rest of the family.

Tommy sat in his study planning his words, rehearsing them, a succinct business-like speech, an honest statement of the facts. Then he anticipated every possible response and prepared an answer.

He'd tell them after tea, while they were still at the table but after eating. That way no-one would be under pressure to stay there. No awkward silences.

Of all of them, Robyn was the unknown quantity. He had no idea how she'd react to his news.

They'd agreed he wouldn't expose her involvement but he couldn't forewarn her either. He'd sat once or twice with the phone in his hand thinking he should call her but decided it was too risky. She'd never keep it to herself and he couldn't have it coming out in dribs and drabs. He needed to know exactly what had been said to whom, at least in the first instance, needed them all to hear the same thing and to hear it from his lips, including his response to any questions. What they said to each other after that was their own business but at least he'd have told them all straight.

The bank holiday weather forecast was dismal but on Sunday the rain held off, though the sky was streaked with dark grey, rising to an edge of brilliant white cloud that billowed against a patch of blue.

They collected Esther en route for Kimble's Top and, ironically, she seemed in better spirits than when they'd seen her last. Tommy hoped she'd be able to stay that way as the afternoon progressed.

As they approached Hunsbury Hill he'd thought that today of all days his mind would be full of James, the awakened memories as fresh and pungent as the newly ploughed fields that lined the dual carriageway. In fact his head felt empty, dead to everything but the three of them in the black car nearing Kimble's Top and the silence between them as they passed through the familiar pillars of the gateway.

Surprisingly the drive was full of cars. The others had arrived before them and as they got out of the car, Laurel appeared from the direction of the country park with Paul and Lee close behind her.

'We got here early!' she called happily.

The boys were in good humour too as Tommy followed them round the side of the house and across the lawn towards the terrace where Maurice was stretched out comfortably with his feet propped up on the balustrade and Lorraine was handing round a tray of drinks.

There was a bank holiday mood in the air. Doreen and Robyn looked relaxed and it was rare to see Doreen sitting back when there was entertaining underway.

Seeing them already assembled he wondered for an instant if there was something afoot but had no time to dwell on it because the others had caught sight of Esther now, trailing along beside him and Bryony, and he realised that he hadn't even thought to tell them she'd be coming.

Richard got to his feet, obviously delighted, and Maurice and Lorraine were quick to offer a hug. Doreen and Robyn just stared, deadpan.

There was a moment of awkwardness while Doreen hurried indoors to set an extra place at the table and Lorraine found she didn't have enough glasses of her home made cordial on the tray.

'Have mine!' said Bryony smoothly, taking one and handing it to Esther. 'Tea's fine for me.'

It was a tricky start and, seeing the contempt on Robyn's face, Tommy wondered if he wouldn't have been better to warn her what was coming but it was too late now.

The wind picked up banging the French windows closed and threatening to upset the empty glasses on Lorraine's tray so they decamped indoors since it was 'about that time anyway!'

At the long dining table the black leather chairs had been pulled up and the white china set out with the usual cold meats and salads, while the sideboard held an extravagant display of homemade desserts.

Doreen must have seen Tommy's glance at them because she murmured in his ear, 'Bit of a landmark occasion. Robyn's going to say a few words.'

Esther glanced his way, looking worried, but Tommy kept his expression neutral as he nodded faintly to reassure her.

They'd barely taken their places before Robyn began her announcement from the head of the table. 'Now we're all here,' a slight emphasis on the 'all' as she glanced at Esther. 'I've got something to say. I've been thinking about it for a while and now you've confirmed it, asking me to host again three weeks in a row. So I'd like to suggest that we hold Sunday tea at Kimble's Top every week. I know it's not the same as it was but I think it's what Gina would have wanted. She must have known when she left me the house that I'd keep it at the centre of things.'

Bryony turned to Tommy wide eyed and Esther was looking his way too. Maurice, who'd been nodding at Robyn's words had opened his mouth to speak but stopped mid-sentence and suddenly everyone was looking at Tommy.

'Well, now's clearly the moment,' he said, ironically, and to Robyn: 'You always did have a talent for the dramatic.'

There was no rancour in his voice but she glared at him all the same.

'What exactly is your point?' said Doreen crossly.

'My point is that I too have something to say. And you're not going to like it,' he addressed himself again to Robyn: 'Especially you.'

He began his carefully rehearsed words. 'The fact is: I haven't been entirely straight with you. Any of you,' this to Robyn again, with a meaningful look, hoping to quell any interruption. 'The week before Gina died. At the end of November. I was here late one night. Things were bad. It looked like . . .'

. . . he tailed off, not wanting to say 'the end'.

'Looking for the doctor's number,' deliberately economic now, eyes on Robyn again, mentally impressing on her the let-out he was offering. 'I ended up going through Gina's things and I found her will. Two wills. The one you all know about, leaving Kimble's Top to Robyn. And a later one leaving it to Esther.'

He glanced swiftly round the table and saw puzzled looks from Maurice and Lorraine, from Doreen, Richard and the boys. Robyn's face was defiant, cold and accusing.

'I took the will,' said Tommy frankly. 'The later one. I shredded it. I didn't realise Gina hadn't sold her shares in RSG. I thought that Esther would still inherit a lot of money.'

There were looks of blank incomprehension all around him.

'I took the will and destroyed it,' he spelt it out slowly. 'There was no other copy. Nothing with the solicitor. I wanted Kimble's Top to stay in the family and I believed Esther would sell it. So did Gina, presumably. Ideally she'd have left the house to Robyn if she could. She changed her will because RSG crashed . . .'

He broke off suddenly, this was Esther's argument not his own. He glanced her way uncertainly and she nodded encouragement.

Meanwhile Maurice had leaned forwards to look down the table at him, his already lined face doubly furrowed with frowning. 'What are you saying?' he asked.

'I'm saying I took Gina's will,' said Tommy. 'Her valid will. And destroyed it.'

Now they'd grasped it. Lorraine turned to say saying something to Maurice beside her, troubled angry words in a tone of disbelief and the boys sitting nearby exchanged looks at it, while Doreen bit her lip unsure of herself and Robyn stared, white faced and stunned.

Richard had half turned in his chair to confront him. 'You took her will? Here in this house? While she was lying there, dying!' He gestured with his head in the direction of the bedrooms.

The emotional tangent caught Tommy off guard.

'You were here when she died,' said Richard. 'Here with Dad. And you said nothing, knowing you'd done that?'

The memory of that night flitted through Tommy's mind. His concern had been for his dad, how he'd cope, yet it had been his own tears that had fallen. He remembered the warmth of them as he'd put his arms round the old man, crying against his neck.

'It was a difficult time,' said Doreen now in a decisive tone. 'Tommy did what he thought was right.'

'Right?' Richard turned on her. 'He destroyed our sister's will?'

'Only one of them,' said Doreen. 'They're not that different. And he's right. If it hadn't been for the shares . . . this is what Gina would have wanted.'

'I don't think that's the point,' said Maurice slowly. 'The fact is, it was dishonest. Isn't it against the law?'

Tommy nodded. 'Except you'd have to prove it,' he said. 'Which you can't.'

'No one else knew!' said Maurice contemptuously. 'You made sure of that.'

That was when Robyn stepped in. 'Actually,' she said loudly. 'I knew,' and then, pointedly to Tommy: 'Were you planning on telling them that?'

'That had better not be true!' said Richard.

'Why not?' said Robyn. 'Because I don't deserve Kimble's Top? The will we kept was valid once. Gina did want me to have this house. And why shouldn't I? I was here day and night with her,' she looked over at Esther: 'Where the hell were you?'

'It's none of your business,' said Esther.

'It's all of our business,' said Robyn. 'We cared about Gina.' A slight emphasis again, on 'we'.

'You cared enough to lie to her,' Esther's voice trembled but she lifted her chin and carried on: 'You were here day and night but you didn't tell her what you'd done, did you? Don't come the angel of mercy with me!'

Robyn got to her feet, furious, and moved towards Esther. For a moment Tommy thought she might actually slap her cousin but Laurel dissolved into tears first and Lorraine and Maurice intervened to calm things down, which was when Richard pushed his chair back to leave the table.

'I can't get my head round this!' he headed for the door. 'I'm going for a smoke.' He turned back to Maurice still seated. 'Come with me, mate. I can't get my head round this.'

As Richard and Maurice left the room, Robyn sat down again and began assembling ham and tomatoes on Laurel's plate. 'Eat your tea! It's grown up stuff, that's all!'

Lorraine and Doreen reached for the bowls of salad and soon they were all helping themselves to food in a tense silence.

Tommy had had enough.

'I need to talk to Richard,' he said, getting up from the table.

'I wouldn't!' said Doreen, but he went anyway.

His brothers were round by the greenhouses as he'd expected, Richard sitting on the edge of the cold frame angrily smoking a cigarette while Maurice looked on.

'You can fuck off,' said Richard as Tommy approached. 'Just fuck off, Tommy!'

'Look, I know you're angry,' said Tommy.

Richard blew smoke in a derisive 'hmph'.

'I know what I did was wrong.'

'Wrong?' Richard's face was hard with anger. 'It's this that's wrong!' He waved a hand around. 'All this! It isn't Robyn's! How could you do it?'

'I thought Esther would sell the place. You know I couldn't have that.'

'Why?'

'You know why,' said Tommy coldly.

He glanced at Maurice who looked away but Richard's expression remained accusing, he refused to be enlightened.

'Because of James,' said Tommy furiously. 'Because of my son who died here. Remember?'

Richard looked away too then. He breathed out a long sigh but said nothing.

'Esther doesn't even want Kimble's Top,' said Tommy. 'She's got Hartley Rise.'

'Yeah, thanks to Dad. At least someone in the family's honest.'

'Oh come on, Richard!'

'No, you come on!' said Richard. 'All that grief you gave us when Robyn got pregnant!'

'I didn't give you grief.'

But Richard wasn't listening. 'And I took it. You know why? Because I respected you!' he laughed harshly. 'My brilliant older brother. The one people talked about. And I did too. At work. Down the pub. When people started up, I didn't hold back. Yeah, what a great guy! Real head for business. And now it turns out you're no better than the rest of us! You and Robyn together.'

He threw his cigarette down and stood up to grind it underfoot. 'I'm going home. I've had it with the lot of you.'

Tommy could only watch him go. He stood there beside Maurice powerless to stop him.

'I screwed up,' he murmured when their brother had gone.

'Big time,' agreed Maurice.

42

An Invitation to Belong

Back at the house the anger was palpable. Robyn eyed him with coldly when he went indoors, Lorraine and the boys avoided his gaze altogether and Bryony and Esther suggested it was time to go home.

The three of them were silent in the car all the way back to Wellingborough. Tommy glanced back at Esther once or twice in the rear view mirror. She was texting on her mobile phone and when they pulled into Hartley Rise Fleur was waiting, arms folded, outside number fourteen.

She greeted Esther with an ironic look which made Tommy fume. He swung the car into a three point turn and pulled swiftly away.

Bryony had little to say but he sensed she was relieved the afternoon was over, slightly triumphant even that the truth about James hadn't come out at the table. He'd told her, though, that it had come up with Richard and Maurice in the garden and God only knew what they were all saying now in the privacy of their own homes.

Either way, it had been a hell of a day. They resorted to the television and sat up late into the night watching the repeat of some predictable action film.

The next morning he got up early and made a tray of blueberry muffins for breakfast. He was just taking them out of the oven when his mobile rang and it was Robyn.

'Just what the hell did you think you were doing?'

Tommy sighed. 'I needed to tell the truth.'

'And drop me in it without warning?'

'The aim was not to drop you in it at all if you'd got my drift at the table.'

'All I got was you spilling your guts to everyone. And Esther clearly knew the whole story, didn't she? Well? Didn't she?'

He couldn't deny it.

'You total bastard,' she said. 'Don't you ever do that to me again!'

'I'm hardly likely to,' said Tommy drily. 'Unless you've been up to anything else you shouldn't have.'

'Oh, go to hell!' and she slammed the phone down.

Within a couple of hours Maurice had rung too. 'We're pretty disgusted, Tommy. There's no getting round it. Lorraine and I have been talking. We're not having this happy families charade every Sunday. Not with things the way they are.'

'We'll stay away,' offered Tommy. 'Until it settles down a bit.'

'Will we?' said Bryony crossly when he told her. 'It was you who started this. Not me!'

'Well you go then,' he said, exasperated. 'You can tell them all what a bastard you married! No doubt they'll sympathise.'

He was restless, frustrated and could have done with a walk, but it started raining heavily that afternoon and carried on into the week until he was sick of it running down the windows all day and dripping from the gutters.

On Wednesday Doreen called by in her lunch hour. 'I want you to know: as far as I'm concerned, I don't have a problem with it. Maybe Gina was right. Obviously the shares . . . that's another matter. But when it comes to the house, Robyn belongs at Kimble's Top. She really belongs there. And Esther doesn't, that's plain to see. She's always turned her nose up at money. It's not as if she even appreciated what she had.'

Bryony must have seen his anger because she led Doreen away into the living room. 'Come and sit down. Tommy was just going to make some coffee.'

He stood in the kitchen listening to the percolator bubble and wondered if Richard knew his wife was here. He'd tried to ring his brother a couple of times since Sunday and received the same greeting as in the garden, followed by the phone being put down. On impulse he tried his brother's mobile again but there was no answer.

In the living room he could hear Doreen was still pursuing the same argument. 'What's Esther got to complain about anyway? She's ended up with Hartley Rise. What did Paul and Lee ever get?'

Fresh coffee was splashing into the jug. He'd set out three cups and a plate of shortbread but, listening to her tones rise and fall, he abandoned it all, picked up his umbrella from the hall and let himself out of the front door.

Bryony wouldn't thank him but he couldn't get drawn into all that. He'd only say something he shouldn't and make things worse. She was far better than him at handling that kind of conversation; letting things blow over.

He crunched his way along the wet gravel and into Ise Avenue. The rain fell fast like a silver beaded curtain before his eyes and his shoulders and chest were damp from the drops cascading off the umbrella but he hadn't seen Dominic for a couple of weeks. Suddenly he needed the priest's calm quiet sanity.

It was only as he reached the main road where the drains streamed with water and the traffic sent up a constant spray that he realised the priest would hardly be out working in this weather. He carried on anyway, glad of the walk.

In the cemetery the tarmac path was muddy and riddled with puddles but the trees at least offered some shelter. Tommy made his way across the grass, the wet earth squelching underfoot, and it was then that he realised Dominic was there. He saw him in the distance, wearing a blue waterproof jacket.

The priest was brushing lichen off a gravestone in the pouring rain. He looked up as Tommy drew near sheltering under a big yellow golf umbrella.

'You're completely mad,' said Tommy. 'What are you doing out in this?'

'The wetter the better,' said Dominic. 'It's ideal for cleaning the stones.'

Tommy shook his head in amused disbelief.

'And how are you?' asked Dominic.

'Last Sunday was the anniversary of the worst day of my life,' said Tommy, full or irony.

The priest looked at him for a moment then dropped his brush back into the bucket of water.

'Why don't we go inside? We can't talk in this.'

Tommy had never been inside a priest's house before. He was curious to see what it would be like. The presbytery was solidly built, local brown ironstone with pointed windows, and stood beside the Catholic church.

Inside the sitting room was plain and functional with a motley collection of second hand armchairs, plain cushions and a hard-wearing grey carpet underfoot. He imagined the rest of the house was much the same.

While Dominic went to put the kettle on, Tommy wandered over to look at the bookshelves that stretched from floor to ceiling along the far wall. They held heavy tomes of philosophy, church history and doctrine. He turned away, uninspired, and something bright and attractive caught his eye: an icon propped up on a table in the corner.

In the centre of the image was a golden chalice, perfectly proportioned with a hint of decoration. It stood on a marble slab and sitting around it were three dark, curly haired figures.

Looking more closely Tommy saw they were angels with golden wings and grey haloes. The one on the left had blue and gold robes, his feet rested on marble and his hands were placed in his lap, not folded but open-handed, as if gesturing. His eyes were dark and ringed with dark, his face gentle.

His companions had the same elegant brows and cheeks; one wore red and blue, the other, blue and green.

All three of them held long thin staffs, like reeds, and their heads were inclined equally. The one in the centre was looking to the angel on the left of the composition and the one on the right likewise, so that they seemed to sit in gracious calm, regarding one another.

Tommy stared at the scene. The angels' robes fell in swathes of rich colours but it was the faces that drew him, the incline of the woolly heads, the solemnity of their shared expression and, between them, the golden shape of the cup.

'Do you like it?' asked Dominic from behind him.

Tommy nodded.

'It's called the Holy Trinity,' said the priest. 'Also known as the Hospitality of Abraham. The space here . . .' he pointed to the blue directly in front of the marble slab. 'Is for you: it's the one empty place at the table and the space the viewer occupies. You could say it's an invitation to belong.'

He offered Tommy a mug of coffee from his tray and put a plate of biscuits down on a nearby table.

Tommy stayed where he was, still attracted to the icon, strangely conscious of the three figures looking at one another.

'Would you like to borrow it?' asked Dominic.

'Don't you need it?'

The priest shook his head. 'Just let me have it back when you've finished with it.'

He'd gone to sit in an armchair and Tommy followed suit, sinking into the deep brown cushions and balancing his coffee cup on one knee.

'Tell me about Sunday,' said Dominic.

'I came clean,' said Tommy. 'Got everyone together and told them about the will.'

'That was brave.'

'Yes!' Tommy laughed cynically. 'So now they know what I'm really like.'

'We all sin,' said Dominic. 'None of us is everything we ought to be.'

'So that's it, is it?' said Tommy. 'Hellfire and damnation!'

Dominic shook his head. 'Repentance? Reconciliation.'

'I don't think we're going to be reconciled,' said Tommy.

'Give it time.'

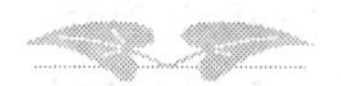

When he got home Bryony was out. Tommy propped the icon up against the computer on his study desk and sat down to look at it. There was something compelling about the scene, even beyond the physical composition that was designed to draw you in. This was different.

As he looked at it now, the angel on the right seemed to be glancing more at the chalice than at his companions and the one in the middle was almost smiling, there was a lift in the dark eyes that Tommy hadn't noticed before, an upturn in the mouth. Meanwhile, the third angel in blue and gold kept his vigil over the others so that the completeness of it all was fascinating.

Tommy had a sudden fleeting sensation of the three of them watching him, as though he were the one being contemplated. He blinked and refocused.

Ridiculous!

He was getting as crazy as a priest who washed gravestones in the pouring rain.

'No-one ever comes here, Dominic!'

'You came.'

'Whatever it is, I hope it does you some good,' said Bryony. 'Something needs to!'

She was standing at the open door of the study with a bag of groceries in each hand. Tommy had heard her car on the drive but stayed where he was, hoping to escape an argument. Now he got up to take the bags off her but she turned away sharply. 'Don't bother!'

'Look, I'm sorry about Doreen,' he said. 'I just didn't have anything constructive to say.'

'And I did?'

'You're the PR expert,' he said weakly.

'And you're the hotshot businessman!' she retorted. 'Broker of a thousand deals.'

'Hardly.'

He followed her into the kitchen and began emptying the bags she'd dumped on the counter. 'Wow!'

She'd been to Waitrose and managed to come home with two bottles of red Sancerre. He held them aloft, one in each hand. 'What a find!'

She smiled in spite of herself. 'You don't deserve them! You've got a nerve, Tommy. I don't like Doreen's attitude any more than you do.'

'I'll make it up to you,' his mind was already on the best dish for a red Sancerre. 'Lamb steaks. Rare. Filet mignon style. And something delicate. Redcurrants. Just a touch of mint.'

'All right.'

It was a token of good fortune, a splendid coup in spite of everything. The Sancerre region, famous for its white grapes, but these rare reds: he loved their delicate pinks, the nose so much richer than any rosé.

He and Bryony sat down to eat and with every mouthful he tasted strawberry, honeysuckle and the faintest hint of some deeper fruit: the whole bouquet redolent of early summer.

It was a brief respite. On Saturday morning Esther dropped by.

'They've all taken it quite badly,' she told Tommy. 'We're all supposed to be going for a picnic at Abingdon Park tomorrow. Doreen's organised it. There's a band playing in the bandstand apparently. But really it's because no-one wants to go to Kimble's Top. I think I'll give it a miss myself. I'm not really big on the whole family scene anyway.'

He went back to his study and found the angels still regarding one another calmly. He wished he had their serenity but the fact was his whole family were at odds with one another and it was all his fault. Family had always been important to him. It was what you invested yourself in: the next generation, giving the essence of yourself to the future.

And you've done spectacularly well at that!

He hadn't even told Chris and Elisabeth yet about what he'd done, dreaded to think what they would say. He'd been so proud of them, self-satisfied if the truth be known.

That's how you bring children up. Teach them respect. How to make the right choices. He'd had Richard in mind when he'd thought like that but, for all his brother's leniency towards Robyn, Richard hadn't taken someone's will and shredded it.

He looked at the icon, at its visual clarity where the three figures created the empty space that was his, and a single thought went through his mind: the problem isn't out there, it's me!

The angels surveyed him sorrowfully, the shared gaze that was constant and gentle while the empty place remained at the table, still inviting.

43

Finding A Solution

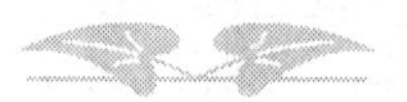

On Sunday they stayed at home, conscious of the family meeting for a picnic without them, but at least there was no reproach from Bryony. She joined him on the sofa, curling up beside him and slipping her arm through his while he flicked through the satellite sports channels.

'I admire you for telling everyone the truth. No-one can ask more than that!'

'Except that I shouldn't have done it in the first place.'

'We all make mistakes, Tommy.'

He nodded silently, appreciating her words, and she nestled beside him, looking through a magazine until they both dozed off, drowsy from the Sunday roast they'd cooked to compensate for not going out to tea.

It was early September by now. The weather had improved from the long week of rain but he still didn't feel much like going out.

Tommy was still waiting for an opportunity to meet the Taiwanese supplier with his new business contact, but the man's visit to England was a few weeks away. In the meantime he tried to occupy himself with American tennis and was engrossed in replays when the phone rang. An awkward moment of silence followed his greeting before Lorraine's voice said, 'I was hoping to catch Bryony.'

'I'm afraid she's out.'

'Oh.'

'Shall I tell her you called?' he said icily.

'Please. And could she call me back? It's important.'

He put the phone down, livid.

'Whatever it was, she obviously couldn't tell me,' he fumed when Bryony came in.

'I expect she was embarrassed,' said Bryony. 'Probably forgotten you're at home all day.'

'Well she knows now,' said Tommy. 'That'll save her ringing again.'

His wife just smiled and began unzipping the dry cleaning bags she'd spread across the kitchen counter, pulling out their winter coats to put on hangers.

'Go and call her back, then!' said Tommy. 'Don't keep me in suspense.'

He loitered in the hall, picking dead heads from a vase of flowers while he listened to her end of the conversation. It was pointless. Lorraine was doing all the talking and he only heard Bryony's, 'Oh, I see . . . yes . . . right . . . okay.'

'They want a meeting,' she said when she'd put the phone down. 'Myself, Richard, Maurice and Lorraine with a solicitor. To see what they can do, legally, for Esther.'

'Great!' he said. 'A very select committee!'

'Well, don't worry,' said Bryony. 'Doreen and Robyn haven't been invited either. I gather Doreen's put out.'

It was no consolation. Tommy followed her back to the kitchen and stood aiming gentle kicks at the wooden doorframe while she folded up the empty cleaning bags.

'Don't take it to heart,' she said. 'At least they're trying to do something positive about it all.'

'And I haven't?'

'You've done what you can. Now it's down to us. Just let it go.'

It was late morning and he'd lost interest in the tennis. He walked up to the graveyard in search of Dominic.

There was no-one around but then Tommy was earlier than usual. He wandered over to the patch where Dominic had been working most recently, under a group of trees where the graves were covered with orange pine needles and heaps of curling sycamore leaves. The ground there was devoid of grass, the earth dry and powdery underfoot as Tommy made his way across it.

There was no bench so he sat down instead on the low wall enclosing an obelisk handsomely mounted on a succession of diminishing plinths. For a good half hour he sat and waited but the priest didn't come and it was a nuisance, he really could have done with talking to him.

He set off half-heartedly along the route to Dominic's house, hoping he might still meet him half way, but by the time the church came into view he realised the priest must be occupied elsewhere.

He was about to turn towards home when he noticed that the church door was ajar and there were lights on inside. He hesitated for a moment, wondering if there was a funeral, but there were only a few cars parked in the street so it seemed unlikely. He made his way over to the church and stepped inside.

It was a relatively new building but old in style, a barn of a place with high rafters. Rows of wooden pews stretched ahead of him while at the east end steps rose to an altar, then more steps, red-carpeted, to a higher one flanked with pillars and overhung with a decorative stone canopy. There were statues of saints, three on either side of the high altar and, in the centre, a silver cabinet with ornate doors and an onion dome. Elegant silver lamps hung from the stone buttresses, the one on his right with a red candle flickering in it.

Dominic was there, fully robed in green and white, with a teenage boy and girl and an older woman. They were busy discussing something, standing round the lower of the altars which had a collection of chalices and other objects.

Tommy drew near along the aisle and Dominic glanced up and saw him, raised a hand in welcome. 'Tommy! Come on in!'

The others turned to look at him.

'We've been making a video,' said Dominic. 'For the infants and juniors. Church in their own words. Saves me doing all the talking. Anyway we've finished now.'

Tommy sat down in the front pew while they cleared the things from the altar, packed up the video camera and said their goodbyes. Then he followed Dominic into the sacristy and watched him remove his heavy vestments and hang them up.

'Isn't it all rather familiar ground for a video?' he asked the priest. 'I thought they drank it in with their mother's milk.'

'Not any more,' said Dominic. 'Technically if they're in the church school they're meant to come to Mass but in reality a lot of them don't.' He'd slipped the long white robe off now and turned to face Tommy looking his usual self in the blue shirt and dark trousers: 'And how are things with you?'

'Oh, I'm an outcast!' pronounced Tommy. 'Right out in the cold. They won't even talk to me on the phone. Got any suggestions?'

'You could pray about it,' said the priest.

'Great!'

It was a cop-out, of course, prayer: the last resort of mindless fools, and it would have been sheer hypocrisy in him. People did pray once. Some of the great industrialists had been church goers but they'd been men of their time. No-one believed in that kind of thing nowadays, except Dominic Palmer and he was a breed apart. The saintly charismatic type.

He was still drawn to the icon, though, sat with it in his study and enjoyed the sense of peace it conveyed. It smacked of a bygone age, a time of simple devotion, like a medieval cathedral. Lots of people felt spiritual in a place like that: a combination of architecture and craftsmanship with a sense of history. It moved you, even if you went out of the doors and never thought about religion again. It was the aura of the past, the ghost of a faith impossible in modern times. Except for Dominic Palmer.

Tommy sat back and focused on the three figures, noticing their bright white haloes, staring at the scale and brilliance of them and the golden curves of their angelic wings.

Are you expecting me to pray?

Their eyes were downcast today, demure, but the smiles were evident again, certainly there was the semblance of a smile on the angel seated to his left.

You'll have to wait for the priest, thought Tommy. I'm no Dominic Palmer.

No! You're Tommy Allbright.

The strong clear voice came from within and it took him by surprise.

The meeting with the solicitor was on a Thursday afternoon.

He watched Bryony gather her things and let her go without saying a word, determined not to show his fury at being left out of the discussions.

In the kitchen he set about sorting out the cupboard where he kept his culinary bits and pieces. It had been overflowing for some time and he'd requisitioned the adjoining one but Bryony had been given an ice cream maker for her birthday and it needed a home. Apparently he'd agreed to clear out his overspill to make space for it.

He opened the cupboard and began pulling its contents out onto the counter: an old tin of goose fat, maple syrup from Canada, a jar of paprika purée from Austria. Within an hour he'd emptied everything out, got a cloth and detergent and wiped the empty shelves down. He was supposed to be deciding what to throw away but, apart from a box of jasmine tea none of them liked and some ancient icing sugar, he couldn't identify a single thing he might not need in the future.

It was obvious he needed far more space than just this one cupboard anyway. He began looking into the others to see what space could be made there. They had some ridiculously old crockery that should have gone years ago. He'd just got it all out onto the work surfaces when he heard Bryony's car on the drive and, looking at his watch, he saw it was already half past four.

He went to meet her in the hall.

'Well, we didn't achieve much,' she said, hanging her coat up.

'The solicitor says it's too late for a claim against the estate. Not that Esther really had grounds for maintenance anyway. Too late for a caveat to allow an investigation. That has to be within six months of probate too. So the only possibility is a law suit disputing the terms of the will and none of us wants that. It'd cost the earth and might not get us anywhere.'

'So that's it, then?' said Tommy.

She shrugged. 'There are possibilities around putting Kimble's Top in trust with, say, me, Maurice and Richard as Trustees deciding who could live there. But really the house should go to Esther. And who would act as Trustees after us?' She offered him a folder of papers. 'Do you want to read these?'

'No point,' he said, turning back towards the kitchen. 'Let's have a drink.'

'I'll make it,' she said. 'You file these somewhere.'

He took the folder into his study and slipped it into the filing cabinet just as her outraged tones echoed from the kitchen.

'You were supposed to be clearing out ONE cupboard!'

'Ah!'

He went down to find her glaring at the clutter all over the work tops, spread his hands wide in surrender, 'There's just not enough space.'

They'd made it plain he wasn't in on the discussions but Tommy just couldn't resist calling on Maurice. He went over to his brother's house at five o'clock the next Tuesday, knowing Lorraine had a keep fit class and Maurice would be home late afternoon, having started his day at seven.

They lived in Hatton Park; a tight Victorian villa inherited from Lorraine's mother in what passed for a stylish address in old Wellingborough. The leaded panes and gothic chimneys of Hatton Hall were still visible there beyond a high stone wall, the preserved façade masking its development into flats for the elderly.

When Tommy rang the doorbell Maurice let him into the house without a word and indicated the front room with a silent nod.

Tommy settled back against the embroidered cushions on the sofa while his brother took the armchair opposite.

'Bryony told you about our meeting, no doubt?' said Maurice.

Tommy nodded.

'I keep asking myself, what would Gina have wanted,' said his brother. 'What would she have hoped we'd do? I know she wouldn't have wanted to see us driven apart like this. She'd have wanted it sorted.'

'How?' asked Tommy.

Maurice shrugged. 'Robyn won't give up Kimble's Top. Not without a fight and Richard's adamant the house is Esther's. She doesn't want it, not now anyway. She's talking about renting Hartley Rise out and going travelling. But at some point it's got to be hers. It's a right mess. You saw to that.'

Tommy sighed. 'I'm sorry.'

'We're all sorry,' said Maurice. 'Sorry you lost your boy. Sorry it's come to this.'

Tommy's throat swelled with emotion. 'I still have to tell Chris and Elisabeth about James,' he said. 'And the will.'

Maurice shook his head, looking sorrowful. 'I don't envy you that.'

Tommy went back to his icon, just sat in his study looking at it.

In the background was a tree and an eastern house with an arched window and a long, black door: a family home like his own, a domestic scene, where people screwed up and got angry with each other. Only this one looked exotic. It had a pitched roof with curved orange tiles and there was something of the desert in the brightness beyond it, a golden white background resonating with desert heat.

In the foreground the angels' robes draped elegantly from the shoulders to their neatly folded feet. They wore long sleeved garments with a different coloured mantle thrown over them.

You're very foreign he observed.

Should I be like you?

He often heard a response when he ventured a remark, words he didn't expect and they intrigued him. It was his mind, no doubt, playing tricks. A psychologist would have an explanation.

'I suppose it's my subconscious?' he said to Dominic when he saw him next.

'You think so?'

'Don't you?' said Tommy.

'I wouldn't know,' said the priest. 'I'm not there. Why don't you ask them!'

Are you my subconscious?

Even as he said it, he knew it wasn't true.

Maurice and the others had pressed on with a trust deed: Robyn would make over the ownership of Kimble's Top to Esther provided she could live there rent free until a designated point. The suggested date was Esther's thirtieth birthday in a few years' time.

'It all works out on paper,' Bryony told Tommy. 'It's just a question of whether Richard can get Robyn to agree. She's already refused to come to the solicitor's once but Maurice thinks we'll get there in the end.'

'Do you?'

'I don't know,' she said. 'Robyn's utterly belligerent and Doreen's backing her. For them it's all about Esther not coming home when Gina was dying. And it's got to be driving a wedge between Richard and Doreen. They can't both win.'

Doreen clearly meant to try, though. She came to see Tommy that Friday afternoon when Bryony was out at the Civic Society.

'Can't you do something?' she demanded. 'If we both stand firm with Robyn they'll have to back down. I know it's not ideal but it's not that far from what Gina originally wanted. If the shares hadn't crashed Robyn would have had Kimble's Top.'

'I'm not so sure of that any more,' said Tommy. 'You don't know what Gina might have done in her final months even if the shares had still been worth something. In any case, I'm not going against Bryony and if you're wise you'll stick with Richard on this. Otherwise we're heading for rift none of us will be able to retrieve.'

'I've got a duty to Robyn too,' said Doreen. 'It's not just Richard.'

'Robyn's in the wrong and she knows it,' said Tommy. 'Take my advice and give it up now.'

'We released equity in our house to fund Robyn staying at Kimble's Top,' said Doreen. 'We'll never get that back.'

'Get her to pay you back,' said Tommy. 'She'll be earning at some point.'

'It's easy for you to say,' said Doreen. 'You've always had money. Has it occurred to you that Esther's going to end up with Kimble's Top and Hartley Rise?' And we should have had a share in that. It should have come to you, Richard and Maurice.'

'And much good that would have done us,' said Tommy. 'You wouldn't have been looking at more than thirty grand apiece.'

'You might be above thirty grand,' said Doreen. 'But it wouldn't have gone amiss in our household. And it's not just Robyn. We've got Paul and Lee to think about. And it's all your fault. You started this.'

'Look, if I hadn't taken the will, Robyn would have got nothing anyway. She'd have been no better off, in fact she'd have been worse off. At least this way she gets to swan around at Kimble's Top as long as the trust allows it.'

'It's just tantalising. Offering her something that'll never be hers.'

'Tell her to move out then,' snapped Tommy. 'You can't cut it all ways, Doreen.'

'You never should have said anything,' said Doreen. 'It's bad enough what you did in the first place but at least you could have kept your mouth shut and let it ride. You've made yourself ridiculous with all your confessions. You've made twice the mess you would have done if you'd just left it at one mistake.' She got up to go. 'It was a waste of time even talking to you. I might have known you'd be difficult.'

He let her go without even seeing her to the front door but the conversation had made him uneasy. He went to the phone, withheld his number and dialled Richard's direct line at the office.

'Don't hang up!' he said as soon as his brother answered.

'What do you want?'

'Doreen was here about opposing this trust deed,' said Tommy. 'I gave her short shrift. I want you to know that I'm not backing Robyn.'

'And I'm supposed to be thankful?' said Richard. 'You're the one who created all this. Robyn might have been a lot of things but she was never dishonest until she got caught up in your big plan.'

Wasn't she? Tommy wanted to say. *And you always knew where she was, did you? When she was out getting herself pregnant?*

He couldn't say it, closed his mouth, then the phone clicked dead.

His brother had hung up.

Bryony was still out with her civic friends.

He got the icon out but his mind was still on Kimble's Top, Gina's will and his dead boy. He thought about Gina, dependable and strong, digging the rose garden as a memorial for James. Then he thought about his dad, at Gina's side every day, watching her fade.

Staring at the icon with its three figures he saw himself at that table with his dad and Gina, one on either side.

I've lost you both.

If only they'd talked about things. What Kimble's Top meant to him and Bryony. What Gina wanted when she was gone. But he'd been angry: angry with Gina for getting ill in the first place and angry with Robyn for being in the way.

'You were born angry.'

They were Gina's words from when he was a small boy. 'Terrible labour mum had with you. Not long. But my God, you were trouble.'

His mother would never say it. She'd wrap an arm round him, hug him close and kiss his hair when Gina spoke like that. His sweet smelling mother, dabbing four seven eleven behind her ears with a wink at him in the mirror. 'For my fancy man!' She'd put her face close to his.

'That's your dad of course,' she'd whisper. 'He's my fancy man.'

'I've destroyed the family,' he whispered back to her now. 'Split them in two. And I don't know what the hell to do about it.'

'Pay 'em off,' said his mother cheerily. 'There's few things money won't cure.'

'I've been thinking,' he said to Bryony when she got home. 'Esther's going to end up with Kimble's Top at some point and an income from Hartley Rise. Robyn's got herself all het up and backed into a corner, thanks to me. She's going to feel short-changed. And she needs to pay Richard and Doreen back. What if I took the hundred grand from Lister's and gave it to Robyn to set things right?'

She looked at him with a resigned grimace. 'That's an awful lot of money!'

'Yes,' he said. 'But I think it might actually help.'

She thought about it for some minutes and finally nodded.

'Yes,' she said. 'I suppose it might.'

44

THE PAY OFF

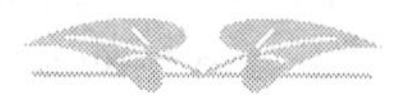

The more Tommy thought about it, the more appropriate it seemed to give his pay off to Robyn as compensation for the mess over Kimble's Top.

He'd never wanted the money in the first place. It had been shameful and meagre: not even a fraction of what he was worth to Lister's. He'd saved that company through pure acumen in the face of die-hard traditionalists without an ounce of commercial sense between them. If they'd paid what he'd been due the sum would have been ten times the figure they'd offered and that was before you looked at the shameful way they'd despatched him.

It had been a dirty, hole-in-a-corner gesture to get him to go quietly. Even now it made his blood boil. He'd have thrown it back in their faces and fought to the end if JG hadn't persuaded him, urged him to cut his losses and put the rest down to experience.

He'd had no appetite to spend the money. It still sat untouched in the bank where he'd deposited it: Robert Hartman's judas money. Robyn might as well have it. In a way it belonged to her: part of that whole shameful debacle he'd created.

Besides, Tommy's commercial instincts had awakened now with the opening for these set-top boxes and the digital switch-over. He'd been down to London with his old retail contact for a meeting with the Taiwanese supplier who was prepared to offer them a deal on the digital decoders. The foreign guy knew his stuff when it came to technology and, talking to him, Tommy had a feeling he was looking into longer-term possibilities around interactive media too. For his own part he knew the UK electricals market and how to sell.

They'd agreed an initial order with a fifty per cent down payment and he'd negotiated a discount for subsequent purchases too. He was making a sizeable investment but nothing too risky. He and Bryony had the money even apart from the Lister's pay-off. Bryony had inherited hers from her mother.

Old man Richardson's choice would have been to leave the family money directly to the grandchildren, Tommy suspected, bypassing him and Bryony altogether given his objection to their marriage. But he'd never got round to acting on that. Bryony's dad had died suddenly and everything had passed to his wife. She'd had her own ideas about Tommy and Bryony.

With that and their own savings he'd been able to buy into this new venture without even touching the hundred grand from Lister's. Now all he had to do was to persuade Robyn it was worth her while to take the money and walk away from Kimble's Top.

He picked his moment carefully, driving over to see her late on a Friday afternoon when she was most likely to be at home with Laurel.

Sure enough, as he made his way along the drive and Kimble's Top came into view, he saw Gina's old Citroen was parked by the front door and there were lights visible at the windows.

When he rang the doorbell it was Laurel who answered. She pulled the door open and stood there staring at him. Tommy hadn't seen her since the Sunday afternoon in August when he'd sat at the tea table and told the family he'd destroyed Gina's will. Now she studied him with an unequivocal look in her blue eyes.

'Is your Mum in?' he asked.

'Who is it, Laurel?' Robyn's voice sounded from inside the house.

Laurel didn't answer and then the door was pulled back further and Robyn was there in a blue sweatshirt and jeans. A look of anger crossed her face at the sight of Tommy.

'Whatever it is, we don't want to know,' she said harshly and moved to close the door.

Tommy lifted both hands in a placatory gesture. 'Just give me a couple of minutes,' he said. 'Even if it's here on the doorstep. Whatever's happened between us, we need to move forward. We can't carry on like this. I know the family's against you staying here. They want Esther to have the house. So you're in a mess and it's my fault. I got a cash pay-off when I left Lister's, in the region of a hundred grand. I want you to have it. To make things right between us.'

Robyn laughed sarcastically. 'You could give me half a million and it wouldn't make things right. Might come in useful. Get me out of the mess you seem to think I'm in. But it won't ever make things right between us.'

'We all make mistakes, Robyn,' said Tommy.

'Really?' She folded her arms and leaned a shoulder against the door with a sardonic smile. 'Do we? That's not really your way of thinking, is it? Some of us don't make mistakes, not in your view. At least you don't. Tommy Allbright doesn't make mistakes. That's for other people. People like me. We make mistakes. In fact I made one hell of a mistake once, didn't I, in your view? And you never let me forget it.'

She looked down at Laurel who was staring open-mouthed.

'Do you know what mistake I made, Laurel?' said Robyn in an ironic tone. 'You're a big girl now. You're old enough to know what a bastard Uncle Tommy was when he found out I was going to have a baby on my own, without being married.'

She glared at Tommy. 'You thought I was a right slut, didn't you? That was your view. That I should have been brought up better.' She stared at him with open malice. 'Well now the boot's on the other foot. And, I've waited long enough for it. So don't come to me saying 'we all make mistakes'!'

'Fine,' said Tommy, all his desire to find a resolution vanishing. He turned away: 'If you don't want the money.'

'Oh, I didn't say I didn't want it,' she said without haste, cold and resolute. 'I only said it wouldn't make things right. Especially now. The whole family's against me, thanks to you with your lying and thieving.'

'You'll take the money then?' said Tommy. 'And leave Kimble's Top?'

'I can't afford to be proud,' she said contemptuously. 'Not with you playing holier than thou and dropping me right in it.'

'You did that for yourself,' said Tommy. 'I was all set to take the rap but you couldn't keep your mouth shut. You just couldn't stay out of it.'

'So, maybe I'm like you,' said Robyn. 'I might make a few mistakes, screw things up. But I'm not afraid to be who I am.'

She drew herself up to her full height as she spoke and she looked dignified suddenly: solid, redoubtable and the image of Gina. He felt as if he were back in one of their old battles and he gave voice to the notion, without thinking. 'It's not me you're like. It's Gina. She'd have been proud to see you fighting your corner.'

His obviously words caught her off-guard and he could see her suddenly stifling her tears.

Embarrassed, he spoke again, quickly. 'I am sorry for how things have gone. I'm not proud of what I did. And if I'm honest, I'm sorry you didn't inherit Kimble's Top. You deserve it in many ways and you've made the house yours. But it is Esther's and we can't deny that.'

Robyn said nothing, her face was frozen in hostility.

'Take the money,' said Tommy. 'Walk away with a good grace. And make things up with your Dad. We can't afford a feud. Go and do something with your nursing. You've got a gift there. You were great with Gina at the end.'

She stared at him, wordlessly, and he'd said more than he'd meant to and needed to take his leave. He glanced at Laurel whose eyes were downcast, staring at the floor.

'Whatever your Mum says,' he told her. 'I was never sorry you were born.'

She looked up with her sombre blue eyed gaze but said nothing.

Tommy took out the cheque he'd brought and offered it to Robyn. 'Please. Let's move on from here.'

She took it silently and, as Tommy moved towards his car, he heard the front door of Kimble's Top close with a thud even before he'd reached the driver's door.

He saw the cheque had been banked within a couple of days and was eager to establish that everything was settled. He badgered Bryony to ring Richard or Maurice and find out how things stood with the legal paperwork but she refused.

'We're in no position to put pressure on. They'll let us know. I'll have to go to the solicitors with them to sign the deed anyway.'

'The lawyers won't be in any hurry to move things along,' grumbled Tommy. 'It'll take weeks if someone doesn't chivvy them.'

The following week he was put out of his misery. Richard rang and wanted to talk to him over a beer at The Golden Lion.

The pub was a favourite with Richard and his work colleagues. Tommy arrived well after six, hoping to avoid the crowd and any banter or speculation. He needn't have worried. The September evening was sunny and most of the regulars were sitting in the garden.

Inside the pub was quiet and Tommy spotted Richard sitting at the bar while the landlord poured what looked like his second pint. His brother's voice reached him across the empty tables.

'Funny how people turn out. You think you know them. And then you find out they're nothing like what you thought.'

The landlord let the last drips of the head form on the new pint and lifted the glass with practised ease to Richard. 'Get that down you then. That'll cushion you. Life's too short to be maudlin!'

He glanced at Tommy as he said it and nodded a welcome.

'Mine's a scotch,' said Tommy taking out a ten pound note. 'And whatever you're having.'

Richard turned to him and lifted his foaming pint. 'Cheers!' he said. 'Cheers to the man who's just given my daughter a hundred grand.' He sipped contentedly and put the glass down then spoke to the barman: 'Nice to have that kind of cash to throw around, eh?'

The landlord simply raised his eyebrows and nodded philosophically.

'Didn't even win the lottery,' said Richard. 'Made it all himself, didn't you?' turning again to Tommy. 'My smart big brother. Pity he's a lying cheating bastard. But hey, he probably can't help that!' he leaned in mock intimacy to the landlord and dropped his voice. 'I blame the parents!'

Tommy took his glass of scotch and gestured towards an empty table by the window:

'Shall we?'

Richard followed him over and they sat down.

'So Robyn's okay about it?' asked Tommy, anxious for confirmation.

'She can't afford not to be,' said Richard. 'Not with a hundred grand on the table. No-one can turn that sort of money away. Except you, apparently. I bet Bryony's thrilled?'

Tommy sipped his scotch and ignored the provocation.

'Bryony wants an end to this rift,' he said deliberately, looking Richard in the eye.

'Ah, you want back in,' Richard nursed his beer glass. 'Sunday tea in the bosom of the family. Well why not? You're one of us after all, for all that you're a lying bastard. Anyway Bryony's a classy lady. We miss her. She deserves some support, putting up with you all these years.'

Tommy said nothing, closed his mouth on any retort.

'Come on Sunday,' shrugged Richard. 'We're meeting at ours. Bring a dessert.'

Tommy nodded, downed his scotch and got up to go, then remembered it had been Richard who'd suggested they meet.

'What was it you wanted to talk about by the way?'

His brother looked up at him, glass in hand, and took a sip of beer that left foam on his upper lip.

'Thank you,' he said. 'I wanted to say thank you. For the money.'

45

CHRIS & ELISABETH

Tommy sat alone in the living room, the day's newspaper and a cup of black coffee untouched beside him. It was a Saturday morning, the 30th September, the day Chris and Elisabeth were arriving home so he could tell them about James.

At the end of August when Bryony had made excuses to stop Chris and Elisabeth coming home for the bank holiday and Tommy's confession to the rest of the family, she'd made it clear that it would be up to Tommy to rearrange their visit.

He'd done it by email . . . *'there's something we need to tell you, preferably both together'* . . . asked them to suggest a convenient weekend.

Elisabeth had telephoned within a couple of hours. 'What's going on?'

'Nothing,' he'd lied. 'We just wanted to see you both together.'

'Are you ill?'

'No, nothing like that!'

'Is it work then? Something's come up in America? You're moving overseas.'

'No! It's nothing. Really. There's been a bit of a row in the family, that's all. We wanted you to hear about it from us.'

'Oh,' she'd sounded instantly bored. 'Well it's not a good time. Work's manic. And I haven't got a free Saturday until the end of September.'

He hadn't known whether to be relieved or frustrated. '30th September, then,' he'd confirmed. 'I'll let Chris know.'

'You're doing the talking,' Bryony had said when he told her the date. 'I can see I'll have to be there. But you're telling them.'

He'd nodded and carefully picked his moment. 'I thought . . . the photos . . . might help.'

Her expression was closed. She shrugged. If you think so.'

'Will you get them for me?'

He knew where they were, the handful of photos they'd taken of James. They'd been hard up in the early days, barely able to afford film for the camera but they had a dozen or so pictures of their boy. Bryony kept them in a box in her dressing table.

She'd fetched them, handing him the flat box without a word and he'd lifted the lid to look down at the delightful grinning face of his son.

There were one or two baby pictures: James as a very young infant, lying on his stomach gurgling and then, more alert, propped up on his elbows and beginning to crawl. The others were from his pre-school days, the mischievous three or four year old, looking up smiling.

Tommy had sat alone, looking at them, wondering what he'd say to Chris and Elisabeth and he couldn't visualise anything beyond handing them a photo each and saying: 'This was your brother.'

Perhaps that was the only way.

Tommy sipped his black coffee. It was after nine o'clock and the sun was casting shadows across the wall as he sat doing nothing in the living room where he never sat alone and inactive like this. The living room was for socialising, family time or watching television.

Bryony was still upstairs, he'd taken her toast and coffee on a tray and now he could hear snatches of music from the radio programme she liked to listen to while she got dressed.

Tommy sat on in silence, thinking how empty a house could feel once its children had grown up and gone.

It was after ten thirty when Elisabeth's silver volkswagen Beetle came to a crunching halt outside the front door. She had picked Chris up on the way and, now they were here, Tommy felt choked up at the sight of them. Bryony had reached the hall ahead of him and was already embracing Chris who was all long limbs as he reached down to hug her back.

Elisabeth came to hug Tommy. 'Is everything all right?'

He smiled reassuringly. 'Don't worry.'

They brought the living room to life, Elisabeth plumping down on the sofa where Tommy had just been sitting alone and Christopher sprawled in the arm chair. Bryony sat down on the opposite sofa by the tray of hot drinks and muffins Tommy had prepared to tide them over to a late lunch.

When they'd all got a drink, Tommy sat down beside Elisabeth and, with a quick glance at Bryony whose face was unreadable, he opened the box of photos.

He handed a picture each to Elisabeth and Chris, then lay the rest of them, one by one, face upwards on the coffee table.

'We asked you home so we could tell you about your brother, James. He died when he was five years old.'

Elisabeth seemed to freeze and sat staring silently at the picture in her hand while Christopher's eyes were wide and fixed on Tommy.

Tommy had no idea what to say next but to his relief Bryony was already speaking.

'We thought it best not to tell you when you were little.' Her voice was quiet and controlled. 'Now we realise we should have let you know.'

'Let us know?' Elisabeth's head jerked up and she looked from one to the other of them. 'When was this?' Her voice was indignant.

'It was a long time ago,' said Tommy. 'When you were still a baby,' and, to Chris: 'Before you were born.'

He'd given them the baby photos. In front of him on the table was James the little boy, culminating in the proud schoolboy of class 1E staring up from among his school mates, arms behind his back, head up.

'What happened to him?' asked Chris.

'He was run over by a lorry,' Bryony's voice was calm.

Chris and Elisabeth looked at one another.

'Why on earth didn't you tell us?' demanded Elisabeth.

'We didn't want you to grieve,' said Bryony. 'Not when you didn't need to.'

'But you must have grieved,' said Elisabeth. 'You must have been grieving all the time. Watching us grow up and being reminded.'

'We put it behind us,' said Bryony decisively. 'It was the best way.'

Tommy nodded agreement, conscious of Elisabeth turning to look at him.

'We looked to the future,' Bryony said. 'We didn't want to look back.'

'Well you're telling us now,' said Chris.

Bryony glanced hesitantly at Tommy.

'You said there'd been a row,' said Elisabeth, seeing the look.

'Let's stick with this for now,' said Tommy. 'The rest is complicated.'

Elisabeth held her photograph of James up in front of her and said nothing. Chris had leaned forward to look at the pictures on the table and was turning them round one by one to face him.

'Is there a grave?' he asked.

'At Kimble's Top,' nodded Tommy. 'It's where he died.'

'Whereabouts?' asked Chris.

'Where the statue of Peter Pan is?' said Elisabeth slowly, questioning, looking at Tommy.

'Yes. It's where the front gate used to be. Where the drive met the road.'

He could see they were, dumbstruck, lost for words and struggling to comprehend it all. They exchanged perplexed glances with one another.

'So who else knew?' asked Elisabeth. 'Gina did, presumably.'

'All your aunts and uncles,' said Bryony. 'Your grandparents of course. But beyond that we didn't want to talk about it. None of your cousins was born then. It seemed easier to leave it alone . . .' she tailed off as if realising how unconvincing it all sounded.

'It's completely bizarre,' said Chris. 'I suppose you thought we wouldn't understand?'

'How could you?' said Bryony. 'You never knew him. Anyway it wasn't your grief to bear. It was ours.'

Chris looked across at Elisabeth and she stared back at him. 'I think we'd better go for a walk,' he said. 'Just the two of us.'

'Yes,' she nodded. 'Clear our heads.'

They left the room and Tommy sat transfixed, looking at Bryony who was staring down at her hands again. Out in the hall Chris and Elisabeth were putting their jackets on and exchanging murmurs he couldn't quite catch.

'Do you want a key?' called Bryony, lifting her head at last at the sound of the front door opening.

'Got one,' said Chris and then the door closed and footsteps sounded on the gravel as the two of them set off down the drive.

Tommy looked at Bryony. 'What now?'

'How should I know?'

Their late lunch didn't happen. They'd agreed Tommy would make his favourite seafood lasagne for dinner that night but later on, while Chris and Elisabeth were still out, he found Bryony in the kitchen peeling the prawns.

'Thought I was doing that?' he said.

She shrugged. 'It's as easy for me to do it.'

He watched her for a minute working rapidly to prise the scales away, then went and stood behind her, slipping his arm around her waist and resting his face against the smoothness of her hair.

'We've done it,' he said. 'We've told them. Thank you for being there.'

She didn't answer or relax into him but carried on working.

'I promise we won't dwell on it,' said Tommy. 'It's over now.'

In the absence of any communication he wandered back into the living room by himself and sat wondering where his two grown up children had got to.

It was nearly three o'clock when they got back.

'We had a coffee in the Pump Room down on the Embankment.'

They'd come to find him in the living room, plumped down on the sofas still in their jackets.

From the kitchen Tommy could hear the strains of the food mixer going: Bryony preparing double cream and mascarpone for the Tiramisu. It drowned out the host of questions they'd brought back, their voices urgent and demanding as they put them to him:

'What was he like?' 'Where did he go to school?' 'When was his birthday?' 'Was he killed outright?' 'Who else was there?'

By way of an answer he took them upstairs to the front bedroom that had belonged to James, opened the cupboard and lifted the boxes down from the top shelf, then sat on the floor with them, watching as they opened the boxes up and looked at the toys and clothes.

'It's because of Mum that you didn't tell us, isn't it?' said Elisabeth. 'She can't handle it.'

'It was a joint decision. It seemed right at the time.'

'It wasn't right,' she said. 'You shouldn't have kept it from us.'

He didn't argue, just sat and watched her handling the toys, remembering her as a little girl, always clinging to him in company: a little girl with her head against his shoulder, refusing to be put down on the floor.

Chris had made no move to look at the toys. He lifted a couple of jumpers out of one box, looked at them briefly and replaced them.

'I'd rather go up to Kimble's Top,' he said. 'I want to see where he died.'

It was problematic and he should have foreseen it.

'Perhaps tomorrow,' he told Chris. 'Tonight what your Mum needs is to have you home. To hear what you've been up to.'

They ate dinner early, facing each other across the table as if in an interrogation. Normally Tommy and Bryony would have sat opposite one another, each with one of the children at their side, but tonight Chris and Elisabeth sat down first, side by side, forcing him and Bryony to take their places opposite.

Elisabeth opened in an unsympathetic vein. 'What else haven't you told us through the years?'

'Nothing,' said Tommy.

'I don't think either of us understands why you didn't tell us about James. How could you cut us off from all the feelings and memories you must have had?'

'We didn't,' said Bryony. 'I told you. We put it behind us.'

'But you must have thought about him. Every time we went up to Kimble's Top. All those visits to the rose garden.'

'And what about the anniversary?' said Chris. 'You must have been thinking about him? And on his birthday?'

Bryony looked vexed, shaking her head at the volume of questions.

'You were our focus,' said Tommy. 'When your Mum and I went out to the garden it was about our being together and looking forward. Of course James was on our minds whenever we went to Kimble's Top, but our lives were about you.'

'So you just forgot about him,' said Chris.

'No!' said Bryony.

Elisabeth flashed a warning look at Chris and for a few minutes they all concentrated on eating their lasagne. Tommy noticed Bryony's hand trembling as she lifted the fork to her mouth.

'I know it's difficult, he said to them after a while. 'But we really did do what we thought was best.'

There was no response and the meal continued in a strained atmosphere.

Chris finished first, sat back and announced to Bryony. 'Elisabeth and I want to go up to Kimble's Top. Tomorrow. We want to be where he is.'

Bryony's face was expressionless, her mouth set in a rigid line.

'Just the three of us, then,' said Tommy. 'We'll go in the morning.'

'Better hope you don't run into Robyn!' said Bryony ironically.

Tommy rose to gather the plates.

'Is that because of the row?' asked Elisabeth.

'We'll talk about it tomorrow,' said Tommy dismissively. 'I think we've all heard enough for one day.'

There was a strained silence and, for a moment, he wondered if there was going to be a scene but Elisabeth was ever his ally. 'Let's watch a film together then,' she said. 'We haven't done that for ages.'

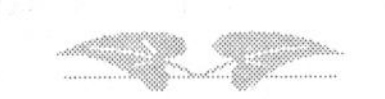

46

Peter Pan

Sunday morning: Tommy was up at five. He made fresh bread for breakfast, brewed coffee and laid the table ready with cereal and fruit juice.

He'd gone to bed late and heard Chris and Elisabeth still talking in Elisabeth's room, the light showing under her bedroom door as he passed it on the landing. He wondered now how long they'd sat up talking.

Normally Elisabeth was an early bird like him. On a weekend like this she'd be down before the others and they'd have one of their chats about work and business. Her absence today unnerved him.

Instead it was Chris who came down first. Tommy had busied himself tidying the kitchen and turned with a handful of cutlery from the dishwasher to find his son standing there, bleary-eyed in his dressing gown.

'Coffee?' suggested Tommy.

Chris shook his head and went to pour himself a glass of milk from the fridge, then sat down on a stool at the central counter. He'd brought the box of photos from the living room and began looking through the snapshots.

Tommy sat down opposite with his coffee and watched his son take out a picture. It was of a three year old James sitting solemnly on the settee at Gina's with a big book resting on his knees. He was turning the pages, utterly absorbed.

'I was thinking,' said Chris frowning down at the image. 'Why didn't he hear the lorry coming and move away? Was it all just too quick?'

Tommy forced himself to think about it, remembering that last sight of his boy, feet strapped into the roller skates. He saw again his son's clumsy manoeuvres, the struggle to make headway, arms swinging wide.

'You said he was on the drive,' said Chris still seeking an explanation.

Tommy nodded. 'The lorry swerved. There were a couple of girls on bikes, out on the road. It slopes there. Maybe they did something unexpected. James was wearing roller skates.'

'He couldn't get out of the way?' mused Chris, and again: 'Did he hear the lorry?'

'I think he must have done.' Tommy remembered the sound of it across the lawn as he'd fetched ice for the drinks.

'Did he see it? Before it hit him?' asked Chris. 'Did he know?'

Tommy looked at the troubled face of his son, the dark eyes looking to him for reassurance, and set his mind to consider the question. 'I don't know,' he said at last. 'I don't know what he saw or how he felt. Whether he had a chance to register . . . fear.'

He could feel the warmth of his tears rising as he spoke.

'Maybe he cried out?' suggested Chris.

'No.'

It had been Bryony who'd screamed. On and on. He didn't want to tell Chris that.

'Your brother died very quickly,' he said instead. 'Almost instantaneously. By the time your mother and I got there . . .'

He broke off and Chris nodded, dropped the photo into the box and closed the lid.

'We're still going up there, right? Today?'

'Before lunch,' promised Tommy.

Chris picked up the box: 'I'm going to scan them. For me and Elisabeth.'

He went off then to the study and Tommy sat there alone in the kitchen, pondering the questions and his son's need to reconstruct how it had been for James. They were things he'd never dared to dwell on himself but he hoped it had been quick. That his boy had been knocked senseless by the initial impact, unconscious even before he'd hit the ground. It was possible he hadn't seen the lorry coming or heard it, engrossed in his little boy's excitement, up and down the drive on his new skates.

The grief of it was piercing. Yet he had a sudden sense of how James might have been today, not unlike Chris but older, steadier and more robust, perhaps, more like Tommy. For an instant he had a sense of him there, present, and it filled him with a desperate longing, a yearning for all that his son might have been if he had lived.

They went up to Kimble's Top shortly after breakfast, which was a quiet affair with little conversation beyond the occasional comment on the weather and news headlines.

Tommy cleared the breakfast things away swiftly and, as he, Chris and Elisabeth, left, Bryony suggested a pub lunch later, somewhere really nice with a carvery. She named a couple of places but Tommy shook his head. 'It's not a good idea.'

She shrugged and he sensed her resentment, as if it were all his fault, putting a damper on things, but he couldn't help it.

It was a dull day with slight traces of blue visible among the clouds, not a day for playing out in the garden he noted thankfully with Laurel in mind. He hadn't been up to Kimble's Top since his doorstep conversation with Robyn and had no desire to encounter the rest of the family up there.

He parked just inside the gate, pulled in close to the hedge and switched the engine off. It would be easy enough for them to walk through the rhododendrons towards the rose garden.

'You haven't told Robyn we're coming,' said Elisabeth.

'This is our grief,' said Tommy. 'Our time.'

He led the way through the trees and shrubs towards the perimeter path. At one point they had to skirt the lawn but at an angle barely visible from the house and then they were hidden again. Thick shrubbery lay to their right and the wire fence to their left with the great trees and red earth banks of the country park beyond it. The path continued straight for some time and then turned suddenly into the secluded space of the rose garden.

It was October now and several of the bushes that had bloomed in the spring were in flower again. The smallest ones at the heart of the garden had clusters of blooms, whiter than white, like frothy old lace. Surrounding them were the larger plants, dark leaved and heavy with golden roses, pink tinged on the outer petals. These had scores of new buds with petals tightly folded upwards and lined with pink.

At the centre of the concentric beds was Peter Pan, stepping over his tree stump as always and staring back at some unknown point on the horizon.

Elisabeth made her way through the roses to stand beside him.

Christopher followed her and knelt down to touch the smooth marble figure, reaching out a hand to the face that looked up and away into the distance. 'Is this where he died?' he asked Tommy. 'Right here?'

Tommy wasn't sure. He found it difficult to reconstruct the arrangement of the drive as it had been, before the gates were moved and the rose beds dug. It belonged in the past.

'It's where his ashes are,' he told Chris.

There were childish voices on the wind coming through the trees from the country park and Tommy couldn't help listening for them, turning his head now and then to make sure they really did come from over there.

'Let's cut some flowers,' Christopher said to Elisabeth. 'We could press them to keep.'

They began selecting the golden blooms for Chris to cut off with his pen knife until they'd assembled quite a posy, and it was as they were debating whether to include some of the white roses too that they all heard the sound of a car on the drive. It was moving slowly and with a window since they could hear the radio playing.

Tommy turned sharply towards the sound but whether the car was arriving or leaving he couldn't distinguish through the trees. Either way, they'd have seen the Audi, know he was here.

Elisabeth picked up the roses. 'It's time you told us about this family quarrel.'

'Not here,' said Tommy.

'In the car then,' she said and led the way.

It was awkward, sitting half-turned to face them, with Elisabeth in the passenger seat at his side and Chris leaning forward from behind; the two of them confronting him while he tried to explain and worried about their being discovered and interrupted.

Outside the birds rustled in the shrubs. In the car his children watched him, waiting, and he didn't want this to be happening, not here, like this, where his boy had died, as if all the losses of his children were destined to happen in this place.

'Was it over James?' asked Elisabeth impatiently. 'The fact that you hadn't told us?'

The two had been related, the fact that Kimble's Top meant so much to him. He put it as plainly as he could and without expression because the familiar words had become wearisome to him. They stared at him blankly as he talked about the two wills, destroying one, about Esther, Robyn and the shares.

Elisabeth's face became a mask of shocked disbelief and Christopher was full of anger: 'How could you do it?'

'I wasn't thinking straight.'

'You left Esther with nothing!'

'I left her with the shares,' Tommy corrected him. 'They should have brought Esther a good half a million. It never occurred to me they'd be worthless.'

'Well it should have occurred to you!' stormed Christopher. 'It's pretty obvious if someone changes their will there's a reason for it.'

'Anyway, it's irrelevant,' said Elisabeth coldly. 'Gina meant Esther to have Kimble's Top. That's what matters.'

Tommy could only nod silently.

'So that was the row?' said Elisabeth. 'Someone found out?'

'I told them,' said Tommy. 'I couldn't go on with it so I came clean.'

'That was big of you!' said Christopher scathingly.

'And what about the house now?' said Elisabeth.

'It'll go to Esther,' said Tommy. 'Robyn's agreed. I gave her my pay off from Lister's to compensate.'

'That makes sense,' said Chris. 'You always did think money solves everything.'

Bryony must have seen the hostility on their children's faces as soon as they arrived home. She stood silent at the front door as they all stepped into the hall.

Elisabeth held up the roses. 'We brought these from James's grave. We're going to press them, to keep.'

Bryony nodded. 'Richard rang,' she told Tommy. 'He seems to think we're going for Sunday tea.'

'Not today!' said Tommy in alarm. 'Some other time.'

'Oh I don't know,' said Elisabeth. 'I think now's exactly the time since Chris and I are here.'

This wasn't what he'd wanted. When he'd dared to anticipate his reconciliation with the family he'd thought of it as a quiet, discreet affair, not in an atmosphere of antagonism, but Elisabeth was adamant.

'Will Esther be there?' asked Chris and, when Bryony said she thought not, that Esther usually did her own thing on Sundays and might even be working, he and Elisabeth decided they'd call their cousin themselves and find out.

Tommy watched them searching for her mobile number, knowing it was stored in his own phone but perversely refusing to offer it. Things were moving at an alarming rate and he felt entirely unprepared.

It was a lavish tea, covering the kitchen counters as well as the dining table in Richard and Doreen's living room.

'That's quite a spread,' said Bryony.

'Thought I'd make an effort,' said Doreen. 'Put the past behind us! I gather even Esther's coming.'

'We persuaded her,' said Elisabeth. 'She's out with friends but she'll pop by later. We wanted her to be here.'

The space for sitting was cramped as always and Tommy felt ill at ease, aware of glances exchanged around him, the rest of them no doubt wondering how much Chris and Elisabeth knew and what they'd made of it all, though no-one so much as mentioned the rift.

When Esther arrived Richard ushered her into the living room. 'Look who it is! Now we're all here.'

The rest of them were eating dessert by then. Doreen went to fetch Esther a cup of tea and Maurice offered trifle or cheesecake or maybe both, while Elisabeth got up to offer her seat. 'We're so glad you came, we haven't seen you for ages.'

Tommy could see Esther was embarrassed to be the centre of attention. She took her cup of tea, shook her head at the seat Elisabeth offered and came to perch on the arm of Tommy's chair with a mock grimace. For once he knew exactly how she felt.

'How are you?' she asked him.

'Great,' he said drily and she smiled briefly at that.

In answer to her cousins' questions she spoke haltingly of her job at Ariadne's, the pub where she still did a few shifts and her plans to go back-packing but even Chris and Elisabeth gave up quizzing her after that. The conversation moved on to Robyn and her nursing course and Esther relaxed then, leaned back against Tommy's chair and finally picked at some cheesecake.

'Things are coming together then?' said Tommy quietly.

'I suppose so,' she shrugged. 'I just want to get out of here. Not this,' she gestured at the living room. 'I mean England. Wellingborough. Have you noticed how the sun never shines here? You get the odd day of it and everyone thinks it's amazing. There's countries where the sun shines all the time. Where it really warms you. I can't stand living here. There's just no warmth. No life.'

Tommy listened silently, caught off guard as he always was by her particular view of things.

'No wonder everyone's so miserable all the time,' said Esther. 'Arguing and picking holes in everything.'

'Where will you go?' he asked. 'Thailand? Goa?'

'I haven't decided,' she said. 'But somewhere hot and colourful. Where people know how to live.'

Tommy thought of his decoder business and recognised her sentiment, hungry to move on from all this too. For once in his life he found himself in total agreement with her and at odds with the rest of the family.

'What about Kimble's Top?' he asked, not caring if the others heard him.

'Robyn's staying til she's thirty,' said Esther. 'After that I might turn it into a hippy commune. Probably not what Dad had in mind!'

'Oh, I don't know,' laughed Tommy. 'He might have been pleased. If it made you happy.'

'Do you think he even knows?' she asked. 'That he's looking down seeing us? Do you believe in all that? Life after death?'

Tommy thought of James. *'Romping through paradise,'* Dominic had said. *'Surveying the universe in the company of angels.'*

'I don't believe in death,' he said slowly. 'I think they must still be with us. Just in a different place.'

He'd never contemplated such an idea in his life but she didn't question it. Her green eyes met his with a look of openness and agreement for the first time in all the years he'd known her. Thankfully, though, nothing more was said because he had no idea what he'd have come up with if she'd pressed him further.

Meanwhile the conversation around them had become raucous. Richard was dominating, celebrating the family together again, all animosity forgotten. He proposed a toast to that effect:

'The family!'

'And absent friends!' said Maurice. 'Gina. Dad.'

Lorraine protested then that they needed alcohol for toasts like that and Doreen went to get the sherry. After that a round of nibbles seemed in order, nuts and crisps, and it was nearly seven when the giggling and banter stopped and the party broke up.

'That went well then,' said Chris facetiously when they got home. 'Major family break down. Fraud and skulduggery. And everything restored over a glass of sherry.'

'Oh I wouldn't be surprised,' said Elisabeth. 'Let's face it, nothing's ever been what it seemed, has it?'

'I think that's a bit of an exaggeration,' protested Bryony.

Elisabeth just shrugged at that and exchanged a glance with Chris.

'I'm going to chill out upstairs,' she said. 'Have a hot bath or something.'

'Good idea,' said her brother. 'And I think I'll watch television in bed for a while.'

The next morning they were in a hurry to leave. Elisabeth's mobile phone had a back log of messages from work and Chris had decided to leave early with her, so she could drop him at a train station on a direct line to Kingston.

Tommy could see there was no point in arguing.

'Call us when you get in,' said Bryony. 'Let us know you've arrived safely.

Elisabeth nodded: 'I'll see you at Christmas probably, not before. It's been a bit much.'

Chris just hugged them briefly on his way to the car and made no suggestions about his next visit home.

It was only when they'd gone that Tommy found they'd forgotten to take the roses from Kimble's Top. They lay in two neat bundles on the kitchen counter, wrapped in polythene for the journey home.

47

ADVENT

Roses were difficult flowers to press, according to his online research, but Tommy was determined to master the art nevertheless. He lined the pages of an encyclopaedia with kitchen towel and picked out a bloom from the selection Chris and Elisabeth had gathered.

He snipped off the stem at the base of the flower where the leaves that had once enclosed the bud extended out in a succession of five light green points, like a star. Examining it more closely, he found the flower intriguing: the softness of its deep gold petals, wide and velvety at the outside while the inner petals were smaller and still formed something of a tight bud at the centre. Within each petal was a delicate pattern of lines, like little veins, marking the golden surface.

He lifted the flower to his nose for a moment but its scent was gone.

Laying the flower head down on the kitchen towel, Tommy closed the book tight and set more volumes on top of it.

By the time he'd worked his way through the entire posy, the shelves in his study were piled high with telephone directories, dictionaries and old almanacs that his parents had collected.

He emailed Chris and Elisabeth and suggested they meet up in a few weeks' time so he could hand the pressed flowers over but their replies were non-committal. Christopher was busy with walking fixtures while the weather held and Elisabeth's deadlines meant she'd be working long hours, including weekends.

Their response unnerved him but he didn't protest, just sat in his study thinking about the roses and how they reminded him of James, the gentleness of his little boy.

When Christopher had used the home computer to scan in the photographs of his brother, he'd saved them onto the desk top and Tommy had come across them as soon as he'd switched on the machine. He'd sat and looked at the beloved face, suddenly alive again, and realised that Chris and Elisabeth's discovery of James had unleashed a fresh wave of grief within him.

He tried to distract himself with the icon but its bright desert scene jarred with his wintry mood and he was afraid to sit too long with his thoughts.

He put his coat on and walked up to the cemetery.

It was October: cold and dry, the sky layered with clouds of light and dark grey, moving constantly.

In the corner of the cemetery where Dominic had been working the ivy was still prolific. A few weeds and nettles were coming back but, on the whole, the undergrowth had been cleared and it no longer felt so lost and abandoned.

Tommy sat down on the familiar bench among the yews, taking in the silence and stillness of the trees and gravestones.

When Dominic arrived he stopped several times to pick things up on his way along the path and Tommy saw that he'd gathered a collection of pine cones.

'If you're planning to keep the place clear of those you'll have more than a full time job!' he remarked as Dominic set them down in a pile on the bench.

The priest smiled.

'I'll concede you've made a real difference, cleaning the place up,' said Tommy. 'But if you think about it, and you really believe they're in a better place, it's actually nothing but an empty space, is it? So what's the point?'

Dominic looked around. 'A memorial?' he suggested. 'A remembrance? And a reminder of what's ahead for us.'

He took a pair of secateurs from his pocket and began snipping away at strands of ivy and holly, gathering a pile of winter greenery.

'Christmas decorations?' asked Tommy.

'It's for an advent corona,' said Dominic. 'For St Hubert's at Harrowden. Do you know it? Old Catholic chapel in the grounds of the hall. We're holding Advent Vespers there in the four weeks to Christmas. Sundays at six o'clock. Come along! You might enjoy it.'

Tommy muttered a vague apology, remembering how out of place he'd felt on the Sunday he'd driven off to mass. Anyway, he didn't want to think about Christmas when he wasn't even sure if Chris and Elisabeth would come home for it. He dreaded to think what Bryony would say if they made other plans.

He was still anxious to hear back about the flowers, sending them inconsequential texts about the weather and local news, with only the occasional one-liner in response.

Keeping busy was the only solution. He'd finished drafting his business plan for the decoder distribution and, by the middle of October, had picked thirty retail outlets within a sixty mile radius, offering them a performance related discount structure and seasonal deals.

All the big brands were promoting set top boxes and satellite channels and that meant smart consumers would be looking for cheaper options.

He was sitting at the computer one afternoon, looking at the latest digital packages, when Bryony arrived with a tray of coffee and biscuits and a collection of glossy magazines.

'How's it going?' she asked.

'Plenty of deals out there. But nothing too radical. The market's strong.'

'Not much for you to do then,' she suggested.

Tommy sipped the coffee, sensing there was more to come.

'I want a holiday,' she said.

Friends of theirs had just come back from a cruise and the magazines she'd brought were brochures with exotic destinations and discounts for late bookers.

'This isn't our kind of thing,' said Tommy.

'Isn't it?' said Bryony. 'Foreign travel? Fine dining? Good company. I want a break, Tommy. Something different.'

'We can get a break . . . .'

'This would be relaxing,' she said. 'We need it. Losing Gina. Your Dad . . .'

She left it there but the rest was obvious: the grief he'd caused over the will and by reawakening the past. Tommy reached for a brochure:

'What did you have in mind?'

They booked a Caribbean itinerary with a free upgrade to an ocean view, a cabin with a balcony, providing they flew out within two weeks.

They'd be back by the end of October with plenty of time for Tommy to pick up with his retailers before Christmas.

He fussed and fretted over his half-dried roses before they went, gingerly pulling back the kitchen towel to examine the fragile petals. All trace of moisture had gone and the different hues of the gold petals were more pronounced, some lighter and others deeper in colour. He touched them gently, probing the dry layers and central buds.

Unsure what else to do, he left them to compress for another couple of weeks under their heavy volumes while he and Bryony flew off to the Caribbean.

The food was the best part, plenty of genuine local produce and always a special dish of the day with the wine well-matched. Bryony insisted it was like their early courtship all over again but privately he'd have preferred to cook the food himself and eat, just the two of them, in the intimacy of their own home.

Their dinner companions were well travelled people, accustomed to five star luxury. They reminded Tommy of Lister's Board, of Hartman and Penelope Leys, and it made him nostalgic for the straightforward company of his old market traders and retail friends.

His mind turned frequently to Chris and Elisabeth. They responded cordially to Bryony's daily email and photos: *glad to see you're having a break . . .* but there was no intimation of what they were really thinking or when he and Bryony could expect to see them again.

They arrived home at the end of October to the news that Tommy's accountant had been having heart problems and could no longer act as his company secretary. There was a younger colleague eager to take on the role but Tommy wasn't keen. He'd set up a limited company for the decoder business with himself as sole Director and named his accountant as secretary precisely because he was mature and experienced.

'This young guy will only be interested in his fee,' he told Bryony. 'It's all about bringing in new business for them. He won't want to spend his time on a small client like me. I suppose I'll just have to appoint a second Director within the company but I can't imagine who.'

'Does it have to be an accountant?' asked Bryony.

Tommy shook his head. 'Just someone good at paperwork. Statutory filing. Keeping the record books, that kind of thing.'

'Why don't you ask Richard?' she suggested.

He looked at her aghast.

'Well, why not?' she said. 'He's experienced. He knows you. And he won't be looking for his next big fee.'

'Richard hasn't got the slightest idea about business.'

'You've just said he doesn't have to. He knows about record books and filing.'

'No!' said Tommy. 'Definitely not.'

It went right against the grain. He'd always believed in keeping business and family separate. Lister's Board had taught him that. Family companies were disastrous, in his opinion, unless there was genuine expertise to run the business as a true commercial enterprise.

He needed someone though. He looked through his old contacts and called Jim McKenna, his Brand Manager at Lister's, but Jim wasn't interested:

'You know me, I'm a shop floor man, Tommy. It's all about the people. Not much of a one for paperwork. You could try JG.'

Tommy hadn't thought of that. As far as he was aware his old PA had stayed on to work for Roper so there might be conflicting loyalties. Still, McKenna would know the lie of the land.

He tried her home number a couple of times and left a message but heard nothing back then, after a week or so, he went to see Richard.

He found his brother at home, early evening, sitting at the kitchen table with a beer, flicking through the *Evening Telegraph*.

The boys were out, Doreen was doing an extra shift at the hotel and only Laurel was around, playing on the computer upstairs.

'She stays over most nights,' said Richard. 'Now Robyn's all taken up with her course. Good holiday?'

Tommy nodded as Richard handed him a can of beer from the fridge.

'And work wise?' asked his brother. 'Or don't you need to work?'

There was a note of envy in his voice.

'That's what I wanted to talk to you about,' said Tommy, and explained his new distribution business. 'I'm looking for a second Director. To be company secretary. Thought it might be your kind of thing.'

He'd never made such a limp proposition in his life. Never proposed anything without being specific about the terms and conditions. Even as he spoke he could hear his voice tailing off without enthusiasm.

'No thanks!' said Richard.

'It'd be a directorship,' said Tommy. 'Obviously it's only a small operation at the moment but I've got plans. This could really go somewhere.'

Richard smiled, beer can raised halfway to his lips. 'I appreciate what you're offering, Tommy, and I won't deny it means something to be asked. But it's not my line. Anyway I've said I'll keep an eye on dad's old place when Esther goes travelling. Manage the rental and so on. That's enough to be going on with.' He took a sip of beer. 'Besides we'll only fall out. And I don't want that. Not over work stuff.'

Tommy shook his head in bitter amusement. It had seemed simple, just a matter of making the offer and he hadn't even been able to achieve that. He must be really losing his touch.

He said so to Bryony when he got home and she smiled and said that she wasn't really surprised.

'Well why did you suggest it then?' asked Tommy exasperated. 'You could have saved me looking an idiot.'

'Oh I doubt you looked an idiot,' she replied. 'And it probably it did mean a lot to Richard that you asked him.'

They were into the second half of November, the wintry days short, evenings closing in by four o'clock, when Christopher finally rang.

Elisabeth was planning to stay with him in Kingston over the first weekend in December so Tommy and Bryony might as well drive down and meet them for Sunday lunch. He suggested a pub they all liked near the river.

'We'll meet you there,' said Chris. 'Save you trekking all the way to my place. You can give us the roses then.'

'I'm glad you've come back to me on it,' said Tommy, feeling relieved.

'Well, it's about James,' said his son. 'We don't want to just forget him.'

We didn't just forget him.

The accusation hurt but Tommy bit back his response, thankful they'd agreed a date.

The day before they met up was December 2nd, the anniversary of Gina's death.

It was on Tommy's mind all week but Bryony hadn't registered the date. She'd agreed to attend a ladies fundraising event at Wellingborough School, so Tommy sat at home alone with a glass of scotch thinking about the previous year.

He remembered the long evenings watching his sister decline and the night she'd died, picking his dad up and taking him over to Kimble's Top. It was only as he raised a glass to the two of them that he realised he hadn't even thought about what Esther would be doing tonight.

He called her mobile. She was having dinner with Fleur.

'I'm glad you rang, though,' she said. 'I wanted to ask a favour.'

She was heading off to Bali in mid December.

'You couldn't take me to the airport, could you? It's an early flight so the train's no good.'

'I'd be delighted to take you,' said Tommy. 'At this rate I might even come with you!'

She laughed.

The following morning he arranged the pressed roses in two gift boxes he'd prepared, lining them with blue velvet from the old sewing shop in town.

Bryony had filled Tupperware containers with home made mince pies and, as they drove south, she was full of excitement at the pleasure of seeing Chris and Elisabeth again, as though all the aggravation of their last meeting had been resolved.

Tommy hoped she wasn't going to find it a difficult afternoon.

As they pulled into the pub car park, Tommy spotted Chris in the thatched porch of the building, waiting to meet them. When they got inside it was clear he and Elisabeth had been there for some time. There were empty glasses on the table and a sense of conspiracy between the two of them which stung Tommy. Bryony seemed thrown by it too.

'What'll you have?' asked Chris, as Elisabeth handed him a twenty pound note. 'This one's on us! You're buying lunch.'

The pub was busy but they'd settled themselves into a cosy nook beside the log fire where comfortable chairs surrounded a polished wooden table.

When they'd all got a drink in front of them, Tommy handed over the gift boxes.

'Thank you for agreeing to meet,' he said. 'I know it wasn't easy last time.'

'You should have told us about James,' said Chris, lifting the lid from his box and pulling back the velvet cover to reveal the pressed roses. 'You should have given us a chance to understand.'

Tommy nodded: 'We're sorry,' he said.

'We're both sorry,' said Bryony. 'It was just so . . .'

'Painful?' suggested Chris.

'Private,' said Bryony. 'James was ours. It was our loss.'

Chris and Elisabeth exchanged looks and Tommy could see they didn't understand but at least they didn't argue.

'So, you're dropping Esther at the airport,' said Elisabeth to Tommy, catching him off guard.

'We've been texting,' explained Chris, sipping beer. 'And you've signed the paperwork so Kimble's Top will be hers?'

'Robyn's staying for a few years,' nodded Bryony. 'But that's all. She'll probably have her own plans by then anyway.'

'Oh well, that's okay then,' said Chris with a trace of sarcasm and another glance at Elisabeth but nothing more was said and the conversation moved on to holidays.

They managed to stay civil over lunch and after coffee, when things seemed to be drawing to a close, Bryony asked when they were planning to arrive home for Christmas.

Tommy was relieved to hear they were at least coming for some, if not all, of the holiday. Chris thought he might be in London for the new year and Elisabeth murmured something about an invitation to go skiing with friends.

'It was the best we could hope for,' he told Bryony when they were back in the car.

There had been no confrontation, no recriminations, but he sensed she felt flat, as he did, deflated at parting from their children with unfinished business and the feeling of an exclusive alliance being formed against them.

'Shall we go for a drink somewhere?' he suggested doubtfully.

They'd already had wine and weren't big drinkers but he'd expected the afternoon with Chris and Elisabeth to last into early evening, and he wasn't in the mood to go home.

Bryony shrugged but didn't dismiss the idea and he guessed she shared his feelings as she stared in silence at the dark trees and bare hedgerows lining the road.

The dim afternoon light had all but gone and it felt like the dead of winter but at least they were into December now, with the shortest day in sight.

Tommy was reminded suddenly of Dominic's advent services. What was it he'd said? Six o'clock at Harrowden? He glanced at the clock on the dashboard. They could probably make it.

'I've got just the thing for you,' he said to Bryony. 'Country house ambience. Christmas carols.'

'Oh?'

She was intrigued. He put his foot to the floor and picked up speed on the country road.

The old family chapel had an intimate feel. It was small, neatly furnished and smelt of old stone.

The pavement underfoot was worn. A narrow aisle divided a dozen rows of wooden seats and there were statutes: a virgin and child and some other ancients Tommy couldn't identify.

An elderly gentleman with an unhurried manner was lighting candles around the altar. He smiled a greeting at them, as did the other individuals already seated when Tommy and Bryony entered and found somewhere to sit half way down the chapel.

Tommy noticed Dominic's advent wreath on a stand at the front: an evergreen circle of spruce, holly and fir cones with four thin tapering candles standing up in it, three purple and one pink.

By six o'clock the chapel had completely filled up and Dominic entered from a side door near the altar, with two boys in white robes each carrying a large candle stick.

The service began with a blessing of the wreath and the lighting of one of its purple candles. It symbolised hope, apparently, looking forward to the advent, the coming of the Lord. The other candles symbolised faith, joy and peace and would be lit in the weeks that followed, giving out an increasing light in the darkness as Christ's birth drew nearer.

There were carols, readings and a homily from Dominic. Tommy realised then that, for all their conversations, he'd never actually sat and listened to his friend talk at length, building an argument for what he believed.

The reasoning of it went over Tommy's head. There were references to mountains dropping sweetness and a fountain coming forth that would water the thorns. The fountain would come from Christ, the baby soon to be born who would die young and violently and bring the promise of resurrection and life for all.

What stayed with him was the priest's calm, thoughtful way of speaking, his easy, compassionate manner and gentle delivery. Sitting there, listening to him in the quiet stillness of the old chapel, it was as though something of Dominic himself was sinking into him and Tommy had a sudden, yet deep-rooted, feeling that everything was somehow going to be all right, not just for his life but for everyone: everyone, everywhere and always, for eternity.

At the back of his mind he wondered what Bryony was making of it all. She sat quietly at his side and passed no comment, making no move to attract his attention or exchange a glance. Afterwards, though, when prayers had been said and a final carol sung, she went over to look at the advent wreath.

Tommy followed her. Observing it at close hand, he saw the corona was fresh and green, its strands of holly with smooth pale stems and prickly leaves wound tightly round the base of each candle. These were set firmly among the bristly needles of spruce and fir.

'We could have one,' said Bryony to Tommy. 'It'd be something different for Christmas.'

'Lots of families do have them,' said Dominic, coming up from behind. 'It's a good tradition, lighting the candle together in the run up to Christmas. Time and space to pray for your family.'

Tommy was amused to see Bryony nod, as though lighting candles and praying for the family were normal occurrences in the Allbright household.

'It's good to see you here,' said Dominic, with a smile and a handshake for each of them, before moving to greet other visitors sipping mulled wine nearby.

'So that's your Catholic priest,' said Bryony.

'Yes,' said Tommy. 'You've met him before. At Gina's funeral.'

Bryony was watching Dominic, laughing in conversation with an elderly couple.

'Perhaps we could remember Gina with our advent wreath,' she said. 'Gina and all our dead.'

Over the next few days she was busy assembling greenery on a circular frame she'd bought from the garden centre.

Tommy remembered Dominic's pine cones from the cemetery and walked up to gather a few of his own.

They were sharp to the touch he discovered, as he gathered them, particularly at the base where the hard segments were bigger and more open. They tapered at the top, the succession of 'v' shaped sections growing smaller and becoming more closed in a way that reminded him of the rose buds he'd recently handled.

He found their interleaved intricacy fascinating, the repetition of perfectly proportioned sections, pointing outwards and upwards, drawing the eye and his finger to the very top of each round, sharp end where the curled brown points were tightly closed.

He half-filled a plastic bag with them and took it along to the lunch he'd arranged with JG. She'd finally responded to his telephone message about the company secretary role.

'Nice,' she commented when he showed her the pine cones. 'Is there a market for that kind of thing?'

He laughed. 'These are definitely not for profit! So how are things?'

She gave him with a familiar wry smile. 'Oh, you know how it is. Life in the fast lane. Trying to keep up with these hot shot businessmen. No change there! So tell me about this new venture of yours.'

He outlined it in brief and was delighted when she agreed to join him as a director.

'I'll have to clear it with Roper first,' she said. 'But he won't object. There's no conflict of interest in business terms. Anyway he's rather intrigued by you. He respects what you achieved at Lister's. I suspect he'd quite like to meet you sometime.'

Tommy took his pine cones home and laid them out on the kitchen work top for Bryony to inspect.

The wreath, by now, was all but ready from what he could see. It was more intricately woven than the one in the chapel: the darker, thicker foliage held in place by stems of light green ivy with leaves like fleur de lys springing out at angles, full of life. The darker needles were cypress, whose knobbly brown stems gave rise to green feathery strands of needles which diminished at the end of each twig, so that each one looked like a miniature fir tree.

Bryony selected a few of his shorter pine cones.

'What will you do?' he asked. 'Intersperse them all around then add the candles?'

'You'll see,' she said mysteriously. 'It's not nearly finished yet.'

'Isn't it?' he was surprised. 'I thought we might light it tonight. Celebrate JG coming on board.'

'All right, Tommy, we can do it tonight,' she said. 'But it's not ready yet.'

She disappeared with it into the study for the rest of the afternoon while he kept busy, preparing a seafood lasagne and selecting a bottle of Touraine Sauvignon to chill.

By seven thirty the main course was cooking nicely, the wine was uncorked and he'd already sampled its crisp lemon depths while setting the table with candles and silverware.

Bryony had cleaned up an old plant stand to hold the advent wreath, twining ivy and gold ribbon around the base, and Tommy set it in pride of place at the head of the table.

When she finally carried her handiwork into the room, he saw at once that she'd been right: the wreath hadn't been nearly finished before.

Now the ivy and cypress were interspersed with patches of dark glossy moss that housed the triangular points of his pine cones and woven among the ivy strands, the glossy needles and pine cones was golden twine and shiny gold ribbon. Along this she'd strung the real feature of the wreath, tiny laminated photographs: the heart-shaped faces of all their loved ones, past and present.

A photograph of James was there; Tommy's mum and dad; Bryony's parents side by side; images of Gina, Arthur and Esther; himself and Bryony; Chris and Elisabeth; Richard's family and Maurice and Lorraine.

'It's to help us remember,' said Bryony handing him a box of matches.

There were four candles set around the wreath, as in church. Tommy lit one for the first week of advent and stood there with an arm round his wife. Together they watched the flickering light pick out glossy segments of the pine cones and shine through the multiplicity of green fronds, while the gold ribbon twinkled round the faces of their loved ones, nestling among the foliage that would be forever green.

'What shall we pray for?' asked Bryony. 'What shall we wish?'

'That we'll all be together again,' said Tommy. 'Even those we've lost.'

Standing there, looking at the familiar faces so loved and so irrevocably lost, he thought of Dominic at the advent service, remembered the conversations in the cemetery, the gentle, reassuring certainty of the man and, for the first time in his life, he actually believed that one day it might be so.

THE END

Acknowledgements

My heartfelt thanks to Roberta Dewa, Diana Peasey and Joy Armstrong for their honest and constructive feedback on every draft of Kimble's Top in our monthly writers' group: without such help and encouragement I would not have reached a conclusion.

Grateful thanks also, to everyone who taught on Nottingham Trent University's MA in Creative Writing course 2005-2007; to Anthony J Murphy for his original recipes and insight into wine; to Martin Paterson who shared the male perspective and technical knowledge on the Audi A8 and to my brother-in-law, Paul Taberner, for refining my proposed financial, business and retail models behind Tommy's success.

I am particularly grateful to Sheila Bone who so generously arranged my visit to Joseph Cheaney & Sons, Northamptonshire shoemakers since 1886. The opportunity to experience the sights and sounds of such an environment and to ask my naieve questions about the business of making and selling hand-made shoes was invaluable. I would like to establish that any technical errors or incongruities in the story of Tommy Allbright and Lister's arise entirely from my own shortcomings and not from any failure in the information I gathered on that visit.

Finally, to my husband, Alan, for his patience with my time-consuming writing habit and his willingness to review my grammar and attempted eloquence—you are a treasure!

Lightning Source UK Ltd.
Milton Keynes UK
UKOW04f0021290813

216132UK00004B/80/P